The Deadly Debutante

The Perfect Poison Murders, Book 4
A Georgian Mystery

E.L. Johnson

Text by E.L. Johnson
Cover by Dar Albert

Dragonblade Publishing, Inc. is an imprint of Kathryn Le Veque Novels, Inc.
P.O. Box 23
Moreno Valley, CA 92556
ceo@dragonbladepublishing.com

Produced in the United States of America

First Edition July 2023
Trade Paperback Edition

Dearest Reader;

Thank you for your support of a small press. At Dragonblade Publishing, we strive to bring you the highest quality Historical Romance from some of the best authors in the business. Without your support, there is no 'us', so we sincerely hope you adore these stories and find some new favorite authors along the way.

Happy Reading!

CEO, Dragonblade Publishing

Additional Dragonblade books by Author E.L. Johnson

The Perfect Poison Murders

The Strangled Servant (Book 1)
The Poisoned Clergyman (Book 2)
The Mistress Murders (Book 3)
The Deadly Debutante (Book 4)

Chapter One

Hertford, late November 1806

Poppy Morton was frowning at her sewing when a knock came at the parsonage door, much to her relief. She despised sewing, hemming, and altering, and if it wasn't completely necessary, she would give up the practice altogether. When the sharp knock came, Poppy looked up.

The family's maid, Betsey, hummed an offkey tune in the kitchen, oblivious to the visitor at the door.

Poppy got up to answer it, and came face to face with… "Father." She beamed at the man she'd only met twice before.

"Poppy," he said with pleasure, which warmed her heart. He bowed and squeezed her hand. "I hope this isn't a bad time. I did send a letter."

"You did?"

"Yes. Did it not arrive?"

"No." She grew sad at the prospect of missing a letter from him.

"I can come back later if you prefer," he said slowly.

"No, no. It's fine. Please do come in." She stood back, allowing him to enter. She smoothed down the dull black crepe folds of her mourning dress as he stepped inside the parsonage.

"Who is it, Poppy?" her Aunt Rachel called.

"My father's here," Poppy said, leading him to the comfortable blue sitting room the family used for visitors. She stood in the doorway. "Aunt, may I present my father, Lord Blackwood."

The offkey humming from the kitchen stopped. Her aunt's mouth opened and she instantly stood up, and then promptly sat down on a pile of ribbons, turning red in the face.

Poppy stepped inside the room and let her father fill the space. He removed a dark gray hat, revealing a head full of silver hair that was tousled from travel. He wore a dark navy traveling coat with a black mourning armband over a light jacket, and a slate gray waistcoat over dark trousers. But that didn't matter, for he had a smile just for her.

It filled her with happiness to see him standing beside her. The very sight of him filled her with pride, for he looked every inch a gentleman. And now he was here, standing in her family's sitting room. She hoped this would be the first of many such visits. Her thoughts wandered to their very first meeting, and her smile fell. She had only met him briefly but had felt an instant connection. It was just a shame that the cause for finally bringing them together was brought about by the sudden death of her mother, her father's mistress.

"Oh, my lord," her aunt said, rising and dipping into a curtsey. "My lord, how wonderful you have come. I'm so sorry. If you'd sent word of your arrival we would have been ready for you. The parsonage is a mess, you see, and–"

"Nonsense, Mrs. Greene," Lord Blackwood said, "This looks like a very comfortable room. But it is I who am at fault. I sent a letter but too late, for as Poppy informs me, it did not arrive."

Betsey said from behind them, "Excuse me, but this letter came for you this morning."

Poppy and Lord Blackwood turned around.

Betsey blushed and fished out a letter from her apron. "Sorry. It came and I forgot."

Poppy took the letter and saw the firm hand of her father's handwriting and personal wax seal on the back of the envelope.

"Thank you, Betsey."

Betsey lowered her eyes and curtsied deeply before hurrying back into the kitchen.

"Please, do sit down." Aunt Rachel gestured to the fine, stiff hardback chair reserved for visitors. "Would you like some tea?"

"That would be most agreeable." Lord Blackwood put his hat on the floor and sat on the chair as Poppy sat on the overstuffed pale green sofa beside her aunt.

He asked, "Pray, is the rector about?"

"Yes, he's just upstairs, working on his next sermon. I'll just go fetch him. Excuse me." Aunt Rachel rose, took the pile of ribbons she'd been hiding behind her rump, and carried them out of the room, her thick black mourning dress swishing around her legs.

Poppy flashed her father a smile as she heard the clatter of the tea things being put together in the kitchen nearby. She happily put her sewing aside and closed up her sewing box, to set it at her feet.

"I'm glad to see you," he said.

"And I, you." Her cheeks almost hurt from smiling.

All at once, things happened. Betsey walked in with a tea tray and set it on a small wooden table between the chair and sofa. Aunt Rachel walked in, followed by her husband, Poppy's uncle, Reginald.

"You are Mr. Greene?" Blackwood asked, rising and giving a small bow.

"I am, sir. You must be Lord Blackwood." Mr. Greene said, taking a seat nearby as Aunt Rachel joined Poppy on the sofa and began fussing with the tea things. "I am the rector for Hertford." Uncle Reginald's mouth pursed with displeasure as he surveyed their visitor.

Lord Blackwood accepted a cup of green tea from Aunt Rachel and sipped it delicately, waiting as she served the others. Once everyone had a cup, he said, "Forgive the sudden visit, but I felt I should come in person, rather than communicate by letter."

"He did send one to tell us of his coming, but it only arrived today," Aunt Rachel told her husband, whose face had darkened.

"You bring news from London?" Uncle Reginald asked.

"Of a sort." Lord Blackwood set his teacup down on the table. "There is no delicate way to put this, so I will speak plainly. Poppy, I'm not sure how much you knew about your mother's financial affairs—"

"Oh no. Tell me she's not in debt," Aunt Rachel started.

"How much is this going to cost us?" Uncle Reginald asked.

Lord Blackwood cleared his throat. "Nothing." He turned to Poppy. "Your mother left a will. I invested for her in some things, but also guided her finances so that if…" He reddened. "If our relationship ever did end, she would not be left destitute."

Poppy bit her lip and blinked hard. Just hearing him talk about her mother brought the loss fresh to her mind. She drank her tea as a distraction, feeling the hot liquid course down her throat. "That's very kind of you," she said.

Lord Blackwood glanced at her. "I loved her. There's nothing I wouldn't do for her."

Someone snorted.

Uncle Reginald's face remained dark. "Why have you come calling, sir?"

Poppy and Aunt Rachel looked at him. That Reginald had been burdened with raising the child of a mistress for two decades was bad enough, but now, facing the man who had led his wife's sister into ruin…it required a lot of self-control. But that was no excuse for rudeness.

"The fact of the matter is, your mother had a small fortune," Lord Blackwood said.

"She did?" Aunt Rachel's mouth dropped open. "How much?"

"Respectable," he said, "As well as a townhouse I bought in her name, Celeste had a small collection of art, and no small number of clothes and jewelry. I'm pleased to say that her investments are very profitable indeed, and… she left everything to you, Poppy."

"What?" Poppy almost dropped her teacup to the floor. Instead, she set it down on the table and rubbed sweaty hands on her knees. "She left her things to me?"

"Yes. All of it. I have a letter from our solicitor, Mr. Harding, who wishes to meet you. He can explain the details of her will more fully." He smiled at her. "You have a townhouse in London if you wish to take it up."

"I have a house?" Poppy said.

"And servants. Celeste owned the freehold of a townhouse on Orchard Street. She had a small staff, good hardworking people. If you like, I can write and tell them to stay on."

"Oh my." Aunt Rachel's hand darted to her mouth.

"Now, wait just a minute," Uncle Reginald said.

"Or you can sell the house if you wish. The choice is up to you," Lord Blackwood said.

Poppy's mouth dropped open.

Lord Blackwood added, "It is in a good neighborhood, so it would bring a sizeable profit your way."

"Just think, Poppy, you could sell it and use the money for a dowry," Aunt Rachel said, "or we could come to stay in London…" Her voice took on a dreamy quality.

"No," Uncle Reginald said.

The others looked at him. "Poppy will not be moving to London or taking up in her mother's house. I will not have my niece stay in the house of a whore."

Poppy's face fell. Aunt Rachel stared at him, a fierce rebuke on her lips, while Lord Blackwood gripped the arms of his chair, so hard the wood creaked. The violent sound filled the stunned silence of the room.

"Reginald," Aunt Rachel began.

"I mean it. Poppy will not be going to London. She already fell into extremely undesirable company whilst she was there before, and I'll not see her tempt fate a second time. Had we not been notified as to the indecency of her situation, we might never have—"

"Uncle, I was a companion," Poppy interjected.

"To a whore," he almost spat. "You allied yourself to a band of mistresses."

"I was helping those girls. They were in danger from a murderer," Poppy shot back.

"And you were lucky you didn't get killed yourself. There was no need to take such risks, Poppy. I did not raise you to be a good, god-fearing girl only to see you throw yourself away in the city at the first temptation." Uncle Reginald pointed at Lord Blackwood. "And you. You, sir, led my sister-in-law into sin for decades and got her with child. You ruined all hopes she had of making a good and decent marriage. I wonder how it is you imagine yourself to be welcome in my home. How can you sleep at night, knowing you ruined the life of a good woman?"

Poppy's eyebrows knit with worry. "Uncle…"

Lord Blackwood picked up his hat and rose to his feet. "I can see I've disturbed you all. Do accept my apologies. I will call again when things are not so uncomfortable."

"Do not call again." Uncle Reginald set down his teacup with such force it clattered, and hot tea slopped over the side onto the saucer. "You are not welcome here. Not while I am still alive."

"Uncle," Poppy said, "That's my father you are talking to."

Her uncle slowly turned to look at her. "He is also the miscreant who ruined your mother. She was so ashamed of how she had been led into sin that she cut off all contact with her family and gave her baby to us to raise. Us, with hardly a penny to live on but the goodwill of our parishioners. I once blamed your mother for all her sins, but I see now that it is this man who is at fault. He pretends to be charming with his fine manners and clothes, but instead is looking to steal you away and probably introduce you to his friends, as an easy mark."

"I would never," Lord Blackwood interrupted, his blue eyes blazing. "She is my daughter."

"You say that now, but I don't believe a word you say. Poppy is a good girl and like any impressionable young woman, can all too easily be led astray. No, sir. You may have money and a title, but as long as I am the rector of this parish and still alive, you are not welcome here. I suggest you leave." Uncle Reginald looked down his nose at the lord, as if he were a sinner of the vilest nature.

Lord Blackwood needed no more prompting. He quit the room without a word.

Aunt Rachel set down her teacup and shuffled past her husband, hurrying after him. "Please, my lord, don't take what my husband said to heart, he does not speak for all of us." Her voice carried. "I loved my sister, and I still do!"

The front door opened and shut with a slam, making Poppy jump. She turned to her uncle. "How could you say that to him?"

Her uncle was visibly trembling and sat down.

"You were so rude. When all he did was come to pay his respects and tell me of my mother's will."

"He plans more than that, I assure you. I've seen men like him before. He may act like he has your best interests at heart, but in truth, he wants nothing more than to lead you into a life of sin and set you up as the mistress of one of his friends. Do you really think he cared for your mother?"

"Yes." Poppy didn't bother to hide the tears in her eyes. "He said he loved her. Would he have done so much if he didn't?"

"You forget your mother was a whore," her uncle said bluntly.

Poppy sat back on the green sofa and let out a noisy breath, tears streaming down her face. "Then I am the daughter of a whore. There, are you happy? Is that how you think of me?"

"No. You are a good, decent, innocent girl. You're nothing like her."

"You were so horrible to him. He's my father."

Her uncle looked at her. "I'm sorry, but that's the way I feel. You must see how it looks. He comes into our lives now, seemingly wanting the best for you? I find that hard to believe."

"When I was a companion in London, my mother revealed she had hidden all knowledge of me from my father. He never knew I existed. Now that he does, he wants to make amends. Is that so hard to accept?" she asked.

"Yes. This man led your mother into sin and ruined her life. I refuse to let you follow in her footsteps."

Aunt Rachel stomped into the room. "Well, Reginald, I hope you're happy. You've sent that man away with a flea in his ear and don't be surprised if he never comes back here again." She saw Poppy's face. "Oh honey, don't worry."

Poppy wiped her eyes on her sleeve. "What if he hates me?"

"Why would he? You weren't rude to him. And don't mind, I'm sure he didn't take it to heart." She surveyed Poppy for a moment, eyeing her tearful expression. "I know. What you need is a distraction. And those dull clothes aren't doing you any good."

Poppy and her aunt had spent the past few days in mourning dress, out of respect for Celeste, Poppy's dead mother, and her aunt's sister. For years, Poppy, along with the townspeople, had been told that her mother had died when she was just a child. But Poppy had recently learned that not only was this not the case, but that her mother was alive and well, and living as a mistress in London. Poppy had found a position there as a companion and with the help of Sergeant Dyngley had found Celeste, only for them all to get embroiled in a murder investigation and her mother to suffer the deadly attentions of a killer.

"Let's think about what you're going to wear to the dance on Saturday."

"Aunt, I'm not going. Mama died just a short while ago. I'm still in mourning."

Her aunt sighed. "Don't you think you'd like to at least attend?"

Poppy shook her head. "Not for at least six months. Maybe a year."

"A year? In these black rags? You'll make me wish for death if you're not careful."

Poppy sniffed and wiped away a tear, smiling. "Since it was your sister, you're allowed to wear black for just three months."

Her aunt sniffed with indignation.

Poppy rose and hurried outside the parsonage. She ran, feeling a crisp autumn wind through her thin black plain dress. She could just spy her father's carriage leaving when she waved and ran after it. Her father saw her through the window and tapped on the roof, causing it to stop. He opened the door. "Poppy?"

She came up to him, slightly winded. "Please, don't go. I'm sorry my uncle was so rude. I had no idea he would…"

"It's of no consequence. I should have expected that reaction. But I would speak with you about your mother's estate. Is there somewhere we could go to speak in private? I will be staying in town a few days."

"Yes. We could meet at the sweet shop in town, or take a walk along the riverbank."

He smiled faintly. "That would be pleasant. Your mother loved to walk along the Thames. I'll call tomorrow and escort you. Would early afternoon be suitable?"

"Yes. Goodbye." She waved as he drove away.

Poppy returned to the blue sitting room where her aunt and uncle sat. Her uncle said accusingly, "You've been talking to him, haven't you? I tell you, Poppy, that man is a bad influence."

"He is my father."

"Not all fathers are good men. They've only managed to procreate. That's not a sign of good character, only anatomy."

"You cannot stop me from talking to him," Poppy said.

"Maybe not outside this house. But Poppy…" His mouth pulled into a frown. "Cannot you see he is devious?"

"I disagree, Uncle. He has only been kind to me."

"That is how it starts," he muttered.

"Reginald, please," Aunt Rachel said.

Poppy sat in the hardbacked chair left for visitors. "Uncle, I mean to speak with him about my mother. And I want to know what we are going to do about this." She gestured to her mourning dress.

"What about it?" Aunt Rachel asked.

"The entire town thinks my mother died when I was a child. If Aunt Rachel and I continue to go around wearing mourning attire, it will raise questions."

"Goodness, I never even thought—" Aunt Rachel started.

Her uncle's bushy gray eyebrows firmed into a hard line. "I did. Do you wish to continue wearing them?"

"I wish to do right by my mother," Poppy said, meeting his eyes.

"I understand. But you are still my niece and a part of this family. It is my duty to look after you."

"Reginald, what are you saying?" Aunt Rachel asked.

"Rachel, we've told everyone her mother is dead. What do you think they're going to say when you and Poppy walk around in all black? It's already been a few days, and you cannot hide away in the house forever," he said.

"We tell them we've had a death in the family. A distant relative," Aunt Rachel said.

"You could always tell them the truth," Poppy said.

Her uncle's face darkened. "I hope you appreciate our situation, Poppy. What we choose to say to our neighbors reflects on all of us. If you go spreading tales about our personal business, you'll be damned as a gossip, and all our names will be dragged through the mud, including yours. Is that what you want?"

"No," Poppy said sullenly, "but neither do I think it is right to tell a falsehood. My mother is dead. Can we not simply say that?"

"They already think she's dead. Poppy, let me make a deal with you," he said. "I will say nothing more about your father if you agree to say that we are mourning a relative. No word about your mother to anyone."

"But I am planning to meet my father for a walk tomorrow."

His eyebrows rose. "Rachel, go with them."

"Why?" Poppy asked.

"You know as well as I do that he is a stranger here. A young woman, walking alone, unescorted, with a strange man? In a town like this where everyone knows everyone else's business, a few loose tongues will have half the townspeople talking. They'll either think I've let you run wild, that your time in London last month has loosened your morals, or that he's a predatory man looking for a mistress. Either way, you cannot be alone in public with him. Ever."

Her mouth dropped open. "That's not fair. He's my father."

"It's how it has to be. You wanted the truth, there it is. Now, can I trust that you will keep our secret?" he asked.

Her mouth snapped shut. A minute later, she nodded.

"Good. Let us talk no more about this." He moved upstairs, leaving Poppy alone with her aunt.

"Don't worry. It won't be so bad as you think," Aunt Rachel said, "And you've only been here a few days. I bet you a sixpence that that constable will be calling on you any day now."

At that, Poppy's heart lifted a bit, and her stomach filled with butterflies at the same time. Constable Dyngley was her good friend, who some months ago had helped clear her name in a murder investigation. He had been one of the very few people who believed in her innocence and didn't dismiss her views as the witticisms of a silly young woman. Instead, he had encouraged her, and together they had teamed up to solve a series of murders, but over time, her feelings had grown to care for him as more than just a friend.

She had kissed him once, and he had kissed her back. He had taken a liberty by kissing her recently, and the warmth was reciprocated. Now that she was back from her time working as a companion in London, she hoped she would see him again.

There was another knock at the parsonage door.

Betsey went to answer it. A moment later she entered the sitting room doorway and announced, "Constable Dyngley to see you, ma'am."

CHAPTER TWO

POPPY'S HEART LIFTED. He was here. The man she'd fallen for had come. She touched her hair and smoothed her black skirts, trying not to blush.

Betsey stood aside for the man to enter the sitting room, then left.

"Constable Dyngley," Aunt Rachel said, curtsying.

"It's Sergeant now, Mrs. Greene," Henry said, bowing.

"Sergeant," Poppy murmured, looking at the floor as she curtsied.

"Miss Morton," he said.

She rose from the curtsey and their eyes met. For a split second, it felt like time stopped and it was just the two of them. Then it passed in the blink of an eye.

"Sergeant? Do tell. You've gotten a promotion," Aunt Rachel said.

"Yes, my work on the murders in London earned me a title. Not that it matters much. All I can see is it requires more work, but I don't mind. I like to keep busy," he said.

"And how are you, Sergeant?" Aunt Rachel asked, gesturing toward the chair for visitors.

"Very well, ma'am. And you? You are in good health?"

"We are all very well, thank you."

Poppy felt his eyes on her black gown. She wore a gown of

black crepe, simply cut. It was dull and drab aside from some shining black thread that caught the light. Her aunt wore a similar deep purple gown, not so dark as Poppy's.

They made polite small talk until Henry said, "I wonder if Miss Morton might show me the garden out back?" Sergeant Dyngley enquired. "It has been some time since I've seen it."

"Poppy would be delighted, Sergeant," Aunt Rachel said.

Poppy rose and walked out of the room and into the faded corridor, not taking the time to put on a bonnet. She had purchased a new one in black, but the day was bright if a little chilly. She opened the door when she felt a touch at her elbow. She turned. "Constable?"

He stood not a foot away from her, a corner of his mouth curled into a smile. "It's Sergeant now. You had a piece of lint on your sleeve."

"Oh. Thank you." She tried to ignore the blush rising on her cheeks.

THE LAST TIME they had met like this, in the entryway of the parsonage, they had just solved a murder and had dined together, when he came in the middle of the night and kissed her, then stole away like a thief. It had shocked her and then months later, when she had taken a position as a companion in London, their paths had crossed again to solve another murder. It was becoming a pattern with him, she realized. Solve a murder, celebrate with a kiss. Except it was extremely inappropriate, for they were not officially courting, and she had no idea what his attention meant. Did he happen to lose himself in the moment or did he care for her?

He shot her a confident smile, his brown eyes seeking hers. She blushed again and said weakly, "Just this way."

She walked ahead, confident her posture was straight and her steps steady. She could feel his eyes on her back and hoped her mousy brown hair wasn't in disarray. She stepped outside the parsonage, hearing the birds call and the quiet rush of the wind through the trees. After a hot and dry summer, the late summer rains had come, drenching the land. What had been a brown and barren field was now green, although, with the impending chill in the air, Poppy wondered how long that would last.

"Congratulations on your promotion," she said.

"Thank you. I'd hoped it would be more than just a title, but the remuneration is… less than I had hoped. It's barely enough to help my family, much less allow me to save for something of my own." His step was heavy beside her.

"What you need is a rich heiress to fund your estate," she said.

He laughed. "If only. Do you know of any?"

"Sadly not. But as soon as I meet one, I'll be sure to recommend you to her."

Dyngley was a quiet presence beside her. "I have not seen you since London. I wrote you a letter," he said.

"I know. I was happy to receive it."

"Yet you did not write back."

"I did not know what to say."

They walked on, around the back of the parsonage and past the small stable, to the garden and chicken coop out back. Chickens ran wild, darting across the field in short bursts of speed, then pecking at the ground. Poppy smiled at the sight of them and said, "It was good of you to call. You're the second visitor we've received today. My father came."

"He did? What did he say?" Dyngley asked.

"He wanted to talk with me about my mother's estate."

"And?"

"My uncle threw him out of the house before he could say much."

His eyebrows rose. "And will you see him again?"

"Yes, but with my aunt present. I hate having a guardian. I'm nineteen. Surely I don't need an escort every time I go out."

"Perhaps not, but I can well understand your relatives' concern. He is a stranger and not without influence. How much do you know about him, aside from the fact he is your father?"

Poppy felt a flash of anger. "I had thought you would agree with me."

"I want to, but look at the facts. You've only met him a month ago. That's hardly enough time to get to know a person or their true intentions."

She frowned at him.

"You've been crying." He noticed her red eyes. "Not over me?"

"No. But how am I to have a relationship with him when my uncle won't even let him into the parsonage, and he doesn't want us to say why my aunt and I are in mourning dress? My uncle wants us to lie about my mother's death and say it was a distant relative."

Dyngley's eyebrows furrowed. "Why would he do that?"

"Since I was a child, he and my aunt told the town that my mother was dead. To mourn her now would raise questions my family would rather not answer."

He brushed away a tear from her eye. "Don't cry. You'll figure this out. And if you need help, you can always talk to me." He laughed. "I may be a poor second son of a baronet in Hertfordshire, but I can always listen if you need someone to talk to."

"I know."

"Do you?" He looked past her, seeing a flutter of a curtain at a kitchen window. "I will call on you again if that is amenable to you?"

She nodded.

He squeezed her hand before leaving.

AFTER DINNER AND a tense but quiet evening of reading by the fire, Poppy excused herself early and went upstairs. As she heard her aunt and uncle climb the stairs and get ready for bed, she overheard her aunt say, "You should not have been so hard on Lord Blackwood. He's the girl's father. There's no indecency with them being seen together."

"There's every indecency," her uncle said.

"Reginald, it's no use blaming him for Celeste. You can accuse him all you like, but she was sleeping around long before she met Blackwood. I'm just glad she met him and not some lout who'd abandoned her once she turned thirty."

Her uncle snorted. "I do not like him. I can already see him exerting his influence over Poppy. She needs to make up her own mind about these things."

Aunt Rachel said, "And she will if you let her. But the more you force them apart, the more they will come together behind your back. And worse, you push her away from you. Wasn't that what you feared most when she went to London?"

He grunted.

"It is, even if you do not want to admit it. Now, I will go with Poppy and listen to what her father has to say. You trust me, don't you?"

"You know I do."

"Then trust that I will not let Poppy get into any trouble. I think I can handle a lord. He may have a fancy title, but at the end of the day, he's just a man. I can handle that."

THE NEXT DAY, Poppy and her aunt stood by the riverbank, waiting. The day was pleasant enough with a blue sky and few clouds, and there was a pretty thicket of trees and bushes that still boasted flowers.

They soon spied a welcome sight in the image of Lord Blackwood, who raised a hand in greeting. He wore a light gray morning suit, black armband in place, with a lighter waistcoat and trousers. He carried a silver-topped walking stick and met Poppy with a smile. "Hello, Daughter, Mrs. Greene."

Poppy and her aunt curtsied, and as she rose, Poppy saw his eyes sparkle with amusement.

"Hello, Father." Poppy grinned.

The three walked along, then Lord Blackwood said, "As I

tried to explain yesterday, your mother left you an inheritance. You'll own her house, her clothes, jewels, art collection, and the funds she set aside for your dowry."

Poppy stared at him.

He smiled. "I didn't know it myself until I spoke with the solicitor. But apparently, she's been writing and sending money for your upkeep. I assume your aunt and uncle handled this."

"Yes. I found that out a little while ago." She frowned and walked on, annoyed that they had kept this secret from her for so long. She kicked a small pebble with her shoe. "Since I was little, I thought she was dead."

He kept walking. "That is unfortunate. But I can understand their need for discretion then, just as I can comprehend your uncle's dislike of my company now."

"Oh, your lordship, don't you worry a bit about my Reginald, I'll see him straight," Aunt Rachel began.

"It is all right, Mrs. Greene. To him, I must seem like a villain out of a gothic novel." He turned to Poppy. "Whatever he may think of me, I did love Celeste, which is why I wish to do right by you." He led them to a small bench, on which he and Poppy sat. Aunt Rachel stood by and waved away his invitation to give her his seat.

"Poppy," he said, "You are an illegitimate child."

She bowed her head, feeling the breath rush out of her. What a thing to hear. She blushed and lowered her eyes to the ground. She had mud on her shoes.

"Back home at my estate I have a wife, and two children, around your age. A boy and a girl. James and Susan. When I leave here, I'll be going back to them," Lord Blackwood said.

Poppy turned away to hide her hurt. She didn't expect him to take her hand.

"But you are mine. And as my daughter, even illegitimate, I want to help you."

"What do you mean?" Poppy asked.

"The wealth your mother left you means you can live a good

life for as long as the money lasts. I'd like to guide you, so you always have an income and won't need to work as a companion or in a shop or anywhere else. She's left you a dowry of £4000 and I've arranged for you to have an annuity of £300 a year until you are married."

"That is very kind," she said.

"That is not all. I know that coming from your present circumstances, any dreams you entertained for your future might not have extended to this, but I should like to give you a Season."

"Oh, my lord!" Aunt Rachel exclaimed. "Really? A real Season?"

Lord Blackwood laughed. "Yes. I know this must all seem overwhelming, but it's the least I can do. I cannot recognize you formally, I'm afraid. But I can do this if you'll let me."

Poppy glanced at her aunt, who was practically jumping up and down. "What is a Season? I don't understand."

"Oh Poppy," her aunt started. "A London Season is wonderful. It's the chance for all young women of quality to dance and meet desirable young men."

"For what purpose?"

"To marry, of course!" Aunt Rachel gushed. "Oh, this is wonderful news, just wonderful. Reginald will be delighted. Just think, Poppy, a London Season, just for you. He'll be overjoyed!"

BUT LATER, HER uncle was not so keen to accept Lord Blackwood's seemingly kind offer. Outside of the blue sitting room, Poppy could hear her Aunt Rachel railing at him, saying, "Don't you understand, this will change her life. Poppy being a debutante will see her married off to a charming young man."

"A wealthy one, you mean," he said.

"And what is the matter with that? There is no shame in wealth."

He frowned and raised his newspaper.

"Oh please, Reginald, can't you see what good this will do for Poppy? She is already an heiress. What is wrong with her marrying a young man of property?"

"Just because a man is rich does not mean he is of good character. We raised Poppy to be calm, good-natured, and satisfied with her life."

"Is that your problem? You have raised her to accept a humble living and now don't want her to leave it? I tell you, Husband, this does not become you."

He ignored her. A moment later he lowered his newspaper. "I do not wish Poppy to get ideas above her station. What if she comes back unmarried, and with haughty airs about her person and situation? What then?"

"Do you think a few dresses and dances will change who she is? She is still the same bright young woman we raised. But now she has a chance at something greater. Don't you want the best for her?" Aunt Rachel asked.

"Of course I do. I—"

"Uncle," Poppy stepped into the blue sitting room. "I'm sorry to interrupt. I heard what you both were saying. If it helps, I'm as trepidatious about this idea as you are."

He gazed at her and folded his newspaper on his lap.

"I don't know what to think. My father comes and offers me all these gifts from my mother, and wants to do this for me. But I don't know what it will do or if it will change me. I can't promise I won't come back with different ideas or airs about myself or the world. But what I'd like to do is accept his gift for what it is. I think he wants to do something for me as his daughter, and this is his best idea of how. I'd like to accept it if that is agreeable to you."

At that moment her uncle looked older. Poppy could see the red veins lining his nose, hinting at many a drink enjoyed, and the laugh lines around his eyes, as well as the pair of horn-rimmed spectacles that sat on the edge of his nose. She loved him, and even if she had to hurt him, she wanted to tell him the truth. Open honesty was the key to repairing their relationship, she felt sure of it. Now if only it would work.

He said, "It's not my decision, it's yours."

There was a knock at the front door. Uncle Reginald rose to his feet and set aside his newspaper. "We'll talk about this later."

"Are we expecting someone?" Aunt Rachel asked.

"I am," Uncle Reginald replied. "Excuse me."

He rose and quit the room. A moment later he answered the door. "Ah, hello. So good of you to come. The journey wasn't too long, I hope?"

"Not at all, sir. I spent the hours reading *Fordyce's Sermons*. That is, until I got sick. As it turns out, I got a bit stomach-sick from the carriage. The motion, I think. The roads can be a bit bumpy."

A minute later Uncle Reginald entered the doorway and said, "Rachel, Poppy, please meet Mr. Terrence Terrell. My protege."

Chapter Three

INTRODUCTIONS WERE HASTILY made. "Your protege?" Aunt Rachel repeated.

"Yes. He'll be staying with us for some time, as he learns under me about the clergy."

"And very excited I am too, Mr. Greene. So grateful for the opportunity." Mr. Terrell grasped Uncle Reginald's hand and shook it, then beamed at Aunt Rachel and Poppy. "So glad to meet you all. I've been looking forward to this for weeks."

"Weeks?" Aunt Rachel said.

"Oh yes. When Mr. Greene sent an open invitation to my college at Cambridge for a chance to stay with him and learn about the clergy, I was the first to see it. I tore the notice down so no one else would see it and wrote immediately. Fortuitous now that I'm here, even with the journey." He swallowed.

Almost everything about Mr. Terrence Terrell was brown. Hair the color of mud, a light complexion with freckles on his nose, a vulpine face and chin, and he wore a brown jacket, brown waistcoat, and matching brown trousers. He even had brown eyes. That, right down to his overly familiar and cheery demeanor, made Poppy dislike him on sight.

"How good of you to come," Aunt Rachel said politely.

"It is very generous of you to host me." He bowed again, eyeing Poppy. "And who are you?"

"This is my niece, Poppy."

Poppy curtsied politely and avoided the man's eyes.

Her uncle cleared his throat. "You will no doubt be tired from your journey. Come take tea with me in my office and our maid will see you get settled in."

Poppy stood quietly as Terrence looked her up and down and said, "You're very tall, aren't you?"

"Yes." She looked down at him. He stood almost a foot shorter than her.

"I like tall women. So statuesque," he said, walking away.

Once they had gone upstairs, Aunt Rachel plonked herself back on the pale green sofa. "Well, what do you make of that? A new guest to stay with us, and so…"

"Brown."

"Yes, that is just what I was thinking. He does seem to have a favorite color, doesn't he?"

MR. TERRENCE TERRELL was very nice, and so Poppy relaxed as the weeks passed. Her father wrote letters to her, asking whether she had agreed to his gift of a Season, but she deferred to her aunt and uncle.

After a quiet Christmas, during which her father sent the family a large ham, and for Poppy, a card and a set of drawing pencils, paints, and paper, Poppy quietly sketched Betsey, her aunt and uncle, even Mr. Terrell, as the household settled into a pleasant semblance of domesticity.

Poppy's uncle and Mr. Terrell spent the days working on sermons and discussing religion, and the young man took tea and spent the afternoons writing, studying, or conversing with Poppy and her aunt, or doing errands around the household to make himself useful. He sat for Poppy to sketch him, studied divinity literature, and wrote sermons, only to scratch them out and start again.

As the weather slowly improved, Mr. Terrell cut and trimmed the hedges and roses, helped Aunt Rachel weed, till, and hoe the vegetable garden, and assisted Poppy in feeding the chickens. The young man seemed to enjoy a life of quiet study. Poppy did not mind as long as he did not disturb her.

But having been a companion before, Poppy missed the sights, the scenes, the hustle and bustle of London. She missed the regular companionship of her employer, a former mistress, and made do with reading her uncle's newspaper. The letters from her father became less frequent, and Sergeant Dyngley did not write at all. His new promotion must be keeping him busy, Poppy supposed.

She and her aunt spent the months in mourning dress, but now that period was mostly over. Her aunt had switched to wearing purple and mauve after three months, and soon it was just Poppy's turn to put away her dull, drab black clothing.

AS HER AUNT entered Poppy's room one morning in May, Poppy noted the change in her aunt's dress. The black dresses had disappeared and now she wore a black mobcap and sheer black shawl over a deep plum dress. Poppy adjusted her own black shawl and looked up from her book. "Yes?"

"Why are you hiding up here? The day is very fine out and we could use some feed for the chickens. It's not good to be inside all day. Will you go into town and get some? I need fresh bread as well."

"All right." Poppy rose.

"Also, I think it's time you changed your clothes. Why not wear one of your other dresses, instead of the black?" Her aunt said, "It's May already."

A knock came at the door and it opened to reveal Mr. Terrell. "Mrs. Greene? I was just thinking I needed more paper and wondered if you needed anything from the market."

"How kind of you. Yes, Poppy was just going to walk down herself. You can go together."

Poppy glanced at her aunt and raised an eyebrow.

"It is convenient, Poppy."

Poppy gave an unladylike snort and knelt to lace up her boots.

IN THE CART drawn by their horse, Poppy sat beside Mr. Terrell, who managed the reins confidently. "I am learning so much from your uncle, Miss Morton. He is so intelligent. I would be lost without him."

Poppy glanced back at their maid, Betsey, and winked.

"I am glad you are enjoying your time here, Mr. Terrell," Poppy said.

"Oh please, call me Terrence," he said, rubbing his nose. "I find that a nice drive in the country is very refreshing. Do you agree?"

"Yes, very." Poppy smiled politely as he drove the way into town. With such company as this, she missed London society and Sergeant Dyngley very much.

"Do you read much, Miss Morton? I often see you with a book in your hand."

"Yes, my—" she paused. "I was left some literature by a relative and have been reading through it. Have you heard of the *Mysteries of Udolfo*?"

"Mysteries? No. Although I rather like *Jerusalem: The Emanation of the Giant Albion,* by the poet William Blake. Have you read it?"

"No."

"We live in a great age for poetry, I'd say." He carried on.

They eventually arrived in town. As Betsey went to purchase vegetables, Terrence left to seek out some parchment, whilst Poppy stayed with the cart. She stood by and patted the horse as she watched the Euston Flyer come into town, stopping briefly in the center to let passengers disembark. A few people did, and Poppy thought nothing of it, keeping an eye on the increasingly grey clouds that spread across the sky.

Poppy winced as she felt the first few drops hit her face. She turned her head from the sky and wished she'd had the foresight to bring an umbrella. It was going to be a wet ride back.

But as she waved to Betsey and Terrence, one of the female passengers from the carriage came up to her. Poppy deduced the woman to be in her late twenties, and from her plain clothes and air, she was a domestic servant.

"Excuse me, are you Miss Poppy Morton?"

Poppy blinked. "Yes?"

The young woman curtsied and said, "Oh good. I'm Barbara Cooke."

"Nice to meet you." Poppy gave a small curtsey.

The woman looked at her and hoisted her travel bag over her shoulder. "This cart yours, then?"

"Yes. I—what are you doing?" Poppy said as Miss Cooke slung her bag into the cart.

"What's it look like?"

"Yes, but why are you putting that there?"

"Where else would I put it?" She looked at Poppy askance.

Terrence and Betsey returned, arms full of bags of vegetables, chicken feed, meat, and paper. At the sight of the new woman, Terrence said, "Miss Morton, is this woman bothering you?"

"I don't—"

"I'll have you know you are harassing a clergyman's niece. State your business and leave. Unless you are in need of spiritual comfort?" Terrence asked the woman.

"No." Miss Cooke said bluntly and turned to Poppy. "Oh. I know what you need. The letter."

"What letter?"

"Here, hold on. This'll explain everything." The woman pulled open her bag, fished out a somewhat crumpled envelope and handed it to her.

Poppy turned the letter over in her hands. She could have recognized the seal anywhere. "This is from my father."

"Lord Blackwood, yes. He's the one who sent me."

Poppy looked up.

"I'm your lady's maid," Miss Cooke said with a smile.

CHAPTER FOUR

"MY WHAT?" POPPY blurted.

"I'm your lady's maid. Your father sent me. I used to do for your mum."

"Do what, exactly?" Terrence asked.

"Who are you?" Betsey asked, hefting her baskets of vegetables and packaged meat.

"My name is Barbara Cooke," the newcomer said, nodding to both. Exasperated, she said, "Read the letter."

Poppy opened it and read:

Dear Poppy,

When I last visited London I took the liberty of shutting up your mother's townhouse. The servants have joined my household but only briefly until you decide to open up the house again. Your mother's lady's maid, Miss Cooke, seemed open to the prospect of working for you in the same capacity, and so I sent her to you with this letter. Your mother liked her very much. But if she doesn't suit, you may write to me in London and I'll arrange for a replacement. From what I understand she was an excellent source of gossip, which amused Celeste very well. I hope I will see you in London for the Season, which starts this June, to coincide with the sitting of Parliament. Many esteemed families will be in Town and attending the assemblies. Whilst I cannot arrange for you to be introduced to the Queen without raising eyebrows, I would like to do this much for you. Write to me at this address and tell me when I might see you in Town.

Your obedient servant,
Hugh Blackwood

Poppy folded up the letter and clasped it tightly in her hands. Her father had written her. And sent her very own lady's maid. She brightened at the feeling of her mother's touch there. "Miss Cooke, I am very glad to meet you. Welcome to Hertford."

Miss Cooke, who was short, thin, and with comely light brown locks, looked around as if seeing the place for the first time. Then a fly buzzed around her face and she swatted it away with a gloved hand. "So this is the country."

Betsey frowned. "You've come to stay with us?"

"With Miss Morton. I am her new lady's maid."

Terrence looked at Poppy. "Did you order a lady's maid? Did you place an advertisement?"

"No. Um, let's go to the parsonage and sort this out. I'm sure my aunt and uncle will want to discuss it."

AT THE PARSONAGE, Miss Cooke's arrival was even less well-received. Uncle Reginald took one look at her and said, "You're what?"

Miss Cooke raised her chin. "I am Miss Morton's lady's maid."

Uncle Reginald turned to Poppy. "Did you know about this?"

She shook her head.

Her uncle ran a hand through his thinning hair. "And presumably you've come to stay with us."

"Wherever Miss Morton needs me," Miss Cooke said simply.

"And if she needs you in London?" he asked.

"Then that's where I'll go."

"Fine. She needs you to return to London and stay there."

Miss Cooke narrowed her eyes at him. "Begging your pardon, sir, but I takes my orders from Miss Morton, not you. If she bids me to go, I'll go. Otherwise, I'm staying."

"Oh my," Aunt Rachel said.

Uncle Reginald fumed. "I cannot handle this. Not now." He made to leave, then turned around. "We have no room in this parsonage for you. Every room is taken."

"Now Reginald, really," Aunt Rachel started, "That's no reason to be uncharitable. The girl's come all the way from London."

"Uninvited," he pointed out. He looked at Poppy. "Are you sure you didn't have a hand in this?"

"No. I didn't know she existed until this afternoon."

Miss Cooke looked hurt. She stood and said, "If I'm not wanted, I'll go." She started walking.

"Stop," Poppy said. Seeing Miss Cooke pause, she said, "Please, don't go. You've traveled a long way. Please sit and we'll figure this out."

Miss Cooke sat.

"We need tea. And biscuits," Aunt Rachel said, as Uncle Reginald quit the room. Betsey quickly removed herself and soon the clinking sound of tea things could be heard from the kitchen.

"Well, Miss Cooke. Perhaps you might tell us why you've come." Aunt Rachel said.

Miss Cooke shifted on the sofa and clasped her hands in her lap. "I did for Miss Morton's mama, Missus Grey. When she passed on, I was sent here to see if I could do for Miss Morton too." She glanced at Poppy and said, "You can call me Cooke, miss. I can do your hair, mend dresses, and fetch and arrange everything you need."

Poppy blinked. "What do you mean everything?"

"Before you know you're hungry, I'll have dinner waiting for you. I'll have your bedsheets warmed when you're feeling tired, and know which dress you'll want to wear to tea." She looked boldly at Aunt Rachel and Poppy, and said in a quiet voice, "I don't have anywhere else to go."

"Oh, my dear," Aunt Rachel began, when Poppy said, "All

right. You can stay."

"I can?"

"She can? But Poppy, where will she stay? And how will you afford her?" Aunt Rachel asked.

"I'm not a horse," Miss Cooke said, "I'm sitting right here."

"You are, forgive me. It's just, this is quite extraordinary. We've never experienced anything like this before, you see," Aunt Rachel said.

Poppy said, "Perhaps you might share Betsey's room for the night, and give my aunt and I a chance to discuss?"

Miss Cooke picked up her traveling bag and joined Betsey in the kitchen.

Poppy sat back against the green sofa with a loud sigh. "Goodness."

"Well there's a clear answer for what you must do," Terrence said, jolting Poppy into sitting up.

"Mr. Terrell, I forgot you were there."

He smiled at her. "Of course you did. It's easy to understand when you have a stranger in your home. Now, this woman is a stranger and has forced her way in here, but there is no reason you need to allow her to stay. You are too kindhearted, Poppy,"

Aunt Rachel sniffed loudly at his familiar use of her niece's Christian name.

"Besides, your uncle tells me your mother died in childbirth. Why would this woman appear on your doorstep now, decades later? It makes no sense."

Poppy exchanged a look with her aunt.

"Besides, you are a good, sensible girl with no airs of vanity. What need have you of a lady's maid?"

Poppy gripped the sofa cushion she sat on with her hands, digging her nails into the stiff fabric. She swallowed. "Mr. Terrell."

"Call me Terrence, please," he told her.

Poppy saw her aunt's eyebrows rise, and she said, "Mr. Terrell, the fact is that my mother is the one who passed, not a distant relative. I only learned of her existence recently, and lost her too soon. I did not know she had a personal maid, but if this woman really was her lady's maid, it feels like an injustice not to take her on."

His eyes widened. "But you have no use for her. Your family already has a servant. Can the living afford such an extravagance?" he asked.

"I beg your pardon?" Aunt Rachel said.

"From what Mr. Greene said to me, the living is small and suitable enough for two, but not much more." He gave Poppy a full look. "It does you credit to have lived in such economic circumstances."

Poppy stared at him. "That is kind of you to say, but any economical arrangements and the credit for them go to my aunt and uncle, not me."

"I am certain you are too humble to admit to your talents." He smiled and said, "I will leave you to make up your own mind, but if you want my opinion, I would send the girl packing." He left the room.

"Well. What a pickle," Aunt Rachel said. "What will you do, Poppy?"

"I'd like to keep her. If my father sent her to me, it's like a piece of my mother. Does that make sense?"

"Sort of. But Poppy, you can't just go around taking on servants. There's the money for one thing, and where will she stay? You can't expect Betsey to share her room forever," Aunt Rachel said.

"I know. I'm not sure what to do. She could stay in my room."

"Certainly not. No well-brought up girl goes around sleeping in the same room as the servants." Aunt Rachel looked up. "I suppose we could clear out the loft."

"Isn't that old and full of furniture?"

"And dust and spiders. But it's as a good a time as any. In any case, you should go feed the chickens and I'll speak with Reginald about keeping her on for a time."

"Aunt, do you think Father will let me have a London Season?"

"Didn't he say the decision was yours?"

"Yes, but I don't know the first thing about what to do or how to go about it. I'd need more than a lady's maid to guide me. I'd need you."

"Oh." Her Aunt Rachel thought on this, then beamed. "Us in London for the Season? What an idea."

"I'd need help. I'd like to do it but… I don't feel I can without Uncle's approval."

"It does rather seem like a scatterbrained idea. But… Hmmm. I will think on it. Best go feed those chickens before it gets dark."

Poppy rose and put on a household apron that she didn't mind getting dirty. It was a cream-colored linen that washed easily. She was about to leave when a knock came at the parsonage door. Poppy answered it, and came face to face with…

"Sergeant Dyngley," Poppy said. "I was just about to feed the chickens."

"Then I shall join you," he said amiably. He wore a nice dark navy suit and smart dark hat.

"Who is there, Poppy?" her aunt called.

"Sergeant Dyngley."

"Hello, Sergeant," her aunt called.

Sergeant Dyngley was too well-bred to take part in a shouting match. He marched to the blue room and greeted Aunt Rachel, then returned to Poppy's side.

Poppy took a bag of chicken feed and stepped outside. She led him around the stables and around the back, where he stood by as she scattered handfuls of chicken feed and smiled at the sight of the hens and rooster running around pecking at it. Once she had finished, she stood back and watched from beside him.

"Poppy." Dyngley stepped closer to her and said, "There is something I wished to talk to you about, I… there is a dance on Saturday. Will you be attending?"

"I—hadn't planned on going. I'm still mourning my mother," she said.

"But your months of mourning are almost over, surely. Will you think about it?"

"All right."

"Good." He kissed her hand. "I demand the first dance."

"Sergeant..." she said, feeling shivers down her spine. Damn him for making her feel this way.

He pulled her to him. "When I last saw you, I did something very untoward."

"What would that be?"

Two spots of color blossomed at the corners of his temples. "I came to visit you after the murderer had been led away."

"Oh yes?" She paused as if trying to remember.

"That horrid man Tom was just leaving."

"Mmhm. A nice young man, Mr. Harris. So handsome," she said.

"And I kissed you," he growled.

"Did you? I must have forgotten." She gave him an impish smile.

"Perhaps you need a reminder."

He was very close. He clasped her hands and looked into her eyes. They seemed warm and inviting. But the impropriety of it all was enough to make her blush. They stood too close for comfort, too close for propriety, too close for anything else. She closed her eyes, when suddenly a familiar voice said, "Poppy?"

She opened her eyes and whirled around. "Mr. Terrell."

Chapter Five

Poppy blushed. Her family's houseguest had caught her in a somewhat compromising situation with Sergeant Dyngley.

Mr. Terrell stood there, stony-faced. "Your uncle bids you come inside the house, Poppy. Right now."

Poppy blushed down to her toes. "I'm coming."

Mr. Terrell looked pointedly at Dyngley, who bowed. "Sir."

"Who are you?" Mr. Terrell asked.

"Sergeant Dyngley. I'm a sergeant for Hertford parish. I was just paying a social call."

"I see. Don't let us keep you from your business, Sergeant." Terrence held out his arm to Poppy, who blinked and took it.

She looked back at Dyngley, who nodded to her. "'Til Saturday, Miss Morton. I do hope you will consider attending."

Poppy allowed Mr. Terrell to escort her back to the house. Upon entering, she dropped her arm from his.

"What did that man want from you?" he asked.

"Sergeant Dyngley is my friend," she said, "we have solved crimes together."

"Pish-posh. A woman, solving crimes? I'll believe that when pigs fly. What's happening Saturday?" Mr. Terrell asked.

Poppy frowned at him. "It's a dance at the local assembly rooms in town. He's asked me for the first dance."

"Has he? Well, then I claim the second. It's only fitting as I am staying at the parsonage."

"I wasn't aware you danced, Mr. Terrell."

"Terrence, please. And yes, I enjoy a good country dance. Of course, if your uncle does not approve, then I will gladly stay at the parsonage and work on my sermons, but once I tell him we are to be dancing together, I am sure he will not oppose the idea."

Poppy winced. Two dances, two partners. At this rate, she'd need a proper dance card just to keep track.

AUNT RACHEL WAS delighted at the idea of Poppy returning to society and together with Miss Cooke, made a quick perusal of the dresses Poppy had brought back with her from her time in London. As it was a simple country dance, they decided on a mauve-colored dress with cap sleeves and a high-cut bodice for Poppy to wear.

Poppy was less enthused by this discussion, but after a time realized they were enjoying themselves, and so abandoned them and left to read in the blue sitting room.

BY THE TIME the day of the dance rolled around, Miss Cooke had become a surprisingly welcome addition to the household. They did have more mouths to feed, but she too assisted Betsey with the baking, adding her own recipes to the household collection, cleaned and showed no distaste at getting her hands dirty, and even trimmed Mr. Greene's wicks for his candles and sharpened the writing nibs of his quills. But Saturday was when she truly outdid herself, for she styled Poppy's hair with a ribbon that made a simple bun look like a Greek muse. With a touch of rouge on her cheeks and a red tint on her lips, Poppy moved down the stairs to join her family amidst many appreciative glances.

"Oh Poppy, you look wonderful," Aunt Rachel said, taking her by the hand. "Miss Cooke, you have done well. I've never made her hair look so pretty."

Poppy smiled at her aunt and looked at her uncle, who

coughed. "You look very well, Poppy."

"Very well indeed," Mr. Terrell echoed. "Shall we?" He held out an arm to Poppy, who looked at her uncle and aunt before taking it and sailing out the front door.

The Hertford assembly rooms were very nice, and a place that Poppy knew well. From its high pillars and cream-colored walls to the many dozens of candles that gave the place a golden-tinged hue, Poppy's chest filled with happiness as she entered on the arm of Mr. Terrell. Tonight he wore a dark brown suit with a fussily tied white cravat, knee breeches, and dark knee socks with shined black shoes.

Poppy's aunt and uncle quickly abandoned them in search of their friends and neighbors, whilst she looked around for Sergeant Dyngley. Where was he?

"Well I don't see the Sergeant around anywhere, Poppy, perhaps he forgot. Allow me the honor of engaging you for the first dance," Mr. Terrell said.

"That won't be necessary, Mr. Terrell," Sergeant Dyngley said, bowing to Poppy. His face bore a trace of amusement as he ignored Terrence and held out a hand to Poppy. "May I have the pleasure?"

Poppy smiled and took his hand, letting herself be guided away by her favorite sergeant, unaware of Mr. Terrell's withering gaze.

"That man has taken a fancy to you, I think, Miss Morton." Sergeant Dyngley said.

She laughed. "He is very amiable and good. I think my uncle likes him very much."

"What a shame it is not your uncle he is interested in."

"Sergeant, you sound almost jealous," Poppy teased.

He winked at her and led her into the first set. The dance began, a cotillion, where they joined a set with three other couples. As the music picked up a lively tune, Poppy lost herself in the movements and concentrated on the dance steps. Every once in a while she would see a familiar face watching from the sidelines, and inwardly wished the dance would never end. But it did, and before she had completed her curtsey to Sergeant Dyngley, her attention was claimed by Mr. Terrell, who stood before her.

"Poppy, I hope you have not forgotten but you promised me the next dance," he said.

As she allowed him to lead her into the next set, he added, "I love a country dance. Would you like to dance the next dance after this?"

This was getting out of hand. She said, "No, I think not. I have just come out of mourning, so it wouldn't be appropriate for me to join in too much of the excitement right away."

Terrence's face fell slightly. "Of course, I understand. You're quite right. It would be unseemly for a clergyman's niece to behave with too much frivolity right away." He paused, "But you see, I had rather hoped I might spend time in your company this evening."

"I… That is too kind—" The dance began before she could finish speaking. Thankfully, she thought, as she stepped in time with the music. This was a quadrille, which suited her well, as the quick music demanded she not lose her place in the formation with the other couples. The dance ended all too soon for her liking, and she suddenly felt overwarm.

Mr. Terrell was at her side in an instant and she waved off his arm, saying, "Excuse me, I need some air."

She moved away from him and circulated around the crowd of townspeople, until she entered one of the outside balconies and breathed in the fresh night air. It felt cool and pleasant against her skin, and she wished she had had the foresight to bring a fan. The evening had barely begun and she was already ready for bed. Had she re-entered society too soon? What would her mother think of her actions, dancing with two men right after mourning her loss?

Dyngley soon came outside. "Miss Morton, are you all right?"

She placed her gloved hands on the stone balcony, taking

comfort in its solid weight. "Yes, I'm fine."

He stood by her, a quiet shadow. "Is it too much? Too soon? Your coming out into society?"

"I think maybe, just a little."

"You look very pretty tonight," he said.

She glanced at him. He blushed and tugged at his cravat. "I mean, you look nice every day, but—"

She laughed. "Are you practicing your charms for when you meet a wealthy widow or rich debutante, Sergeant?"

He gave a little laugh. "No, I was just paying you a compliment."

She snorted.

"Do you miss it? London, I mean?"

"Yes. I wish I could be back there. I miss my former employer, Miss Hayes, and the ladies we socialized with." She politely did not mention Mr. Tom Harris, a young man of a similar age who acted as a procurer of female talent for the highest bidder, and who had taken a shine to her recently.

"London is certainly freer in some regards, but in others, I find it just the same," he said.

"What do you mean?"

"There is a greater variety of sights and sounds. The city itself doesn't sleep, and we are only in the nineteenth century. But I find that there is still an expectation to go out often, to see and be seen, and that for many people it doesn't matter how silly you look, as long as you are driving a barouche or traveling in the right circles." He looked at her and rubbed the side of his face. "Sorry. Since we returned, my work has kept me busy and I've barely had time to look in on my brother and his wife."

"How are they?"

"Well enough, from what their letters say. What about you? Have you heard from your father much?"

"Some. At Christmas he was very generous. And he wishes to give—"

"Poppy, there you are. I've been looking for you." Mr. Terrell appeared at the balcony. "Oh. This man isn't bothering you, is he?"

"I was just enquiring after her family," Sergeant Dyngley said, giving him a dirty look.

"They are all in excellent health, thank you," Mr. Terrell said, turning to Poppy. "I know you have no wish to dance but may I escort you around the festivities? Your aunt and uncle will be wondering where you are."

"All right."

The rest of the evening was spent either in the company of Mr. Terrell by her side or in conversation with her aunt and uncle. Within an hour, Poppy was ready to go home and drank far too much to console herself as she watched Dyngley talk with other people. Their eyes met across the room more than once, but he did not approach her again.

THE NEXT DAY, the group had just finished breakfast and were sitting in the blue room. Poppy's uncle was sitting in a comfortable chair reading the newspaper, Mr. Terrell sat nearby reading, whilst Poppy and Aunt Rachel mended shirts. Betsey and Miss Cooke tidied the house and were preparing luncheon when there was a knock at the door.

"Who could that be? It's too early for visitors," Aunt Rachel said.

Poppy glanced at the doorway when Miss Cooke went to answer it. A moment later she introduced, "Sergeant Dyngley to speak to you."

Poppy said, "Sergeant? Is something the matter?"

Sergeant Dyngley came into the blue sitting room. He bowed and said, "Excuse the interruption, but I could not wait."

"Good heavens, Sergeant, what is the matter?" Aunt Rachel asked.

"I have heard a rumor that Miss Morton is to go to London shortly."

"I am?" Poppy asked.

"I have heard she is to have a London Season," Dyngley said.

Aunt Rachel set aside her sewing. "Yes, she may. Her father has offered to fund it and so gentlemanlike too. But her uncle has not yet made up his mind yet whether to allow it." Aunt Rachel turned to her husband, "Think of the dresses, Reginald. She could look so beautiful at a ball in a new dress. I can't wait to see what she'll wear…" Aunt Rachel stopped at his serious expression.

"Why do you ask, Sergeant?" Mr. Greene lowered his newspaper.

"Because, Mr. Greene," Dyngley started. He looked at Poppy for a fleeting moment and said, formally, "I would like permission to court your niece."

Poppy's mouth dropped open. "You would?"

Dyngley looked at her and blushed, then gave a quick nod. "That is, if it is acceptable to Miss Morton."

"Oh Sergeant," Aunt Rachel gushed and darted to her feet. "Finally!"

Poppy blushed from head to toe. Her heart beat as fast as a hummingbird's.

"You want my permission to court Poppy?" Her uncle murmured.

"Yes, sir," Dyngley said.

"And so do I," Mr. Terrell said, standing up.

CHAPTER SIX

THE ENTIRE GROUP looked at Terrence, who blushed. "Since my arrival at the parsonage, I have become enamored of Miss Morton. Her charms and beauty are second to none and I know that she will make any clergyman a good and proper wife."

Poppy's mouth dropped open again. Aunt Rachel winced. Sergeant Dyngley looked ready to strike the man, while Uncle Reginald beamed.

"No," Poppy said, clapping a hand to her mouth. "I mean, Mr. Terrell, you are too kind."

He turned to her, fixing her with his gaze. "I think you are very smart and sensible. Those are amiable qualities I must have in a wife, and when I do marry, I hope you will consider me as a prospective husband," Mr. Terrell said, touching his heart.

Sergeant Dyngley fumed quietly as Uncle Reginald said, "What a wonderful idea."

"Uncle?" Poppy asked.

"I have made up my mind," Uncle Reginald said. "You shall have a London Season, Poppy."

"I will?" she echoed.

"Yes."

"Oh, thank goodness. I thought you'd never say yes. Oh Poppy, how wonderful," Aunt Rachel began. "Just think of the dresses and the balls you'll attend."

"On one condition," Uncle Reginald said.

"What is that?" Poppy asked.

Her uncle looked at the sergeant, then at Poppy. "I will agree to your London Season, and to allow the sergeant to court you, provided he promises to be a devoted and honest suitor."

"I will," Sergeant Dyngley said.

"He will," Aunt Rachel echoed.

"Then you may have him as a suitor, Poppy, but you must allow my candidate as well."

"Uncle..." Poppy started.

"You may see the sergeant for social outings, as long as you see Mr. Terrell also. Accompanied by another woman or your aunt, of course. I have made my mind up and think this is the best solution. Mr. Terrell is a fine young man and I will not have you chasing after one young man when there is a perfectly good gentleman right here."

Poppy felt the air go out of her. Two suitors and only one she wanted. If she could have, she would have reached for an alcoholic drink at that moment. She glanced at Mr. Terrell, who grinned, then at Sergeant Dyngley, who looked firm and forbidding in his dark suit, but had eyes only for her. "Very well, Uncle. I accept your proposal."

She heard a loud cheer from the kitchen and then Miss Cooke appeared. "Begging your pardon, but me and Betsey just saw our bread rose. So sorry for the noise."

Sergeant Dyngley left with a bow and fleeting look, but no final words for Poppy. The group soon broke up after that, with Poppy spending the morning writing a letter to her father, to tell him the news. She had Miss Cooke post it straightaway, and listened as Miss Cooke and her aunt discussed what would happen.

MEALTIMES BECAME DIFFICULT, as Poppy felt the added burden of Mr. Terrell's weighted looks upon her almost every waking moment. When he was not upstairs writing sermons or studying with her uncle, he took pains to be in the vicinity nearby. She'd even found a poem left on her pillow one evening that made her laugh out loud, then cringe, as she found the words "orange" rhymed with "challenge" to be genuinely meant. At least in London she need not see him so often as in the parsonage.

FINALLY, IN MAY, a most desired letter came. Poppy was studiously avoiding Mr. Terrell's gaze when a messenger knocked on the front door of the parsonage. Betsey delivered it to Poppy, who recognized the handwriting immediately. She tore it open.

"What is it, Poppy?" Aunt Rachel said.

Poppy read it and handed her the letter.

"Oh my." Aunt Rachel read it and looked at her husband. "Poppy's townhouse has been opened up and is ready for her stay."

Poppy shared a smile with Miss Cooke, who put aside her sewing. "I shall start packing at once."

"So will I," Aunt Rachel said, rising from her seat.

"You? You're not going." Uncle Reginald looked up from his newspaper.

"Of course I am. Who is going to look after our niece? It's all well and good that Poppy is going to London, but she's still barely twenty. What is she going to do in her mother's house all alone? She needs someone to guide her."

Mr. Terrell paled. Uncle Reginald frowned. "I did not think this would happen so soon."

"It is May. The Season starts in June to coincide with the sitting of Parliament, so we need to make haste if we are to prepare Poppy in time."

"For what? She has a sound mind and good manners. What other attributes does she need?" Uncle Reginald asked.

"Gowns, hats, gloves, and petticoats. You can't allow her to go to parties inappropriately dressed. Come Miss Cooke, we have work to do," Aunt Rachel said.

COMPARED TO THE packing, the trip to London was relatively short. After hours of packing, unpacking, and repacking hats, dresses, shifts, undergarments, shoes, petticoats, gloves, Poppy was ready to scream. Instead she walked out of her bedroom while Aunt Rachel and Miss Cooke were in a discussion about which set of gloves to wear when she went for a daily walk.

The family decided to take their carriage, a secondhand purchase from her uncle's patroness, Lady Cameron, and made the journey to London. Poppy, her aunt, and maid all piled into the carriage amidst trunks of clothes and other necessities, along with Mr. Terrell, as her uncle drove. Poppy's uncle did not approve of all the fanfare, but neither was he comfortable with letting his wife and niece go off alone, so the men came too and took turns driving.

By the time they stopped in Enfield to rest the horses and stretch their legs, Poppy was ready to get a breath of fresh air. She and the other ladies climbed out of the carriage and took lunch at an inn. Less than an hour later they were on the road again, hoping to reach the city of London by nightfall.

Luck was with them and they entered the city through Moorgate, and made their way down the busy roads. At a brief stop, Miss Cooke climbed to sit up top and direct Poppy's uncle as he drove through the London streets. As darkness was setting over the city, they drove down the busy Oxford Street, past Bond Street, and turned right, to eventually pull up outside a pleasant-looking building on Orchard Street.

Miss Cooke climbed down and hurried straight down to the tradesmen's entrance. In a matter of minutes, all manner of servants came out of the building, taking boxes, trunks, and traveling bags, and a footman helped each of the ladies disembark from the carriage. Poppy had been inside her mother's house just twice before, and neither had been a positive experience. Now that she stood there in the well-lit foyer, feeling tired from her journey, it all felt surreal.

Servants hurried by and then stopped. Whispers flew and in

moments, they all lined up before Poppy. Each wore a smart uniform of black with aprons or smart jackets, all in a muted dark gray color. They looked at her and she felt their eyes weighing her, from her overly tall height to the quality of her traveling clothes. Would she fill her mother's shoes? Would she be a good mistress? Or would she stay no more than a week? There was so much to decide.

Miss Cooke did the introductions. Standing there in a dark traveling cloak and bonnet, she introduced two footmen, a butler, a fearsome cook, a fierce-looking housekeeper, a housemaid, two scullery maids, two groomsmen, as well as a man and maid of all work. These last two Miss Cooke referred to as dogsbodies, who took on any task, no matter how dull.

Poppy gave them a polite smile. "Thank you for coming and returning to your posts. I don't know what you have been told, but I am looking forward to staying here for some time." She introduced her aunt, who stood beside her.

"My uncle and his student are outside with the carriage. Perhaps one of you could assist them? I have no idea where the carriage should be kept."

The two groomsmen left to assist, as a heavy-set woman curtseyed. "Miss Morton, I am the housekeeper, Mrs. Pratt. I will show you to your mother's room, Lucy will assist your aunt, and Johnny and Scott will escort your uncle and his student to their rooms, if that is agreeable to you, miss?"

Poppy felt dead on her feet. "Yes, most agreeable. Please." She began to follow Mrs. Pratt up a narrow flight of stairs, then paused. "Did you say my mother's room?"

"Yes. It has been made up for you."

"Um, I'd rather not stay there. Could you make up one of the guest bedrooms for me instead?"

Mrs. Pratt blinked. "Yes, miss."

After some deliberations, everyone had a bedroom to their liking. Poppy stayed in a guest bedroom, her aunt and uncle in another, and Mr. Terrell in one. It was not a large townhouse, but very tall, with long narrow staircases. From a central foyer at the entrance led a small dining room to the right, a drawing room to the left, and servants' kitchen and pantry downstairs. Upstairs was another sitting room that had been transformed into a private library, and then bedrooms. Above them was the loft, where the servants slept.

As the hour was getting late, the group dined on a small dinner of roast pork with crackling, carrots, boiled potatoes and peas on china plates, served with a smooth red wine. Poppy felt a bit lightheaded after the meal and bid the others good night early, for after such a long journey she could barely keep her eyes open.

As the others settled in, Miss Cooke accompanied Poppy to her room and helped undo her hair from its messy bun and laid out a simple shift for her to sleep in. Poppy's eyes felt heavy and she gratefully accepted Miss Cooke's help to undress.

"That Mr. Terrell has got his eye on you," Miss Cooke commented.

Poppy snorted. "He can look all he likes, provided that's all he does. Although, I'm rather surprised by the whole thing. I never thought he liked me so much."

"Didn't you? I could see it from a mile away. The man's besotted. He looks at you like a ripe cheese he wants to eat."

Poppy glanced at her maid. "I am a cheese?"

Miss Cooke's stomach grumbled. "Sorry. I was thinking about food. Mind you, I wouldn't put it past him to try something while he's staying here."

"What do you mean?"

"He was very put out you were leaving, until it became clear that your uncle was coming too. Now that he's here as a suitor in your household..." Miss Cooke shook her head. "It wouldn't surprise me if he were to try and put pressure on you to accept him."

"Hah!" Poppy laughed. "He wouldn't dare."

"Just mind what I said, miss... I'd keep the door locked if I was you." Miss Cooke left, taking Poppy's dusty travel boots and dress with her.

There was a small fire in the hearth and the bed looked inviting. Poppy closed the door, glad to have a few moments to herself. She was currently in a guest's room which suited her fine, as she undid her traveling dress, stays and stockings and put on the comfortable shift. As she slipped into bed, she pulled the covers over her and soon drifted off to sleep.

But Poppy wasn't used to the noise of London at night, and something awoke her. She didn't open her eyes, but a sixth sense told her she wasn't alone in the darkness. She opened her eyes.

A dark figure stood over her, its mouth open in a rictus smile. Poppy screamed and punched it with all her might.

Chapter Seven

THE GHOST GRUNTED and crashed to the floor.

Poppy shrieked and tangled herself in the blankets, thrashing and trying to get away. She fell out of the bed, ran to the fireplace, and picked up a poker, brandishing it like a weapon. "Who are you? Whoever you are, get out!"

The ghost cried, "Miss Morton! I meant no harm. I was only coming to check on you."

Poppy held out the poker like a fencing foil and peered into the darkness. "Mr. Terrell?"

"Yes." He slowly got up from the floor, holding his nose.

"What are you doing here?"

"You hit me! My nose is bleeding," he accused.

"I thought you were a ghost. What on earth are you doing here?"

He stepped closer and stopped at the poker. "I wanted to check on you, make sure you were all right," he said, his voice thick.

"Why wouldn't I be?"

The door to her bedroom stood open. Her aunt filled the doorway. "Poppy, are you all right? I heard a noise."

"I am fine, Aunt. But Mr. Terrell is here."

"What? Why is he here?" Aunt Rachel stepped into the room.

"That's what I would like to know," Poppy said, still holding the poker.

"There has been a misunderstanding," Mr. Terrell said, pulling his robe around himself and holding his nose. He said, "these old houses are often uncomfortable and noisy. I thought perhaps Miss Morton might have trouble falling asleep, so I went to see if she was awake. If she was, I was going to offer to bring her a glass of warm milk."

Poppy inwardly couldn't think of anything worse.

"That is very kind, I'm sure…" Aunt Rachel looked at him oddly. "But why would you think to go walking into her room in the middle of the night? Surely a simple knock would have sufficed."

Mr. Terrell shrugged.

"You woke me, sir. However kind your intentions, perhaps you might leave me here. I am positive if I cannot sleep I will ring for a servant," Poppy said, her voice taking on an edge.

"Of course, of course. Forgive me." He swept from the room.

Poppy gripped the poker hard, her hand trembling. She stood in near darkness as the fire in the hearth had mostly succumbed to mere glowing coals now. How dared he come into her room at night? What was he thinking?

"Poppy, are you all right?" Aunt Rachel asked, "That must have given you a fright."

"What's happened? I heard a noise. Is that Mr. Terrell who just left?" Miss Cooke arrived, dressed in a nightgown and robe.

"I'm fine. Mr. Terrell decided to pay me a nighttime visit," Poppy said darkly.

"Did he?" Miss Cooke frowned. "Was your door unlocked?"

"Yes. I fell asleep and didn't think of it." Poppy glared at the door. "I'll lock it now."

"I'd say so. Although there's no reason you should have to. This is your house. I'll have a word with Reginald about this in the morning," Aunt Rachel said.

"No, don't, Aunt. It was hard enough getting Uncle's agreement for us to come to London for the Season. I don't want him to change his mind."

"It doesn't matter if he disagrees, this is indecent behavior. Mr. Terrell is a guest; he has no right or proper reason to be wandering around the rooms so late at night," Miss Cooke said.

"You're right."

"And he could have put you in a compromising position," Aunt Rachel muttered.

"Do you think that was his intention?" Poppy asked, lowering the poker. She rested its point into the wooden floor, feeling its solid iron weight.

"I do not want to consider it. He is your uncle's student, and comes highly recommended from the divinity school. Likely he was just thinking of your comfort and acted without thinking of any possible impropriety," Aunt Rachel said. "Yes, that must be it. Good night, Poppy."

Poppy watched her aunt go. As Miss Cooke took the poker and built up the fire, Poppy said, "It looks like you were right, Miss Cooke."

"Never mind that. What are you going to do if he tries that again?"

"There won't be a next time. I think I hit him in the nose."

"Serves him right." Miss Cooke rose. "Will you be all right now?"

"Yes. Thank you." Poppy smiled as Miss Cooke left.

But as the door shut behind her, Poppy's smile vanished. Her hands trembled. In truth, she was furious at Mr. Terrell. He had interrupted her sleep and somehow had thought it acceptable to creep into her room at night while she slept. How monstrous. It was like a scene out of Matthew Lewis's gothic novel, *The Monk*.

She frowned at the fire and hoped his nose hurt. Her aunt might be right in that he was only thinking of her comfort, but to go wandering around so late at night was odd. She did not like it, not one bit. It sent an eerie feeling down her spine.

Poppy quickly locked the door to be safe, taking comfort in hearing the bolt turn with a satisfying click. She leaned a chair beneath the door and laid the poker beside her bed. Still, as she stared up at the ceiling from beneath the bedcovers, she despaired of getting sleep any time soon. Even with those safeguards, she did not feel safe, and was wide awake. Every subtle noise and creak of the house made her tense and stare around the room. She could not shake the feeling Mr. Terrell had abused her hospitality and her family's goodwill in order to compromise her. But had he, or was it all just an innocent mistake?

THE NEXT MORNING, Poppy washed her face in a basin of water Miss Cooke had left out for her and unlocked the door to let her maid in. Miss Cooke took one look at her bleary eyes and gently helped Poppy dress in a dark purple dress with flowers on it. It was perfectly innocent, high-cut, and with a dark shawl over her shoulders, she presented a picture of calm respectability.

Miss Cooke dressed her hair in an ordinary bun and pinned up the flyaway hairs to give a simple appearance. The effect was a trifle severe, but allowing no nonsense either, which was what Poppy wanted at that moment. Or at least that was the effect she imagined as she looked in the mirror.

She wandered down to breakfast to a meal of toast, preserves, eggs and coffee, and found her aunt and uncle there already. She said good morning and filled her plate, when her uncle dropped his fork. "Mr. Terrell!"

Poppy and her aunt looked up. Into the dining room walked Terrence, dressed in a brown suit as usual, but with a bruised and swollen nose. He looked very sheepish as he cleared his throat and sat at the table across from Poppy.

"Mr. Terrell, what happened to you? Did you have a tumble in the night?" Uncle Reginald asked.

Mr. Terrell avoided Poppy's eyes. "An unfortunate accident."

Poppy exchanged a look with her aunt, who raised an eyebrow. "Mr. Terrell wanted to check on Poppy, but she thought him an intruder."

"An unfortunate mistake on my part," Mr. Terrell said, turning red.

"Yes, well. Your Christian kindness is to be lauded, but maybe let's let the ladies sleep. They need their beauty sleep, or so Mrs. Greene keeps telling me," Uncle Reginald said, smiling at his wife.

Aunt Rachel shot him a look that Poppy interpreted to mean if they weren't in mixed company, she'd have stuck her tongue out at him.

The group quietly ate their breakfast as Uncle Reginald helped himself to porridge and asked, "So Poppy, what will you to do today? Start scouting the area for husbands?"

Poppy smirked at her uncle's teasing. "I thought I might take a walk and see the neighborhood."

"Very good. I shall read the newspaper."

"Perhaps I might join you, Miss Morton," Mr. Terrell said, biting into his toast.

"Oh, but Mr. Terrell, surely you need to focus on your studies. We wouldn't want our trip to London to distract you," Poppy said.

Mr. Terrell opened his mouth to object, when Reginald said, "Quite right. The boy needs no such distractions as parties and dances. After breakfast, we'll head to the drawing room for your studies and later perhaps we'll visit the local church, and see what we can do to help."

Mr. Terrell said, "Would you care to join us, Miss Morton?"

Poppy restrained herself from kicking him beneath the table. "No, thank you. I might see what events are on. I'm sure I'll hear from my father soon." And she studiously avoided his gaze for the rest of breakfast.

AFTER THE MEAL, Poppy had a servant go out for newspapers and pick up a copy of the *London Daily Advertiser and Oracle*. Sat comfortably in the parlor on a light gray sofa of comfortable material, she spotted on the very front page, "Aunt, here is something. The Royal Academy at Somerset Place has an exhibition open."

"An exhibition of what?" her aunt asked, sipping tea.

"Art. And there's a production at the Theater Royal tonight, a comedy called 'The Poor Gentleman.'"

"Nonsense, Poppy, we can't afford that. You shouldn't go filling your head with such idle fancies as attending the theater," her uncle said over his book.

Poppy looked at her uncle, then raised her eyebrows at her aunt. She did not wish to contradict him, but felt strongly that those sorts of idle fancies were exactly the reason she was in Town.

"Aunt, look at this." Poppy leaned closer to her and pointed at a section labelled *The Oracle of Fashion*.

"Oh my. This is what we need to see." Her aunt peered at the fine print. "How exciting. Let's visit the exhibition. We're in Town, some culture would be good."

THAT MORNING POPPY was given a tour of the building by the housekeeper, Mrs. Pratt. As Poppy learned the ins and outs, she did wonder if she would be able to handle the responsibility of taking her mother's place and owning an entire household.

Poppy and her aunt dressed in light-colored walking dresses and were delighted to take her mother's barouche to the royal exhibition, where they paid the shilling entry fee and spent an enjoyable afternoon looking at art. Until something caught Poppy's eye.

There were many finely dressed men and women in attendance, including some very finely dressed to go out. "Those are most likely members of the *ton*," Aunt Rachel whispered in her ear. "Too good for us."

Poppy stood by and watched, as a dirty young woman in shabby clothes wandered closely behind some of the fashionably dressed women and then walked away. A minute later a loud voice said, "My reticule. It's gone!"

People stopped. A well-dressed woman in an excellent green hat with feathers, looked around the room. People gathered around her as she looked frantically around.

Poppy spotted the questionable young woman start to pass by, who avoided all eye contact. She stuck out her long leg and tripped the girl.

"Poppy, watch out!" Aunt Rachel said.

The girl went flying and out of her hands flew—

"My reticule!" The well-dressed woman cried.

The girl scrambled to her knees when Poppy trod on the hem of the girl's dirty gray dress so she couldn't escape. The thief, her blonde hair hidden by a straw bonnet that had seen better days, scowled at her. She pulled out a pair of scissors and cut at Poppy, who veered back.

They were quickly surrounded by people.

"This girl is a thief," Poppy's voice carried.

"Somebody stop that girl," a voice called out.

The thief tugged but couldn't escape, as her skirt had not only been stamped on by Poppy's boot, but her dress had also caught on an unobliging nail in the floor.

Soon they were surrounded by people, including two men who pulled the girl up. One said, "Pickpocket, eh? You're going straight to the watch."

The girl spouted profanities as she was dragged away. Poppy picked up the now dirty red velvet reticule and dusted it off, then handed it back to the approaching woman.

"Thank you," the woman said, taking it firmly. She was tall, near fifty years of age, with strands of gray among her fashionably coiled brunette hair. "How did you know the girl was a thief?"

"She didn't belong here. Her clothes gave that away. And she wandered too close to you and your friends. I thought it was a bit odd. Then when you cried out your reticule was gone, I suspected she had taken it."

"But you didn't know for certain."

"No, I didn't. But she seemed out of place here. I rather suspected she had done something to take it, rather than you losing it."

She surveyed Poppy closely. "What is your name? I do not recognize you."

Poppy curtseyed. "Poppy Morton, and this is my aunt, Mrs. Greene."

Aunt Rachel curtseyed as well, keeping her eyes lowered beneath her straw bonnet.

"I see. And do you often catch thieves whilst at the Royal Academy?"

"No, ma'am. We are newly arrived and I wished to take in the sights. Catching a thief was rather the low point of the day." The quip came so quickly to her lips, Poppy wondered at the cleverness of her tongue.

The woman's mouth curved into a smile. "Indeed. And do you have much planned in the way of entertainment, Miss Morton?"

"Not yet. We are in Town for the Season."

The lady's eyes widened a fraction. "How delightful. If you are looking for amusement, you might visit the Fashionable Institution and purchase a subscription from the Secretary, Mr. Boyle. Mention my name and he is sure to sell you some tickets."

Poppy curtseyed. "That is most kind, Mrs.…"

"Devenshaw." The woman clutched her reticule tightly and left.

Poppy rose from her curtsey. "I wonder what all that was about."

"Oh my goodness. Do you not know who that was?" a feminine voice asked. "You must be new in Town."

Poppy turned to see three young women, all fashionably dressed, facing her. The first was an impetuous looking redhead with a light walking dress, her auburn coils curling around her shoulders. Beside her stood a black-haired girl who looked pale and washed out, with a pointed nose and a bit of acne on her chin. The third was a blonde, who stood a bit shorter and plumper than the others, who wore a straw bonnet with green ribbon, and had green in her walking dress. She smiled warmly at

Poppy.

They all curtseyed and Poppy said, "I am new. My aunt and I arrived just last night. I am Poppy Morton."

The redhead introduced herself as Lucretia Dobbins. The girl with black hair was Mary Gibbs, and the blonde waved hello was Emily Munden. "We are all here for the Season," Lucretia said, "That must be why you're here."

Poppy nodded.

"Is it true you caught a thief?" Emily asked.

"Shush, Miss Munden, of course she didn't. Good girls don't do that sort of thing," Lucretia told her.

"I didn't catch her, but I did trip her." Poppy gave Emily a warm smile. "She looked suspicious and when Mrs. Devenshaw said her reticule had been stolen, I saw the girl getting away."

"You're certainly tall," Miss Gibbs commented, looking up at her.

"Yes," Poppy said, not sure what else to say.

"Have you been presented to the Queen yet? We all were," Miss Gibbs said.

"No, I'm afraid not."

Miss Gibbs smirked.

"Never mind. We can't all have a knight as a father." Lucretia rolled her eyes at Miss Gibbs. "You're out, and Mrs. Devenshaw has given you an introduction to the Fashionable Institution, so you'll be attending the same balls and concerts as us, no doubt." Lucretia eyed Poppy's smart blue spencer and matching blue bonnet with white ribbon. "We'll see each other soon, I'm sure. Good day." She marched away, leading Miss Gibbs with her.

Miss Munden stayed. "It's a pleasure to meet you. Where are you staying?"

"On Orchard street. Number 56."

"I'll pay a visit if you're in. Unless you're riding the parks?"

"What do you mean?"

Emily giggled. "That's what some men call it. This time of year, the three parks, Hyde, Green and St James's Park, are where people go to see and be seen. But they are so busy, we have to stand out in some way, so many girls taking to riding horses instead of promenading. It's called 'riding the parks.' Do you have any plans for tomorrow afternoon?"

"No. Will you be riding the parks?" Poppy smiled.

"Not a chance, I'm a terrible rider. But I will walk with you around Hyde Park if you like. Say we meet at the entrance at three o'clock?"

"I'll look forward to it."

The girls curtseyed, and Poppy watched Emily dart after the others.

Aunt Rachel appeared at Poppy's side. "I'm so pleased you've made friends already. This is excellent news. And such pretty girls. I shall tell Reginald. This will be a treat."

Poppy and her aunt spent a few more minutes wandering through the Royal Academy before popping outside to the street sellers for a light luncheon, purchasing what one food seller told them was a "Cornish pasty." Poppy bit into the light golden pastry, shedding crumbs all over her gloves. The pasty was piping hot, and she got a mouthful of minced beef with seasoning and vegetables. Altogether, it was delicious. "Mmmm."

"I've heard of these. Miners in Cornwall apparently eat them," Aunt Rachel said.

Once they'd eaten, they made their way to the Fashionable Institution and enquired after Mr. Boyle. A short, fastidious man with a round pate and spectacles, he surveyed them up and down with a practiced eye. Poppy rather suspected he missed no detail and was prepared to turn away, but his mouth opened when she gave him Mrs. Devenshaw's name.

"Mrs. Devenshaw bid you apply here?" he repeated.

"Yes. Is that…" Poppy hedged.

"You'll be wanting tickets, of course."

"Of course," Aunt Rachel said, nudging Poppy aside. "For all the assemblies and concerts if you please."

Once Poppy and Aunt Rachel had paid the man, Aunt Rachel

grinned and took the first set of tickets and stuffed them in her reticule. "Just think, Poppy. All in one day you've saved a woman from a thief, made some new friends, and now have tickets to London assemblies! You're sure to find a husband in no time."

CHAPTER EIGHT

UNLIKE HER AUNT, Poppy wasn't so keen to find herself a husband. At the ripe old age of twenty, she felt naive and inexperienced in the ways of the world, and yet also jaded and cynical. When she had briefly celebrated her birthday last June, she had enjoyed sugared ices with her family in Hertford and tried her best to ignore the happy mentions of engagements and beaus from the young women nearby, all of whom were younger than her. She wanted to enjoy herself, not throw herself at the feet of the first eligible bachelor. London boasted so many diversions, she wanted to try them all.

But her aunt had other ideas. That early afternoon as they returned to the townhouse, Aunt Rachel chatted about the parties, balls and new clothes Poppy would need. "You cannot go walking around in old clothes. I saw the way that Mr. Boyle looked at you at the Fashionable Institution. You're lucky I spoke for you. Why did you decide to dress so severely, Poppy?"

Poppy looked down at her plain white walking dress. It was a bit faded from wear, but it was comfortable and she liked it. Plus it was light and airy, which was a blessing in the early summer warmth. "No reason, I suppose. Although, after Mr. Terrell's intrusion into my bedroom last night, I felt I wanted to cover up."

"Nonsense, the man was only paying you a kindness. You make it sound like he was a scheming mastermind like out of a gothic romance. Don't go filling your head with such silly ideas, Poppy."

"Aunt, he did say he wished to court me."

"Oh, yes. That is true. I had forgot. Well, never mind. You can't blame the man for caring."

But Poppy could and did inwardly blame Mr. Terrell for impropriety. She had not yet forgiven him for his nightly visit and wanted no repeat turn of events. Instead she turned her head and looked at the passing scenery, as the barouche turned into Orchard Street.

As the barouche approached the townhouse, Poppy saw a familiar face. "Miss Munden." She waved.

"Miss Morton!" Emily Munden waved back. She looked very fetching in a light green walking dress and matching bonnet. "You have just come back from your errands, I see. Is this a bad time to call?"

Poppy looked at her aunt, who quickly nodded hello and disembarked from the barouche. "Not at all, dear girl. Come, Poppy will show you the way."

Poppy led Emily into the townhouse and into the parlor, where within moments, tea and biscuits were provided. As the girls dined on green tea and spicy ginger biscuits, Poppy made a mental note to speak with the cook and try to arrange some lessons for herself. She was not a talented baker by any means, but these were a good snack.

Emily dived in, "So is this your first Season?"

"Yes. Is it obvious?"

Emily grinned, revealing dimples in her cheeks. "A little, but that's not bad. What you want to avoid is being like me. I've had a London Season three years in a row and still no luck."

Poppy shifted in her seat. "Is it not a bit..." she shrugged.

"Horribly like a cattle market? I suppose so. I've never been to cattle markets, so I don't know, but I can imagine. Our parents truss us up in these dresses and parade us around in front of men. But it's all a great game. So unless you're a girl with a title, great beauty, or wit, a handsome dowry, or you're a bit scandalous, you'll be as unnoticed as last year's fashions."

Poppy winced.

"Not to worry. You don't have any scandals, do you?" Emily asked.

Poppy bit her lip. The girl seemed friendly enough, but how much of her background should she share?

"Have you always lived in London?" Emily asked.

"No, I've just come up from Hertfordshire with my aunt and uncle."

"So this townhouse isn't yours?"

"It is. It was a relative's of mine, but they died recently and left it to me."

"That's lucky. Were you very close?"

"A little." Poppy blinked and tried not to think of the tragedy of her mother's death that had landed her here. "But what about you? Are you a Londoner?"

"Me? I suppose so. Papa owns a rotten borough so he has a seat in the House of Commons as the MP of Barcote, near Littleworth, in Bedfordshire." She added with pride, "But before that he was an apothecary and did very well. He owns an apothecary's shop in London, and belongs to the Royal Society of Apothecaries."

"Oh. That's very impressive," Poppy said.

"People sometimes like to remind us of our background but I don't care. Papa worked very hard and now he can vie with the rest of them for the number of carriages they have. We have a country house in Littleworth which is nice enough. Is this your first time in London?" Emily asked.

"No, I have visited." Seeing as she wasn't going to get anywhere without sharing a little bit about herself, she added, "I was a companion to a lady before, but it didn't work out."

"Oh, that's a shame. But I'm glad, for then we wouldn't have met. And the way you were talking back to Mrs. Devenshaw, I never would have thought you to be a companion."

"What do you mean? Is she that fearsome?"

"Completely. One word from her and you'll either be getting tickets for the assembly, or be deemed unfit to shine her boots. She's perfected the way of looking at someone into an art form."

"She sounds very fierce," Poppy said. "if you don't mind my asking, what happened with your three Seasons? Did you not find anyone you liked?"

"I had offers. But… something always seemed to go wrong at the last minute. The man had a change of heart, was suddenly penniless, or was discovered to have a disreputable background. Something always seemed to get in the way of my future happiness." Emily sighed. "But never mind that. I'm sure we'll both meet handsome men at the parties this year."

They made plans to walk around St James's Park the following day, and Poppy bid Emily good day. As she walked back to the parlor, she ran into… "Mr. Terrell."

"Miss Morton," he said and bowed, dropping the book in his hands. As she bent to retrieve it, he knelt, too, and clasped the book at the same moment as she. Poppy froze and he dropped the book.

She handed him the book, a small tome with an aged brown cover. But as he took it, he stroked her fingers with his own. She stiffened at the touch. His eyes looked daring, hungry, even. She did not like the look of them at all.

"Excuse me," she said, rising to her feet.

"I wondered where you were."

"My aunt and I went to the Royal Academy."

He gave her a hard look, almost accusing. "I thought I heard voices just now. You weren't with him, were you?"

"Him?"

"That sergeant. Dingme or some other common name. It escapes me."

"Sergeant Dyngley, you mean," she said.

"That's it. He's not lurking around here, is he?"

"No, he is not. I was just chatting with a new friend." She

wanted to tell him off, but also heard her uncle's words in her head. She had to be equally nice and friendly to Mr. Terrell if she was to have Sergeant Dyngley as her suitor, especially as he was staying with them.

"I'll leave you to your book."

"Poppy, wait." He put a hand on her arm.

She tensed, slowly tugging her arm free. "Yes?" She glared at him. "How is your nose?"

His expression turned sour. "I'm fine. None the worse for wear."

"I trust you won't feel it necessary to visit my room tonight."

"Would you mind if I did?"

Her mouth dropped open. She stared at him, at a loss for words. "Excuse me." She walked out, oblivious to the smile that spread across his face.

THE NEXT DAY Poppy joined Emily for a walk around Green Park, where they were joined by Miss Dobbins, Miss Gibbs, and another girl in pink named Sarah Haskett, who had hair the color of wheat and striking blue eyes. Once pleasantries had been exchanged, the five girls walked together through the park, chatting amongst themselves. Emily stuck close by Poppy, when Lucretia stopped short and hushed, "Stay back!"

Poppy glanced at Emily in confusion as the other girls kept a steady distance from Lucretia, who walked ahead with her parasol, seemingly unaware of the handsome young men who walked toward them.

Emily's smile vanished at the sight.

"What's wrong?" Poppy asked.

"Nothing. I'm fine."

"Who are they?" Poppy asked.

"Montague Fletcher and Peregrine Grant. Best friends and two of the more eligible men in Town. Montague has an income of £7000 a year, while Peregrine has £5000," Miss Gibbs whispered.

Montague stood tall and athletic with a shapely, muscular form. His smile looked close to a sneer, his eyes ranged over the girls with confidence, right down to the cleft in his chin and curled blond hair.

Peregrine was the leaner of the two, with smooth dark hair cut close to his head, in a blue suit. Compared to Montague's light tan fashionable suit, Peregrine looked like a clergyman, so dull and severe he appeared. At the very thought of that, Poppy grimaced and turned her head. She'd had enough of clergymen in her life.

"And Lucretia's interest?" she asked.

"She wants Mr. Fletcher, of course. She's fancied him for ages, and he knows it," Miss Haskett whispered.

"Sssshhh." Miss Gibbs shushed them.

The girls watched as Lucretia declared, "Good afternoon, Mr. Fletcher."

Montague tipped his hat as Peregrine nodded hello. "You're looking well, Miss Dobbins."

Lucretia preened at being the center of attention.

"And who are your pretty friends?" Montague asked.

Lucretia's smile faded as she hastily made introductions. Poppy stood by as Montague flashed a smile at each of them, whilst Peregrine ignored them all. She felt overlooked and ignored, but didn't particularly mind.

Emily turned and said to Poppy, "God, this is dull. I thought a walk in the park would be pleasant, but I can't stand to see Miss Dobbins act like this. She's practically throwing herself at him when he's clearly not interested."

"Sshhhh, lower your voice," Poppy said.

"Ah, Miss Munden. Fancy meeting you here." A low voice said behind her.

Poppy and Emily turned to see Peregrine standing there, curiosity in his eyes.

Emily reddened. "Excuse me."

"Miss Munden?" Poppy said.

"Please, don't go. I was hoping to speak with you," Peregrine said.

"The sun is giving me a headache. Good day." Emily walked off toward the shade of some trees.

Poppy watched her go. "I'm sorry, I don't know what's come over her."

Peregrine's expression was dark, then he blinked and gave her a pleasant smile. "That's all right. I find these excursions dull, too. But they have the benefit of allowing us to make the acquaintance of attractive young women. Now tell me, Miss Munden, what would you suggest instead?"

"I am rather partial to museums," Sarah interjected, looking at Peregrine's handsome face. "And sweets."

"Who isn't?" he murmured.

Sarah pouted.

Poppy saw Emily waving her over. "Do excuse me. It was a pleasure to meet you, Mr. Grant." Poppy excused herself and joined Emily beneath the shade of a large tree.

As they were a short distance from the others, Poppy glanced back to see her thoughts confirmed. Peregrine stood watching them depart, whilst Sarah whispered into his ear, or so it looked.

"Come on, let's go," Emily said.

"Why did you leave? He seemed nice."

"He's not. Mr. Grant is a deceitful rake who's not to be trusted."

"What makes you say that?"

"I just don't trust him."

"Surely you can give me more than that to go on," Poppy said.

Emily gripped her hands with surprising strength. "Take my word when I tell you that you cannot trust him. Believe me, Miss Morton, as my friend. Will you promise to stay away from him?" Her dark eyes were serious.

Struck by her reaction, Poppy uttered, "All right."

Chapter Nine

At the Dyngley family manor in Essex, Sergeant Henry Dyngley had been in a fine mood that morning until he had come downstairs for breakfast. The clatter of cutlery over china plates stopped as Petunia Dyngley, his elder brother's wife, waylaid him over eggs, toast, and marmalade. Now very clearly pregnant, he wondered why she did not go into her confinement soon. But if anything, the unsightly bulge of her belly acted as a poignard that seemed to emphasize her point when she spoke. It was so comical at times he wanted to laugh, but dared not, for her grim expression was enough to make any man quail in his boots. He didn't mind the sour set of her mouth or the sight of her disheveled jet-black hair. He had gotten used to her tartness and acerbic tongue, regardless of the hour. What he could not abide by, however, were her stratagems.

Not content to be a calm and sweet loving wife to his brother, John, Petunia had made a nuisance of herself recently, following her husband and Henry to London a few months ago, where she had found John arm in arm with his mistress, an actress. When the girl had been killed on stage at a live performance, Petunia had briefly been considered a suspect, but that was no longer the case. Thanks to Poppy's investigative skills, she and Henry had caught the culprits. A celebration had ensued, only for them to discover that Petunia was acting strangely.

When it came out that she was with child, it changed John.

Henry and his father were delighted. Finally his brother, ever the rake, with tousled blond hair and roving eye, might settle down at last and be a dutiful husband to Petunia. Perhaps all that was needed was a little babe on the way to set the world right. And for at least a month, it had.

But then John had gotten bored, as he was wont to do, and soon renewed his forays into society, much to the disgust of Petunia and Sir Dyngley, a baronet. Henry did not care at the moment, for all he thought of was Poppy. As such, he missed what Petunia was saying and munched his toast. "Mmm?"

"Henry, are you listening to me?"

"Yes, of course." He chewed his toast, swallowed, and poured himself a drink. "Go on."

"You weren't paying attention at all, were you?" Petunia said.

"Of course I am."

"Then what was I talking about?"

"My brother."

Petunia frowned.

Henry grinned. He'd been right.

She looked down her hawklike nose at him and said, "John's gone off riding again. He's gone riding every day since we've been back from London."

"There's no harm in that. The exercise will be good for him."

"Not if he comes back smelling of women's perfume," Petunia snapped, "He's been talking of going to London again. I'm sure he's waiting for the right moment. You'll speak with him, won't you?"

"What is it you want me to say?" he asked, pouring a cup of hot tea.

"Stop him from going. I can't very well have a baby whilst he's gallivanting around London and the countryside. I want him here, with me."

"Men generally stay outside the birthing chamber, or at least that's what I've heard," Henry said.

"I don't care. All this riding and going about has me nervous. You all need to be thinking about my nerves, Henry." She glared at him. "I don't see what you're so happy about. This is all your fault."

"Me? What are you talking about?" he asked.

"John's jealous of you. He doesn't want to be hassled with a wife, he wants to be free and unattached like you. He wants his independence. Even that little mistress he had offered him some entertainment. Now he just mopes around the house, drinks too much, and eyes the servant girls."

"And just how is that my fault?"

"He would pay less attention to the help and more attention to his family if you were settled, Henry."

"Me?" Henry drank his tea.

"Yes. You. Married. When is it going to happen?"

Henry choked and spat it out, wiping his mouth with a napkin. He looked Petunia in the eye. "Forgive me, Mrs. Dyngley, but I fail to see how that is any business of yours."

She laughed. "Of course it is. Especially when the sanctity and steadfastness of my marriage depends on it. John may be older but he looks to you for guidance. Are you seeing someone?"

Before Henry could speak, she cut in, "Of course, you are not. Never mind, I will prepare a list of suitable candidates for which to make your acquaintance. One of them will, I'm sure, take your undivided attention."

Henry bit into his toast savagely. "Petunia, there is–"

"And of course, we will have to travel to London for the Season. I know you're kindhearted, but really, you must be picky about these things. I can't spend the rest of my life with a silly twit for company just because she looks pretty in a corset."

Henry's eyes widened. "Petunia."

She colored. "Forgive me. It's just the stress of this child, Henry. I'm at my wit's end."

"What are you worried about?" he asked.

"Never you mind. That's women's business." She nibbled a

piece of toast and turned slightly green and pushed the offending plate away. "You have no objection to going to London for a time?"

"None at all. I think it's a grand idea." He thought of Poppy.

"Splendid. I'll tell John and start making the necessary arrangements. Tell your valet—never mind, I'll tell him what to pack for you. And not to worry, I'll have a list of suitable girls prepared for you very soon. I'll tell you all about each and every one of them in the carriage ride to London."

"Oh good." Henry swallowed the last bit of toast and felt a lump in his stomach. Petunia was scheming again, and that was never a good sign. He'd have to warn Poppy.

THAT AFTERNOON, HENRY rode to the parsonage in Hertford. It was a few hours' ride, but he could use the exercise. To his surprise, it was locked up. A note on the door read: *Gone to London. For all inquiries contact Mr. Ingleby in Waterford.*

Henry read the statement in surprise. London. So Poppy was to have a London Season after all. A smile lit up his face. Perhaps they might court in London. He could add her to Petunia's list. He'd listen to his sister-in-law for hours if itmeant he could see Poppy again.

HENRY RODE BACK to the family estate in Essex, where things were in an uproar. Not one, but two, of the family's carriages stood outside in the main courtyard, with boxes being loaded up top of one of them. As he entered the foyer of the crumbling mansion, servants carrying hat boxes, clothing trunks and cloaks walked past. Henry stopped and removed his hat. "What is going on?"

"Oh, Henry. I'm glad you're here. I'm supervising the packing." Petunia said, sitting in a padded chair against the stairs. "We're going to London. You haven't forgotten already, have you?"

"No. But does that really necessitate two carriages?"

"Yes. One for us and another for the servants and luggage. We can't have my trunks traveling alone."

"I see," Henry muttered and removed his coat.

"I've already spoken with Geoffrey about what to pack for you."

Henry tugged at his white cravat. "Thank you, Petunia." He knew better than to cross words with her. It was like willingly entering a saber match with a foil—ill advised.

As he took the steps up the main large staircase, two at a time, he shed his dark blue traveling cloak and tossed it on his bed, then went to find his brother. With any luck, John would be in the billiards room.

He was. Henry could smell the scent of John's tobacco from outside the room, and as he walked in, he heard the crack of the ball against the others. He nodded hello to his brother, John, and his father, Sir Dyngley, who sat in a comfortable chair, a glass of wine in his hand. "I thought I might find you two here."

"Damn it Henry, you've ruined my shot," John said, bemoaning the white ball bouncing off the side of the green felt, missing the other balls.

Henry smirked and poured himself a glass of wine. "Have you seen all the chaos downstairs?"

"Petunia's making herself known. It's good for her to focus on something," John said. "Keeps the servants on their toes."

"She'll have that babe to care about soon enough," Sir Richard Dyngley said. "John, you've not been giving the girl any cause to worry, have you?"

"Me? Surely not. You're thinking of Henry. He's the wild one." John winked at Henry.

Richard guffawed, a deep sound. "I may be old, but I'm not senile."

John grinned. "The way I see it, we just sit back and relax whilst she gets the servants in order. Once she's had her way of things, we'll just follow along and do what she says."

"Sounds like you're a bit henpecked, boy," Richard said.

"Nonsense, I'm nothing of the sort. I know when to pick my battles, that's all. She's got to have her way over them, otherwise she'll turn her attention to me, and that I can't abide."

"That seems like a grim situation," Henry said.

"That's marriage," Richard said sardonically.

John's smile faded, then rose again. "Never mind. There'll be lots of entertainment in London. And all thanks to you, Henry."

"Me?"

"Yes. why else would we be going? Petunia is determined to see you wedded, and to a girl of her choosing."

Henry groaned and drank his wine. "Tell me you had nothing to do with this."

John rubbed his chin. "Well… the fact is you've been running wild for too long. You're twenty-seven now. It's time you put down roots. Sowed those wild oats. Found a filly who—"

"Stop yourself there, John. I understand. But why? I've just been promoted to sergeant a few months ago. I've got too much to do. I've no time for courting," Henry said.

"Don't be daft, of course you do. And who better to sort you out than Petunia? She knows every eligible girl in the county and she's bound to find you a good match."

"For her, you mean."

John shrugged. "She'll have exacting standards, so woe be it to any girl who doesn't measure up. You'll have no riffraff here, Henry. Petunia looks after us Dyngleys. No servant girls or poor social climbers will enter these walls, so help me God."

"Here, here." Sir Richard Dyngley held up his glass in agreement.

Henry frowned and walked out of the room.

"What was that all about?" Sir Richard asked.

"Damned if I know," John said, lining up his pool cue for another shot.

Henry walked through the corridor and across to the east wing of the house. The walk did him good. He entered his private rooms, passing through the dressing chamber, where his valet,

Geoffrey, stood packing two traveling trunks.

Henry nodded hello to the manservant and sat in a comfy cushioned chair and stretched out his long legs. He watched as Geoffrey Piggot, a man previously falsely accused of murder, was now folding one of shirts with delicate care.

Geoffrey looked up as Henry sat down and said, "You'll have heard we're off to London in the morning, sir."

"As early as that?"

"Yes, sir. Mrs. Dyngley wants to be off early." Geoffrey crossed the room. "This came for you, sir." He handed Henry a letter.

Henry walked to a writing desk in the room and took a letter opener, slicing through the dull wax seal. He opened the letter and said, "It's from Judge Parkinson. He's invited me to dine with him this evening."

"I'll lay out your evening clothes."

"Nonsense, it's just a casual dinner. It'll just be the two of us dining in his study."

Geoffrey raised an eyebrow and Henry knew he'd lost. The man may have come from humble origins, but Geoffrey knew the ins and outs of modern dress and etiquette better than some butlers twice his age.

"Very well." Henry sighed and pulled a book off the nearest bookshelf.

THAT EVENING, HENRY took a horse from the family stables and rode to Stonefax Manor, not far from Harlow in Essex. Being early April, the weather had begun to shift and was a touch warmer than the previous months. Fortunately for him, the roads were dry. He made good time and was greeted by Judge Parkinson, a tall gentleman with long features and a shock of graying hair. Henry knew that the man was easily underestimated by people as a kindly older gentleman, until he donned his white wig and presided over a court. Then he was a force to be reckoned with.

Henry bowed, handed his coat to a footman, and was introduced to Judge Parkinson's family, including his wife, and his daughter, Julia. The daughter stood just as tall as him and Henry looked at her, trying to recall where he'd come across her before. He was sure he hadn't met her, yet why was her name so familiar?

As they sat down to dinner, dining on roast lamb, buttery herbed potatoes, and beans, Henry listened as Judge Parkinson chatted over the latest cases he'd judged. Henry drank and paid attention, all whilst a bit wary that there were eyes on him. He glanced over and saw both Mrs. Parkinson and the daughter watching him. He quickly drank more wine.

Then it hit him. The daughter, Julia Parkinson, was one of Petunia's girls on her list of suitable marriage partners. He could have slammed his head into the wall. He should never have come. But how could he have known? He wiped his mouth with a napkin and listened more closely to judge Parkinson. Fortunately, dinner came to an end, and Henry was glad to join him for a glass of port afterwards, separate from the ladies.

As he stood by and accepted a fresh glass of port from his host, Henry sat in a comfortable chair in a large library with impressive floor to ceiling bookshelves, and was admiring the dull warm glow of the candlelight reflecting off the titles, when Judge Parkinson said, "Sergeant, I wouldn't have called you here if it weren't a serious matter."

Henry blinked. "I thought I was here by your invitation."

"You are, of course. But… I had an ulterior motive for asking you here this evening."

Henry raised an eyebrow.

"My daughter, Julia, is of age. This will be her first Season and I'm afraid my health won't allow me to properly look after her."

Henry sat up in alarm, but the judge held up a hand. "Nothing for you to worry about, Sergeant. But, the doctor's told me my lungs don't do well in London's air. Too smoky. I'd dismiss him as a quack, but my wife won't hear of my going. Just as well, as I have work to do, but that means that it's only Julia with her mother to look after her..." He looked at Henry. "She needs a male protector. Julia is young and inexperienced in the ways of the world and I need someone I can trust to keep an eye on her. You won't mind looking in on her from time to time, will you?"

"You're assuming I will be in London."

"I heard it on good authority from my wife, who heard it from one of your servants in the village. You're leaving tomorrow and staying in Park Street, correct?"

"You are well informed, sir."

That earned him a smile. "I am. In my profession, it serves me well. So what of it, Sergeant Dyngley? We have a small townhouse two streets away from yours, along Duke Street. Will you look after my daughter?"

Henry tugged at his cravat. "Would it not look unseemly, sir, for me to escort her? Rumors might start."

"Nonsense. My wife will provide an additional escort at all times. But I find myself uneasy at the prospect of them both alone navigating London. You'll look after them, won't you?"

Henry set down his glass. He owed this man so much. It was the very least he could do. But he knew very well that as soon as Petunia had word of this, she would bring Julia into the fold and in no time at all, set her up to be his wife, when he wanted nothing of the sort. And most of all, how would it affect Poppy, to see him escorting another girl around town?

"I would ask that you do this small favor, Sergeant. You're a man I trust, and I do not say that lightly, for there are many young men who would seek to abuse my family and make loose with my daughter. You are no such man, and are the only one I could think of. Please, Sergeant."

Henry looked in the judge's eyes, and for the first time, noticed the man's ill health. The hearty, hale, tall forbidding figure that had judged fiercely over miscreants and thieves, saving lives and destroying others, now looked like a shadow of a man. His nose was red with veins from too many nights drinking, and his sharp blue eyes now looked watery. His eyebrows appeared bushy and overgrown, and his beard needed trimming. His stately yet severe clothes hung on him, and Henry realized he'd lost a considerable amount of weight.

"Of course. I promise," Henry said, wondering how on earth he was going to explain this to Poppy.

"Excellent. Thank you, Sergeant. I'll write to your wife and make the introductions. I'm sure the ladies can sort out any details between them."

"Pardon, sir, but you are mistaken."

"Are you certain? I heard your wife was with child."

"You are thinking of my brother, John. It is his wife you are thinking of. I am unmarried."

"Indeed." It was the judge's turn to raise an eyebrow.

From the slightly predatory look in his eye, Henry wondered if the judge had known all along.

WHAT HAD BEGUN as an ordinary day ended up with him riding toward home with a thick letter addressed to Petunia. As he had suspected, Petunia had been delighted upon receiving the letter from Mrs. Parkinson, even at the late hour. She woke up servants in a hurry and began giving orders, including more instructions to their long-suffering cook, Mrs. Langland, to prepare more baskets of food and drink for the journey.

By the next day the Dyngleys' simple trip to London had grown to four carriages; two for the servants and luggage, one for the ladies, and one for John, Henry, and their valets. Henry could hardly think of anything worse, but thanked his lucky stars he was not sat in the carriage with the ladies, and having to put on a pleasant expression amidst hours of Petunia talking with two ladies she'd never met before.

After hours of traveling on bumpy roads and sleeping fitfully, they arrived in London. The smells were what Henry recognized first. The sweet country air of cows, flowers and grass had been replaced by the stink of manure, butchers' bloody carcasses of animals, the noise of construction work, and the ongoing calls and chatter of people, not to mention the regular clop-clop of horses going up and down the streets. The daylight had faded and Henry was glad they had reached the familiar parts of the city. Night had definitely fallen, but he didn't mind that at all. Now that the carriages came to a stop on Duke Street, they let the ladies adjourn whilst footmen removed the Parkinson's traveling trunks. Henry felt restless, when there came a soft tap at his window. He sat up and looked outside. There, illuminated by the street lights, stood Miss Parkinson.

He cracked open the door. "Yes?"

"Mr. Dyngley, I wonder if you might stand by as we go inside. It looks awfully dark."

Henry looked outside. She was right. Their house did indeed look dark inside. Almost as if… no one was home.

He got out of the carriage and walked up to the entrance. It was a respectable building, and whilst the street itself was fairly quiet due to the late hour, it was not at all suitable for two ladies to go about at night, unaccompanied. He breathed out through his nose and scratched his chin. He needed a shave.

Petunia opened the door of their carriage and called out, "Henry, what is happening? Why haven't we left?"

He walked over to her. "Mrs. Dyngley, it seems the Parkinson's servants have not prepared their house yet."

"What a pity. They'll have to hire better servants. I can tell them—"

"The ladies will need somewhere to stay for the night," he said.

"I—oh. Well of course, they must stay with us." She called out, "Mrs. Parkinson, Miss Parkinson, you must both stay with us. Come back inside the carriage."

Henry turned to find Julia standing there, looking up at him. "Thank you," she said shyly.

"Of course," he said, and turned back to his own carriage. Once he explained the situation to the footmen, they all drove on to the Dyngley townhouse.

Once the ladies had been settled into guest bedrooms and the group had said goodnight, Henry waited until the household quieted, then put on a robe and slippers and padded outside. The corridor was dark, but he'd known the ins and outs of the family townhouse for years, and so felt comfortable moving about without a candle. Besides which, he didn't want to be seen.

He walked down the stairs quietly, only walking on the parts of the stairs that did not creak so loudly as others, and made his way down to the foyer, with a corridor that led down to the kitchen. But then he heard a noise.

He froze, waiting. He held his breath, not making a sound.

He heard it again. Muted steps inside the dining room.

He walked inside the room and said, "What are you doing?"

The person banged into a chair and let out a cry.

Henry hurried forward and said, "Stop!"

The person crashed to the floor. He was on them in a second and pinned them down, gripping their hands to the floor. "What are you—Miss Parkinson?"

He released her at once and backed away. "What is the meaning of this?"

"Mr. Dyngley!" she breathed, her eyes wide. "Oh, I'm so embarrassed. Forgive me for intruding. I was hungry after the long journey and it's been so long since we ate, I couldn't help it. I thought I'd look for the kitchen and have a small bite to eat, but I forgot this wasn't our house and I got lost." She smiled up at him in the darkness, the moonlight shining through the windows to alight on her face.

"I see. Forgive me for… Eh…" He blushed as he saw that she wore a nightrobe that had gaped open, revealing a night dress that in the moonlight, looked somewhat sheer. He stood and said, "Let me find a candle. It's no good to have you tripping in the dark, you'll hurt yourself."

"Oh yes, thank you." She got up and brushed herself off.

"What is going on?" Petunia's voice came out loud and clear

at the entrance of the room. She held a candle, its warm light casting shadows on her features. "What is all that noise?"

"Miss Parkinson was hungry and looking for the kitchen. I had the same idea and I found her in here."

"I got lost, Mrs. Dyngley," Julia said, offering her a winsome smile. "I'm so sorry to have disturbed your rest."

"Yes, well, I was hungry, too. I couldn't sleep," Petunia said.

"Petunia? Darling, what are you doing down here? I've told you before, you can just use the chamber pot on the side of the bed. I don't care and won't think less of you," John said, coming to her.

"Oh, John, not now. Look who I found."

"Eh?" John said sleepily, then glanced into the room. "Henry, what are you and Miss Parkinson doing here—oh." His eyebrows rose.

"Nothing, John. We all had the same idea to go searching for the kitchen. Shall we all go together?"

Petunia led the way, marching like a general as she took the candle and moved downstairs in the direction of the kitchen. In minutes the four of them sat around a table, slicing into cold ham, cheese, bread, and cold milk. John made the ladies smile and laugh with his chatter about late night ghosts and apparitions, but as they all cleaned the plates and stowed them away, Henry couldn't shake the feeling that something was amiss. Something wasn't quite right, he just couldn't think of what it was. As he stood by as Petunia and John showed Julia the way back to her guest room, he fell into his bed, wondering what it was.

CHAPTER TEN

THE NEXT MORNING Poppy rose early, hoping to get a head start on the day. She wanted to see the gardens of St James's Park for herself, and knew that her aunt had taken full advantage of ladies' ways in London. No self-respecting lady got out of bed until after eleven, or at least she did not go downstairs. Poppy herself was a morning person, and felt excited and spritely, ready to start the day. But she was to be disappointed, for it rained, the skies a dull gray hue. Not to be deterred, she dressed, ate an early breakfast, and armed herself with thick boots, a sturdy walking coat, a stiff bonnet, and an umbrella. She made her way out of the house, shutting the door quietly behind her, and slipped outside.

Raindrops pelted down as she opened the umbrella, but it soon changed to a misting rain as she walked in the direction of the nearest bookseller and lending library. There was McNally's Books just a few streets away. Gripping her umbrella tightly, she crossed the streets, keeping an eye out for horses and carriages, and made her way through the foot traffic. She felt lightness in her heart for being able to be alone in the city. She loved her family, but London symbolized freedom and independence, whereas her uncle's presence had the effect of stifling her, making her feel obliged to follow his way of life, and devote herself to a future of caring for the sick, poor, and needy. She'd rather devote her time to a good book.

As she crossed the street and approached the welcoming sign that hung above the shop, she spotted a man dressed in brown and gave a little sigh. She did not particularly dislike Mr. Terrell, and it likely was genuine concern for her person that made him wander into her room that night. But she also felt no affection for him, and believed she would be ill-suited to be a clergyman's wife. Yes, she knew the lifestyle and expectations, she understood the frugality and economy needed to keep a household and to live within one's means, but she also felt that her uncle and Mr. Terrell viewed this background knowledge as something more, as if just because she understood what it involved, she should jump at the chance to continue that way of life, and be grateful for it.

She wanted nothing of the sort. As she'd left the house, she'd overheard her uncle comment on the townhouse, adding there was much that could be done to improve the place.

Her aunt had replied, "I know what you are about, Reginald, but leave it be. We did not come all to the way to London just to turn Poppy's townhouse into a pauper's hospital."

"But Rachel, think of all the good that could be done. We could wipe the stench of sin from this place and—"

Poppy had left silently, not wanting to hear more. Having her aunt there was a help, but Poppy wanted her as a foil for her uncle. She did not want to spend her days doing good works. She'd feel defeated and resigned. No, she wanted something more out of her time here. She didn't even particularly mind if she didn't meet anyone suitable for her Season. She just wanted to be free, and if dancing at a few parties was the price, she would pay it. But then she felt a wave of guilt, and of a serious lack of appreciation for her breeding. Her aunt and uncle had spent their lives raising her to be a good, kind, caring Christian. Not a girl who snuck away in the early morning to find books.

She opened the shop door and a bell jingled, signaling her arrival. Everywhere she looked, there stood towers of books, piled high. The effect was messy, random, and chaotic. Poppy loved it.

The owner, presumably Mr. McNally, nodded to her from behind a desk. He said, "Purchase anything you wish, but if you wish to partake in the lending library, you'll need to purchase a subscription."

Poppy nodded and said, "My mother's personal book collection is full of works from here. Did you happen to know a Celeste Grey?"

"Miss Grey? Yes indeed. She was a regular customer, and with a subscription." He glanced at her, taking in Poppy's tall height, semi-fashionable dress, and said, "I was sorry to read about her passing. You are her daughter?"

"Yes."

"Do you wish to resume her subscription?"

"Um, sure. What sort of books was she reading?"

"She was due to return *The Mysteries of Udolpho,* but hasn't yet. Have a look around. We restrict customers to a maximum of two books at a time, but as it's your first time, I'll allow you to take one with you today, unless you just wish to purchase some."

She began wandering around the tall shelves and columns of books, perusing the titles. There was a lot of poetry, pamphlets, legal texts, works on geography, history, languages, and some fiction.

She was just looking at a volume of poetry when she bumped into someone. "Oh, excuse me."

It was Peregrine Grant. He said, "It was my fault, I wasn't looking where I was going." He glanced at her. "You look familiar. Have we met?"

"The other day, at St James's Park. With Miss Dobbins."

"Oh yes." His eyes glazed over in boredom. "I didn't think many young women liked to read books." He moved to leave, then turned. "I remember now. You were walking with that girl, Miss Munden."

"Yes." She remembered Emily's warning.

"I wonder… Are you very close?"

She gave him a stern look.

"Sorry, it's just..." he frowned. "You look like an honest person. Who are you again?"

"Poppy Morton," she said.

"You're not from around here. Your accent isn't from London."

"No, it's not."

He blinked and waited for her to tell him, then raised an eyebrow. "It would be polite to tell me."

"That's assuming that you recall we've met, which you don't. We might as well be strangers, since you don't recall our being introduced."

Both his eyebrows rose. "Have I offended you in some way?"

"No, not at all." She met his eyes.

"Do you really not mean to tell me?"

"Is it so important?" she asked.

"No. But I asked a question. To refuse to answer would be impolite."

"I would agree, but as you are asking questions to which you do not care for the answers, I fail to see the point."

He stared at her. "And you are friends with Miss Dobbins. Now I see. Like attracts like."

"What is that supposed to mean?" she asked.

"Only this. That if you are anything like her, then you're right, I have no wish to learn anything about you. Tell your friend to keep away from Mr. Fletcher. He's not interested in her. She's only making herself look a fool by throwing herself at him."

"She is not my friend," Poppy said.

"Could've fooled me. Excuse me." He turned and exited the shop, the bell ringing angrily in his wake.

"Mr. Grant, you left behind your book!" Mr. McNally called.

Poppy went up to the counter. "I'll take it to him." She took the book and hurried out the door.

The rain continued to fall but she didn't care, she moved quickly after him. She looked left and right, then spied him, a dark figure walking purposefully down the street. "Mr. Grant!" she called.

He stopped and turned, but seeing her, he looked away.

"Mr. Grant." She darted through the rain.

"What?" He waited as she caught up to him.

Now dripping wet, she extended the book to him. "You left this in the shop."

He took it from her. "I would have come back for it later. There was no need—"

"I'm sorry," she said, cutting him off. "For my behavior in the shop. You didn't deserve that."

He looked at her, weighing her words. "It's raining. Shall we step indoors for a moment?"

They stood outside an alehouse, with a hanging sign that dripped on them, bearing the image of four geese. "Very well."

He opened the door for her and she went inside. It was early morning, so there were not many people around. He led her to a small wooden table for two and said, "What'll you have?"

"Oh I don't know. What do they serve?"

He smiled faintly. "Ale, wine, small beer."

"Tea?"

"Not so much. I'll bring you something."

He left the book with her and disappeared. She wiped her gloves on her walking coat, and peeked at the book. It was little more than a pamphlet on criminals in England. Moments later he came back with two cups of steaming black liquid.

"What is this?"

"Coffee. Just the thing for the morning. Try it."

She took a cup and sniffed it. It smelled bitter. "Thank you. But won't the owner be mad?"

"There's a coffee shop next door. The man behind the bar won't notice. Now, why did you come racing after me?"

"I wanted to give your book to you," she said.

"You could have waited. Why really?"

She sipped the black coffee. "I wanted to apologize for my behavior. It was rude."

"Why were you acting that way? I was just making conversation."

"When we had been introduced in the park, the girls in my company were so excited to meet you and Mr. Fletcher, it annoyed me that you couldn't remember who I was."

"So that's it. Miss Morton, do you have any idea how often I am introduced to groups of young pretty girls?"

She tried not to think of herself as included in that generalization. "No."

"Almost every day. And twice on Sunday." He smiled.

"You're joking."

"I am. Did it amuse you?"

She smiled then. "A little. Why are you two so popular?"

He shrugged. "Montague has always been popular with the ladies. He's all smiles and everyone knows he's an eligible bachelor, whilst I'm just his friend. Quiet, observant, and easily overlooked." He met her eyes. "I'm sorry I didn't remember you from our first meeting. I won't make that mistake again."

She blushed. "Thank you."

"Where are you from?"

"Hertfordshire."

"What part?"

"Hertford."

"Are you really? I have an uncle who lives in Hitchin, but we don't see him so often. What brings you to the city?"

"The Season."

"Ah, of course. And have you had any luck so far in attracting suitors?"

She smiled. Soon they were chatting like old friends. She felt warm and comfortable around him, as if he were a trusted older brother, if she'd have been lucky enough to have one. She asked, "Why did you ask me about Miss Munden?"

His smile disappeared. "Why do you ask?"

"You first."

"How close are you with Miss Munden?" he asked.

"We became acquaintances only a few days ago."

"And are you friends?"

"I'd like to think so. Why?" She cocked her head at his expression. "Do you have an understanding?"

His expression hardened. "No. Nothing like that."

"Then why the interest in her?"

He sipped his coffee and said, "Have you heard of Stuart Horley?"

"No. Is he an acquaintance of yours?"

"He was my best friend. We were like brothers." He gazed at her. "Last year, he went up to London for the Season. We both did. But one day riding in the park, my horse slipped a shoe and threw me, and I broke my ankle."

"Oh, I'm sorry."

He waved a hand. "It's fine. I recovered in a few weeks. But whilst I was abed, he went out to a party, at the Fashionable Institution. Do you know it?"

She nodded. "I have a subscription to their parties, yes."

"So did we. He went, but never came back. I thought nothing of it, until the next day when it was all anyone could talk about. He had fallen from a balcony, having had too much to drink."

"Oh, my lord. Mr. Grant, I'm so sorry."

He stared into his coffee cup. "Don't be. It was a year ago, and besides you had nothing to do with it." He was quiet for a moment. "Everyone thought it was just an unfortunate accident. But one of the ladies present that evening is a friend of my mother's. At tea a few days later, she said it was rather odd about the way Mr. Horley had died."

"How so?"

"It was suspicious circumstances. She said that when he had walked out onto the balcony, he was not foxed—"

"Foxed?" Poppy repeated.

"In his cups. Drunk. The lady said he hadn't had much to drink at all that evening, instead mostly dancing with pretty young women. But the strangest thing, was that the girl he walked out on to the balcony with…"

Poppy sat up straight. "You mean to tell me…"

"It was none other than Miss Emily Munden."

Chapter Eleven

Poppy was at a loss for what to say. She curled her hands around her coffee cup for warmth and stared at Mr. Grant, whose smooth dark locks had fallen into his eyes. She asked, "Do you think Miss Munden had something to do with your friend's death?"

"I don't know. But I can't help but wonder. I've tried to talk to her, to see if she knows something, anything that could help explain how Stuart died. But she refuses to talk to me."

"Why is that?"

"I don't know. Maybe she's afraid I'll think she had something to do with it? Accuse her maybe? She's like a shy little wallflower, easily overlooked. Some girls are like that. They prefer to be on the sidelines rather than in the spotlight." He glanced at her. "Which type are you?"

"Neither."

"There's a third type?"

"There must be, for I am no wallflower, nor am I a girl who wants to be the center of attention all the time. It sounds exhausting."

They shared a smile. He said, "So now you know my story and the reason for my interest in Miss Munden. Miss Morton, do you think you could help me?"

Poppy shrugged. "If she doesn't wish to speak of it...Our

friendship is new. I do not wish to test our relationship so soon."

Mr. Grant looked hurt. "I understand. Forget I said anything." Glancing out the window, he said, "The rain has stopped."

She followed his gaze. "So it has."

Together they walked back in the direction of the bookshop. Outside in the morning light, the sky was a dull whitish gray, and rain dripped off the eaves and buildings, falling into puddles that they stepped around. Once outside the bookshop, he bowed. "It was a pleasure to meet you again, Miss Morton from Hertfordshire."

"Mr. Grant..." She started. "I'll ask Miss Munden. If she does know anything, I'm sure she'll tell me."

"Thank you." He bowed. His expression was serious, but his eyes were full of hope.

POPPY WALKED BACK to her townhouse and slipped inside just as the housekeeper was passing. "Oh, good morning, Miss Morton."

"Good morning, Mrs. Pratt." Poppy leaned her umbrella against the wall, then unbuttoned her damp walking coat.

Mr. Terrell was just passing by. "There you are. I was looking for you. Have you eaten already?"

"Yes. Good morning, Mr. Terrell."

The housekeeper gave them a knowing look and walked on, leaving them alone.

"You go ahead, Mr. Terrell. I was just out."

"In the rain?" he said, surprised, as she fumbled with the strings of her bonnet. "Here, let me." He stepped toward her and before she knew what was happening, he was in her personal space, his fingers undoing the tangle of her bonnet strings.

She became keenly aware of his face near hers and could feel the warmth of his breath. His eyes were focused on the task at hand, but then he finished and said, "There. All done."

His gaze darted to her lips. She held her breath. His Adam's apple bobbed as she met his eyes. This was the moment, where she felt that if she wanted, she could encourage his attentions.

But she felt nothing. No warmth or depth of feeling, no passion or desire. He was just an acquaintance, helping her untie her bonnet strings. Who happened to be male.

She swallowed and stepped back. "Thank you, Mr. Terrell. That was very kind."

"Where did you go?"

"Oh just for a walk. But I got stuck in the rain."

"Alone? Poppy, you shouldn't be going out alone. A young woman like you has no place wandering around the streets unaccompanied."

"Who's unaccompanied?" Aunt Rachel yawned as she walked into the foyer. "Poppy, you're looking a bit damp. Were you outside?"

"Yes, Aunt. I just came back."

"She was unaccompanied, Mrs. Greene," Mr. Terrell pointed out.

"Poppy?" Aunt Rachel asked.

"It was just a walk," Poppy said.

"It's not the end of the world, but we don't know this neighborhood and it's a big city. What if you got lost and couldn't find your way? No, I'm afraid Mr. Terrell is right, Poppy. You shouldn't have gone out by yourself. Please take one of us the next time you go out."

Poppy frowned, feeling slightly betrayed by her aunt. "Yes, Aunt." She shed her bonnet and hung it on a coat stand, along with her coat.

SHE SPENT THE day reading and wondering about the incident of the death of Mr. Grant's friend, Mr. Stuart Horley. If what he was saying was true, then Emily Munden might well know something. Why would she not speak about it? Was there something she wished to hide? And odder still, Emily had warned her to stay away from Mr. Grant. Why?

Poppy closed the history book she was reading and thought on this, gazing out as rain dripped down the windows. She sat in her mother's library, which afforded a good quantity of books, but many were a bit risqué for her taste.

THAT AFTERNOON THE weather cleared, and within an hour, there came a knocking on the front door. Moments later, a footman entered the parlor and said, "Pardon, miss, but you have a visitor."

Poppy looked up from her book. "I do?"

He nodded. "Four, in fact." He stood back as Lucretia, Mary, Emily, and Sarah all walked in.

Poppy rose to receive them all, and bid them sit on the comfortable sofa and chairs. She asked the footman to bring tea, and the girls sat.

"This is a pretty sort of room," Sarah said, admiring the fine walls decked with paintings and thick curtains. "It seems very comfortable."

Poppy smiled at her.

"It's not so fashionable as the rooms in Chawton, but it's respectable," Lucretia said.

"Chawton?" Poppy said.

"Where Lucretia's family have a country house," Miss Gibbs informed her.

"I see."

"Nothing is as good as Chawton Manor," Emily whispered with a smile.

Poppy restrained herself from grinning as a servant arrived with a silver tray of tea, china cups and saucers, whilst another servant came with two plates of ginger biscuits and freshly made scones. At this, Miss Gibb's eyes widened and she helped herself, shedding crumbs of flaky golden scone across her lap.

Lucretia said, "We've come to pay you a visit."

"How nice," Poppy said.

The girls looked at each and a beat later, Poppy busied herself by pouring tea for everyone. It was her mother's stock of black tea, which she found perfectly pleasant.

As the girls politely sipped their tea and munched on biscuits and scones, Lucretia said, "It's true, isn't it? That you actually helped Mrs. Devenshaw recover her reticule that day in the Royal Academy."

"Yes. But you were there. Didn't you see it?"

"No, I just heard about it. I was in the next room and came to see what all the commotion was about. Is it true that you… find things?"

"What do you mean?"

Lucretia daintily wiped her mouth and said, "Mrs. Devenshaw is telling everyone that you stopped that dirty girl from stealing her reticule. It was apparently a gift from her husband, so it's precious to her. She's been singing your praises all around Town."

"Is she?"

"You didn't know?"

Poppy shook her head. "I wasn't aware."

"It is impressive," Emily said, just as Lucretia said, "Well, never mind."

Lucretia shot Emily a look, who stayed silent. Lucretia said, "Do you do this often? Finding things and helping people?"

Poppy shrugged. "I just happened to be there at the right time."

"Poppy, what are those voices? Do you have visitors?" Aunt Rachel entered the room. "Oh, hello, girls. I remember you all, you met at the Royal Academy the other day."

Poppy made introductions and Lucretia said, "We were just discussing Miss Morton's luck in stopping that thief from taking Mrs. Devenshaw's reticule."

"Hah, that's no luck. Poppy's always catching criminals. She caught a murderer before, and thieves before that."

"Aunt…" Poppy started.

"What? There's no sense in being modest, you know it's true. Even the papers covered it the last time. I saved a copy."

"Really…" Lucretia exchanged a look with Miss Gibbs.

"Oh yes, my Poppy's always getting involved in business that she doesn't belong in," Aunt Rachel said. "But it always turns out for the best."

She left just as Mr. Terrell walked into the room. "I thought I heard voices. Oh, hello." He bowed, looking at each of the girls. "Are you friends of Miss Morton's?"

"Yes," Emily said.

"I am Mr. Terrell."

"Are you Miss Morton's relation?" Sarah asked.

"No. But we are good friends," he said.

Poppy snorted, but so inaudibly only Emily heard her.

"I am a divinity graduate, lately from the divinity school at Cambridge. I am studying with Mr. Greene before I take orders."

"You are to be a clergyman?" Sarah asked.

"Yes," he said brightly, his gaze landing on Poppy.

Lucretia shifted in her seat. "That is all very well, but Miss Morton, I wonder, will you be attending the dance tonight at Almack's?"

Poppy blinked. "No, I don't have an invitation."

"Oh." Lucretia smiled to herself.

"Almack's is rather prestigious. They don't let just anybody in," Mary said, munching on a ginger biscuit.

Emily glared at her.

"I do have tickets to the Fashionable Institution, so I might go there," Poppy said, "Mrs. Devenshaw invited me to apply."

Lucretia's eyes narrowed. "She did?"

Poppy nodded, noting Emily's smile. Sensing a challenge, she added, "Will I see you there?"

Lucretia gave a little shrug. "Perhaps. You really should try to get tickets for Almack's though. It's where you really do want to be seen. Not just anyone can get tickets, and Miss Gibbs is right, it is very exclusive. But with the right sort of connections..." She gave a half shrug and waved a hand in the air.

"And if one does not have those proper connections?"

"Then she'll miss out on the dances, balls, parties and meeting the right sort of gentlemen this Season."

"Who are they?" Poppy asked.

"Well no one in trade, but any man between the ages of twenty and thirty, who is highly advanced in the navy, the law, the army or militia, and of course gentlemen of good fortune," Lucretia said.

"And what of the clergy?" Mr. Terrell asked.

Lucretia glanced at him, as if surprised to see him still standing there. "Oh, I suppose. With the right connections and breeding…"

At first he began to turn pink in the face, then thought better of it and said, "Miss Morton, I would be honored if I might have the first dance this evening. The Fashionable Institution is holding a dance tonight, is it not?"

"Er… um…"

"It is," Emily said, casting a triumphant glance at Lucretia. "It is. I'll be there, too," she said, glancing up at Mr. Terrell.

"Jolly good. Good day, ladies." He bowed and left.

"How long is he staying with you, Miss Morton?" Sarah asked.

It was Poppy's turn to shrug. "I do not know. My guess would be for the Season."

"But what of your suitors?" Emily asked.

"What suitors?" Poppy and Lucretia said.

"Well, you're bound to get some. Won't he scare them away?"

Poppy smiled. "If I was lucky enough to receive any, I don't think Mr. Terrell would stand in their way."

Emily mused quietly, "I rather think he would."

The girls did not stay long after that. Emily lingered behind, as Lucretia said, "I'm sorry, Miss Munden, but you'll have to excuse us. There's something particular that Miss Morton and I need to discuss."

"There is?" Miss Gibbs said, scratching at a spot on her chin.

"Yes," Lucretia said.

"But you've only met her twice."

"Three times, and that is enough to form a friendship. Now do leave us." Lucretia said imperiously, and stared at Miss Gibbs until she led Sarah away. Emily shot Poppy a questioning look as she followed, to which Poppy shrugged in reply.

Poppy, surprised, bid Lucretia sit and poured her a fresh cup of tea. "What did you need to discuss, Miss Dobbins?"

"Oh, that. Someone's trying to kill me," Lucretia said over her cup of tea.

Chapter Twelve

"What?" Poppy sputtered over her tea. "Why would someone be trying to kill you?"

"If I knew that, I wouldn't be asking you for help." Lucretia looked around the room with an indignant sniff.

"Are you sure someone is? I mean, what's made you think this?" Poppy asked.

Lucretia fixed her with a look. "I think I'd know when someone is trying to kill me."

Poppy's eyebrows rose.

Lucretia let out a long-suffering sigh. "Very well. It all started a few weeks ago. I was walking out from church when I heard someone call to look out, and a man shoved me to the ground. If he hadn't, I would have been crushed. A piece of stone outcropping had come loose from the church roof and had fallen. It just missed me, thanks to that man. But that was just one instance. There's more."

Poppy listened as Lucretia sat huddled on the sofa, her gloved hands clasped together. "I was walking along the street and someone pushed me into the way of an oncoming carriage. If the horses hadn't reared, I wouldn't have been able to escape. I was lucky."

"Why would someone want to kill you?"

Lucretia shrugged. "Isn't it obvious? My money, connections, breeding. Anyone would be jealous. I've been introduced to the Queen, and have subscription tickets to Almack's, which are highly sought after. The question you should be asking is, who wouldn't want to hurt me?"

Poppy cocked her head at an angle. "You sound very sure of yourself."

"I am. But I have to be. It doesn't pay to be a meek miss in this day and age. This is 1807, after all. I'm not after a man who wants me to be shy and modest with the personality of a stick. I'm a real woman."

Poppy smiled. She rather felt her mother, god rest her soul, would have approved if she'd been there.

"What would you do?" Lucretia asked.

"Refer you to the watch. They'll be able to help. Or your family could hire some guards for you. A minder or something, to have a care for your safety."

"Hah! As if we hadn't already tried those things. The magistrate properly laughed at my mother when she and I went to their offices, and having extra footmen around did nothing but drain my father's checkbook. They weren't of any use at all, so we let them go."

"Did the attacks keep happening whilst they were protecting you?"

"Yes. My father let the men go. But...I can't let anyone know this is happening to me."

"Why not?" Poppy asked.

"It's unseemly. What proper girl has a London Season where some deranged person tries to kill her? It would ruin my marriage prospects."

"I see. But Miss Dobbins, why are you telling me this? We barely know one another."

"Isn't it obvious? I wish you to find whoever is behind this."

"What makes you think I can do this? You should go back to the magistrate."

Lucretia shook her head, her auburn ringlets swinging. "And

be laughed out of the building for causing trouble? You fail to understand the importance of this situation. I am a Dobbins. We don't just go around asking for help. We sort out our own problems—"

"Or pay people to fix them for you," Poppy said.

"Exactly. Now are you going to help me or not? You stopped that thief in the Royal Academy…" Lucretia said, as if that explained everything.

"So?"

"Everyone was around, but no one saw her. I didn't even notice the girl until you had her pinned and Mrs. Devenshaw was calling for help." Lucretia gave Poppy a queer look. "I think you've got an eye for trouble."

"Excuse me?"

"I mean, you notice things. Sordid, unseemly things and characters. People who might be untoward, or who have alternative motives behind their actions. Genteel people like me wouldn't normally notice such persons, but you…" Lucretia seemed to remember where she was, namely, being a guest in Poppy's home. "You're different. I cannot make you out. You seem wealthy and have good breeding, but I've never heard of you. You're not in Debrett's Peerage, I checked. You're a clergyman's daughter–"

"Niece. My mother passed away and my aunt and uncle took me in."

"Right. So…" Lucretia sat back and surveyed Poppy. "Your background is beside the point. Will you help me or not? I'll pay you."

For the first time in her life, Poppy didn't need money.

Poppy blinked. Before she could respond, Lucretia said, "Very well. I can see you're uncomfortable around the subject. Hmmm. Yes, I know. I've got the perfect way to help you."

"Help me?"

"I'll help you help yourself. Besides, you'll need it anyway," Lucretia said.

"What are you talking about?"

"Tickets to Almack's. I'll purchase tickets to the Fashionable Institution and put in a good word for you with the ladies at Almack's. I can't promise you'll be allowed to attend, but I'll need you with me, in case the person tries to attack me again."

"Miss Dobbins, don't you think you're getting a bit ahead of yourself? I mean, there's only been two incidents you've told me of and they both seem like harmless accidents."

"Are you calling me a liar?" Lucretia's cheeks sported angry spots of pink.

"No. But how can you be sure those were murder attempts? You could have slipped in the road and thought somebody had pushed you. You might have just been unlucky, walking around the church at the wrong time. It could all be happenstance."

"Not very likely. But I can see I shall have to prove it. Come with me to dinner tonight," Lucretia said.

"Where?"

"Oh, it's just a small gathering at the Prices's. A little dinner, some dancing. Excellent wine and good music. Plus plenty of eligible men around," Lucretia said.

"Did I hear something about a dinner?" Aunt Rachel walked back into the room.

"Yes, Mrs. Greene. I was just inviting Miss Morton to join me at a small get together this evening, as my guest. I think we are to be great friends." Lucretia flashed Poppy a smile so bright, it was blindingly fake. "You'll come, won't you, Miss Morton?"

Poppy blinked.

"That is very kind of you, miss." Aunt Rachel said. "Of course Poppy will go."

Lucretia wore a satisfied smile and rose to her feet. "Perfect. I'll pick you up in my carriage at seven."

THAT EVENING, POPPY dressed in a nice light blue evening dress, trimmed with shining embroidered thread on the hem and cap sleeves, with a matching blue embroidered sash at the waist.

Paired with a matching pair of sky-blue evening gloves and pearl white dancing shoes, she was ready to charm.

Miss Cooke had done her hair in a stylish updo, trimmed with another blue ribbon. The effect was very pretty. As Poppy looked for a fashionable cloak to wear, Miss Cooke pulled out a dark blue cloak with a hood, that looked very warm. She handed it to Poppy and joined her downstairs, where her aunt was waiting. "I'm so pleased for you, Poppy. This is sure to be a nice evening."

"Where is she going?" Mr. Terrell came out from the parlor. "My, Miss Morton. You look very fetching."

Poppy turned her head, willing the spots of blush to fade from her cheeks. "Thank you." She moved to pull on the cloak, when Mr. Terrell came forward and said, "Let me."

Poppy stood stiffly as he closed the distance between them, pulled the cloak around her shoulders and tied the strings at her collarbones. She could smell his breath, his scent, and wished he had taken a bath recently. He had a spot forming on his nose, and sported a day's growth on his chin. The effect was unappealing, but then he distracted her by putting his hands on her arms. "There. You're ready. I do hope you won't stay out too late. It's not good for a young woman to be out alone with no one to look after her."

Poppy stepped back, to have some distance between them. "I won't be alone. My friend Miss Dobbins is coming to collect me. We shall be together the entire time."

His face clouded. "And how well do you know this Miss Dobbins? She was dismissive of the clergy, if I rightly recall."

"You will just need to persuade her," Poppy said, turning from him. She felt his fingers graze her arm, and looked back. She pulled her cloak away and said, "Don't stay up waiting for me, Aunt. I don't know how long Miss Dobbins will want to stay."

Her aunt shrugged. "You know me, I'll just read a book by the fire until you return. It's no trouble."

Poppy bid them good evening and stepped outside. Lucretia's carriage, a grand affair with a family coat of arms on the side, was fast and comfortable, with very stylish inner furnishings and cushions. Inside, Poppy was delighted to see Emily and Miss Gibbs as well. They took off at a merry pace, whilst Lucretia chattered about the Prices. "They're an older family, very distinguished, but I've heard rumors that the second son gambled away a lot of the family fortune, so now they are in less grand circumstances. So they are here, holding a little get-together."

The carriage pulled up outside a townhouse where there were queues of people going inside, with many dallying, drinking, laughing, and talking. "Miss Dobbins," Poppy said, "What sort of place is this?"

"Why, it's a party. Just a small gathering," Lucretia said, opening the carriage door. "Come on."

But what Lucretia described as a small party, Poppy found to be quite large, with at least twenty people waiting to go inside, and indoors a further hundred talked, laughed, danced, and caroused. People were everywhere, and Poppy instantly regretted looking so fine. She had no doubt that before the evening was done, her gown would be torn or stained, her feet would be stepped on and her hairstyle mussed, through no fault of her own. Indeed, she clutched her cloak tightly around her as she followed Lucretia, Mary, and Emily inside.

At the first sight of Montague, Lucretia abandoned them, and went in search of him, slipping away.

Emily said, "Oh, there's Mr. Grant. Excuse me." She left, with Mary following her. Before Poppy could ask them to wait, they were lost in the crowd. Poppy leaned against a wall of the crowded corridor. Couples were chatting, men drinking, ladies laughing, and now abandoned by her party, she knew not a soul.

A servant pressed a drink into Poppy's hand and she drank, for lack of anything else to do. The corridor she stood in was warm, but she guessed that the rooms were hot, and so she removed her cloak. Fortunately for her, she stood taller than most women and some men, so she was easily able to look around. There indeed, came Mr. Peregrine Grant, who walked toward her.

"Miss Morton." He bowed. "I did not expect to see you here. It didn't strike me as your sort of party."

"Mr. Grant." She curtsied and quipped, "The booksellers were all closed."

He stared at her, then laughed, his eyes crinkling. On such a serious man, the effect was heartwarming. Mr. Grant wore a dark navy blue suit jacket, a gold embroidered waistcoat and matching navy breeches over white knee socks and shining black buckled shoes. With a stiff white cravat and smoothly combed hair, he looked every inch what he was, a prim and proper gentleman with no fuss or frills in his life or appearance.

He looked at her. "And how are you enjoying the party, Miss Morton?"

"It's very hot."

"Yes, it is." He smiled.

"What is so amusing?"

"Are all Hertfordshire girls so direct in their speech? A normal girl of my acquaintance would have made eyes at me behind her fan, whilst trying not to sweat."

"And would you prefer me to be coy, rather than say how I really feel?" she asked.

"Not at all. Your directness is refreshing, if eye-opening."

They shared a smile, then Poppy heard a scream. She looked, and above the crowd, saw Lucretia tumble down a large set of stairs.

Chapter Thirteen

Poppy and Peregrine pushed their way through the crowd. Lucretia lay in a heap at the bottom of the stairs, lying still as a ghost on the marble floor.

"Miss Dobbins!" Poppy said, going to her.

"Don't touch her," Peregrine said, "She could be hurt. You could make her injuries worse."

Poppy shot him a look then turned back to Lucretia. A small crowd had gathered around them as Poppy sank to her knees, gently trying to wake up the girl. "Lucretia? Lucretia? Miss Dobbins? Can you hear me? Miss Dobbins?"

Poppy told Peregrine to call for a doctor, when he knelt and began assessing her injuries. "I'm training to be a doctor," he told her.

"Oh." She moved aside to let him work.

Meanwhile, Sarah, Mary and Emily came from all directions. "Miss Dobbins," Mary said. "What happened? Is she…"

"She's not dead," Peregrine said brusquely.

"Thank goodness," Mary said.

"Did she slip on the stairs? I saw her fall," Emily said.

"Oh, there's blood. I can't stand the sight of blood." Sarah paled.

"Lord, you're going to faint. Come on, I'll get you a drink." Mary rolled her eyes and tugged Sarah away. Emily shot Lucretia a glance, then frowned at Peregrine as Poppy said, "I'll stay with her."

Emily nodded and followed the girls, casting a long look at Lucretia's still form.

A moment later, Lucretia's eyelids fluttered and she shrieked, lashing out and smacking Peregrine and Poppy. "Miss Dobbins, you're all right," Peregrine told her, "You're safe."

Lucretia uttered a low moan. She looked at Poppy and asked in a small voice, "What happened?"

"You fell. Are you all right?"

"No. My head hurts..." She reached behind her head to touch her hair, and her fingers came away speckled with blood. "Oh...."

"Lie still." Peregrine gently felt along her head. His brow knit seriously. "You've got a nasty bump on the head, Miss Dobbins."

"I say, Perry, what's happened? Oh, Miss Dobbins, hello there," Montague said, peering at them.

"Go away, Montague," Peregrine said. "Wait, fetch me a towel, or a bandage."

"Where am I to find that?" he asked.

"Ask a servant. They'll know," Peregrine said.

"I'll go," Poppy said, "I'll find one."

"No, Miss Morton, stay with me," Lucretia said, grasping Poppy's hand. "Don't leave me alone, please."

"All right." Poppy stayed.

"You go, Montague," Peregrine said.

"But I don't see any servants anywhere." Montague looked around.

"I say, does the lady need some assistance?" a familiar voice asked.

"Harris? What are you doing here?" Montague asked.

"I could ask the same of you. This isn't your sort of rout, is it?"

Poppy said, "Could one of you please fetch a servant or bandage? Her head is bleeding."

"Poppy?"

Poppy's head whipped around. "Tom?"

Standing before her was none other than her friend, the pimp, Tom Harris.

Her eyes widened, his mouth opened. He bowed and said, "Miss Morton. What a pleasure to see you again."

She smiled at him. "Hello, Tom."

"Why are you calling him Tom?" Montague asked. "Do you know who it is you're talking to?"

Poppy looked at Montague. "Yes."

"I don't think you do."

Poppy looked at him in confusion.

Tom cleared his throat. "Monty, let's go find a servant. They need a bandage and you need a drink. The Prices won't care for some girl's blood on the floor." Tom led Montague away.

Poppy turned back to Lucretia, who gave a little sniff.

"What is it?"

"You have interesting friends, Miss Morton," Peregrine said.

"What do you mean?" she asked.

"You are acquainted with that gentleman?"

"Yes. why?"

"Perhaps you are not aware that he is the third son of Lord Markham, of Wyck, near Tisbury, in Wiltshire."

"What does that matter?"

Peregrine and Lucretia looked at her.

Poppy said, "What?"

Lucretia rolled her eyes, whilst Peregrine attended to her and said quietly, "There are many young ladies who would like to boast an acquaintance with that young man. That you are so familiar with him will raise their ire."

"They'll be jealous of you," Lucretia said.

"Jealous? Of me?" Poppy laughed, then cast a glance behind her. Sure enough, two pairs of young ladies stood by talking and watching her.

"I think you are mistaken, Mr. Grant," Poppy said.

They were interrupted by Tom returning with a handful of

bandages. He passed these to Peregrine and said, "Is the girl all right?"

"She will be," Peregrine said, taking them and helping Lucretia sit up.

Tom fetched her a glass of wine, which Lucretia took and sipped, casting glances around. "Thank you. And you are?" She gave Tom a glance, pursing her lips.

"Uh, no one. But I wonder if I might steal your friend for a moment." Tom offered Poppy a hand up, and pulled Poppy to her feet. Once he led her a few feet away, he gave her a sly smile.

"Tom, what are you doing here? And dressed so?" Poppy looked him up and down. His hair was artfully tousled, his white cravat messily tied over a rich rust colored suit jacket and matching waistcoat, along with dark breeches and pristine white knee socks. His face was no longer so weathered looking; it was as if he were an entirely different person.

"You look…" She started. "Different."

"You look beautiful. What you doing here? I didn't know you were back in London."

"I've practically just arrived. I'm here for the Season."

Tom's eyes widened. "You are?" His smile grew big. "So am I."

"Miss Morton, I need you," Lucretia called.

"Don't tell me you're a companion again," he said.

"No, that's a friend."

Tom squeezed Poppy's hands. "May I call on you tomorrow?"

"Of course. But Tom, why are they saying you're some son of a lord?"

Tom laughed and ran a hand through his tousled hair. The effect was rakish and handsome. "I'll explain everything tomorrow. Two o'clock? Where are you staying?"

"At my mother's townhouse, on Orchard Street. Number fifty-six."

"I'll see you there." He lifted her hand to his lips, kissed it, and winked, before walking away into the crowd.

Poppy blinked and returned to Lucretia, who had been watching the exchange. "Hmph. You're barely in Town five minutes and already have men kissing your hand." She finished her wine in one large gulp and winced, setting down the glass. "Poppy, help me up."

Peregrine helped Lucretia to her feet as Poppy helped steady her.

Peregrine said, "You shouldn't be doing any dancing tonight."

Lucretia pouted. "But that's why I came. What's the point of coming to a rout if I can't enjoy myself?" She clapped a hand to the back of her head. "Oh, that hurts."

"Let's call you a carriage," Peregrine said, escorting Lucretia to a chair. "Stay here. I'll come for you when it's arrived."

"Oh, very well." Lucretia pouted and crossed her arms beneath her chest. "What a waste of an evening."

"I agree. Quite pointless," a feminine voice said. "You would think they would have more chairs, but apparently providing seats for one's guests is out of the question."

Poppy turned to see the source of the voice. "Mrs. Dyngley?"

"Poppy?" Petunia's mouth dropped open. "Upon my word. Hello, Miss Morton, how do you do?"

"How do you do?"

Lucretia muttered a curse. "Is there anyone in London who you don't already know?" She rose and said overly sweetly, "Ma'am, won't you take this chair?"

"I will, thank you, child." Petunia Dyngley, her stomach round with child, sank into the chair with a little sigh of relief. "Now, Miss Morton, what are you doing here?"

"That is the question," Lucretia said.

Petunia ignored her. "Well?"

"I'm here with my aunt and uncle, for the Season," Poppy said.

"You're having a London Season?"

"Yes."

"My word." Petunia fanned herself and glanced at Lucretia. "Thank you. Who are you, again?"

"Lucretia Dobbins, ma'am." Lucretia gave her a pretty curtsey, but it was lost on Petunia.

"I see. Your dress is dirty." Petunia pointed.

Lucretia frowned. "Yes, I had a fall."

"She fell down the stairs," Poppy said.

Petunia said, "That was clumsy of you."

Lucretia turned pink, when Poppy asked, "Mrs. Dyngley, are the rest of your family in Town?"

Petunia said, "No, just John and myself. Preparing for my lying in, you see. We wanted to have the baby in London. The best doctors, you know."

"And what of Sergeant Dyngley?"

"He stayed in Essex. There is a young lady there and he's quite besotted."

Poppy breathed in. Henry was besotted? With someone else?

"Who is Sergeant Dyngley?" Lucretia asked.

"My brother-in-law. Second son to Sir Richard Dyngley, of Essex. My husband John is the eldest and he will inherit the title of baronet someday." Petunia said with pride. "Did you say your surname was Dobbins?"

"Yes, ma'am. We are in Debrett's," Lucretia said brightly.

"I see." Petunia looked away as if the girl had said something vulgar.

Peregrine came in to say, "Miss Dobbins, your carriage is here. May I escort you out?"

"Very well." Lucretia allowed herself to be led by Peregrine and said, "Miss Morton, you come, too. Tell the girls, will you?"

"Of course." Poppy turned to Petunia, who waved her away.

"Would you tell Sergeant Dyngley I said hello if you see him, Mrs. Dyngley?"

"I'll tell him in my next letter," Petunia promised, crossing her fingers behind her back.

Poppy curtseyed and left in search of the girls. Once she had corralled the group, they were quite happy to leave. The carriage dropped them off at their homes one by one, stopping by Poppy's second to last. Once Lucretia and Poppy were alone in the carriage together, Lucretia's polite smile fell away, and she clapped a hand to her head. "God, that hurts."

"Are you all right?" Poppy asked.

"Yes, my head hurts but I'll be fine. But Miss Morton..." Lucretia said.

"What?"

"I didn't fall down those stairs. I was pushed."

Chapter Fourteen

"Tell me what happened," Poppy said.

"I was upstairs chatting with some of the people there, when all of a sudden, I felt a hard shove and I fell. When I woke up, I was on the ground and you were there."

"Who were you talking to at the time?"

"No one in particular. Miss Gibbs, Miss Munden, and a few others. We were looking for Mr. Fletcher and I thought I saw him, so I started down the stairs."

"Could you have slipped?"

Lucretia thought, the moonlight's beams playing shadows on her face. "No, it was definitely a shove. Someone did that on purpose, I'm sure of it."

After saying a concerned good night to Lucretia, Poppy exited the carriage and made her way up to the entrance of her mother's townhouse. Or her townhouse, depending on which way she looked at it.

She did not like this. It could have been an accident, she supposed. Lucretia might not have been paying attention to where she was going and could have slipped and fallen down the stairs. But something didn't feel right. What if Lucretia was right, and someone was trying to kill her?

As Poppy walked up the steps and opened the door, she shut it closed behind her. Shedding her cloak into the waiting hands of

Miss Cooke, she gave her a smile as Miss Cooke said, "You look troubled, miss. Something wrong?"

Poppy said lightly, "No, nothing to worry about."

She wandered up the stairs to the first floor and turned right, to follow the corridor that led to her bedroom. Once inside, she allowed Miss Cooke to help her out of her fine dress, shift, and stays and pulled on a light, clean white nightgown over her head. She felt troubled about Lucretia's accident and made a mental note to visit her on the morrow. But with seeing specters everywhere, Poppy eyed the warm fire in the hearth in her bedroom, kept the poker by her nightstand, and leaned a chair beneath the door handle. If someone did try to come upon her in the night, she would know.

THE NEXT MORNING Poppy rose and dressed simply in a light gray dress. She did not feel very light or good-humored, even though her white stays were new, her white stockings were clean, and as she washed her face in the cream-colored ceramic basin, her skin felt refreshed. But she had not slept well and worries plagued her dreams.

She had dreamt of Lucretia falling down the stairs again and again, and she was powerless to save her, except each time Lucretia fell to her death, or raised a finger accusingly amidst a death rattle, pointing at her for doing nothing. Poppy had woken up, shivering and once she had washed her face, looked in the large looking glass on her dressing table. Dark circles hung beneath her eyes, giving her a hollowed gaze. Her skin was pale and she felt a little weak, as if she might trip and fall. She allowed Miss Cooke to dress her hair into a comfortable hairstyle and went downstairs to breakfast.

"You're looking tired, Poppy," her aunt said, as Poppy helped herself to tea, pound cake, toast, and preserves.

"I didn't sleep well." She sat down across from her aunt.

"You should not have stayed out so late," Mr. Terrell said, drinking from his teacup. "A clergyman should always be well rested each morning."

"Quite. You never know when a parishioner might come by unannounced, or if there's work to be done," Uncle Reginald said, helping himself to more tea.

Poppy felt bleary-eyed indeed, but did not care for the men's musings on her social hours. To keep a civil tongue, she kept her focus on her food and did not endeavor to make eye contact with Mr. Terrell. She could feel his gaze on her, weighing on her countenance like a stone.

"When I take a wife someday, you can rest assured, Mr. Greene, that she will not stay out late and keep odd hours," Mr. Terrell said.

"I should hope not. No rector's wife would dare."

"But what of family dinners, Reginald? There was that time we stayed out at the Wilsons's until after eleven," Aunt Rachel pointed out.

"Well, yes."

"And that time just a few weeks ago, when we dined at the Proctors, and they are such a drive away, completely across town, it took us ages to get back that night."

"Quite..."

"And you must recall that instance at the assembly rooms where we were so in company, we did not return home until very late," Aunt Rachel said pointedly.

"Yes, yes, I take your meaning." Uncle Reginald shot his wife a look. "One cannot keep proper hours and spare oneself for all the social engagements required. But it behooves a clergyman to rise and retire early and to live in moderation. Mr. Terrell sets a good example for us all. Especially you, Poppy," Uncle Reginald said, shooting Poppy a look.

Poppy glanced up from her tea. "What? Yes, Uncle."

Mr. Terrell shot her a winning smile. "I'm glad you agree."

Poppy finished her slice of pound cake and toast and drank her tea quickly. She felt uncomfortable with Mr. Terrell's eyes on her.

"How was your evening, last night? Rachel said you went out with a friend," her uncle asked.

"Yes, a young lady invited me to a small get-together."

"Were there many people there?" Mr. Terrell asked.

"Not so many as some parties," Poppy hedged. "But the girl who took me, Miss Dobbins, had a tumble down some stairs and hurt her head. She was taken ill and had to go home. I was going to visit her today and see how she was feeling."

"Very kind of you," Mr. Terrell said, cutting off Aunt Rachel.

"Yes, that's very nice of you to do, Poppy. Did you see anyone of our acquaintance there?"

"Yes. Mr. Harris, and Mrs. Dyngley."

"That awful woman with the black hair and firm opinions?" Aunt Rachel said.

Poppy smiled. "Yes. She's with child and is preparing for her lying-in."

"A lady in her condition should not be attending dinner parties," Uncle Reginald said.

"Perhaps not, but she seemed happy enough sitting down with a glass of wine."

"Are the Dyngleys in Town then? Perhaps we should visit," Aunt Rachel said.

Poppy tried not to wince. "They seem very busy, Aunt."

"What is that when there are such acquaintances to be met? She did us a good turn writing to us before."

"Aunt, I do not think a visit would be welcome right now. She seemed… out of sorts," Poppy said.

"I see." Aunt Rachel frowned and looked away. "I declare, I do not know what young people are about these days. One minute they're paying calls and the next, not. How one is to keep track of it all, I do not know."

"Never you mind, Rachel," Uncle Reginald said. "What concerns the younger generation has nothing to do with us."

Rachel harumphed and sipped her tea as a servant came in with a note on a silver tray.

Reginald reached for it when the servant whisked the tray out of his grasp. "It is for Miss Morton."

"Oh." Poppy reached for the note. "Thank you."

She turned over the note, observing the fine white paper and ornate wax seal. "It's from my father." Her face lit up with a smile. She took a butter knife and wiped it clean with her napkin, then slit open the seal and began reading.

"Well?" Aunt Rachel asked, "What does it say?"

"My father has made an appointment for me to meet my mother's solicitor today. In an hour's time." She looked at her aunt and uncle. "I'll need the carriage."

"Won't he come here?" Aunt Rachel asked.

"No, he says he'll meet me there. May I take the carriage?" Poppy asked.

"Not your barouche, it looks like rain," her aunt said.

"You can't take the family carriage either," her uncle said. "For Mr. Terrell and I are going to visit the local church, and it is some distance away. Too far to walk."

Poppy was aware that the footman who delivered the note was still present. He coughed and got her attention. "Pardon me, miss, but you do have another carriage, besides the barouche. It is serviceable for traveling around the city. We could have it ready for you."

Poppy smiled at him as Aunt Rachel said, "Excellent, that's wonderful news. But oh, I cannot go with you, I have my own errands to run today."

"That's all right. I don't mind going alone," Poppy said.

"Nonsense. I will accompany you," Mr. Terrell said grandly.

"But Mr. Terrell, we need to visit St Botolph's church," Uncle Reginald said.

"I can join you another time. I would like to use this opportunity to spend time with Miss Morton. Besides, we are courting." He looked at Poppy, who subconsciously gripped her butter knife.

"Well, I don't know, Reginald, is that really appropriate?"

Aunt Rachel asked. "Two young people alone, unsupervised? No, the more I think on it, I am certain. They cannot be left alone together."

"Can't we?" Mr. Terrell asked.

"Yes, can't they?" Uncle Reginald said.

"No," Poppy said, at the same time as her aunt said, "Absolutely not. It's indecent. Poppy cannot go out with an eligible man alone, especially her suitor. If they were engaged, it is one thing. But they are not, and so it is not," Aunt Rachel said.

"Very well. Poppy you can go alone. But take your aunt and Mr. Terrell with you next time," her uncle said.

Poppy gave him a thin smile. In half an hour she was smartly dressed in a white day dress, sky blue spencer, matching bonnet, and gray reticule. But as she approached the front door, a voice called her name. Poppy turned around. "Yes?"

"Miss Morton, I hope you will not think me remiss in my duties as your suitor. I promise you, we will spend time together." Mr. Terrell took her left hand in his.

Poppy became very glad she was wearing gloves. "That's all right, Mr. Terrell."

"Please, call me Terrence," he said, and beamed. "And I shall call you Poppy."

"I'd rather not," she said, staring him straight in the eyes. She tried gently tugging her hand from his, but he would not let go.

"Poppy, why are you not gone yet—oh." Her uncle entered the foyer and stopped short, looking at Mr. Terrell holding Poppy's hand. A slow smile lit up his face. "Forgive me, I didn't mean to intrude."

Mr. Terrell gave him a benevolent smile. He had food stuck in his teeth.

Poppy tugged her hand back forcefully. "Excuse me, I must be on my way." Her bonnet strings hung loosely around her face, but she did not care. She flung the door open and headed outside.

She stepped into the carriage as fast as she could and shut the door, tapping on the roof to the driver. As it took off, she tore off her gloves and began tying her bonnet strings into some semblance of decency. She almost snarled as she tied, the audacity of the man. How dare he take her hand and act as if they were lovers, or make it seem like they had an understanding in the foyer of her own home.

She tied the bonnet strings into a firm knot and pulled her gloves back on, gripping her gray cloth reticule tightly on her lap. She did her best to calm herself as the carriage rolled through the busy streets, dropping her off outside the respectable building with a small sign in front, marking Ernest Cartwright, solicitor.

Outside stood her father, all smiles. Poppy exited the carriage and came close to him, and stood by as he gave her a quick hug. "Hello, Poppy."

"Father."

"How are you today?"

"Very well, thank you. And you?"

"Better now that we are together. Shall we go in?" He held out his arm and she took it, appreciating the gesture. He led her inside and up a flight of stairs, to an office with a sign on the door. They were admitted and shown into the office of Richard Cartwright, solicitor, and son of the owner.

Richard Cartwright was a man of average height with round features and a pointed nose, thinning blond hair, and eyes that surveyed Poppy gravely. He stood and bowed, then gestured for them to sit. "Hello Lord Blackwood, Miss Morton."

Mr. Cartwright had her mother's accounts before them and explained the particulars, namely that she had left Poppy everything, including her townhouse in Orchard Street, as well as open credit accounts with milliners, dressmakers, McNally's books, shoemakers, and an annuity of £100 a year, in addition to an inheritance of more than £2000. Poppy glanced at the account ledgers detailing her mother's finances in black ink and was stunned. She blinked and sat back in her seat.

"I can see you are shocked by this," Mr. Cartwright said.

"I don't know what to say. I had no idea my mother was so

wealthy," Poppy said.

"Your mother lived well, but had also saved well, and invested wisely. The inheritance is not a princely sum, but well over £2000 a year, which is very smart indeed," her father said, "You are an heiress, Poppy."

Poppy looked at her father. "Is it true? It's really mine?"

"Yes," he said with a smile.

It was recommended, and she agreed, that they would continue to invest her inheritance and finances in the same way as her mother's. Nothing would change very much, except that in Poppy's mind, everything had changed. In no time at all she owned a townhouse, a carriage, and barouche, lines of credit and a regular allowance each month, to cover her expenses and pay bills.

Mr. Cartwright looked at her. "You seem like a sensible sort of girl, so I will give you some advice."

Poppy glanced at him.

"Continue with your life as if nothing happened. For you, nothing has really changed. Do not go wild buying fancy dresses or hosting dinner parties for hundreds of people, and your finances will survive. Ignore my advice and you will find yourself popular at first, but all the poorer later on."

Poppy cocked her head at him.

"He means for you to not go on any wild drinking or shopping sprees, and to restrain yourself from spending all your inheritance right away," her father said.

"I see. Thank you for the advice," she said.

They agreed she would come by once a month to collect her allowance and stay in contact. Mr. Cartwright gave her a series of paper banknotes and coins to take away with her. Once safely stashed in her reticule, he shook hands with her and her father led her out, giving her his arm. Together they looked like the very picture of respectability.

"Have you eaten?" he asked. "Of course you have, it's after the breakfast hour."

"I have, yes. But I don't mind if you wanted to nibble on something."

He led her toward a food seller's stall, but stopped short. His face clouded as he stared at a sight far away.

"Father?"

Poppy saw a crowd of people, including a young woman who stared at them.

Her father said, "I'm sorry, Poppy, but I must leave you. There is an errand I must run. Do excuse me." He left her in the middle of a crowd, leaving Poppy to walk back through Fleet Street.

Poppy wondered at him but assumed his errand must be very important, and so began to walk on, holding her reticule tightly. She strolled among the booksellers and printers of Fleet Street, where she saw a familiar face standing outside a printer's shop. "Miss Haskett?"

Sarah turned around and blushed. "Miss Morton, hello."

"Good morning. What brings you here?"

"Me? Oh, nothing much. I thought I'd take a stroll," Sarah said, her smile tight. "Shall we walk together?"

"Yes, that would be nice," Poppy said, just as a beefy man stepped outside the shop and said, "Sarah, you forgot this." He handed her a pamphlet and said, "Don't forget to come back for dinner, you know what your mum is like."

Sarah nodded and quickly hid the pamphlet away. She led Poppy away and mumbled, "I'm sorry."

"For what? You did nothing wrong. Was that your father?" Poppy asked.

Sarah nodded.

"He seems nice."

Sarah looked askance at her. "You're not going to say anything?"

"About what?"

"How my family is in trade?"

"Does it matter?"

Sarah stared at her. "To many people, it does." She started walking, forcing Poppy to keep up. Once they were some distance away from Fleet Street, Sarah said, "I'm being sponsored this Season by my aunt and uncle, who are wealthy. They have connections in society, which is how I'm here for the Season at all."

Poppy nodded. "My circumstances are similar. I'm here with my aunt and uncle, who is a clergyman."

"And you've got that other clergyman in your townhouse, too, don't you."

"Yes, that's true."

Sarah said, "You're not like the other girls, are you?"

"What do you mean?"

"Miss Dobbins, Miss Gibbs, Miss Munden. They're a tight-knit group, and they care about things like whether a person has the right connections, enough means to finance their lifestyle, who their family is, how many estates they have, that sort of thing." Sarah looked closely at Poppy. "You don't care about any of that, do you?"

Poppy smiled. "Not in the least."

"Well. You're a curious sort of person."

Poppy shrugged. "I don't see how that sort of thing should matter. If a person has good manners and breeding, why should I care if they have ten thousand a year or work in a shop? I think I would be the poorer for it if I were to ignore such friendships."

"Hmmm. No doubt there are many shopkeepers who would agree with you," Sarah mused, then shook her head. "Sorry, it's just that stepping out with these girls is like walking into another world. It's all dances and beaus and who you know, who have you met at a ball, do you have tickets to this… Sorry, I realize we never truly met properly. I am Sarah Haskett, and my father is a printer. Please don't tell the other girls. I'm not embarrassed, it's just that I know what they're like. They'd kick me out of their social circle for sure, and then I'd have no one to socialize with."

"Think nothing of it," Poppy said.

Sarah smiled and asked, "What about you?"

"I'm Poppy Morton, and I live with my aunt and uncle in Hertfordshire. We're here for the Season, but I too am being sponsored by a rich relative."

"Then we're the same," Sarah said with a warm smile.

"We are." The girls shook hands.

They walked along a bit, and Sarah asked, "Do you know if Miss Dobbins's health has improved after her fall?"

"I don't know. I was going to visit her today. Do you want to come?"

"Yes, let's go. I know where she lives." Sarah led the way to Lucretia's townhouse, which was a grand affair on a more respectable street.

Poppy expected nothing less, she realized, and hoped she looked presentable as she and Sarah knocked on the door. They sent up their names via a footman, who after a tense wait, admitted them inside and led them into a parlor, where Lucretia sat in a simple housedress.

"Hello there," she said. The girls curtsied and at Lucretia's invitation, sat across from her on a rich burnt orange colored sofa. The family had gone for aesthetically pleasing rather than comfort, Poppy decided, as the seat was quite hard. She noted the room's fine yellow-papered walls which bore candleholders and landscape paintings. A small fireplace was located in the west side of the room, across from the entrance, and the girls sat across from Lucretia on one of two sofas.

Sarah rested her hands in her lap. "What a comfortable room."

"It is, isn't it? I love this room. When I have a house of my own, I'm going to design a parlor just like this," Lucretia said, sipping a glass of tea. "So you've come to visit me."

"Yes, we wanted to see how you were feeling," Sarah said.

"I'm all right. Mama would hardly let me get out of bed this morning, for fear I'd hurt myself worse, but I told her that if Montague calls then I want to look presentable and not have my head covered in bandages like an invalid," Lucretia said.

"Montague?" Poppy asked.

"Montague Fletcher. We met him in the park that day, with his friend Mr. Grant. He might not remember you, but he certainly knows me." She gave a little laugh.

"Is he your beau?" Sarah asked.

Lucretia laughed. "I suppose you could say that, yes."

There was a knock at the door, and Lucretia sat up straight. "That's likely him." She set down her tea cup and patted her hair.

A footman entered the room and said, "A Mr. Grant, to see you, Miss Lucretia."

Lucretia's face fell. "What does he want?" She pouted and said, "Very well. He can come in."

"Perhaps he brings a message from Montague," Sarah said.

Lucretia rewarded her with a smile. "Probably. Now, girls, if you'll excuse me..."

Poppy and Sarah rose as Peregrine was led in. His eyes widened at seeing them, and he bowed. "Miss Morton, Miss...." he fumbled for Sarah's name.

"Haskett," Sarah said, "Hello."

"Hello." He looked at Poppy.

"I expect you've come to me with a message from Monty," Lucretia told him.

Peregrine blinked. "No. I came to check on you after your accident last night."

Lucretia pouted. "I'm fine. No messages? Did you not see him? When he heard about my tumble, what did he say?"

Peregrine shrugged. "I do not know, I couldn't find him. He is uncomfortable around the sight of blood. I think he was occupied elsewhere."

"Probably searching for bandages for me, of course," Lucretia said, "What a dear. Tell him I said thank you, next time you see him."

"Of course. And how is your head?" Peregrine asked.

"It's fine. Hurts a bit, but I'll live. Where is Montague now?"

Lucretia asked.

"He has errands in Town. His family keeps him very busy," Peregrine said diplomatically.

Poppy rose to her feet. "Forgive me, I've taken up too much of your time."

"No, don't go," Lucretia started. "Although I am waiting for Miss Gibbs to call. As my oldest friend, she should be here. And then if Monty comes, then he'll want my full attention. All right, you can go. Do call on me again tomorrow, Miss Morton, and we'll talk. Good day."

Poppy curtsied and made her way out. She was soon followed by Sarah, who shut the front door behind her. "Well, that was interesting."

"What do you mean?" Poppy asked.

"Her going on about Mr. Fletcher. Did you ever see anything so sad?"

Poppy's eyebrows knit together.

Sarah looked at her and said, "Her infatuation with him. It's not to be. I heard it this morning from a reliable source. He's already engaged."

"To who?"

"Her best friend, Miss Gibbs."

Chapter Fifteen

Poppy stared at Sarah. "Lucretia's beau is engaged to her friend, Miss Gibbs?"

"Yes. I heard it all this morning from Miss Gibbs herself. Although she swore me to secrecy and said no one must find out, not yet. But it's true," Sarah added eagerly. "And that's not all. They have been secretly engaged these past three years, ever since Miss Gibbs's first Season, but they were considered ill-suited and so decided to wait. Isn't that romantic?"

"It's trouble. How did you find out the news from Miss Gibbs?" Poppy asked.

"I was passing by the flower sellers this morning and caught him holding her hand. She quickly came to me and told me not to say anything about it to anyone, especially not Miss Dobbins. She wants to break the news to her herself."

"Lucretia will be heartbroken."

"Maybe. But I'm sure she'll find other young beaus to take her fancy."

"But what about their friendship? And what did Mr. Fletcher say when you saw them together?" Poppy asked.

"He disappeared right quick. Miss Gibbs said he was shy and wanted to avoid any suspicion, but I know what I saw."

Poppy thought on this. "I didn't know that Miss Gibbs and Mr. Fletcher had an understanding."

"Nor did I. Miss Gibbs said they have kept it a secret these past three years, especially as Miss Dobbins lately developed a fondness for him."

"But why were they considered ill-suited in the first place? Miss Gibbs is a debutante for the Season and he is a potential suitor. What was the problem?"

"He is only the second son of Lord Alesbury in Wiltshire, but he had no one and nothing to recommend him, and rumors were that his grandfather had gambled away the family fortune, so no one would have him. Lately he seems to be well off, but he of course won't say how his family is wealthy again, and it is of course, impolite to ask," Sarah said.

"Of course," Poppy agreed, and the girls parted ways.

Poppy returned to her townhouse and was glad of the walk back, for her mind felt clouded. She liked that Sarah came from a similar background to her, but disliked how eager she was to gossip about others, especially a girl she was supposed to be friends with. Lucretia was clearly the leader of their little band of debutantes, but she certainly didn't inspire any loyalty amongst her followers, for otherwise Miss Gibbs wouldn't have hidden her engagement. As Poppy walked along the pavements, passing by all manner of people, she thought to herself how sad it was, that Miss Dobbins had pinned all her hopes on a man who was secretly engaged to someone else.

"Penny for your thoughts," a voice said.

Poppy looked up. "Tom," she said with a smile. "How are you?"

"Better, now that I'm seeing you. Where are you off to?"

"Just home, I've had to run a few errands today."

"Very well then, I'll walk you back." He gallantly offered her his arm.

She took his arm and felt safer. This was his town. Due to his time as a pimp, he knew so many people, whereas she was an outsider. She looked at him. "You're not the man I thought you were."

"Oh?"

"You're the second son of a lord or something. I felt confused to see the others talk to you as if you were someone else."

"Sorry about that. If I'd known you were going to be at that party, I would have told you first. When did you arrive in Town?"

"Just a few days ago, not long at all." She looked at him keenly. "So what is your real name? Are you Tom? Harris?"

He gave her a smile she thought she knew well, but perhaps she didn't. Part of her wanted him to be the same old Tom she had come to know and trust when she had worked as a companion in London last year, but something was different, and it was him.

"My name is Harris. My middle name is Tom. I'm the third son of Lord Ernest Markham, of Wyck. It's in Wiltshire."

"Why did you hide your background from me?"

"It wasn't anything against you, love, I was making a name for myself," he said. Seeing her expression, he added, "As Tom Harris, everyone thinks I am a certain sort of person. A procurer of female talent, and a man who can be trusted with a secret, to be discreet, and to help a man out when he's feeling lusty."

"Feeling lusty? Is that what you call it?" Poppy asked.

"I can call it something else if you'd like, but I think it's rather coarse for your ears." He said in a low voice.

Poppy tensed. "Tom…"

"Harris. Everyone calls me that. If you prefer to call me Tom, you can. I don't mind." He squeezed her hand. "Poppy, I never meant to hide from you. I only…"

"Wasn't sharing all of who you were. I think I understand," she said. "What were you doing all this time? And why not announce yourself as who you are? You come from a good family, don't you?"

"By good, you mean wealthy, or titled, do you not?" he asked.

"Either. It confuses me exceedingly as to why you would hide your true identity, especially among friends."

He dropped her arm then and pulled her close to face him. He took her hands in his. "Believe me, Poppy, if I had known that I would meet you, I would never have hidden my true name. That is the truth. Will you not believe me?"

She looked down, then back up into his eyes. "Yes, I will. But explain yourself."

He released her hands and ran a hand through his hair. "I… got into a fight with my father. Our family wasn't doing well and my eldest brother was having to retrench and sell off some of our estate to survive. It just about gave my father apoplexy. My elder brother went off into the navy and died in battle, which left me. I've never got on well with my father, we're like chalk and cheese. So I left for London and never looked back."

"But Tom, your chosen profession is so… sordid. Why choose that?"

"London is a town of lovers, didn't you know? Many a man and woman are looking to meet the right partner, they just need a helping hand. That's where I come in. I started off as a waiter in the Shakespeare's Head in Covent Garden and worked my way up. What money I made, I sent back to my family. They didn't ask where it came from, and I didn't tell. It's taken some time, but we're doing better now, enough that I could step into my role as the younger brother and do my family proud."

"By what?"

"Restoring their good name. Putting my name and an appearance in at the right establishments. Making connections amongst the *ton*. It's not a bad life."

"But you're playing them, aren't you? How many of these men you're connecting with have been customers of yours in the past?"

"A few." His eyes became flinty. "Does that bother you?"

"A little. It feels dishonest," Poppy said.

He shrugged. "That is the game, love. Any man who comes to me for help you can bet either has money to burn, a girl back home, or a girl he's looking to escape. I just provide a little extra help, is all."

"Do none of them recognize you?" she asked.

He grinned. "I've gotten a few second glances, but they disappear when I put on my second-son persona." He stood up straight and removed a dainty perfumed handkerchief from his inside pocket. He whisked it out under his nose and sniffed, then tucked it back inside his suit jacket and bent down over her hands, murmuring sweet words. His face took on a pinched look, almost a sneering expression, and his eyes became half-lidded as if he was bored. He spoke in a high-pitched drawl and said, "This is what everyone expects when they see me. I simply give them what they are asking for."

She removed her hands from his. "You should have gone on the stage."

His mouth quirked in a smile.

"And what are your plans this Season, Mr. Markham?"

His smile fell. "There's no need to be so formal Poppy, I kissed you before, remember?"

He reached for her hand, but she kept it from his grasp. "I remember."

"Why the sudden coldness? You're acting as if we are strangers," he said.

"Because it feels like we are. I hardly know you. I thought you were Tom Harris, the man I knew. He was my friend. This man who is an overdressed, perfumed fop, I hardly know."

"Poppy..." he reached for her and she stepped back.

"Last year I worked here for about a month. Why during all that time did you never tell me your true identity?"

"I barely knew you. It's hardly the sort of thing a man tells a girl he's just met." He stepped toward her. "Miss Morton, the reason I kept my true name a secret is my own business. But my feelings toward you are as unchanged as they were last autumn. Will you not believe that I am genuine and true in my attentions?"

"In your attentions, certainly. In your manner and ways of

acting, I'm less certain." She looked at him. "What do I call you? Harris? Tom? Mr. Markham?"

"You can call me yours if you like." He rubbed the side of his face, which needed a shave. He wore knee-high black shined boots, light beige trousers, a rust suit jacket, an embroidered waistcoat, and carried a silver-topped walking stick. His hair was artfully tousled and he had razor-sharp sideburns that framed his cheekbones as skillfully as any artist's palette knife.

In short, he no longer looked like the young man about town that knew everyone, with a free and easy manner. The man before her stood foppish, overly smiling, with an air of indecision, disinterest, and elegance that saddened Poppy's heart. Where was the man she had come to know and trust? This new man before her was unattractive.

"Never mind. I can find my own way back. Excuse me." She curtsied and walked on.

"Poppy, wait," Tom said. "You're going around with those girls this Season, aren't you?"

She paused.

"Miss Dobbins, Miss Gibbs, that Haskett girl, and Miss Munden, is that right?" he asked.

"You're well informed."

"I make it my business to be," he said.

"What of it?"

"You should be careful around those girls. There are some ugly rumors going around about them," Tom told her.

"What sort of rumors?"

"Well, I heard that at a party, a man died. Very suspicious circumstances. Those girls were all present when it happened, but none of them will talk about it."

"How do you know so much about it?"

"I'm friends with Mr. Grant, whose good friend died. He reached out to me for help." Seeing her expression he said, "But you knew this already. He has spoken to you, too?"

"Not as such. But I knew he was inquiring about the matter.

Has your search turned up anything?" Poppy asked.

"No. but if you were to get close to the girls and learn which of them did it..."

"Tom, I am here for the Season. I'm here to find a husband." But even as she spoke the words, they sounded false to her.

"You forget, Poppy, that I know who you really are, and who your father is."

Her head snapped up, out of her reverie. "What are you saying?"

"Just that it is a bit hypocritical for you to be having a go at me for being vague about my background when you are doing exactly the same thing." He stepped toward her. "Or are you going around telling everyone that you are the bastard child of a lord and his mistress? What did the girls say when you told them that?" he snapped.

Poppy glared at him. "You know perfectly well I have kept that a secret."

"As well you should. I would know, since I have been doing much the same. Is that such a crime?"

"No. But you...Knowingly hid it when you had no need to. I know that if I were to tell anyone outside of my immediate family, then gossip would spread that would harm him, and those connected with him. You do it out of a selfish desire for your own ends, nothing else." They stood inches apart, but she didn't care, she was fuming.

He gripped her hands and looked down on her, his eyes seeking hers. His gaze darted to her lips and he said, "If I were not so angry at you right now, I would kiss you, and not care who was watching."

"And how would it look for the son of the Earl of Markham to be kissing the daughter of a mistress?" The words came unbidden to her tongue, as vile as any nasty remark that could be heard in a London slum. Her chest rose and fell angrily with the heat of the moment.

His eyes widened and he glanced at her lips again. "Miss

Morton, I have a mind to take you here and now. Whoever watches can be damned." Tom's eyes blazed and he stepped back, his face furious. "No. I will not. I will behave. I am my father's son, and will not allow the poor daughter of a mistress to distract me. If you know what is good for you, you will steer clear of those girls." Tom gave her a sharp bow and turned, walking away.

Chapter Sixteen

Poppy walked toward home, her face hot. She hoped the air would lessen the rosy blush of her cheeks, and remove the heat from her face. How dared Tom speak that way to her? To accuse her of hypocrisy when he had been playacting as another person for the entire time she had known him.

But she was not the only one with secrets, certainly. Sarah herself had admitted her family's background in trade, which they both knew would make her unwelcome in many social circles and keep her from the drawing rooms of high society. But did that truly matter? Were the only suitable eligible men to be found in the drawing rooms of the elite?

Poppy stopped short. In her anger and confusion at Tom, she had lost her reticule. Her gloved hands were empty. She froze and turned around. The streets were full of people. She hadn't walked very far but in the reticule was…

She fretted. Her hands trembled. What would she do? She had literally just met her solicitor for the first time. It would leave a poor impression indeed to have to go running back to his offices right away to ask for more money. He'd think she wasn't trustworthy at all.

She bit her lip, hard until it hurt. She blinked and her eyes turned watery. How would she get the money? What if Mr. Cartwright refused her and didn't believe her story? How would she pay the servants' wages or buy food? She couldn't ask her aunt and uncle for funds, that would be harsh on them and come with a heavy moral lesson for her that would be almost unbearable to swallow.

She looked here and there, but couldn't see it anywhere. Her reticule was gone and with it the month's wages for the servants, pin money for going out and funds for meals for the month. Her hands shook as she filled with embarrassment.

"Miss Morton!" a voice called.

Poppy tensed. The last thing she needed was to lose her composure and be teary in front of an acquaintance.

"Miss Morton, yoo-hoo!" a feminine voice called. It sounded familiar.

Poppy looked in the direction of the sound.

There came hurrying up was Emily and in her hands… Poppy's reticule.

Poppy gasped. "Miss Munden. You have my reticule."

"I saw you across the street as you dropped this. You were in too much of a storm to notice it fall from your hands." Emily smiled and wiped it off, handing it to Poppy. "It's a little dirty but not damaged. Is it very precious?"

Poppy clasped it to her chest. "Oh, thank you. It is valuable, to me at least." She did not want to say it was quite full of banknotes and coins. "Thank you, Miss Munden. I don't know what I would have done if you hadn't found it."

"Oh don't worry, it was no trouble. I just didn't want anyone else to pick it up. I don't mind getting my hands dirty for a friend." Emily smiled at her, and received a warm smile in return. "Are you acquainted with that gentleman?"

"Tom?"

Emily's eyes grew wide.

"Harris. I mean, the second son of the earl of Markham, er…I always knew him as Tom, but everyone calls him something different," Poppy said. Seeing Emily's confused expression she said, "It's a bit of a muddle."

"Is he a friend of yours?"

"Sort of. We knew each other from before the Season."

"You looked angry."

"We had an argument," Poppy said.

"About what? Sorry, I'm being nosy. But I care about my friends. And it must have been important if you were arguing with Mr. Harris Markham," Emily said.

So that was his true name. How different it was from the man she had come to know and trust as Tom Harris, a likable, fun, cheerful waiter from the Shakespeare's Head who procured female talent for the highest bidder. The man *she* knew knew everyone, and was open and honest about his profession. He wasn't the same man as the fussy, perfumed dandy who spoke with an affected drawl. She didn't like this new man at all and had trouble reconciling the two.

"Does everyone know who he is?" Poppy asked.

"Yes. He and his father, the Earl of Markham, had a huge row in London at a ball and Mr. Markham stormed off. His father left for their country estate in Wiltshire the next day, and Mr. Markham stayed here in Town. No one ever saw him for years, not until recently. He was so popular with everyone, it's like he never left. How do you know him?"

Poppy smiled. "I came to London for a time last year, to work as a companion."

Emily's eyebrows rose. "My word. Really?"

"Yes. But then my mother passed away and I returned home."

"How sad. So how is it you are here?"

"I have a wealthy relative who is supporting me in the Season."

"I see." Emily pursed her lips and said, "Miss Morton, you should know that whilst I have no objection to your background, the other girls might. Perhaps you should keep it to yourself."

Poppy's smile fell. "I don't wish to lie. I'm not ashamed of my background."

"Nor should you be. But… in the Season we all need to present the best picture possible to our suitors and to each other, and the slightest remark in the wrong ear can have disastrous results for a girl. Believe me, I've seen it happen. Take it from a friend," Emily said.

"Is that what we are?"

"I hope so. I'd like to think so. Why else would I return your reticule? I could have kept it for myself. Besides…" Emily paused and dug the toe of her boot into the ground. "I could use a friend right about now."

"Why is that?" Poppy asked.

"I don't know if you've heard but a few months ago an… incident occurred at a party I was at, and a man died. It was nobody's fault, but ever since, the man's good friend has tried his hand at investigating and has made it plain he thinks I am at fault."

Poppy looked Emily in the eyes. "You are speaking of Mr. Grant."

"He is not a gentleman. It's not right for him to be going around asking questions and pointing his nose wherever he fancies. He's like a dog with a bone, but he's barking up the wrong tree." Emily's face twisted in anger.

Poppy couldn't hide the smile from her face. "Any other metaphors you'd care to use?"

"I'm being serious, Miss Morton!" Emily said, her voice rising. "Mr. Grant thinks I did it, and instead of talking to me about it, he's telling everyone else his suspicions."

Poppy frowned.

"I didn't, of course, it was an accident. But it was an extremely painful and uncomfortable experience for all of us, which is why none of us want to talk about it. But Mr. Grant has got his eye fixed on me as his friend's killer, and now I don't know what to do. Wherever I go he is there, shooting me little suspicious looks. It's insipid and immoral and I hate it." Emily stamped her foot and looked at Poppy. "Will you help me?"

"With what?"

"Prove my innocence to him."

"Why not just go talk to him? Surely he'll believe you."

"I'm not certain he will. I think he's decided I'm behind it and doesn't care if he's right or not. But you're good at this sort of thing, aren't you? You helped Mrs. Devenshaw, I remember. Could you help me? As my friend?"

And there came the magic word. *Friend.* She so wished she might have a friend, a true friend she could trust and confide in, not just a mere female acquaintance to attend parties with. Poppy felt pathetic, to be twenty and without a real friend. Each time Emily called her friend she felt a little warmth glow in her chest, and felt almost pathetically grateful to have someone actually want to include her amongst their close acquaintance.

"I'd gladly help, but I don't see what I can do," Poppy said.

"Find out what really happened."

"But this incident happened months ago. And you were there, you know what happened. There is nothing for me to investigate."

"Pooh, you're right. I suppose I got caught up in the moment," Emily said, as they walked away from the streets and along the outskirts of a gated park.

"Miss Munden, what really happened that night?" Poppy asked.

"Who have you spoken to already?"

"I've heard rumors about the man's death, but wanted to hear from you before I draw any conclusions. Will you tell me?" Poppy asked.

"I… I'm afraid I cannot. We made a pact, those of us who were there, not to say anything about it, for fear of damaging each other's reputations."

"What do you mean? Surely you would all just tell the truth and let the law handle it. The man fell to his death, did he not? Like you said, it was an unfortunate accident," Poppy said.

"It was, but… I'm sorry, I don't want to talk about it. I just need you to believe me that I am innocent." Emily blinked hard.

And then Poppy stopped short.

"Miss Morton? What is it? Is something wrong?"

"I… that is…" Poppy stared straight ahead.

"Miss Morton? Are you unwell?" Emily asked.

"I am perfectly fine, thank you," Poppy said.

But she wasn't well, not at all. For not twenty feet away, walked Sergeant Henry Dyngley. And on his arm, there was a young woman she'd never seen before.

Chapter Seventeen

Henry Dyngley gritted his teeth against the warm sunny air. He did not like this heat, the smell of the flowers, the loud cawing of crows, and the jabbering of malicious magpies, nor did he like the press of the hand that belonged to the woman on his arm, Miss Annabelle Grace.

Miss Grace laughed a lot, too much, in fact. She had shining blond curls that hung in ringlets about her face, she laughed when he'd stepped in goose shit on the green and laughed harder as he cursed and tried to walk through wet grass to wipe it off. She had even laughed at her own little jokes at the smell of the company, saying that whilst it was very pleasant to look it, there was rather a smell.

Henry had just about had enough of her and was ready to shake her hand off and send her away with a strong shit-covered boot to her backside, but years of good breeding, modesty, and decorum restrained him. He had promised Petunia that he would meet each of the young women she had selected as worthwhile candidates to bear the Dyngley surname, and unbeknownst to him, had arranged for him to escort one of them, Miss Annabelle Grace, around St James's Park that very afternoon. As he had no prior engagement and could not think of an excuse fast enough, he put on a polite smile and escorted the girl, especially as to refuse outright would be rude. The girl had been sitting in

Petunia's parlor and had risen to her feet when he walked in, declaring she had been waiting and was ready for their walk.

"What walk?" Dyngley had said. But one look at Petunia's tight smile made it clear who the guilty party was.

"Henry, meet Miss Annabelle Grace. Miss Grace comes from one of the best families in Somerset, you know."

Miss Grace looked up at him sweetly, fluttered her eyelashes, and gave him a warm smile.

Minutes later they entered the park, with Miss Grace's gloved hands wound tightly around his left arm. She was shorter than him and took shorter steps. That meant that as they walked together, he either had to slow down or quickly outpace her, causing her to tug and pull at his arm as she dragged behind or hurried to catch up.

"Slow down, Dyngley," Miss Grace said, tugging on his arm.

Henry's mouth withered at the familiar use of his name and pulled up short. "Yes, Miss Grace?"

"You're walking too fast. I can't keep up."

"Perhaps you should walk faster."

"How can I keep up with those long legs of yours? You're as tall as a horse."

His eyebrows rose. "Perhaps we are ill-suited for one another."

"Hardly. With my ten-thousand pounds and your title, we are an excellent match. You just need to walk slower. When we are married, you will keep a stately pace with me."

As if he were an obedient dog, he realized. He breathed out through his nose. "You'll need more than ten-thousand pounds in this family."

"I beg your pardon?" she asked.

"Our estate is falling apart. Your dowry won't even cover the rebuilding of the roof," he said.

Miss Grace's mouth dropped open. She stumbled most ungracefully and renewed her grasp on his arm. "What do you mean? Why are you telling me this?"

"You are the one who spoke so brazenly of money. I was returning the favor."

She turned pink. "I thought I was being honest and open about my situation."

"By telling me you disapprove of my height, my speed of walking, and that I alone should take you as a wife due to your inheritance? Do tell, what more do you honestly think I need to know?" he asked.

Her mouth shut like a trap and she pouted. "For a lord, I didn't think you'd be so beastly."

"I'm not a lord," Henry told her.

"You're not? But Mrs. Dyngley said..."

"She is mistaken. But then, she is married to the heir, who will inherit the baronetcy someday. It's just a pity you missed your chance."

"Your brother, then, will inherit the title?"

Henry's free hand curled into a fist. He'd had enough.

"Yes. Fortunately for us, they are very much in love, which means we no longer have need of your company. Do excuse me, Miss Grace." He did not bow. Even for him, it was rude.

"What? You're leaving me? Here, all alone?"

"I am sure that the honest and open manner you have inflicted on me will no doubt impress another man to escort you around. Besides, with your ten-thousand pounds, what man wouldn't want you? Perhaps you should mention that first, rather than attempt to charm a man with your sense of honesty."

Her mouth dropped open again and she glared at him. "You're insulting me."

"You're hurting my arm. Besides, I'm positive if you were able to find your way into my sister-in-law's parlor, you can find your own way out of a park." He pulled his arm free of her grasp and stormed off, leaving her staring after him.

He walked on, angry, fuming, and not caring about where he was walking. He heard a voice call his name but kept walking. He didn't want to see Miss Grace ever again.

He stopped and looked around. The park was bigger than he remembered and suddenly he didn't recognize where he was.

"Goodness, Mr. Dyngley, are you all right?" a familiar voice said.

Henry turned. There walked Miss Parkinson with her mother, looking very prim and polite. They offered him curtsies as he bowed.

"Good day, Mrs. Parkinson, Miss Parkinson."

"We called earlier but Mrs. Dyngley said you had gone out with a young woman. Did she leave you?" Miss Parkinson walked up to him, looking pretty in a light gray walking coat and straw bonnet.

"No." Henry ran a hand through his hair. "We discovered that upon closer inspection of our characters, we are not suited, and I thought it prudent to let her enjoy the sunshine where she might attract other suitors more to her liking."

"You left her alone?" Mrs. Parkinson asked.

"Um, yes. But she is a grown woman," Henry said.

"You left a poor young girl alone in this park, unescorted? My word, I must look for her. Julia, do stay with Sergeant Dyngley." The mother shot him a disapproving glance and left without a word.

Miss Parkinson took Henry's arm. "You'll have to excuse her, she's very protective of young ladies."

"I can understand that," he said.

"She has her reasons." She let out a little sigh.

Together they walked on, as Henry's temper lessened, in part due to curiosity at what Miss Parkinson had said.

"It is a sad history, our family. You'll never hear her talk about it, but my older sister, Gertrude, well..."

Henry allowed her to steer him along the green, toward crowds of well-dressed men and women.

"A young man had captured her fancy, but mama and papa disapproved of him. He was a sailor, and had nothing but his name to recommend him. Just a poor midshipman. Can you guess what happened?" she asked him.

Before he could speak, she said, "They were wild for each other. One day we were walking together in Town, on a day just like this, when Mama and Gertrude got into an argument, and Gertrude marched off. Mama was so angry, she let her go off alone and didn't bother to go after her. What she didn't know then is that Gertrude had planned it all, and used that opportunity to run away with the man. They were married in Gretna Greene within two days."

"What became of them?"

"He is a lieutenant now, based in Portsmouth. She lives there with their child whilst he is at sea. But Mama and Papa were so angry, they haven't talked to her since. Now she and I exchange letters, and I send her money whenever I can. But I know Mama blames herself for letting Gertrude out of her sight that day," Miss Parkinson said.

"But it wasn't her fault, especially if, as you say, the girl planned it all."

"She did, but that doesn't matter. My father is a judge and holds us all up to his standards of proper character and decorum. For us girls, that includes a strong respect for one's elders, particularly parents. For Gertrude to act as she has done shook them both. Since then they have kept a close eye on me. Not that I mind, however. The company is rather pleasant." Miss Parkinson looked up at him.

He felt his cheeks warm. "Miss Parkinson, are you flirting with me?"

"Is it working?"

He started.

She laughed. "Your face is turning red. I seem to have gotten a rise out of you, Sergeant."

Henry mumbled something and stared straight ahead. Then he stopped.

"What is it? Did my manner offend you?" she asked.

"Uh..." His face grew redder.

"Why have you stopped?" she looked and followed his gaze. "Oh. Do you know them?" She cocked her head and peered at three young women nearby. "Lord, that plain girl in the middle is quite tall, isn't she? Like a beanstalk out of children's tales."

Henry didn't answer, for he stood, locking eyes with Poppy.

She stood with a blond girl he didn't recognize, and the tactless Miss Grace, who glared at him. They were soon joined by Mrs. Parkinson, and Henry quickly found himself surrounded by disapproving women. Everyone seemed to speak at once, except for the woman he most wished to talk to.

"Who are you and why have you left this young woman unaccompanied?" the young blond woman demanded.

"He is a mere county constable and an artless one at that. He is no better than a rake, I tell you," Miss Grace declared. "As soon as we had a difference of opinion, he abandoned me."

Multiple pairs of eyes stared at him. Henry turned red. "I say, that is not—"

"So it is true. You left this young lady alone, to fend for herself," Mrs. Parkinson said.

"I mean—" Henry had no doubt that whatever man so unlucky enough to tangle with Miss Grace would find himself fatigued, tongue-tied, or worse, engaged to the girl.

"How could you? It's not safe for a young girl to be left alone in a public place like this. Anything could happen to her." Mrs. Parkinson continued, "Shame on you, Constable."

"It's Sergeant, mama. And I think we are doing the sergeant a discredit," Miss Parkinson said, earning a look of gratitude from Henry.

Henry looked at the blond girl and Poppy, who looked at him and sniffed. He could well discern her thoughts. This was the man she was supposed to be courting and yet here he was, walking with one woman arm in arm, and having just jilted another within the space of a few minutes.

He could see her expression fall with disappointment. "Miss Morton, I..."

The jaded look she gave him could have stopped a bird in flight. He felt a chill despite the warm weather as she said, "Come, Miss Munden, let us go tour the park. I can see the sergeant has his hands full."

Miss Munden, the blond, shot Henry a dirty look and left him with the others, as Miss Grace trailed behind them, shooting nasty little smirks at Henry.

Henry frowned after them. "Miss Morton, wait."

But Poppy was gone, and with her, her two young companions. Henry was left alone, with Mrs. and Miss Parkinson. "How unpleasant. The girl is just as obnoxious as you warned me, Henry. Let us follow their example and walk in another direction, for they've left a sour taste in my mouth," Miss Parkinson said.

THAT AFTERNOON, HENRY entered the Dyngley townhouse and slammed the front door shut with a bang. He marched up to the parlor where Petunia sat, nibbling a biscuit. He growled, "Did you know that Miss Morton was in Town?"

She paused and looked away.

"You did, didn't you? Why didn't you tell me?"

"What good would it have done? She is the no-good daughter of a clergyman. Leave her to her own sort and let her go marry a farmer or tradesman and be done with it. I'll not see you sink so low as to marry that, Henry."

Henry could barely believe his ears. "How could you keep this from me? I have feelings for her. And stop setting me up on these little dates. They're all unsuitable."

"Hah." Petunia slowly rose to her feet, which was no easy feat considering her bulk. "I'll have you know that these girls come from the very best families, the best stock, and are some of the richest in the country. You would be lucky to attract any of them."

"Miss Grace has no tact. She laughs like a donkey," Henry said.

"She has ten-thousand pounds."

"I don't want to see her again."

"Fine."

Henry glared at his sister-in-law. "Stop it, Petunia. I mean it. No more."

"Very well."

"I'm serious," he said.

"I'm sure you are."

"Does my happiness mean nothing to you?" he asked.

Petunia looked at him with dark eyes. "You know what will make you happy? Money. An income. Your sergeant's income is nothing but a pittance, John told me. You need a wealthy wife, and now that you are nearing thirty, you cannot dawdle. You must take a woman of good fortune and breeding. Someone with at least ten-thousand pounds."

"And if she smells and has no manners?"

"Then I have no doubt you will encourage her to bathe once you are married," Petunia said sweetly.

Henry threw his hands in the air and quit the room. He was certain his face was dark as a thundercloud but it made no difference. His sister-in-law was determined to see him married to one of her caliber, regardless of whether it made him happy.

CHAPTER EIGHTEEN

POPPY RECOLLECTED THE afternoon's events at dinner that evening, and felt sad. She had seen Henry on the arm of a well-dressed pretty girl. But instead of being able to exchange pleasantries with him, she and Emily had been joined by Miss Grace, who laughed with a braying sound and spent the next ten minutes extolling the many vices of Sergeant Dyngley. Once they had shed the opinionated girl and returned her to a group of friends of hers, Emily turned to Poppy. "You know that man, don't you? That sergeant."

"Yes."

"Why do you look so cast down? Is it because of what Miss Grace said?" Emily asked.

"No, I wouldn't believe it. But…" Poppy glanced at Emily, wondering how much she could trust her. "I have known him for over a year, and when we last spoke, we had agreed to court."

"You're courting?" Emily smiled and clasped her hands. "That's wonderful. Oh." Her face fell. "I see. What was he doing with Miss Grace and that other woman?"

"I have no idea. This is the first time I've seen him in weeks, since we were both in Hertfordshire."

"Do you like him?" Emily asked.

Poppy smiled despite her dull mood. She couldn't hide it. "Yes."

Emily laughed. "I can tell by the way your face lights up. What will you do? If he is in fact courting other women?"

"Nothing. He can court whomever he likes," Poppy said.

"But you still like him, even after you've seen him with other women?"

"I guess so. Is that wrong? Am I pathetic?" Poppy asked.

"I'd say yes, definitely. I saw him walking with those women, as if he was a rake of the first water," Lucretia said, interrupting their conversation as she, Sarah, and Mary joined them.

"I don't know how you can just stand there and do nothing. If a man crossed me in love like that, and so openly, too…" Lucretia started.

"I'd kick him in the shins," Mary said.

"I'd step on his foot," Sarah said.

"I'd elbow him during a dance," Emily added.

"I know what I'd do," Lucretia said sharply.

"What's that?"

"I'd kill him."

Poppy stared at Lucretia. "Come now, Miss Dobbins. Yes, it was disturbing to see him with other women, but it could all be a harmless occasion. That's no reason to say such things."

"You have never been truly in love, have you?" Lucretia said, "I can tell. For anyone who truly loved a person, it would cut them to their very heart to see them walking around with someone else."

Poppy and Sarah exchanged a look.

Lucretia said, "You're right, but I am passionate about those I love. My dear Montague adores me. You might not understand, but for those of us truly in love, I wouldn't tolerate the man I love paying another girl attention, however innocent. Not when he's promised to me."

"And when did you see him last?" Sarah asked, earning a look from Poppy.

Lucretia waved a hand in the air. "Not that it's any of your business, but we are meeting at the Fashionable Institution tomorrow night. He's sure to make me an offer soon, though. Especially when he sees me dance."

Mary said, "Someone's been reading novels again…"

The girls laughed, and Lucretia turned pink. "So what if I have? They matter, and the lessons they share are worth noting. The heroines love and are loved as they deserve, and do not waste their affections on anyone less worthy." She eyed Mary. "What a shame you do not have any beaus to think about, Miss Gibbs. It might give you something to do, rather than follow me around all day."

Mary's mouth dropped open and her eyes narrowed. "Be careful, Miss Dobbins, or you might find that you have no one around to listen to you but yourself."

"Hah!" Lucretia laughed. "I shall see you all at the dance tomorrow night, or at least those of you who have tickets. Good luck in attracting a man with an attitude like that, Miss Gibbs. It wouldn't surprise me to see you alone all night." She left in a swirl of skirts, with Mary glaring daggers at her back.

"That girl needs a good kick up the backside," Mary said.

Sarah snorted. "She'll get her just desserts at the ball for sure."

The others looked at her. Sarah colored. "I just mean that she may think she is popular amongst the men, but when she sees all of us dancing, she may change her mind. We are pretty, too. There is no reason to think she will be the belle of the ball."

Mary nodded. "I agree."

IN PREPARATIONS FOR the ball that evening, Poppy consulted with her aunt and Miss Cooke. But she sat forlornly at the dressing table whilst the pair fussed and chattered behind her.

After seeing Henry that afternoon, she had walked home a short while later, despondent. He had seen her but had he said anything to her, or paid a call? No. Instead he was out walking with other women. What was she to think? As she glanced at her ordinary features in the looking glass and blinked as her maid dabbed rouge into her cheeks and a dusting of black kohl on her eyelids, she felt that she was a dark beauty, despite her plain looks. If only Henry could see her.

They had decked Poppy out in a pretty pink dress with gold embroidered thread at the scooped bodice, trimmed around the waist and hem, with matching pink gloves and a simple gold chain for her neck. It wanted a pendant of some sort to adorn it. With some consternation that evening, Poppy, upon the urging of her aunt and Miss Cooke, had looked at her mother's jewelry. But she did not feel right raiding her mother's jewelry collection, however grand it was.

Miss Cooke stood arranging Poppy's hair in a fashionable updo with a small bow, when there came a polite knock at the door. Poppy glanced at her maid. "Who is it?"

Aunt Rachel went to open the door. "Reginald, what is it— Oh. Hello, Mr. Terrell."

"Good evening, Mrs. Greene. Miss Morton." He bowed and said, "I know you are preparing to attend a ball this evening."

"Yes," Poppy said. The man was rather stating the obvious.

"As your suitor, I wondered if you might like to wear this tonight. No young lady should be without some adornment, and as the niece of a clergyman, I do not think it would go amiss. That is, I mean, please do me the honor of accepting this token of my affections and great esteem for your person." He held out his hands.

Aunt Rachel took a small item from his hands and held it up in the light. "Oh, it's perfect. Just the thing. Of course, she will wear it." she crossed the room and showed it to Poppy. "Isn't it beautiful?"

Poppy smiled, feeling everyone's gaze on her. "Yes, it is."

On her aunt's palm sat an ordinary cross, of simple gold. Once, Poppy would have loved to receive such a kind gift, and from a gentleman too. But not anymore. Perhaps London society had spoiled her, or perhaps the acquaintance of a certain sergeant had ruined her expectations of love from any other quarter. She weighed all men against him and Mr. Terrell's gift, however kindly meant, brought with it an unwelcome closeness and connection she did not want.

"That is too kind, Mr. Terrell, I couldn't possibly—" she began.

"Of course she will. How delightful, and very kind of you, son." Her uncle's voice boomed behind Mr. Terrell in the doorway, making him jump.

"If I might be so bold, Miss Morton, I would be honored if you would accept this cross." He strode forth into the room and stood close as Aunt Rachel gently unfastened her gold chain and slid the cross onto it, letting it dangle below Poppy's neck.

"Beautiful, isn't it?" Aunt Rachel said, admiring the cross.

"Yes, she is," Mr. Terrell said, eyeing it.

Poppy blushed at the attention.

Miss Cooke shot her a look, which Poppy deciphered to mean, *You're in a right mess now.*

Poppy stood from her seat and let her maid drape a cloak around her shoulders.

As she moved to tie the cloak strings, Mr. Terrell watched her closely. He watched her like a hawk as they all made their way downstairs, his eyes not leaving her as they were in the foyer, and Aunt Rachel handed Poppy her ticket for the night's assembly.

As Poppy stepped into her mother's carriage, Mr. Terrell hurried forth and gripped her hand. "I hope you like the cross."

Poppy wanted her hand back. "It is very nice. Very pretty."

He held onto her hand. "I hope it is the first of many gifts I will give you."

Poppy swallowed. "That is too kind of you, Mr. Terrell, really." She jerked her hand back. "Good evening." She shut the carriage door, hard.

BUT ONCE SHE had arrived at the dance and gave her ticket to the matron inside, it was a mad crush of people. Beautiful ladies danced and mingled, gentlemen and officers stood by, talking, drinking, laughing, and flirting, as some young women batted their eyelashes whilst others giggled and more than one swooned from the heat. It was a crush indeed.

She shed her cloak and entered the ballroom, only to see Emily standing alone on the sidelines.

"Hullo there," Poppy said.

"You made it, I'm so glad to see you," Emily said, giving her hand a quick squeeze. "You look lovely."

"Thank you, so do you," Poppy said.

It was true. Emily looked fair indeed in a light green gown with white feathers in her hair and painted along the neckline of her bodice. The effect was very pretty, almost waiflike. With Emily's pert nose and cheeky smile, she looked positively elfin.

"Do you recognize anyone?" Emily asked.

"Not a soul. You?"

"I've seen Mr. Grant lurking nearby, but I'm staying away from him. I've seen Miss Gibbs around somewhere, and Miss Haskett too. No sign of Miss Dobbins yet."

But as Poppy looked around the room, she did see some faces she knew, and some curious ones as well. She spied her father standing on the sidelines, who nodded once with a slight smile. Beside him stood a young man and woman, the latter of which looked familiar.

Poppy thought nothing of it and instead looked to find a man standing before her. He wore a very official sort of outfit and stood tall and forbidding, with a razor-thin mustache and a stiff upper lip. "Miss Poppy Morton," he began. "I am the master of ceremonies. There is a gentleman who wishes to become acquainted with you."

"Oh?"

"If you please." He extended a hand for her to follow him.

Poppy followed, and was introduced to a Mr. Harris, of Markham. The master of ceremonies left them as Poppy said, "Tom."

Tom held a finger to his lips. "Shh, I'm the third son of the earl of Markham now." He bit back a smile and bowed deeply. "I thought we should be properly introduced."

"And so we are. What are you doing here?" she asked.

"I'm here to play cards. Don't tell me there's a dance on, too," he joked. "Are you dancing tonight?"

Poppy's gaze drifted to the little paper dance card and pencil that hung at her wrist. "Well..."

Tom laughed. "Of course you are. I demand the first dance." He took her card and scribbled his name on the first line. "There. See? It's official now. We are dance partners."

She paused. She so wanted to dance with him. They had parted in anger before. Were they still angry with each other still? He was her friend, he might be something more, and yet, he had seemed like a different person. She glanced at him, taking in his fine hair, sharp gaze and cheeky smile, and couldn't help falling a little for him. She couldn't be angry with him for long. He might be a former pimp, or the son of an earl, but from the serious look in his eyes, sensing her hesitation, it seemed to confirm her feelings. He was still Tom, the man she knew.

Poppy smiled. Her very first dance of the Season, and she had gained a partner within minutes. This was not to be believed. "Thank you, Mr. Markham, but don't think that you have to. You can play cards if you wish, I don't mind."

Tom clasped her hand and said, "Poppy, I dance with you because I wish to. Not for any other reason."

Under his steadfast gaze, Poppy blushed and ducked her head. "Thank you."

He led her back into the main ball room, pulling her past couples, matrons, gossips, ne'er do wells and homely wallflowers. People started whispering as soon as they spied them together, especially with Tom leading Poppy by the hand.

"There goes a striking couple," one matron observed.

"That is one of the Markham sons, but who is the girl?" another asked.

"Some lucky chit, no doubt. Tall. She's taller than most."

"Yes, but he certainly doesn't seem to mind."

Poppy blushed at the attention they received, even more so when Tom and she joined the queue of dancers and joined in, moving to the music. She didn't recognize the tune but didn't care, for Tom was there to guide her. The rough, rakish young man with tanned skin and unruly hair was gone and in his place, an earnest gentleman with a warm grin and sparkling eyes.

She liked him still, even if he had been less than truthful about his true name and background. "And what do you do here, sir?" she asked.

He blinked, then grinned. "I'm here for the Season. I hope to meet the woman of my dreams. Do you think I will be so lucky?"

"Perhaps. But do you not think that a rather high pedestal to put a lady on, to be the woman of your dreams? Can you not love someone who is of this earth?"

His smile deepened into a roguish look. "I never said anything about love, Miss Morton, and the women in my dreams have heavenly charms, I assure you."

"Mr. Markham..." She blushed further and he laughed as he twirled her about. They came together when the dance partners switched, and she came face to face with another young man. He stood about her height, but that was nothing remarkable. He had thin brown hair cropped closely to his face, with a long round face and intelligent eyes. He led her in the dance but as they were not introduced, neither said a word. He did, however, take in her face, meet her eyes, and look at her again before they parted.

The dance ended and as Tom went to fetch Poppy a drink, she was soon joined by Sarah, Emily, and Lucretia.

"Who was that you were dancing with?" Sarah asked.

"You didn't know? That was Harris Markham, the third son of the earl of Markham. He has an estate in Wiltshire and has at least ten-thousand pounds."

"He does?" Sarah asked.

"Yes. good luck to you, Miss Morton, for I heard he is very popular with the young ladies this Season. You'll have stiff competition, if you ask me," Lucretia said.

"Nobody did," Mary muttered and walked off.

Poppy looked and sure enough, Tom had forgotten all about her drink and was instead chatting amiably to a young woman. At first, she felt disappointed, but then realized she didn't mind at all. She mentally wished him good luck and turned to the other girls.

"There are more debutantes here tonight," Emily said. "Look, there's Miss Grace, who we saw the other day in the park. And then there is Miss Townsend, she comes from a very good family."

"How do you know this?" Poppy asked, eyeing the pretty young women.

"They were here last Season, too. We attended a lot of the same parties together."

"Oh."

"Never mind the girls, it's the men I care about. And speak of the devil, there's Mr. Fletcher," Lucretia said.

"Who's that he's talking to?" Sarah asked, peering at the man and woman, who eventually turned around.

"It's Miss Gibbs. She is probably just looking for me. She's such a good friend," Lucretia said, leaving them and weaving her way through the crowds toward them.

Sarah murmured to Poppy, "I wonder if she'll find out..."

"Find out what?" Emily asked.

"Nothing. I heard a rumor that Mr. Fletcher and Miss Gibbs were seeing each other, that's all," Sarah said.

Emily's eyebrows rose. "Miss Gibbs wouldn't dare. She and Miss Dobbins have been friends for years."

Sarah shrugged. "You know what they say, all's fair in love and war." She walked off.

Emily frowned. "Miss Haskett is not a good friend."

"What do you mean?"

"She joined our little circle just this year, like you. But we don't know her very well. Miss Dobbins, Miss Gibbs, and I know each other like sisters, and we're a close-knit group. We're happy to take new debutantes into our social circle and help them navigate the Season, but… I value loyalty and friendship over catching a man. Perhaps that is why I am still single, but I don't care. I esteem my female friendships more highly. Miss Haskett might want to learn a thing or two."

Poppy didn't agree with all that Emily said, but she understood how she felt. "I think I take your meaning. A true friend would not spread rumors about her other friends, even if one was two-timing another."

"Exactly. You understand me perfectly," Emily said with a smile.

"I'm surprised there are no young men to have caught your eye," Poppy said.

"There have been a few over the years, but I'm not one to fight over a man. I'd much rather he pursue me. I want to be wooed and courted, like any other girl. I dislike this idea of the Marriage Mart, where young women and their mothers are concocting schemes to ensnare or trap a man into marriage. It's despicable," Emily said.

"Do you know of any such occasions where this has happened?"

"Yes indeed. Just last year, Mrs. Fletcher and her daughter, Ginny, hatched a plan for her to marry Harry Swinton. After one dance, Ginny invited Harry into the gardens, where they were soon discovered by her mother and her friends. Needless to say, they were found alone together, in a situation that decorum demanded no other result but for them to marry."

"You mean they trapped him into it?"

"It's one of the oldest tricks in the book, Miss Morton. Start to seduce a man and get caught, and trust in the others to demand the man make the woman a marriage proposal immediately. Ginny could sue Mr. Swinton for breach of promise otherwise, and it'd be his word against hers. To refuse her and her family would be dishonorable, and would be insulting to all involved."

"And are they happy?" Poppy asked.

"Who knows? They married within a month, which is all that

can be said. Although I do think they could have chosen nicer. He was known to be a gambler before their marriage…"

"I see." Poppy looked around the room and wondered just how many of the people present were hunting for a partner. If finding a husband was to be a game of trickery and deceit, she wanted no part of it. And nonetheless, it hurt that she had not heard from Sergeant Dyngley yet.

"I say, is that not your beau?" Emily asked, "Look there."

Emily was right. Henry was walking by not twenty feet away, and with the same young woman on his arm that he had with him earlier that afternoon. Were they seeing each other?

Poppy stiffened and gripped the folds of her pale pink dress. Henry hadn't seen her yet, but the woman on his arm had. Then his gaze fell on her and he stopped.

Poppy could well understand his indecision. Here he was with another woman in his company, yet they were supposed to be a courting couple. What to do?

She smiled at him, and made the decision for him. He had no choice but to recognize her or be rude. And Henry was above all, a gentleman.

He strode forward with his companion and bowed. "Miss Morton. What a pleasure to see you here."

"Sergeant Dyngley, the pleasure is all mine." Poppy curtseyed and introduced Emily.

"Ah. How do you do, Miss Munden? Allow me to introduce my friend, Miss Julia Parkinson. Her father is Judge Parkinson, who resides over the county court in Hertfordshire."

Julia gave Poppy a confident smile and inclined her head. "A pleasure to meet you, Miss Morton. Henry didn't tell me of his old friends."

Poppy blinked. She was twenty, not forty. Did she seem older than she looked?

"Miss Morton and I have known each other for at least a year. She welcomed me and was my first friend when I moved to Hertfordshire," Henry said with a warm smile.

Poppy tried not to wince.

Emily took her arm and said, "Oh dear, Miss Parkinson, I do believe you have something in your hair. It looks like a fly. Did you bring one in?"

Miss Parkinson's eyes grew wide and she dropped Henry's arm, patting her hair. "No."

"Oh dear," Emily said.

"Excuse me," Miss Parkinson quickly left, touching her hair.

"Let me help, I think I see it. It's still buzzing around you," Emily said, and gave Poppy a look.

As the girls disappeared into the crowd of people, Henry asked, "What was that about?"

"I don't know. I think my friend doesn't like your friend."

"Miss Parkinson is not my friend," he said.

"Oh."

Henry closed the distance between them and in the crush of people, took the opportunity to take her left hand. "Poppy, I…There is much to say. When did you arrive in Town?"

"Just a few days ago."

"I am surprised to see you here."

"Why is that? I've heard it's a fashionable place to go."

"It is. That's why I'm surprised to find you here. I would expect you to be much more at home in a library or museum."

"You know I am having my first London Season. What's the harm in attending a few parties?"

His expression grew dark. "It is a harm if I cannot escort you or be there with you. Other young men might get the wrong idea."

"Oh really? And just what am I supposed to think when I find you with two women in the park, and another on your arm just now?"

His eyebrows knit into a frowning line. "Take care, Miss Morton, that you do not sound like a jealous wife."

"From where I'm standing, jealousy might be the only thing I do get," she said. "It looks like other girls are vying for that position at the moment."

Henry released her hand and raked his fingers through his tousled dark brown hair. "Damn it, Poppy, this is not how I wanted our first meeting in London to go."

"Forgive me for disappointing you."

"You don't disappoint me at all. I am the one who is having my time wasted with other women," he said.

They looked at each other. The look in his dark brown eyes was serious and steadfast. He still cared for her, she could tell.

"Well, Sergeant, I hear that dancing is the proper activity for a soiree like this. Do you agree?"

"Yes. Would you like to dance?" He held out his hand.

"I would be delighted." She curtseyed as he gave a slight bow, and he led her through the throng and to the center of the dance floor. He did not let go of her hand as they waited for the previous dance to end, and a minute later, they joined the row of dancing couples.

Violins and pipes played as they moved in time in a row, touching hands, then not. Poppy enjoyed the warm touch of his hand, and the confident smile he gave her as they stepped in time with the dancers. For a brief time, she relaxed, and enjoyed being with him in the moment.

But then a scream rang out, and everything stopped. Silence reigned, and a girl's voice cried, "She's dead! A girl is dead!"

CHAPTER NINETEEN

EVERYONE FROZE. POPPY and Henry looked at each other, and left the dance floor, pushing through the crowd.

Henry cut a swift path through the people as he said, "I'm a sergeant, move aside," and Poppy followed close behind him. They reached the end of the room and a balcony, where Henry asked, "What's happened?"

At the scene stood Emily, Mary, Lucretia, and Miss Parkinson, along with Sarah and one other girl. Each girl either stood in tears or fretted.

"I repeat, what happened here?" Henry asked.

"Someone tried to kill me," Lucretia said.

"She's dead," Emily said.

"Who?" Henry asked, "I see no body."

The girls pointed to the edge of the balcony. Henry and Poppy looked over the side, where on the pavement lay a body, outlined in shadow by the street lights below, their dim light creating an eerie glow around the body. What should have been bathed in warm light now seemed dark and disturbing.

"Good God," Henry uttered. He told Poppy, "Stay here," as Mr. Grant entered the balcony.

"I heard a scream. What's happened? They're saying someone died."

"Who are you?" Henry asked.

"Peregrine Grant. I'm a student at the medical college at St Bartholomew's Hospital."

"Are you experienced?"

"Yes," Mr. Grant said.

"Come with me."

Henry turned and Mr. Grant followed, but not before glancing at the women standing there. His eyes widened but he said nothing and followed Henry out.

Once the men left, Poppy looked at the women. She knew most of them, but it was confusing to be sure. She looked from one woman to another. "What happened?"

"Someone tried to kill me," Lucretia repeated.

"What do you mean?" Poppy asked.

"Just that. Someone gave me poisoned wine."

"What?"

"Are you hard of hearing? I just said, someone gave me poisoned wine."

Poppy blinked. "Then how is it that someone else is dead?"

"Oh, her? Miss Grace took the wine from me and drank, then she choked and before we knew it, she'd fallen off the ledge. It's horrible, isn't it? Someone tried to kill me," Lucretia said.

"Someone did kill Miss Grace," Mary pointed out.

"It's true. We were all here. We all saw it happen," Emily said.

"What makes you think someone meant to kill you?" Poppy asked.

"Aside from the fact that someone has been after me, that was my wine Miss Grace took. It stands to reason that it was poisoned, for the sake of killing me," Lucretia said.

"Why would someone want to kill you?" Emily asked.

"I could think of a few reasons," Mary said.

All eyes turned to her. She shrugged. "Whoever was behind this had a good reason. Why else would they go to such trouble?"

"Are you sure the wine was poisoned? How do you know Miss Grace didn't just lose her balance and fall?" Poppy asked.

Miss Parkinson was pale but began to regain her color, and turned thoughtful. "She was choking and started to gasp for breath. She had started to claw at her throat when she backed up, and pitched over the side before we could stop her."

"So you're saying it was an accident?"

"Her death was. But I rather doubt Miss Dobbins's assertion that it was poisoned wine. Likely the girl just had too great a mouthful and began to choke. None of us knew what to do to help her and she tripped and fell," Miss Parkinson said.

Lucretia gave a loud sniff.

Poppy looked over the side of the balcony and could see below, a crowd had gathered around the body. She could make out the forms of Mr. Grant and Henry surveying the body of Miss Grace.

The master of ceremonies and Mrs. Devenshaw entered the balcony. "What happened? There are rumors going around that a girl has died."

"It's true. She fell off the balcony," Miss Parkinson said.

"My wine was poisoned," Lucretia said loudly.

"What?" Mrs. Devenshaw turned a buzzard-like gaze at her, which stopped Lucretia's protests entirely. The master of ceremonies leaned over the balcony. "My word, it's true. This is tragic. We'll have to send for the watch. Who is it? Did any of you know the girl?"

"It was Miss Grace, one of the debutantes of the Season," Emily said.

"Oh lord, a debutante. We'll have to cancel the party. Call the magistrate and the watch." Mrs. Devenshaw looked at the master of ceremonies with an air of distaste. "The Fashionable Institution will suffer for this. The ladies of Almack's will be laughing behind their fans."

"That can't be helped, Mrs. Devenshaw. A girl is dead," the master of ceremonies said.

Miss Parkinson cleared her throat. "Excuse me. I know someone who can help, and who has the diplomacy and delicacy to make sure that this does not get out of control."

All eyes turned to her. "My father is Judge Parkinson, of Hertfordshire. While I am here in Town, he has appointed Sergeant Dyngley to look out for me. As he is here and has little else to do, I am sure he would be happy to investigate this for you."

"What is there to investigate? The girl slipped and fell, the ladies here said so themselves," the master of ceremonies said.

"Someone tried to kill me, and she died instead," Lucretia said.

The gazes turned to her. "I keep saying it and no one listens to me. For over a week now, someone has tried to hurt me. Then tonight, when I was about to drink my wine, Miss Grace said she was thirsty and took my glass. But then she choked and fell. But that wine was meant for me," Lucretia said.

Sarah gasped. "Oh my."

"Is this true? How do you know?" Mrs. Devenshaw asked.

"I have entrusted Miss Morton with finding out who is behind it. After she helped you catch that thief in the Royal Academy, I thought to make use of her talents," Lucretia said with a self-satisfied smile.

"Indeed," Miss Parkinson said, glancing at Poppy.

"I know. We will have them work together," Mrs. Devenshaw said.

"Who will work together?" Sergeant Dyngley asked, entering the balcony. "Excuse me, but where are the organizers of this event? There has been a death."

"We are the organizers. I am Mrs. Devenshaw and this is Mr. Sedgwick, our master of ceremonies," Mrs. Devenshaw said. "And you are?"

"Oh Henry, we have decided you will solve this crime," Miss Parkinson said, going to him.

"And Miss Morton will assist him," Emily said.

Mr. Sedgwick snorted. "What could a girl possibly do? No offense, miss."

"None taken," Poppy said, although Mrs. Devenshaw's eyes

narrowed.

"Miss Morton is being humble, Mr. Sedgwick, for she caught a thief stealing my reticule, and had it not been for her, I would have lost something very dear to me," Mrs. Devenshaw said. "I assure you, Miss Morton is up to the task."

Henry and Poppy looked at each other, then he snapped into action. "Mr. Sedgwick, Mrs. Devenshaw, we need to end this party. Everyone must go. I'll need to speak with the servants." He turned to Lucretia. "I heard you say the wine was yours. What makes you think it was poisoned?"

"Well, someone has been trying to hurt me for weeks. When I took the glass, it smelled funny, like the wine was off. So I didn't mind when Miss Grace wanted it."

Mary snorted. "You're so kind, Miss Dobbins."

Henry turned to Mrs. Devenshaw and Mr. Sedgwick. "Has anyone else complained of foul wine or gotten sick?"

They shook their heads. "No."

"Miss Dobbins, who gave you the wine?"

"Oh, it was a friend of mine who took it from a passing servant. Mr. Fletcher," Lucretia said.

"We'll need to speak with him, too."

"But he had nothing to do with this. He's innocent, I swear." Lucretia grew alarmed.

"Nevertheless, he may have seen something or someone that may be useful to our investigation." Henry strode out and the others followed him.

The party broke up after that. One newspaper editor was in attendance, but Mrs. Devenshaw paid him not to write anything and threatened not to let him purchase a subscription any more if his paper published an article on it. The man frowned, but left swiftly.

Henry questioned the servants, but no one seemed to know anything. Mr. Fletcher stood by, drinking.

Lucretia came to him. "Oh, Mr. Fletcher, that's so good of you to wait for me, but you should go. This beastly sergeant won't let any of us leave."

"Oh really? But a girl died, didn't she? Everyone's talking about it." He smoothed back his blond hair.

"Not just some random girl. Miss Grace. A debutante." Mr. Grant approached them. He rolled down his shirt sleeves and said, "The watch have come. They want to speak with everyone here."

"Oh no. the newspapers will cover this to be sure. We'll have to close. I should never have paid that newspaperman to shut his mouth and go. I should have paid him to write what we want," Mrs. Devenshaw said.

"Never mind that now, we'll need to speak with the watch," Mr. Sedgwick told her.

"What about the girl's family? Does she have any friends or family here with her? They need to be told," Mr. Grant said.

Henry looked around. "I know her a little. But I don't know where her family lives."

"What's the name?" Mrs. Devenshaw asked.

"Miss Annabelle Grace."

"Hmmm. Mr. Sedgwick?"

"They're not of the *ton,* madam. A middling family. Wealthy. If I'm not mistaken, the family owns a property on Swallow Street, near Hanover Square."

"Very good. Send a servant there immediately to tell them," she said.

The watch took the body away, after which the crowd soon dispersed. It was a grim procession.

Poppy felt lightheaded and parched from the overly warm room and from having nothing to drink, but after that evening's events, she did not want to touch any wine.

Sarah returned from the balcony with a partially broken wine glass. "This was the glass Miss Grace was drinking out of."

"Give it here," Henry said, taking it and sniffing it. He turned to Poppy and held it out. "What do you think of this?"

Poppy delicately sniffed the glass. There was some wine still in the bottom of the glass, even though most had escaped. It didn't smell, but the glass itself looked dirty, with bits of dust coating the inside of it. She said, "The glass. Do you think the servants would have served that to a guest?"

"I'll have you know that our servants uphold the highest levels of cleanliness and decorum. Are you insinuating that our glasses are dirty?" Mr. Sedgwick asked.

Henry took the glass from her, his hand briefly touching hers. "I think what Miss Morton means to say is that no self-respecting servant would dare serve a dirty glass to a guest, especially at the Fashionable Institution."

Eyes darted to Poppy. "That is exactly what I mean."

"This glass has been tampered with," Henry said, holding the glass up to the light. It looked as though dust or powder coated the glass. As he swirled the wine, the remaining red wine coated the powder, making it visible to the naked eye.

"What does that mean?" Mrs. Devenshaw asked.

Henry turned to Lucretia. "I think you may have been the target of an attack, Miss Dobbins. Either you or Miss Grace. Could you tell me again what happened?"

Lucretia pouted, then rallied as she realized that everyone was watching. She removed a speck of lint from her sleeve and said, "We were all at the dance, and Mr. Fletcher had just brought us over some drinks from a servant. I saw that my glass was dirty, so I just held it until I could find a place to put it aside. Miss Grace was complaining that she was so hungry and thirsty, she hadn't had anything to eat or drink all day, so that she would be able to fit into her corset and her dress for that evening. When she looked at me and asked for my drink, I didn't think anything of it."

"Then what happened?" he asked.

"Nothing. Everything seemed ordinary. But then a little while later, we were all outside chatting on the balcony when Miss Grace..."

"I can tell you," Sarah said, "She started to seize up and convulse. She started to choke and… it was so horrifying. It was like her arms and legs locked."

"Locked?" Henry repeated.

"Yes, like she was a toy soldier stuck in place or something. I've never seen anything like it. Her limbs became stiff and she started to choke, but she couldn't breathe. It was horrible. Then when I touched her arm, she seemed to seize up more, I could see the muscles in her arms move on their own." Sarah looked away.

"And then she fell over the side of the balcony. You know the rest," Miss Parkinson said.

Lucretia looked at Henry. "You see, it's true. Someone did try to kill me."

"It's possible. Tell me about the servant who gave Mr. Fletcher the drinks. What did they look like?"

"How should I know? I wasn't paying attention. It was a servant," Lucretia said.

Henry and Poppy exchanged a look. He said, "Very well. Mr. Fletcher, I wonder if you might answer a few questions."

"Why ask him? He didn't do anything." Lucretia stood in his way.

Henry sidestepped her and said kindly, "As I said, he may have seen something useful. Even the smallest detail could help." He turned to Montague. "Did you drink the wine?"

"Me? No. Not the red, anyway. I was drinking white. Don't want to stain my clothes if anyone bumps into me at these things." Montague flashed him a winsome smile. "I know what you're getting at, but I didn't notice anything out of the ordinary. I saw the girls were thirsty and so took a few glasses of wine from a passing servant. But I didn't see anything odd or suspicious. There were too many people around to see much."

"He's right," Lucretia said, linking her arm with his. "It was such a crush of people everywhere, a person could steal and no one would notice a thing."

Henry frowned. "I think that's all we'll uncover for tonight. Please, everyone, go home. If I need to speak with you later, do make yourself available."

As the servants and remaining guests dispersed, Miss Parkinson touched Henry's arm. "So, we'll be investigating a mystery of sorts. Together."

His eyes darted to Poppy nearby, and then back to Miss Parkinson. "Not together. You are a lady. Your mother would not thank me for involving you in this."

"And you think that criminal investigation is not a lady's profession?" she asked.

"It is not for all. It takes a certain type of mind to be able to discern truth from lies and to observe others. There is more to it than asking questions. That is just the start of it."

Miss Parkinson pouted. "You don't want my help. I can be useful, you know. My father is a judge."

"You are not your father." He added gently, "I would hope that you would overlook this evening and spend your time like the other young ladies, enjoying the delights of the Season."

"I would if you were with me," she said, curling her hands around his arm.

Poppy turned away. This was too much. Then a voice said behind her, "Well, you all look miserable. Who died?"

Poppy turned around. "Tom." At his pointed look, she said louder, "Mr. Markham."

"Miss Morton." He bowed.

Henry's face grew dark as he said, "Of course you would be here."

"Course I am. Why wouldn't I be?" Tom grinned.

"How did you get in? This is no place for the likes of you."

"Excuse me, but do you know who you are talking to? That is the third son of the Earl of Markham," Mrs. Devenshaw said.

"Who?" Henry asked, looking Tom dead in the eyes.

Tom grinned and buffed his nails on his thigh, glancing up as Mr. Sedgwick said, "It is as Mrs. Devenshaw says, he is the third son of the Earl of Markham."

Henry disengaged his arm from Miss Parkinson's grasp and

said to Tom, "A girl is dead. Did you see anything?"

"What?" Tom's eyes grew wide. "No. What happened? I can help."

"I don't have time for this. Do not involve yourself in this investigation, Mr. Markham. Perhaps you should stick to your normal pursuits."

Tom's face turned pink. "Enjoy your investigating, Constable. I will continue to admire the genteel company around me. Miss Morton, may I escort you home?"

"I… I should really go with my friends," she said.

"I'll take you both home. After a night like this, young ladies shouldn't be walking the streets of London alone." He held out his arm and she took it, glancing back at Henry. She and Tom were soon joined by Emily and Sarah, as Mr. Grant stayed behind to speak with Mr. Sedgwick and Mrs. Devenshaw. Montague, Lucretia, and Mary followed them to the foyer.

As they turned to the servants to fetch their cloaks and call carriages, Henry said, "A word, Miss Morton. If you please."

Poppy turned. Tom's face was pulled into a frown, but he did not stop her as she let go of his arm. She walked over to Dyngley, who motioned for her to speak with him a few feet away, by a column not far away.

"Sergeant."

"That man is an upstart."

"Is that what you wanted to talk to me about?" she asked.

"No. That is a pretty cross," he said, his gaze going to her neck.

"Thank you. It was a gift," she muttered.

"From who? You uncle?"

"No. Our guest, Mr. Terrell."

"Mr. Terrell is giving you gifts? His eyebrows rose.

"Yes." Poppy looked down. How could she tell him that if he asked it, she would rip the gold cross from her neck that very instant? She would gladly dispose of it and be done, not out of discourtesy toward her faith and religion, but because she wanted no part of anything to do with Mr. Terrell. "You recall, when you requested my uncle's permission to court me, he said he wished to as well. And since I cannot in all good conscience refuse him, I have to accept."

"I am sorry. I have been remiss in my duties as your suitor."

She looked up at him. She did not wish to hurt his feelings, but yes, he had. "I was surprised not to hear from you. When I ran into Mrs. Dyngley the other day, I–"

"You saw Mrs. Dyngley? She never told me she saw you."

"Oh. She must have forgotten," Poppy said, heat rising to her cheeks.

"Yes."

Both of them looked away in embarrassment. Henry, for the rudeness of his sister-in-law toward Poppy, and Poppy, for the hurt and dislike Petunia clearly must have felt toward her, to hide both of their arrivals from each other.

"And now there is a mystery to solve," he said.

"I'd be glad to help any way I can."

"I know. But your days should be filled with parties and suitors, not investigating murders," he said.

"I would much rather be doing the latter."

"But that is not what you are here for, and I would not put you in any situation that risks your safety. No, Poppy. I will solve this on my own. And I will make the time to court you properly. Forgive me, I'm new at this."

"What do you mean?"

"I've never courted anyone before," he said quietly.

"Oh." She smiled at him.

They shared a look when Miss Parkinson came up and took his arm. "Dyngley, you promised to see me home. I'm ready now."

"Yes, of course, Miss Parkinson." He inclined his head toward Poppy. "Miss Morton."

"Sergeant." Poppy watched as Miss Parkinson led Henry away.

Chapter Twenty

The next day Poppy met Emily and Sarah in her mother's parlor and served them green tea. Once they were comfortably situated with tea and biscuits, Sarah began the questioning. "You know Mr. Markham, don't you?"

"Yes. We met when I was in London last year."

"He likes you," Sarah said.

"We are friends."

"It looked to me like he wants to be more than that. I saw the way you were dancing together. He watched you very closely," Sarah said, "What do you think, Miss Munden?"

"I think Miss Morton has a lot of men vying for her attention. What did that police sergeant want to speak with you about, as we were all leaving?" Emily asked.

Poppy sipped her tea. "He told me to stay out of the investigation."

"So there is to be an inquiry," Sarah said.

"It looks that way. But it might be only cursory. It's not every day a girl dies at an assembly," Poppy said.

"But it does happen. Didn't a man die at an assembly a few months ago? There was a big article about it in the papers."

"You take an eager interest in crime, Miss Haskett," Emily said.

"I do. I love reading about the crimes happening in Town.

The things people do. Sometimes it's painful to read, about young children stealing in order to provide for their families. But other times the stories are insipid and horrible, with men and women stealing or fighting." She repressed a shudder. "Part of me loves reading those articles, even if they're horrible. Does that make me a bad person?"

"No, just excitable. I have a tonic for that," Emily deadpanned.

Sarah looked at her askance, and Emily laughed. "I am joking, Miss Haskett."

"Oh." Sarah smiled. "What will you do now, Miss Morton? The sergeant told you to stay out of it."

"There's little I can do. I don't have his connections, and no one will believe me when I say I'm investigating. I've run into this before." Poppy said.

"But what will you do about my situation?" Lucretia sailed into the room. "I heard you talking just now. I came to visit to tell you that this is incredibly serious, and I hope you all believe me now when I say that someone is trying to kill me."

Sarah tensed. Poppy set down her tea cup. Emily said, "I believe you."

"You do?" Lucretia asked, then sat down on an empty spot on the sofa beside Sarah. "I mean, of course, you do. As well you should. This concerns all of us."

"What do you mean?" Sarah asked.

"This all started when I started attending parties for the Season. Someone has clearly decided that I am competition for the man she wants and has decided to remove me from the picture, permanently."

Silence reigned.

Then Emily said, "Goodness, you talk like something out of a gothic novel. That sent a chill through me."

"But it's true," Lucretia said. "They're focusing on me now, but they could attack any of you, especially now that we've all been seen together."

Sarah's hand darted to her mouth. "You think so?"

"What makes you think a woman is behind this?" Poppy asked.

"Who else would do it? In the Season, men are pawns. Women are the ones who make things happen. Where would we be without our mothers, aunts, and grandmothers orchestrating things behind the scenes? Men think they have a choice, but in truth, all I have to do is flash a few pretty smiles at a man, tell my Mama, and he will be at my home, courting me the next day."

"If that is the case, then where is Mr. Fletcher?" Sarah ignored Poppy's look of warning. "I thought you two were courting."

Lucretia said, "We are, but he is busy. That doesn't matter. It's only a matter of time before we announce our engagement."

"Where is Miss Gibbs, I wonder?" Sarah asked.

Poppy glanced at her, and Emily's eyes narrowed. "Miss Haskett, you are new to our little group, and have much to learn about the ins and outs of a London Season. I did not see you dancing with any young men yesterday, so perhaps you think that if a man is not constantly standing attendance upon a woman, they are not courting. I assure you, that is not the case." Emily glanced at Poppy.

"Hear, hear," Lucretia said. "Now, what are we going to do about my situation?"

"Why would anyone want to come after you?" Poppy asked. "You make no secret of your relationship with Mr. Fletcher."

"Isn't it obvious? Some woman wants him for herself. It could be anyone. It could even be one of you," Lucretia said.

The girls exchanged startled looks. Emily said, "Miss Dobbins, I think we can safely say it is not one of us. We are your friends, remember?"

"Then who killed Miss Grace?"

Emily shrugged. "Someone else. We were all with you yesterday, if you recall. None of us could have poisoned that wine."

"How do you know it was poison? Didn't someone say it was an accident?" Sarah asked.

"It didn't look like an accident. Miss Parkinson said so herself, her limbs seized up like a toy soldier's," Emily said.

"Besides, it was busy, anyone could have done something and in the crowd, it would be easy to hide," Lucretia said.

"I think poisoning someone's wine would elicit comment, even in a busy assembly," Emily said. "More likely the girl had an unfortunate accident."

"Miss Dobbins has a point, though." Poppy earned their attention. "I keep thinking about that glass. It had a dust or powder in it, I am sure. But the only way we could see it was when the red wine coated it. No servant would dare serve a glass like that to a guest."

"But if the powder in it was colorless, they might not have seen it." Emily pointed out.

"Even so, if the servant had been taking drinks around the assembly, there's no way to control who would have picked it up. Anyone could have taken that glass. There's no way the servant could have made certain Miss Dobbins or Miss Grace would have taken it."

Poppy frowned, just as Terrence walked into the parlor with a book in hand. "Ah, Miss Morton. There you are. Oh, you have guests. Hello, girls." Mr. Terrell smiled at the ladies present, of which Sarah seemed the only one to return his smile with interest.

"Hello, Mr. Terrell."

He ignored Sarah's greeting. "And what brings you all here today? Visiting Poppy?"

The girls looked at her. He had used her name in a familiar fashion, and it suggested a close friendship or intimacy between them. For him to use her Christian name so casually embarrassed her, for it put her in the awkward spot of either having to correct him and be rude, to remedy what may only be a slight slip of the tongue, or to act as if they were together. She swallowed and said, "We were just having a chat. As I mentioned at breakfast, Mr. Terrell, a girl died at the assembly we attended yesterday."

"My word. Were you all there?"

"Yes."

"Goodness. Well, none of you should attend the assembly there anymore, to be safe."

The girls exchanged looks. Tickets to the Fashionable Institution were not cheap, especially as one needed a word of approval from the organizers to get in. Sarah shot Poppy a look that said, *Without the right connections, how would they meet eligible young gentlemen?*

Poppy smiled politely and said, "Thank you for your concern, Mr. Terrell."

"Of course. I had another reason for coming, however. I wonder, Miss Morton, if you might like to join me for a walk this afternoon."

Poppy stiffened.

"As you accepted my gift yesterday, I think it only right that you might join me for a walk and then you can tell me about your evening."

Poppy swallowed as the girls looked at her. "Mr. Terrell very kindly gave me a gold cross to wear to the dance yesterday." She looked at him quizzically. Did he mean to suggest that because he had given her a necklace, she owed him?

Sarah said, "I love a walk."

Lucretia rose to her feet. "Well, I won't keep you."

"Good, we can set off now," Mr. Terrell said.

"I'm sorry, Mr. Terrell, but I cannot." Poppy paused. "A girl died yesterday and some of us were present when it happened. I cannot in good conscience go promenading as if all is well."

"Oh. What do you mean to do?" he asked.

"I will go and pay my respects to the girl's family. She was very young, and new to the Season, like us. Her family will no doubt be devastated."

"Very good. I shall accompany you there." He smiled at Poppy. "Your sense of showing the proper decorum and restraint do you credit, Poppy. I am sure you would much rather go out walking, but in this case, I agree, paying a call to the girl's family would be best." He nodded to the girls. "I'll just fetch my hat."

As he left, a moment passed before Lucretia hissed, "Miss Morton, are you two courting?"

Poppy looked at her lap. Her tea had gone stone cold. "Yes."

"You seem positively overjoyed by the prospect," Emily said.

Poppy glanced up at her with a slight smile. "Is it so obvious?"

"Why allow him to court you if you do not like him?"

"Because, I..." she paused. All the girls had leaned in with interest, and it struck Poppy that this was a prime source of good gossip.

"He used your Christian name. Do you have an understanding with him?" Sarah asked.

"Tell us," Lucretia said.

Poppy saw Emily flash a warning look. "Mr. Terrell is a guest here. He is studying with my uncle, and has just lately taken orders."

"Is there no living he can take?" Sarah asked.

"Not that I know of."

"Who cares? Forgive me, Miss Morton, but we have more important things to concern ourselves with than your houseguest," Lucretia said. "What are we going to do about this person? My attacker?"

"How do we know it wasn't an accident? The glass could have just been dusty and no one caught it," Emily pointed out.

"Why are you so keen to think it an accident?" Lucretia asked.

"Why are you so determined to think someone is trying to kill you?" Emily countered.

"Because they are." Lucretia's voice rose. "I was pushed down a stairwell just last week and hurt my head. Now someone dies after drinking a glass of wine I'd taken. What else am I to think?"

"That you're incredibly unlucky, or lucky, depending on how you look at it."

Lucretia's eyes narrowed at Emily and she turned to Poppy. "What are you going to do?"

"Miss Munden makes a good point. We don't know if the wine was actually doctored or if it was just dust. Maybe Miss Grace had a physical reaction to it," Poppy said.

The girls stared at her.

"Have you not heard about people's bodies reacting strongly to some things?"

"I had an aunt who could not eat nuts. If she did, her throat would swell and it became hard for her to breathe. Is that what you mean?" Sarah asked.

"I do not think there were nuts in the wine," Lucretia said.

Emily rolled her eyes.

"Miss Haskett, that is exactly what I mean," Poppy said, rising to her feet. "But I think we will know more once we see her body."

There was a little gasp.

"See her body?" Lucretia repeated. "Are you mad?"

"I mean to pay my respects to her family and if possible, learn how she died," Poppy said.

"The girl fell off a balcony. What more do you need?" Emily asked.

Poppy looked at Emily. "Will you come with me?"

Emily made a sour face. "All right. But I think you are wasting your time. Miss Dobbins, Miss Haskett, will you join us?"

The girls, accompanied by Mr. Terrell, who looked most appropriate in somber clothing despite the warm smile on his face, went to the residence of the Grace family. But outside the building, Emily stopped.

"I do not think I can do this," she said.

"What's wrong?" Poppy asked.

"This feels ghoulish, going to see her body. I don't like it. I can't. I won't." She looked at Poppy. "I'm sorry." She walked away.

Poppy's shoulders drooped. At Emily's example, Lucretia

said, "I agree. This is more than just paying respects, it's dishonest. And I have better things to do. I'll see you girls later."

That left Poppy, Sarah and Mr. Terrell. "Take heart, girls," he said, "we must do our duty and respectfully call on the family, who no doubt are in need of spiritual succor."

"Succor?" Sarah repeated.

"Yes. come along." He led the way up the walk and knocked boldly on the door. As a clergyman, he was allowed in, and Poppy and Sarah followed.

Inside they quietly called on Miss Grace's parents, who were understandably distraught. The mother in particular, who wore black mourning clothes and held a handkerchief to her eyes. She was very grateful to see them. "Oh how good of you girls to come, and to bring a clergyman with you too. That's kind. Annabelle was new to Town, we were only here for a fortnight. I didn't think she had time to make friends." Tears streamed down her face.

Miss Grace's body was already laid out on a funeral bier, resting in a coffin and covered with black cloth, surrounded by flowers. Mrs. Grace came up to Poppy as her husband talked with Mr. Terrell. "It's such a tragedy. She was only nineteen." She sniffed, dabbed her eyes with her handkerchief and whispered, "I suppose you heard about her fall."

"Yes, I was at the assembly," Poppy said.

"Didn't she look beautiful? So pretty." Mrs. Grace sniffed. "Her injuries were of such a nature... we thought it best to remember her like this."

"I'm so sorry for your loss."

To Poppy's surprise, Sergeant Dyngley arrived, followed by Peregrine Grant. They paid their respects to the family, and if Henry and Terrence had an animosity toward each other, they did not show it. Peregrine made his way over to the women, whilst Sarah talked with Mrs. Grace. He nodded to Poppy and said, "I'm a little surprised to see you here. Did you know the girl well?"

"No, not really. But I wanted to pay my respects. She was our age, so it feels wrong that she died so young." She paused. "I wonder, Mr. Grant, did you examine her body when you found her?"

"Yes. Why?"

"There were some questions about how she died. Some of the girls were talking, and–"

"I neither know nor care what those girls talk about, and neither should you. There's not a lick of sense in any of them," Peregrine said darkly.

"I'm sorry you feel that way."

He looked at her. "No, I didn't mean that. It's just…All right. What is it you want to know?"

"Before she fell, Miss Grace complained she did not have anything to eat or drink that day. She took a glass of wine from Miss Dobbins and a short while later, the girls said that on the balcony her limbs seized up, and she fell off."

He frowned. "Why are you telling me this?"

"Because it seems suspicious. When we looked at the glass of wine, it was coated with a fine dust inside, but it only could be seen once the wine stained it."

"So there was dust in the glass." He looked at her. "What are you thinking?"

"The dust had no smell. We wonder if the wine was poisoned."

He blinked. "I remember, the girls said she choked."

"If she choked, would her limbs have stiffened like that?"

He paused. "I did think it was strange. When I examined her body, her injuries were consistent with a fall, for there was a lot of blood. But, it was odd. She had lockjaw. And her body already had a rigidity about it, that a normal body would take hours to develop." He looked at her. "Did her limbs seize up before she fell?"

"That is what the girls say."

His shoulders slumped. "Then, Miss Morton, I do think it is possible Miss Grace died from poison."

Chapter Twenty-One

Henry and Poppy did not stay long. Sarah talked with Mr. Grant a while longer and was present as Henry asked Mr. and Mrs. Grace about their daughter. But to hear Mrs. Grace's tearful answers was almost more than Poppy could bear. The woman explained that this was Annabelle's first Season, and whilst she did not have many friends, she was keen to attend the assemblies.

"Did she have any suitors?" Henry asked.

"She was seeing Mr. Dyngley."

Henry had the grace to blush. "That is me. I escorted Miss Grace around the park a few days ago. It was thought we might suit, but our temperaments were too different."

"Oh, how very honest of you. So often she steps out with suitors and seems to think her time with them has gone well, but they never come calling again. I never knew why."

Henry winced inwardly and tried to remain a serious expression. "I am sure she would have found a good husband this Season."

He relayed his sympathies and left, not long after Peregrine, Sarah and Poppy had left. Mr. Terrell, that obnoxious clergyman, was soon at his heels. "Mr. Dyngley," he called.

Henry stopped and waited for the man to catch up. "Yes?" he asked.

"I want a word with you."

Dyngley turned. Mr. Terrell looked very somber and severe in his black clerical clothing, but as holy as the man seemed, there was something about him he did not like. Mr. Terrell had a pinched, square face, with small eyes and a sour expression that seemed as though he permanently sucked on a lemon. His skin was overly pale, not in the fair, attractive sense, but in the way that suggested he spent too much time indoors, and not enough in the sunshine. He had an unhealthy pallor and brown hair that was messy and shabbily cut. But he, too, was courting Poppy, and so Henry gave him the time of day.

"What can I do for you, Mr. Terrell?"

"I want to know your intentions toward Poppy," he said.

Henry blinked. "I know you are staying in the same house, but I would not be so familiar as to use her Christian name in polite company, Mr. Terrell. It would give the wrong impression and could land her in trouble."

Mr. Terrell reddened. "Any trouble she gets into, I will remove her from. Answer the question."

The man was impertinent. "My intentions are entirely honorable, as I hope are yours, Mr. Terrell." There was something delicious in being so formal with his rival. It allowed him to be exceedingly polite and yet chilling in the same breath. Perhaps it was the English way, but he had never met any manner so cutting as the English.

Mr. Terrell balked. "Of course my intentions are honorable. I only ask because I see that she has been attending parties where accidents have occurred. Whilst I cannot accompany her everywhere just yet, I would expect you to do your part to protect her person."

"Where I am present, you may trust that I will."

"I also came to tell you that you may stop your attentions toward her. I have reason to believe that my proposal to her will result in an immediate acceptance."

Henry stared. "Your proposal?"

"Of marriage. We have been living in close quarters and…have become close." Mr. Terrell smiled to himself.

Henry could have throttled the man. "You mean your gift of the necklace."

"She told you, did she? A mere token of my affection, but I take it as a positive sign of her acceptance of my suit."

Henry snorted. "Her accepting a necklace does not mean anything."

"It most certainly does. You're just too oblivious to see it. We are in love. And I mean to propose to her within the week. Once she accepts, we will remove to the country where there will be no more of this investigating or murderous accidents."

"Murder by itself is no accident. For an accident to be a murder, there is no accident about it, only motive, means, and opportunity. An accident is only that," Henry said.

"You quibble words with me, but mark my warning, Sergeant, Miss Morton will be my wife soon enough. I only wanted to do you the courtesy of telling you to stop wasting your time."

"Hah." Henry chortled. "Thank you for your warning, Mr. Terrell. If I believed a word of it, I might even take your advice." Henry stomped away, his thick black boots striking the cobblestone street. He did not care where he went or how stormy his face looked, he only wanted to wipe the smug expression from Mr. Terrell's face and court Poppy, until she declared herself madly in love with him and spared no thought for the obnoxious clergyman.

HE WALKED DOWN the road, furious with himself. He'd gotten so distracted with Petunia's debutantes that he'd lost sight of what he really wanted to do. Meanwhile, Poppy was being courted by the insidious Mr. Terrell, and Tom Harris was back in the mix.

Tom. Henry had dismissed him as an ordinary pimp with an eye for beauty. But the more that he had come to know Tom, the less he liked him. The man had few morals, and now that he had shed his humble facade and embraced his titled background,

Henry disliked him even more. Henry thought back to the previous evening.

He almost hadn't recognized the man, but for the same self-assured smirk he wore. Gone now were the worn clothes, and in their stead was a suit worthy of any decent high street tailor. The man's hair was no longer messy, it was artfully tousled. His voice was higher pitched, like a dandy of the *ton,* and he walked, talked, and moved with an exaggerated foppishness that got on Henry's nerves.

What had changed, Henry wondered. Why now had Tom shed his humble mask to hobnob and dance with the young ladies of the Season? And this death of Miss Grace. Tragic though it was, why did it happen? The organizers of the Fashionable Institution were right, this would reflect badly on their venue.

He wondered where Tom was living now. Was he still working at the Shakespeare's Head in Covent Garden? Henry's feet found their way there, and he repressed the urge to hold a handkerchief to his nose.

The air was different from elsewhere in Town. Grocers, food sellers, and market stalls crowded the space. Ladies-about-town strolled and laughed, their coarse laughter grating on his ears. He was in London to be sure, as the air smelled of fresh vegetables, rotting fruit, and flies buzzed everywhere with a low drone. He walked past drunkards, layabouts, ne'er do wells, sailors, militiamen, merchants, servants, flower girls, and more than one child whom he suspected belonged to an adolescent street gang. He kept a wide berth, and a tighter hand on his coins. He walked to the Shakespeare's Head, which bore no connection to the playwright aside from the name, and strode inside. The smells of wood paneling, urine, stale beer, and sour wine, mixed with sweat and body odor, assailed his nose.

He bought a drink, stood by a wooden post, and looked around. The barkeep appeared unfriendly and the serving girls looked harried and lazy, their blouses undone, with aprons loosely tied around their waists. The resulting appearance was slovenly. When the first prostitute came up to him, he asked, "Where can I find Tom Harris?"

"Tom? Nowhere. He's gone. But if you're lonely, I'm here." She flashed a gap-toothed smile at him.

"What do you mean, gone?" He avoided looking at her openly-bared breasts.

"He left. About a fortnight ago, he told Mr. Higgins he's done and took his wages, and walked out. What d'you want him fer?"

He shrugged. "Wanted to talk to him is all." He gave her his drink and walked out.

So Tom had disappeared, from Covent Garden and his former life. Why, and why now?

LATER THAT AFTERNOON, Henry sent a bouquet of hothouse flowers to be delivered to Poppy. He sent an errand boy to deliver them, with the hope that she might see it as a sign she was not alone with only Mr. Terrell around. He had hopes of courting her too.

He never saw Mr. Terrell intercept the messenger boy and take the flowers for himself.

HENRY RETURNED HOME to the Dyngley townhouse, where he ran into his older brother, John. "Ah, hullo Henry."

"Where is Petunia?" Henry said.

"In the parlor, with the Parkinson ladies, why?"

Henry stopped. "I need you to tell your wife to stop involving herself in my affairs."

John's face clouded and he clapped Henry on the shoulder. "What do you mean?"

"She has been setting me up with debutantes, almost as soon as I enter a room. She has no care for what I want, and only wants to see me married. Tell her this forward approach is unwanted. I do not want, nor need, her help in finding a wife."

John removed his hand. "I say, Henry, there's no need to be

so harsh. She's got little to do now that she's further along. The only thing she can think to do is try and marry off everyone else. She doesn't mean any harm by it, she only wants you to marry well."

"She has no care for who I might want," Henry said.

"Oh, come now. How awful are these debutantes anyway? I'd love to be in your shoes," John said, looked around, then said loudly, "If I was single, of course. I'm a happily married man."

Henry gave his brother a grouchy look. "She set me up with Miss Grace."

"Miss Grace, Miss Grace. Why is that name so familiar…"

"She had a laugh like a donkey, was overly presumptuous and forward, and died yesterday evening."

"Good god. That's horrible. Her poor family…" John shook his head.

"Yes. It is tragic." Henry removed his hat and gripped it in his hands. "We discovered we were not suited and she set about abusing me to anyone who would listen. This is the sort of woman Petunia wishes to set me up with," Henry said.

"Well, she wouldn't have done it without a good reason. The girl was probably wealthy. Surely you could have put up with an obnoxious laugh for a dowry of a few thousand pounds?" John grinned.

"No."

"Well, never mind. I'm sure the next girl Petunia introduces you to will be better."

"I don't want any other girl. I want–"

"Good afternoon, Mr. Dyngley, Sergeant Dyngley." Miss Parkinson walked into the room, looking fair and demure in a light purple dress.

The men bowed. "Hello, Miss Parkinson."

"Forgive me for interrupting your conversation. Sergeant, I think I have a solution to your problem," she said.

"You do?"

"Yes." She said quietly, "My mama wants me to get married

as soon as possible, but she does not care for who I might fancy or take a liking to. I see that you are in a similar sort of situation. I propose we form an alliance of sorts."

Henry tensed. Any mention of an alliance between him and an eligible young woman sent alarm bells ringing in the back of his mind. If he had been a dog, his hackles would have risen. "What do you suggest?"

"We pretend to be courting each other. Just for the Season. That way my Mama and your sister-in-law stop throwing unsuitable people at us, and we live up to their expectations without hurting anyone, for as I'm sure you appreciate, we are wasting their time as much as ours."

Henry felt sheepish. He'd only thought of how much Petunia's plans had inconvenienced him, he'd never spent a moment thinking of how the ladies thrown at him might be feeling.

"And what happens at the end of the Season?" he asked.

"Then we go our separate ways, citing differences. You could insult me, or I could jeer at you in public. Either way, it would be easy to convince the others we are ill-suited."

"And what would I have to do?"

"Escort me to parties and things. Throw a few flowers my way. Tell people we are courting."

He felt uncomfortable about this. "And if we find someone we do wish to court?"

"Then do that as well. There's no need to be exclusive."

Henry paused. What would Poppy think of this? Why couldn't they just court and be happy?

"It's a good idea, Henry. Just think, it would get Petunia off your back, and save Miss Parkinson any unwanted attention," John said.

Henry sighed. He really should think about this more, but hadn't time. "All right. I'll do it."

Miss Parkinson clapped her hands and John squeezed his shoulder. "Well done. Excellent. Just excellent."

Mrs. Parkinson stepped out of the parlor and said, "What's

going on?"

"Did you hear, Mama? We are courting. Henry and I are a courting couple." Miss Parkinson's eyes shone with triumph.

Mrs. Parkinson was all smiles, and shared her congratulations on his wise choice. Petunia had them all join her in the parlor for tea, and was so pleased, she gave Henry a biscuit.

Henry was surprised at her generosity, and bit into the crumbly ginger biscuit, but it tasted like ash. He tried to pay attention to the conversation of the others, but couldn't focus. Why did he have a sour feeling in his gut about this? He and Miss Parkinson were just playacting, that was all. Right?

CHAPTER TWENTY-TWO

POPPY RETURNED HOME. She read her books, joined her aunt in needlepoint, and chatted with her lady's maid about what to wear to the next ball, which was to be a masquerade. She even patiently listened to Mr. Terrell describe the latest sermon he and her uncle were composing, but listened with only half an ear. She was waiting for the telltale sound of the door, which would signal Henry was calling on her.

But he didn't. Instead, she sat facing the bouquet of hothouse flowers that Mr. Terrell had purchased for her. They looked wild and exotic and must have been expensive. She didn't want to like them, but couldn't help it. They were lovely. But as she stared at them, she distantly heard Mr. Terrell say something. "I'm sorry, what did you say?"

"I said, are you going to the next ball at the Fashionable Institution? I hear it's to be a masquerade."

"Yes, I was planning on it," she said.

"What will you wear as a disguise?" he asked.

"I don't know. I think Miss Cooke had some ideas. She and my aunt were talking about it."

"Will your aunt go as well?" he asked.

"Yes. I think it is very hard that she's in London, but can't enjoy the amusements too. Besides, I need an escort."

He stepped toward her. "I would be happy to escort you."

"That's very kind of you, but it would be inappropriate."

He smiled down at her. "Your sense of propriety is truly admirable, Miss Morton," he said. "I have no doubt you will be equally modest at the ball. I shall look forward to seeing you there."

"Are you going as well?" she asked.

"Yes. Your uncle kindly procured tickets for us three. It was no easy feat, I tell you. But when he said we were your family to Mrs. Devenshaw, she had her secretary write our names in the book. I suppose not all the balls are open to the public. Fortunately for us, now we shall all go with you." He grinned.

"Oh good," she said, rather less animated than he.

"And I know your dance card is free, which is why I request the first two dances with you."

"I…" she had no excuse. "Certainly, Mr. Terrell." She tried not to sigh.

THE MASQUERADE BALL approached and Poppy had no idea what to wear. Her aunt was going in an evening dress with a simple masque, as were her uncle and Mr. Terrell in dark suits, wigs, and tie-on masks. Poppy had left the details to her aunt and lady's maid, for she had little interest in dresses at the moment, leaving them to decide what she would wear as a costume. But when the pair returned from one of the masquerade warehouses, they were giggling like old friends, and Poppy wondered if she had in fact missed out on a fun occasion. When she asked what she would be wearing, the pair exchanged a look.

"You'll just have to wait and see, Poppy," her aunt said.

The day of the masquerade was upon them and that evening, Poppy allowed Miss Cooke to do her hair, but in quite an odd manner. Her hair was left long and hardly pinned up at all. Her cheeks and lips were rouged, her skin dabbed with a light white powder to make her reflection pale. "Miss Cooke, what am I going as?"

Her maid's smile widened as she helped Poppy slip inside

stays that were pulled tight, so her chest became exaggerated, and she wore a plain green dress over a tightly cinched corset around her waist, complete with light stockings and dancing shoes. "Miss Cooke?"

"You're a shepherdess!" Miss Cooke crowed in delight. "And a damned pretty one too." She pinned a little lacy cap on her hair and tied a colorful apron to hang around her waist. "There. Pretty as a picture."

"I thought the idea behind a mask was to hide your identity."

"Not always. Some just go in a costume and others try to guess who or what they are. You should see your aunt."

"What's she going as?"

"You'll see."

As it turned out, her aunt bore a striking resemblance to a goose. "Aunt? You're dressed up as a goose?"

"It's a swan. I'm a graceful swan," Aunt Rachel informed her, fluffing down her white dress trimmed in feathers. She wore a pointed white feathery mask with a bright orange bill.

"I see."

Poppy quickly pulled on her cloak and tied it tightly around her, holding it closed. With so much of her skin showing, she did not want to give Mr. Terrell a reason to ogle her.

But ogle her he did, as soon as they had arrived at the Fashionable Institution and she was obliged to remove her cloak and hand it to a waiting attendant. His eyes barely left her chest and when she cleared her throat to get his attention, he glanced briefly at her face, then at her chest again. He was not very good at admiring women peripherally, she supposed.

He tripped his way through the first two dances, and trod on her feet, stumbling and making a general nuisance of himself. "Well, these dances are not the same as in the country, I assure you. Quite different. That man beside me was out of time and threw me off-balance," he said.

Poppy murmured an agreement and looked away. Could no one rescue her from this mess?

And then she saw it. Henry was dancing with Miss Parkinson. The girl wore a light pink evening dress and a mask with pink feathers. To Poppy's critical eye, the young woman looked like a simpering pink bird. Henry looked dashing as ever in a dark suit, almost black, and an ugly silver mask that sneered. It was a departure from his usual character but tonight, Poppy didn't care. Every touch of his hand to Miss Parkinson's was painful to watch.

The dance ended and Poppy turned from the sight. Mr. Terrell said beside her, "You look very fetching tonight, Poppy. Very fetching indeed."

"Please, Mr. Terrell. I beg you would please call me Miss Morton."

"But we are courting."

"But we are not engaged. You are very kind but we are not so close, and I would not have others think us so."

His face suffused with red. "You do not wish to be intimate with me?"

"At a ball, certainly not," she spoke without thinking.

"But Pop…Miss Morton, we are courting with a mind to wed. As your suitor, I think it is my due that you afford me these little intimacies, as a sign of our closeness."

"Mate, I don't think she's interested. Hullo there, Miss Morton," Tom said, giving her a boyish smile.

"Hullo Mr. Markham."

She curtseyed as he bowed and extended his hand. "May I have this dance?"

She nodded and accepted him without a word. As soon as they were away from Mr. Terrell, he said, "You looked like you needed a rescue. Who is that fellow?"

"My suitor."

Tom stopped. "Your what?"

"My uncle's choice, not mine."

"Why are you letting your uncle decide who you should socialize with?"

"Have you any sisters, Tom?"

"Me? No. Two older brothers. Obnoxious sods, both of them," he said.

"And what of the girls you look after?"

"I'm not in that line of business anymore. Gave it up."

"Did you?"

"Yes. I thought it was time."

"Well…And what if you wanted to provide for one of the girls with a suitor. Would you encourage them to accept him?"

"Absolutely. These girls often can't choose and—oh. I see." He paused and looked at her. "Something tells me there's more to this."

Poppy smiled thinly. "If I do not allow Mr. Terrell to court me, then I cannot see Sergeant Dyngley."

"I see. And myself?"

"You haven't paid me a visit. I only have two suitors at the moment."

He snorted and led her into the queue of dancers awaiting the next set. "We'll have to remedy that."

"What for? Tom, I've heard of your background. You are wealthy, genteel, you have a good family and connections, while I–"

"Have a decent heart and a smart head on your shoulders. Not to mention how stunning you look in that dress. I've seen five men eye you already. Do I really need to tell you how much I admire you, Miss Morton?"

Poppy blushed. "Do you not see how ill-suited we are?"

"We're more suited than you and that other fellow."

He had a point.

"What will you do?"

"I don't know. Mr. Terrell has given me flowers and jewelry, whereas Sergeant Dyngley…"

"Hasn't," he said, glancing at Henry and his fair partner. "That's odd. Is he solving a case?"

"Yes. He's investigating the situation of the girl who fell off the balcony before, but I've been told to stay out of it."

"Oh, that business from before. There was some poisoned wine involved, wasn't there?" he asked.

"Yes."

"Well you know what I would do," he said, leading her into the set.

"What?"

"I'd investigate it on my own. You'd be a member of the watch or a magistrate yourself with that brain of yours, were it not for your sex."

She glanced down. There were no women constables, and to even suggest such a thing would make her the butt of many jokes. But maybe someday.

Tom continued, "So I'd learn what I could. Not everyone will talk to him, you know. Especially given his name."

"What do you mean?" she asked.

"People talk, Miss Morton. Everyone knows that his sister-in-law, Mrs. Dyngley, has tried pairing him up with a number of suitable young ladies. He's dancing with one of them now."

Poppy began dancing with Tom and glanced over. There danced Henry with another young woman she did not recognize.

"That there is Miss Simkins, a debutante with naught but one-thousand a year," he said with a little laugh, "Although if the list is right, that's not all she'll bring to her future husband. Knows her way around the bedroom, that one."

"What do you mean? And what list are you talking about?" Poppy asked.

"You recall Harris's List? The list that my relative penned years ago, about the ladies of London?"

"Yes." Poppy looked away. It was a dirty periodical, describing the ladies for sale about town and their assets, right down to their physical charms and temperaments. "You don't mean…"

"Oh yes. I heard the men talking about it. Apparently some enterprising individuals put a new section in there for this year's debutantes. Miss Simkins is in there."

Poppy's hand darted to her mouth. "My word."

"She doesn't know, of course. I haven't seen it, yet. But she'll have to be careful what society she chooses, to be sure."

The dance ended, and Tom led Poppy back to the sidelines, when they were approached by Sarah and Mr. Terrell.

"Sir, I don't believe we are acquainted, but what have you been telling Miss Morton? She seems quite ill at ease," Mr. Terrell said.

The two looked at Tom, who raised his hands. "I simply mentioned that Harris's List this year has a new section, about the ladies of this year's season." He gave Poppy a cheeky smile.

"Harris's List?" Mr. Terrell repeated.

"I've heard of that. Is it true? No one we know is in it, is there?" Sarah asked.

"What is this list?" Mr. Terrell asked.

"It's a naughty list of all the women in London who sell themselves. It talks about everything, right down to where a man can find them, and what kind of intimate relations they prefer."

"Miss Haskett!" Mr. Terrell said. "Really."

"I'm just saying what is in the list," Sarah said.

"Well, never mind. As long as you girls aren't in there, there's nothing to worry about." He turned to Poppy. "Shall we dance?"

"You forget, Mr. Terrell, we have already danced two dances together. To dance any more would be unseemly."

"Would it? But we are courting."

"Still." Poppy shook her head. "I'm sorry, Mr. Terrell. It would cause gossip and be unfair."

"To who?"

"Her other suitors," Sarah said.

"What other suitors?" Mr. Terrell asked.

"Me, for one. Come on, Miss Morton. You've not had a second dance with me yet, and I feel like dancing." Tom took her hand and led her into the dance.

As Poppy glanced back, she saw Sarah say something to Mr. Terrell. What it was she didn't know, but she could guess.

She spied Henry dancing with another girl, who looked

equally fetching in a rose-colored gown and a mask covered with rose petals.

Tom said in her ear. "He'll come around. Give it time."

She looked at him. "I thought you two were rivals."

"We are of a sort, but…" He thought for a second. "I have an idea. Something that will give him a little push in the right direction."

"What's that?"

"Let us court."

"What?" she blinked at him.

"I mean it. I'll court you and with my background, your relatives could hardly say no. Your sergeant can't stand me, so that will put a foot up his backside and get him moving," he said.

She looked back at Tom. "Why?"

"Do you need me to spell it out? You're beautiful, I'm charming, you're smart and I'm witty. Plus, you know…I fancy you."

She smiled. "I've seen you fancy a lot of girls."

He laughed out loud. "Yes, I have. But I mean it. I care for you. If you let me, I'd like to court you. I'll get rid of that nasty Mr. Terrell for you and Dyngley will come running."

"You would do that for me?"

"Let's see, courting a girl I like. Yes, I could manage that," he joked.

But as he twirled her in the dance and her eyes landed on Henry, she wondered…What if Tom's plan failed and Henry never came?

Poppy danced with Tom, and was soon claimed for a dance by none other than her father. As soon as they walked on the dance floor, he said, "Forgive me for not seeing you much. I have been much engaged lately."

"It's no trouble. I'm just glad to see you again," she said.

He rewarded her with a smile. "And what have you been getting up to?"

"Not much. I've made some friends."

"That is good. Who were those young men dancing with you

earlier?" he asked.

"There's Mr. Markham, he is the third son of the Earl of Markham."

"He looks familiar, somehow. Who was the other man you danced with? He tripped all over his feet in the first dance. I thought he was going to step on you."

Poppy smiled. "That would be Mr. Terrell. He is a guest of my uncle's and is staying with us in Town."

Lord Blackwood's eyebrows rose. "He seems to have a fondness for you."

"He is a suitor of mine," she said blandly.

"You don't seem overjoyed by that prospect."

She gave a minute shrug of her shoulders.

"You don't appreciate his attention to you?"

"Not particularly."

She heard a snort from nearby and saw that Miss Parkinson was dancing in the next set.

Poppy asked quietly, "How are you enjoying London?"

"Very well. There are many amusements to behold. I hope we might see more of each other soon, Miss Morton."

"I would like that."

The dance ended and they bowed, but not before Poppy caught Miss Parkinson looking at them. Miss Parkinson smiled at her and walked away.

Poppy saw a young man and woman dancing not far from her, but the blond girl's face was suffused with anger. If Poppy didn't know better, she'd think the girl was glaring at her.

EMILY APPROACHED POPPY later, offering her a glass of wine. The girls drank and looked around. "What a crush of people," Poppy said.

"Yes. Who was that girl dancing with your sergeant?"

"Miss Simkins, I think. Have you met any new gentlemen this evening?"

"No, although I've been trying to hide from Mr. Grant. He's

determined to speak with me and I don't want to be anywhere near him," Emily said.

"You know all he wants is to talk with you about that night, when his friend died."

"And to relive something so painful to me? Why should I go through that just to suit his curiosity? No," Emily said. "As my friend, I wish you wouldn't pressure me to do this."

"I'm sorry. I can see the anguish he is going through and how he wants answers. That's all."

"And what about my anguish? No one thinks of that."

"What do you mean? Were you two...courting?" Poppy asked.

Emily gave her a pained smile. "Yes. That is why it troubles me to talk of it."

The girls stood by and watched as many other people danced.

"What will you do?" Emily asked. "About Lucretia's little problem, and Miss Grace dying?"

"I think I'll investigate a little," Poppy said.

"Even though you were told not to?"

"Even so." The more she thought about it, the better she felt. It would give her something to do, a puzzle to solve. She had felt like she was unappreciated and abandoned by Henry, both in love and as a partner in crime investigation. Maybe this would give her the distraction she needed.

CHAPTER TWENTY-THREE

THE NEXT DAY Poppy was treated to a visit from her father, who sat on her mother's sofa and rested his hands on his knees. "You danced very well last night, Poppy. Your mother would have been proud."

Poppy beamed. "Thank you."

"Any young man would have been honored to stand up with you." He cleared his throat. "I know you have admirers, but you mustn't think you need accept the first offer that comes your way."

Poppy's eyebrows rose.

"You know, of course, that as your father, any young man who wishes to pay his addresses to you must also consult me. I won't give my blessing to just anyone," he said.

Poppy beamed. "Thank you, Father."

Mr. Terrell wandered into the room. "Miss Morton, I wonder...Oh. Who are you?" he asked, noting Lord Blackwood's older countenance and fine clothes.

"I am Blackwood. Hello. You must be Mr. Terrell."

"Yes." Mr. Terrell bowed, but perhaps not as deeply as he should have. "How are you acquainted with Miss Morton?"

Poppy exchanged a quick look with her father, who said, "I knew her mother well. We were good friends."

"I see. A shame the good lady passed away so soon, but I'm

sure it was for the best. From dust to dust and ashes to ashes, I say."

Poppy tensed. "That is my mother you are talking about, sir," she said.

"Yes, I know. I fancy myself as a clergyman to have a keen understanding of people's emotions and inner thoughts when it comes to topics of delicacy like death. And marriage," he said pointedly, looking at her. "Are you thirsty? I'll join you for tea."

"That is all right, I was just leaving. Miss Morton, would you care to walk with me in the park this afternoon?" her father asked.

"That would be nice."

"Say, Hyde Park at two o'clock? Meet at the entrance?"

"I'll be there." she said.

Lord Blackwood took his leave.

THAT AFTERNOON POPPY met her father at the park, followed by the watchful eyes of Miss Cooke and her aunt. Poppy enjoyed a pleasant walk, her boots crunching against the gravel walkways. They passed by carriages and phaetons, and it was rather busy, but Poppy didn't care. She enjoyed every minute she got to spend with her father. But strangely enough, she felt uneasy.

Before they had walked very far, she looked over her shoulder. A figure darted away behind a tree.

"What is it?" her father asked.

"Nothing, I thought I saw something," she said.

They walked on, until she felt the force of a glare on her, like an itch between her shoulder blades. This time, however, the figure did not hide. It was a young woman, with ash blonde hair and a face like a thundercloud.

She turned and said, "There, do you know that girl?"

"Who?" Her father asked, turning around. "Oh no."

"What is it? Do you know that young woman?"

"Poppy, I want you to walk away. Right now," Lord Blackwood said.

"What? What are you talking about?"

The girl came closer.

"Do it. Walk away, now." His tone was stern.

"But why?"

"Trust me, please," he said.

It was too late. The young woman had walked fast and was upon them. Her expression was set in a dirty sneer. "Who are you and what are you doing with my Papa?"

"Your Papa?" Poppy repeated. "What?"

"The man you are standing with is Lord Blackwood. I am Susan Blackwood. He is my father. Who the hell are you?"

"Susan," Lord Blackwood said sharply. "Hold your tongue."

"No. Who is she? Your whore?"

Poppy's mouth dropped open.

"Susan, stop this at once. We are going home. Now," Blackwood said.

"Not until I learn why you're spending time with this chit. She's a bit tall, but you like them that way, don't you?" Susan's brown eyes blazed with anger.

Lord Blackwood's hands trembled as if he wished to strike her, but would not. "Susan, let us go somewhere and talk. Please."

"No. I want to know now. Who the hell is this, and why is she with you? This is the errand you had to run?"

Poppy looked from Susan to Lord Blackwood. "An errand?"

Lord Blackwood's face and neck bloomed pink. "Ah, yes. Let us go somewhere quieter and I will explain." He turned and began walking, with the expectation that they would follow.

"I watched you two outside his solicitor's, and again at a dance or two, flouncing around like you're the bloody queen," Susan sneered.

Poppy stared. "Excuse me, but I don't know you. I can well understand your anger, but do not direct it at me."

Susan blinked. "Papa?"

Lord Blackwood returned, removed his hat, and ran a hand through his silvery hair. "Let us go somewhere more private.

Please." He led them away from the crowds, over to where the Serpentine lake was shallow and had a bit of marsh, complete with ducks and geese floating by. He waited for a carriage to pass, and then said, "I would not have chosen this as your first meeting. Forgive me." He looked from Susan to Poppy. "You are sisters."

"What?" Susan said. "I don't believe you."

"You wanted the truth, girl, here it is. Now listen," he said, his bushy eyebrows knitting into a frown. "Years ago, I took a mistress."

Susan's mouth dropped open. "Whilst you were married to Mama?"

"No. This was before we were married," he said, "Our estate was in dire straits. We needed an influx of money, and marrying well was the only way we could see to remedy our debts and sort out our affairs." He swallowed and said, "I married your mother, Susan. But we did not love each other then. I broke up with Celeste for a time, out of courtesy to Agnes, my bride."

"My mother. Your wife," Susan hissed.

"Yes. But she made it clear that she had no interest in sharing my bed," he said curtly. At Susan's pained expression, he said, "I understand this is painful for you to hear, but it is the truth, every word of it. So before you go attacking this girl, hear me out."

Poppy and Susan glanced at each other, then back at him. Lord Blackwood said, "Agnes bore me two wonderful children, you and your brother. But then she made it clear she wanted no more to do with our marital bed and preferred to sleep alone. As far as she was concerned, her duty was done. She'd given me money from her dowry and an heir. She could live out her days as my wife in peace."

He sighed. "I, on the other hand, was unhappy. I craved love and affection. Companionship. Something that I once thought only a wife could give me, but instead, with my wife no longer willing...I went to Celeste once more. She had been out of Town for a time, but when she returned, she accepted me with open arms."

"Your whore, you mean," Susan scoffed.

"Hold your tongue," he told Susan, and faced Poppy. "For years we were happy together. She understood the pressure I faced, and the secrecy we must keep if we were to remain together. But when she told me about you a few months ago, the child of mine she had borne in secret and kept hidden from me all these years, I was angry. Then she died before we could talk further. And of course, the morning after her death was when we first met."

"I remember." Poppy's voice was thick, and she blinked hard.

"Since then I have tried to look after you. It is the least I could do for my daughter."

Susan glared at him. "Your illegitimate bastard, you mean."

He looked at her. "That's your sister you're talking about."

"She's nothing to me. She's the daughter of a whore. What do I care that it's your whore?"

He took in a shaky breath and let it out. "If you were a child, I would take a switch to you. I would never tolerate such disrespect from a child of mine. Ever."

Susan's cheeks flamed red. "It is you who are disrespectful. To my Mama, my brother, and myself for carrying on with a prostitute. How could you do that to us? To your family?"

He hung his head.

"Do you care for us at all? Do you even love Mama?" Susan demanded.

"Yes. I do."

"Then why? How could you do it?" Susan asked.

"She stopped loving me a long time ago. We are fond of each other but there is no love there."

"Stop being so dramatic. You're not some romantic hero in a novel. You're my Papa, and you've been married for twenty some odd years. Do you really expect to have the same passion you did now as you did back then?"

"I never stopped loving your mother."

"Then shame on you for dishonoring her, and all of us,"

Susan said, tears running down her face. "I came here to find you and tell you that I've had a letter. Mama is sick with a fever, and the doctors do not think she has long."

"What?" Why didn't you tell me this at once?" he demanded.

"How could I when you were walking with this daughter of a whore?"

It took all of Poppy's resolve not to slap the girl.

Susan must have sensed Poppy's emotion, for she turned to her and said, "I hope you're happy. Congratulations, first your mother ruins my family and now you're here to do the same. What, were you hoping he'd take you on as his mistress too? Maybe introduce you to some of his friends?"

Poppy's mouth dropped open, then snapped shut. She wanted to slap the sneer right off the girl's face, but she well understood the anger and emotion she was feeling. She knew betrayal too. Instead, she said, "I hope your mother's health improves." She turned and walked away, when a small clod of dirt hit her back.

Poppy turned around. Lord Blackwood had a hand on Susan's arm, and her face was red as a devil, like out of one of the paintings in the Royal Academy, it was so furious. Poppy brushed off the back of her walking coat, and kept walking. She tried to ignore Susan's taunts, when Susan called, "I'll ruin you, you bastard, if it's the last thing I do."

A DAY LATER, there came a hurried knocking at the front door of Poppy's townhouse. Poppy and her family were in the sitting room when a servant announced Miss Emily Munden, who held a pamphlet in her hands.

"Miss Munden, are you all right?"

"No, I am not." She curtsied quickly to the others and said, "Miss Morton, an alarming bit of news has come my way. Have you seen this?"

"What is that?" Aunt Rachel asked.

Miss Munden held out the pamphlet. Poppy took it and started. "It's Harris's List."

"Yes."

"I've heard of that nonsense. Why would you bring that here? Have you no decency? This is a clergyman's household," Mr. Terrell barked at her.

Emily was not to be deterred. "Look at the extra section toward the back."

Poppy turned the pages with shaking fingers. She read:

A new listing of the debutantes of the season

Miss Mary Gibbs

A brunette of acerbic wit and little beauty, this debutante...

Poppy frowned. "Miss Gibbs is in this."

"We're all in it. You are too."

"What?" Aunt Rachel snatched the pamphlet. She scanned the pages, turning furiously. "My God."

Poppy took the paper back and read,

Miss Poppy Morton

An innocent girl of country-going manners and no fortune, this naive young clergyman's niece is dependent on the kindness of others. She is sure to have an easy virtue for the right price.

"My lord. You're ruined," Uncle Reginald said.

Chapter Twenty-Four

Poppy was shocked. "Ruined? But I haven't done anything wrong."

"It doesn't matter. Do you know what this means? Your name is in a men's solicitous paper. Every man in London will think you are a girl of easy virtue," Uncle Reginald said.

"And what about the suitors?" Aunt Rachel said. "Who will want her now?"

"No one. No one of quality anyway," her uncle mused sadly.

Mr. Terrell cleared his throat. "I can see this is a family matter. I will leave you." He bowed and quit the room.

"So kind, that Mr. Terrell," Aunt Rachel said.

"Yes. You would be lucky to have a suitor at all now, much less one of his stature," her uncle added.

Emily said, "Miss Morton, can we talk in private?"

"Of course." Poppy rose and led Emily to her mother's library.

Once Poppy had shut the door, Emily said, "I think this is no accident. I think someone maliciously did this."

"But why?"

"I don't know. My father came to me this morning, furious because some of his friends read the List and found my name. I didn't know what else to do, so I came straight here," Emily said. "What should we do?"

"Let's think about this. Who is mentioned in the pamphlet?"

"I read it through. It's you, me, Miss Dobbins, Miss Gibbs, Miss Haskett, and even Miss Simkins."

Poppy's eyes widened. "Indeed. Then, there are people I need to talk to." She went to a writing desk in the room, removed a sheet of paper and began writing notes. "I'll invite the girls here to discuss it."

The other girls arrived within an hour, each as might be expected, visibly distressed. Emily stayed with her, fretting, whilst Sarah, Lucretia, and Miss Gibbs were not far behind.

Poppy made sure the parlor was free and served them the best tea and biscuits she had, straight out of the oven, to her guests' delight. But it did little to soothe their worries, and in the case of some, their tempers.

"I am mortified by this. Who would dare do this to me?" Lucretia demanded. "Do they know who I am? I am the most eligible debutante this Season. Why would anyone throw my name in this pamphlet with you lot?"

Miss Gibbs rolled her eyes. "Calm yourself, Miss Dobbins. You'll have us all thinking we weren't your friends."

"I cannot think anyone is a friend who would do this. I cannot trust anyone. First these attacks on me and now this." Lucretia pointed at Poppy. "What do you have to say for yourself? Have you found out who did this?"

"No, not yet. But I wanted to call you all here and ask you in person, who do you think would do this?" Poppy asked.

Lucretia shrugged. Miss Gibbs looked blank. Sarah bit her nails, whilst Emily said, "I don't know. Someone who dislikes us, perhaps. Or someone who wanted us out of the competition for the bachelors this Season."

"Who are the most eligible bachelors this Season?" Poppy asked.

"That was the other thing I was going to tell you," Emily said. "They're listed here, too. In the pamphlet I mean."

"Who are they?" Miss Gibbs asked.

Emily fetched a copy of the list that Poppy and she had taken from the parlor, before her relatives could destroy it. She scanned the names and said,

"There's a whole section dedicated to the men and ladies this season, although only the ladies have descriptions of their um… attributes. The men listed are Montague Fletcher, his friend Peregrine Grant, Thomas Markham, and…" She glanced at Poppy. "Sergeant Henry Dyngley."

Poppy's mouth dropped open. "Dyngley? Why?"

Emily shrugged. "I don't know. But this says it, so it must be true."

"I don't understand. Why would he be listed in it? Montague, I understand, but who is this Dyngley fellow?" Lucretia asked.

"Henry is the second son of Sir Dyngley, a baronet. When his brother inherits, he will gain the title."

"And if he does not then it goes to Henry…" Lucretia mused. "Do they have an estate?"

Poppy nodded.

"There you have it. So who would have wanted to ruin our chances for making a match with these gentlemen?" Lucretia wondered. "And also, this list isn't complete. I know of a few other girls who are equally as prominent as us. And a few more gentlemen."

"Why would this list only focus on us, then?" Miss Gibbs wondered.

"Because they're out to get us. Remove us from the competition by ruining our names in print. It's obvious," Sarah said.

"What's not obvious is who. Who would have a motive for this?" Poppy asked.

"Miss Grace, but she's dead."

"Miss Simkins, but she's too dumb. She heard the rumors about her false chastity and went straight home. Her parents have taken her back to Devonshire. I heard it last night," Emily said.

"In that case, who's left?"

"There's that awful girl Miss Parkinson," Emily said. "She

quite fancies Sergeant Dyngley."

"I heard they're courting," Sarah added.

Poppy frowned. "But why would she go to the trouble?"

Sarah bit her lip.

"There's one person here who hasn't been honest with us," Lucretia said, crossing her arms.

"What do you mean?" Miss Gibbs asked.

Lucretia glared at Sarah. "I saw you in Fleet Street. Your father is a printer. He comes from trade. You hid it so as not to be overlooked, perhaps, during the Season. But if anyone could have done this, it's you."

"It's not me!" Sarah cringed, her nail-bitten hands darting to her mouth. "I didn't do it."

"A likely story," Miss Gibbs said. "Did you think we wouldn't find out about your low background? We all know. I'm surprised you get into the assemblies at all."

"You certainly wouldn't have met the Queen," Lucretia said. "But this is too much. How could you do this to us? To me?"

"I didn't," Sarah said.

"Prove it," Miss Gibbs said.

"Why would I include myself in the pamphlet? I'm there, too," Sarah said.

"To avoid suspicion."

Sarah shook her head, her face turning red. "I swear to you, I didn't do this." She held up the paper with shaking hands and said, "Would I really call myself, 'A snot-nosed girl with a penchant for too many sweets, but without a sweet temperament'?"

"Hold on, there's no reason to think Miss Haskett could have done it. Yes, her father is a printer, but does it print Harris's List?" Poppy asked.

"No. He usually prints bibles, cookbooks, and self-help regimens. Sometimes medical books. He wouldn't dare touch the List. And if he saw my name in it, he'd give me a walloping so bad I wouldn't be able to sit down for a week," Sarah set the offending pamphlet on the table beside the biscuits and tea.

"Do you know how to work the printing machines?" Lucretia asked.

Sarah shook her head. "No, Father never let us. He had us girls manage the shop and deal with the customers instead. He was afraid we'd lose a finger if we worked with the machines."

"Well, who else could have done it?" Miss Gibbs asked.

"Who else knows us all?" Lucretia wondered.

"Could it be one of us?" Emily asked.

The girls looked at her. Sarah opened her mouth to speak, when Mr. Terrell entered the parlor and said, "Excuse me, Miss Morton, I wonder if we might have a word in private. I think I have an answer to your little problem."

The girls all looked at her.

He bowed to the girls and said to Poppy, "If you wouldn't mind."

Poppy rose and left to follow Mr. Terrell into the corridor. Once she was certain they were alone, she said, "Yes?"

He cleared his throat. "As you are aware, the List smearing your character will be read by every disreputable man in the city. No doubt hundreds of men will think you are a woman of easy virtue and thus, easy to prey upon."

Poppy swallowed. As if the day wasn't bad enough, he had to rub it in. "Thank you, Mr. Terrell, I am aware."

His look was severe. "I don't think you fully understand the consequences of this. No man in his right mind will look at you, never mind consider you as a potential wife. Your chances for the Season are unquestionably ruined."

Poppy gasped. "Mr. Terrell."

He held up a hand. "I know what I say may seem harsh, but I only speak the truth. Now that your name is in that publication, doors and assemblies will be closed to you, people will ignore you in the street, and all good society will avoid your company."

Poppy bit her tongue hard to keep her composure.

"Unless you have a person of good standing and reputation to stand up with and say your virtue is unblemished."

Poppy thought instantly of her father. He would stand by her. "I see."

"Someone who will stand by you, no matter what, and not be afraid to escort you in society, even in the face of those who would denounce you."

The faces of her and her aunt and uncle came to mind. They had weathered scandal and gossip before, this would be no different.

"I would offer myself, as this person," he said, with a deep bow.

Her face was resolute. "Thank you, Mr. Terrell, that is very kind. But I have been the subject of malicious rumors before, and this is something I can survive, with my family. There is no need to trouble yourself to get involved, just because you are a guest here."

"It is no trouble, I assure you. It would even be a pleasure, I daresay, to stand by you. Perhaps not at first, but I am sure things would improve in time," he said magnanimously.

"As I said, this is a family matter. Thank you for your concern."

"I trust you will think over what I have said."

"I will, but I am certain there is no need to call upon you for help. Excuse me." She curtsied and returned to the parlor.

"What was all that about?" Emily asked.

"Nothing, he was just offering to help any way he could," Poppy said. Then she asked, "Miss Haskett, Is there a way you could speak to your father, and ask if he could see who turned this in to the printers who produce the List?"

"Yes. I could do that." Sarah straightened and brushed a tear away.

"Good. Then I'll be going. Ladies, let's meet again over dinner," Poppy said.

"Come to mine. I'll treat you all to some venison," Lucretia said. "Besides I have letters to write, and want to be home in case

Mr. Fletcher calls."

Miss Gibbs rolled her eyes. Sarah stood and brushed biscuit crumbs off her dress. Emily said, "Where are you going, Miss Morton?"

"To speak to an old friend."

"Who might that be?"

"A reformed pimp."

POPPY DRESSED IN a simple walking dress, plain bonnet, and stiff walking boots. She pulled her bonnet down low, then realized she did not know where Tom was staying. She called for Miss Cooke, who said, "Ah, him? I'd think he'd be staying with his family in Chelsea. I'll see what I can do."

An hour later she had a visitor. Tom walked into her parlor, removed his hat, and sat down. "That's a good lady's maid you've got, Miss Morton. Not just anyone knows where to find me. She said you needed me to come right over, and I can guess why. This is a sad day, Miss Morton. I never thought I'd see your name in Harris's List."

"Believe me when I say it is untrue," Poppy said.

"Oh, I know. Anyone who knows you will know it's a falsehood. But how many men will judge it to be true, that's the quandary." He scratched his head. "I can't think how this was done. Someone must have gone to the printers."

"Have you learned anything?"

"Not yet. Whoever did it didn't go to our printer direct, but to another, a cheap one off of Fleet Street, who printed an outdated copy of Harris's List." He laughed, "The version they printed is at least ten years old."

The look Poppy gave him sobered his cheeky expression. "Ah, but, I'll get to the bottom of this, I assure you. No one adds to Harris's List, especially with false information. There could be lawsuits from this."

"Does your family not know your connection to the List?" Poppy asked.

"No, and if they did, they'd disown me. Never mind that I've caught my father and my brothers with a copy or two." He smiled. "I'll sort this for you, Miss Morton, I promise."

"Could you see if it was a woman or a man who sent in the addition?" she asked.

"You think a woman could've done this?" he asked.

"I do," she said, thinking of her half-sister, Susan.

But before she could say more, Poppy received another visitor. Her butler came in and announced, "Lord Blackwood to see you, miss."

Tom got to his feet. "I'll not overstay my welcome. Be seeing you, Miss Morton." He bowed and swiftly left, passing by Lord Blackwood.

Poppy's father stepped back to let Tom pass, then he glanced at him as he bowed to Poppy. "Hello, Miss Morton." He waited until they were alone, then he gave her a hug. "Are you all right?"

"Yes, I'm fine. But the rumors that this pamphlet have started will be disastrous for my friends. Do you have any idea who could be behind it?"

He frowned. "I'm afraid not. I came as soon as I heard about it. That fellow looks familiar. Is he a suitor of yours?"

She smiled. "We are more friends, I'd say."

He smiled briefly in return, then his expression fell. "I wanted to apologize for my daughter's behavior toward you yesterday. It was unpardonable."

Poppy shook her head. "I can't imagine what she must be experiencing. I know it took you and I time to come to terms with our relationship. Perhaps what she needs is time."

"That is very kind of you to say, but she had no right to attack you like that, in public, and throw dirt at you. I am ashamed of her behavior." He looked at the floor. "She never used to be like this. She takes after her mother, I think."

"Father, should you be here? Isn't your wife ill?"

"That is why I have come. I wanted to tell you in person, rather than write you a letter. I am leaving, almost within the hour, to return home. I need to look after her."

For a moment he looked older. His face was drawn, and he looked pale and cold, despite the warm weather. His eyes were shadowed, which she had not seen since her mother's passing last year.

"This means that I can't be here to escort you or chaperone you at parties, and I won't be around to meet your suitors, if any of them wishes to ask for your hand in marriage. I'll have to approve by post."

Poppy gave an unladylike snort.

Her father blinked.

"Sorry," she said. "I understand completely. I was just amused, as what you say suggests you think I will find a man to marry this Season, when all I have done is dance and meet unsuitable young men."

"I would not call the third son of the Earl of Markham unsuitable."

You would if you knew his former profession, she thought.

"I am not confident I will fall in love right away," she said.

"That's all right. I didn't either. It can take years to truly develop a fondness for another person. It's not a decision to make lightly," Blackwood said, then cleared his throat. "Although, it's best not to keep a young man waiting. If he's left thinking you are uninterested, he will look elsewhere."

"What are you saying?"

Her father turned pink and tugged at his tightly tied cravat. "Just that if there is a young man whom you fancy, who is equally taken with you, perhaps, you might let your preference be known. To him, anyway. Give him a bit of encouragement. Then once he professes his love for you, write to me and I'll approve him. Assuming he meets our standards."

"And what might those be?"

"That he is smart, capable, kind, and above all else, wealthy, with no debts to his name. I'll not have you marry a handsome young chap only to see your dowry gambled away in weeks to a layabout," he said sternly. "But I trust you."

There was the sound of heavy footfalls, and both her uncle and Mr. Terrell entered the parlor. "Ah, Poppy, there you are–" Uncle Reginald stopped short. His face turned red at the sight of Lord Blackwood. "You, sir, I told you never to come under my roof again. Leave."

Lord Blackwood rose.

"This is my roof, Uncle, and my father can stay if he pleases," Poppy said.

Lord Blackwood rewarded her loyalty with a smile, and said, "No need, Miss Morton. I'll be going. Would you do me the honor of escorting me to the door?"

"She will do no such thing," Mr. Terrell said, crossing his arms beneath his chest.

Poppy stood. "Excuse me, gentlemen, but this is my home. I appreciate the care you have for me, but I will walk my father to the front door if he asks. Do make way." She walked past her uncle and Mr. Terrell, ignoring their stony glares.

Lord Blackwood followed her and took his hat from a footman at the front door. As he put on his hat, he grinned. "You've got the same iron as Celeste. That'll you do you in good stead, Poppy." He added, "I meant to say, I've spoken with Susan about our...situation. She has agreed not to say anything about it."

"What do you mean?"

"We both agree it is best that things stay as they are and our relationship is kept secret, apart from those most close to us. It will harm no one then."

"I see." For some reason, Poppy felt sad. "I'm sure you're right."

"You are very kind, Poppy. I will write to you," Blackwood said.

"I hope your wife is all right."

"She always was strong as an ox. This sudden fever worries me." He tipped his hat. "Good day, Poppy. Take care of yourself."

Poppy curtsied and once she closed the door behind him, she returned to the parlor to overhear Mr. Terrell say, "Not to worry, sir. When we are married, there will be none of that going on. I won't allow her such visitors in our home. She will be a good, biddable little wife, and leave all such unwanted connections behind."

Poppy fled to her room. Was she never to be rid of the man?

Chapter Twenty-Five

HENRY WAS OUT of sorts. At the masquerade, he had danced the allemande with Miss Parkinson, had the misfortune to dance with Miss Simpkins, whose breath smelled like sour wine, and then Miss Parkinson again, aside from one or two other girls he couldn't remember. He'd overheard more than one woman describing him as an eligible bachelor but he didn't care what they said. He only cared about Poppy, but she was nowhere to be seen.

She had to be at the dance, for he saw what he was sure was her aunt decked out as a white feathery goose, and another girl as roses. He thought he spied her dancing with Mr. Terrell but couldn't be certain, for the man kept stumbling over his own feet. But by the time he got near he was claimed for another dance by another partner, and it would be rude not to accept. There were so many mothers, guardians, and young women demanding his attention. He didn't mind it at first, but it was rather a crush of people.

THE NEXT DAY he rose early, breakfasted, and went to a coffee house. He was tired but didn't want to have to deal with Petunia's knowing smiles, or Miss Parkinson's triumphant gaze. So he bought a cup of steaming coffee, sat down at a small side table, and took up a paper that had been left behind. He barely noticed the words as he heard a man behind him say, "That party last night at the Fashionable Institution was mad. I'll not be taking my wife there again."

"What do you mean?" another voice asked.

"My wife goes and wears a gold bracelet, a gift from me, and what happens? She loses the damned thing. She swears it was stolen, but I told her, 'Mrs. Townsend, you're being daft.' Who would dare steal at a dance like that? It's hard to get in, you have to be known and approved of by the proprietors. They won't let just anyone inside, and they certainly wouldn't let thieves in."

"Shame about the bracelet, Mr. Townsend," the man's friend said.

"Yes. I told her that was the last piece of jewelry I'll buy her. She's that clumsy, there's no use buying her any more. She'll lose it the next day for sure. And yet..."

"What?"

"Well, she's never lost anything like that before. Frances is usually so orderly. She even remembers where I've misplaced things around the house. This isn't like her. Not at all."

"Could she be right? Could someone have stolen it?"

The two men debated this as Henry sipped his coffee and tried to organize his thoughts. So someone had stolen a gold bracelet at last night's assembly. He glanced behind him for a second, and vaguely remembered the man dancing with his wife, close to himself and Miss Parkinson. They were in some of the same dances, so he'd gotten to see the man's face a bit that evening. He thought briefly about offering his services, but decided he had enough on his plate at the moment.

There was the case of the dead girl, Miss Grace. Henry felt a pang of guilt that he had treated her so poorly during their time together. But now it was too late. A word with the medical student, Mr. Grant, and a close look of the girl's body before she was buried suggested that she had in fact been poisoned. The question was why, and was it true that someone had meant that poisoned wine for someone else? Miss Grace's parents were distraught, understandably so.

Henry drank more coffee and closed his eyes. Nearby, another pair of men chatted. One of whom spoke in a lazy drawl, "I don't know what I'm supposed to do, Peregrine. She writes me letters every day and demands to see me. It's supposed to be the man chases after the girl, not the other way around."

Henry smiled. It sounded like he wasn't the only one being hunted by matrimony-seeking women.

"At least you have her undivided attention," Peregrine said.

"How is that little search of yours going? Have you found out anything about Stuart?"

"No. Miss Munden refuses to even be near me in public."

Henry blinked.

"Sounds like she's got something to hide. Those girls, they all do. Did you hear how they're all mentioned in the List?"

"What?"

Henry sat up straight.

"There's a new section added to Harris's List. Some other printer printed an old edition of it, it's years old, but the new addition has the names of all those girls in it, and their charms, or lack thereof." The man laughed.

"Montague, don't be coarse."

Henry turned around. "Mr. Grant?"

Peregrine Grant and Montague Fletcher looked at him through tired eyes. "Sergeant Dyngley?"

Montague tensed, and Henry nodded hello. "I thought I recognized your voices. Is a friend of yours missing?"

The young men exchanged glances. Montague rose and said, "I'm off. We'll talk later, Peregrine."

Once he left, Peregrine faced Henry and said, "It's our friend, Stuart Horley. He's not gone missing, he's been dead these past few weeks."

Henry listened as Peregrine told him of their friend, Stuart, who had lately fallen in love with a lady, but whom he wouldn't say. He had been planning to ask her that night to marry him, but instead, he had a dreadful encounter and fell to his death.

"But the circumstances are odd," Peregrine said. "Like I told Miss Morton, our friend Stuart Horley refused to say who he wanted to propose to, just in case he got rejected. But he was not an anxious sort of man, and the manner in which he died..." Peregrine frowned. "He fell off a balcony, but he was surrounded by those girls. Miss Emily Munden, Miss Lucretia Dobbins and Miss Gibbs. I have tried to question them, but they refuse to speak to me. I can't figure out why."

"They may feel traumatized by having witnessed his death."

"They can't have been bothered that much. They've seen it often enough. The girl, Miss Grace, died in the same way just a few days ago," Peregrine said.

"Was it the same way? We know that Miss Grace drank poisoned wine which contributed to her fall. We don't know whether your friend was clumsy or just had an accident," Henry said.

Seeing Peregrine's mutinous expression, Henry added, "I appreciate this is harsh but we must look at the facts. What do you actually know about your friend's death?"

"Only when it happened, and the company he was with at the time. He died from a fall."

"Was Mr. Horley a heavy drinker?" Henry asked.

"He liked his drink as much as the next man. That's no reason to think he was drunk," Peregrine said.

"It happens all the time. Men can handle their drink better than women, but young men can often underestimate how drunk they really are," Henry said grimly. Peregrine was of a similar age as him, perhaps a few years younger at most. "Tell you what. I will look into this for you. The fact that those girls were in the presence of two accidental deaths seems strange, and not a mere coincidence."

"You'll help me?" Peregrine asked.

"Yes. But don't go following the women or harassing them at all. They'll be less likely to talk to me if you do." Judging from the guilty look on Peregrine's face, he already had. "Or rather, don't question them anymore. Leave it to me."

"What about the girls in the List? You'll investigate that too?"

"What do you mean?"

"I thought you knew, or overheard us talking. Those girls, they are all mentioned in the new addition of Harris's List."

"Sounds like someone is playing a practical joke."

"It's not funny. Every man in town will be thinking they're girls of loose morals. Their fathers will have to keep them indoors for the next century to save their reputations."

Henry frowned. "I'm sure these girls' families can look after them."

"Don't you think it odd, that they're all mentioned? Even the girls in their society this Season, like Miss Morton, are listed too."

"What?" Henry stared. "Do you have a copy of this List?"

"No, but go down to Fleet Street. They're doing a third print run of it by now. It's a bestseller."

Henry left without a word.

HE HAILED A hackney carriage and took it to Queen Street, where he met members of the watch, as well as Magistrate Tomlinson. The overweight man scratched at his chin and said, "What's a toff like you doing here?"

"Remember me, Magistrate? Sergeant Dyngley."

"Who? Ohhh. You. You dealt with that letter-writing criminal last year. Yeah, I remember. What you want?"

"I presume you've seen Harris's List, and the new addition?"

"Who hasn't?" One of the men snorted and pulled out a copy.

Henry said, "Unless you stop this printer, there will be lawsuits."

"What's it to me? I don't care."

"It's a trusted guide of females," a man of the watch said.

Henry restrained his anger and said, "The new addition is false. Those girls are debutantes of the Season and their reputations will be ruined unless something is done."

"Too bad for them. Why should it bother me?" Magistrate Tomlinson said.

"Who do you think they'll come to, in order to make it stop? Who will they blame for letting the printer print lies about their daughters? It's libel. The least you can do is stop the printers from printing any more."

At the word libel, the magistrate sat up in his chair and cursed. "Bugger. All right boys, let's go."

HENRY JOINED THE group of men on their way to Fleet Street, where they quickly disbanded a fight. The printer, a large, heavy-set man, was brawling with a young man of quality, who knew his way around the boxing ring. The young man swerved and knocked the big man out with a right hook across his jaw.

There were whistles and claps, as the man came up to shake the young lad's hands and clap him on the shoulder. Henry stood by, stony-faced, as the magistrate whistled between his teeth and men scattered.

The young man stood by and spat on the ground, kicking the man when he was down. The unconscious man didn't move.

"Serves you right, you animal."

"Mr. Harris?" Henry said.

The young man turned around. "Oh, it's you. I should've known you'd be here later rather than sooner." He nodded to the magistrate and his men.

"Tom Harris, as I live and breathe, what are you doing here? Aside from kicking the shit out of this man. I haven't seen you around the Shakespeare's Head in weeks," Magistrate Tomlinson said.

Tom rolled his sleeves down and dusted off his suit jacket. He rubbed the side of his face and said, "I gave it up. Thought I'd move out to the country and try my luck there. I'm back for the Season."

Some of the men shared smiles. "Good luck with that."

"Hey, do you know this man?" the magistrate asked.

"No, but I know the girls he was printing about. I was asking him questions when he pulled a knife on me, and we started fighting. I'd just finished when you all showed up." He avoided Henry's eyes.

The constables quickly stopped the printing press and held the gradually awakening owner for questioning. Henry and Tom listened as Magistrate Tomlinson said, "All right, why have you been printing Harris's List?"

"I can print what I want." The printer, an overweight bald man with an apron and ink-spattered hands, said with a sneer.

"The List you're printing is out of date. It even says 1785," one of the constables said.

The man shrugged.

"Who gave you the new addition to print, about this year's debutantes?" Henry asked.

The man looked at him and kept his mouth shut.

Magistrate Tomlinson socked the man in the stomach. The man doubled over and coughed. The magistrate said, "Do you know how much trouble you're in? You've been printing lies, mate. Those girls you printed about, they come from some of the best families in the city. You know what that means?"

The man looked up at the magistrate with piggish eyes.

"It means, you sorry arse, that you're printing a retraction right now to go on your shop window. You're going to stop printing this List that isn't yours to print anyway, and you're going to give back the money you earned to any that want refunds."

"If I don't?" The man put his hands on his knees, coughing.

The magistrate laughed. "Oh, you stupid arsehole. If you don't, then you're going to have a nice stay in jail whilst you await trial at the Old Bailey. Newgate Prison isn't that far away, and I'm sure you'll have lots of families wanting to testify against you."

The man spat on the ground. "How was I to know it was false? The man said it was all true."

"What man was this?"

"The man. I dunno. Tall. Brown hair. Brown clothes. Not from around here."

"So it wasn't a woman?" Tom asked.

"A woman? No. Only woman around here is my wife," the man said, spitting blood.

"Why would you ask that?" Henry asked.

"A hunch." Tom dusted off his clothes and began chatting with the constables.

Henry turned and came face to face with a young woman who looked familiar. "Yes?"

She was well-dressed, suited, and booted for walking around. She was pretty enough with dirty blonde hair pinned beneath a straw bonnet. She stood about average height for a woman, and looked up at him. "I know you. You're Sergeant Dyngley. I'm Sarah Haskett."

He blinked. "You have the advantage of me, Miss Haskett. But this is no place for a young woman. You shouldn't be here."

"That's why I'm here. We are investigating the same thing."

"Pardon?"

She pushed a sweaty tendril of hair out of her face. "We are both looking into the matter of the printing of Harris's List, with the debutante section."

"How do you know about that?"

"I'm one of the girls mentioned in it," she said quietly, looking around for any men that might have heard. "And my father is a printer. I came here to ask questions, but when I got here, the men were already fighting."

"This isn't a place or a matter for young ladies. You should go home," Henry told her.

She beamed at him, as if she rather enjoyed being told not to involve herself. "I knew you'd say that. It's just like what Miss Morton said, you telling her not to investigate. Well, I won't give up so easily. You'll see. I'll find out who did this."

"Please, Miss Haskett, don't. You don't know who is involved in this and it could be dangerous."

"How so? Your constables have already apprehended the man responsible. What danger could there possibly be?" she asked.

He didn't have an answer, but he also disliked the excited look in her eye. "Nevertheless, please go home. This is a matter for the constabulary." *Not wayward printers' daughters*, he thought.

"You'll see." She winked at him. "Perhaps we could talk over dinner later?"

He stared at her. The girl was bold, and it rankled him. "I'm afraid I have plans."

"Shame." She curtsied and left.

"Who was that?" Tom asked, looking after her. "She's a pretty one."

"She's a busybody," Henry said.

"Fair enough. Excuse me. Magistrate, good seeing you." Tom waved and left.

Henry followed Tom outside. "Mr. Harris, a moment please."

Tom turned around. "What is it, Constable?"

"It's sergeant now."

"My mistake. I do wish you'd call me Markham, everyone else does." Tom said.

"Why did you go to the printer? How did you know?"

"It's all anyone's been talking about for the past twenty-four hours. An old, outdated version of the list, printed with a new addition about this year's debutantes? But not even all of them, only a few? This would damage any girl's reputation."

"Have you spoken to Miss Morton?" Henry asked.

"Yes. But I'll wager that you haven't, as you didn't even know. She's the one who thought a woman might've done it."

"What gave her that idea?" Henry asked.

"Ask her yourself. You haven't seen her much, and she's getting a lot of unwanted attention lately," Tom said. "I'm courting her myself to help her along."

Henry laughed. "How could you courting her possibly help? You're not trying to help her, you just want her for yourself."

"So what if I do? At least I'm trying, which is more than I can say for you."

"You're nothing but a boy playing a pimp," Henry said.

"A very successful former pimp, I'll have you know. Aren't you the same, just playing at the constabulary? You're not a judge or a magistrate."

Henry and Tom glared at each other.

"I could ruin your reputation. Tell the world what the third son of the Earl of Markham has been doing with his free time in London."

"Who would believe you?" Tom challenged.

"Everyone. Especially the lords who are loyal customers of yours."

"Not a chance. Not if they want to keep their noses clean. No one will admit to it, once they realize that once they do, there goes their sterling reputations," Tom said. "Dyngley, what do you want from me?"

"Leave Miss Morton alone."

"I'm doing her a favor," Tom said.

"Are you? Sounds to me like you're just causing trouble."

"I like her. I'd do right by her too. Besides, it's better than that Terrell chap chasing after her. He's giving her jewelry and flowers non-stop."

"Flowers? I gave her flowers," Henry said.

"No, you didn't. The only flowers she's got are from him," Tom said.

"What?"

"Aye, and sad about it she is, too. It's time to do a bit more to win her affection, Sergeant, or perhaps in your case, do anything. She doesn't deserve to be shuffled off to the country to waste away as that man's bride."

CHAPTER TWENTY-SIX

THAT EVENING, POPPY dressed for dinner at Lucretia's. Miss Cooke helped her dress in an evening gown of rose-pink satin with cap sleeves, a high waist, and rose embroidery along the round scoop bodice, sleeves, and hem. Finished with a pair of long white evening gloves, some rouge to her cheeks, and a comb with pinned rosebuds for her hair, Poppy looked every inch the well-dressed lady.

As Miss Cooke was patting down flyaway hairs from her face, she said, "I've been meaning to tell you, Miss, but I never got the chance. Your uncle today told Mr. Terrell of your relation to Lord Blackwood."

Poppy stiffened in her chair. "He did?"

"Aye. Seeing as your father visited you earlier when Mr. Terrell was here, once you left, I overheard him ask your uncle if that man was another one of your suitors. Your uncle disabused him of that notion."

"What did he say?"

"That you have an unfortunate connection with that gentleman which is not to be spoken of, er, or something like that," she said, seeing Poppy's expression. "Not to worry, I don't think Mr. Terrell will say anything. He's too keen to stay in your uncle's good graces."

"Of that, I have no doubt." Poppy donned her cloak, bid her

relatives goodbye, and went off to Lucretia's for dinner.

It was not necessarily a merry party, but certainly a small one. Lucretia lived with her mother and father in a respectable part of Town, in a decent-sized townhouse. She welcomed Poppy, wearing a pretty purple dress trimmed in white lace. She led Poppy to the drawing room, where the other girls sat and stood, drinking small glasses of wine.

Poppy bid hello to Sarah, Emily, and Mary, and joined them at the dinner table for a fine meal of roast venison, potatoes, peas drowned in a butter sauce, as well as miniature fish pies.

Once they had finished and were on dessert, Lucretia said, "So what are we going to do about this List? This affects all of us."

"Have you heard from Mr. Fletcher?" Sarah asked.

"No. I'll wager he thinks it will raise eyebrows if he continues to court me with this scandal happening. He'll wait for things to quiet down. But until that happens we can't be together, and I need this scandal to stop, right now." Lucretia's voice was shrill.

Sarah said, "You don't need to worry, Miss Dobbins, I've got it well in hand."

The girls look at her. "Pray, enlighten us," Miss Munden said. "Whatever do you mean?"

"I'm investigating this sorry business, along with Sergeant Dyngley," Sarah said with a smile.

Poppy knocked over her drink.

"Pooh, Miss Morton, you are clumsy," Lucretia said, as a footman instantly came by to sop up the mess. Fortunately, most of the wine was drunk, so there was little to clean.

"I'm sorry, I was just taken by surprise." Poppy sat back and let the footman do his job.

Emily shot her a look of concern, and glanced at Sarah. "Tell us, Miss Haskett. You're investigating this matter?"

"Yes. Since I am a printer's daughter it's only right I look into it, especially as I was one of the people mentioned in the pamphlet," Sarah said.

"And? What have you learned?"

"It was a wayward printer on Fleet Street, who said a man had come and given him the addition. It was an outdated edition of the List anyway, so few people will actually believe it's accurate."

Lucretia frowned. "Outdated?"

"Yes, the edition this man printed was from years ago. The only new thing about it was the addition of our names," Sarah said.

"So it was a man who gave the addition about us, not a woman?" Poppy asked.

"That's what I said."

"I wonder why the printer didn't print a newer edition of the list?" Mary asked.

"He doesn't normally print the list. He's not the printer of it. He prints other things," Sarah told her.

"So why didn't the man go to the normal List's printer?"

"Probably because they would have refused," Poppy said, thinking of Tom. If he'd known, he would have put a stop to it before their names got anywhere near a printing press.

"What makes you say that?" Lucretia asked.

"Well–" Sarah started, but Lucretia said, "I was asking Miss Morton."

Poppy said, "Think about it. The List and the printers of it pride themselves on it being the primary source of information for men on where to find the loose women of London. Their information is likely brought to them by pimps, or the ladies themselves. The reason it's had numerous editions is because the information changes over time."

"So?" Mary asked.

"So, if you've got a business periodical that's valued by customers based on the quality of your information, you won't accept new additions from just anyone. Any new additions would have to be from someone you trust."

"This printer didn't know who the man was, he just took the list and printed it," Sarah said.

"I'm still none the wiser," Mary said, tracing her finger around the rim of her wine glass.

"The real printers of Harris's List would have made sure the information regarding our characters was accurate, not hearsay. Otherwise they could get sued," Poppy said.

"That's right. My father is furious about all this," Lucretia said.

"And mine," Mary added.

"Mine too," Emily said.

"We're all concerned. But you needn't worry, Sergeant Dyngley and I will sort this," Sarah said confidently.

Miss Munden and Poppy exchanged a look. "Miss Haskett, I think you should leave this matter alone. If Sergeant Dyngley is looking into it, as you said, he wouldn't want you to put yourself in danger."

"Oh, you sound just like him. But he took extra care in discussing the investigation with me. So thoughtful. And handsome," Sarah said, "We may have dinner soon to chat about it. Amongst other things."

Emily said quickly, "I would take the sergeant's advice and not trouble yourself in this, Miss Haskett. We wouldn't want anything to happen to you."

"What could possibly happen? The dodgy printer was apprehended and jailed. He'll be sitting in prison waiting for a trial. No one would hurt me," Sarah said.

"Except for the person who was behind this," Poppy said, "Whoever gave our names to the printer did this for a reason. Did the printer give a description of the man?"

Sarah screwed up her face in thought. "No, I can't remember. I don't think he said much."

"Well, that's no help. It could be anyone," Lucretia said. "Who would want to get all of us in trouble?"

"I know who," Emily said.

"Who?" the girls asked.

"The man who has been hounding me since we were present

at the death of Mr. Stuart Horley."

"You mean..." Lucretia started.

"Precisely. Mr. Peregrine Grant."

"No. Him? Why would he?" Lucretia asked.

"To cause trouble. None of us would answer his questions so...This is his way of taking revenge on us," Emily said.

"That's horrible. Are you sure it's him?" Poppy asked.

"Who else could it be? There's no other man who knows all of us." Emily said.

"And he's bookish, and he reads a lot. He could have done it," Lucretia said. "Miss Morton, you'll tell the sergeant, won't you? He'll want to know."

"I'll speak to him," Sarah said, "We're very close."

CHAPTER TWENTY-SEVEN

THE NEXT DAY there was a retraction notice in the paper, from the printers, apologizing for the printing of false information regarding the new addition in Harris's List. Henry read the retraction with grim pleasure and got to his feet.

He'd eaten an early breakfast with his brother and read the paper in their library. Now that he had some business to take care of, he needed to go. He walked out the door and turned left, down the corridor and to his bedroom, to find the door was open. He paused, and slowly entered the doorway. There stood a robed figure, bent over his table that held his cufflinks.

"Miss Parkinson?"

She whirled around. "There you are. I've been looking for you."

"I'm here. What are you doing over there?"

She straightened. "I was looking for you and then something caught my eye so I went to see what it was. I love shiny things."

"I see." He crossed the room and took a suit jacket and hat from his wardrobe.

"And where are you off to in such a hurry?" she asked.

"Constabulary business."

"I see. I just thought..." Her voice sounded wistful. She wore a thin pink nightrobe over her shift and walked up to him with her hair hung long around her shoulders. Her eyes sought his and she said, "I wondered if we might walk together a little. Alone."

"Another time," he said.

"When?"

"I'm not sure."

"Why not?"

"I am investigating a matter, and do not know when I will return."

Her expression darkened. "We are supposed to be courting. How can we do that when we are not together?"

"We were at the dance the other night."

"That was only good for then. Mama and Mrs. Dyngley are already asking me how it's going and what we will be doing next. What am I to tell them?"

He shrugged. "I'm sure you'll think of something. I have to go. If you wouldn't mind, Miss Parkinson." He politely waited for her to exit the room, then closed the door firmly behind her.

A VISIT TO the printer's revealed it was shut down for the time being, as he expected. But he needed no further delays. He stopped by an open-air market and walked until he spotted flowers for sale. He purchased a simple bouquet of violets, pink and purple sweet peas, ivy, and forget-me-nots, and walked on until he reached Poppy's townhouse. At his knock, the door was opened by a servant, who let him in and brought him to the parlor, where Poppy sat with her aunt, uncle, and Mr. Terrell.

The servant announced, "Sergeant Henry Dyngley."

Poppy's face lit up. "Sergeant.

"Miss Morton." He bowed and nodded to her aunt and uncle. "Mr. and Mrs. Greene." As an afterthought, he said politely, "Mr. Terrell."

"Sergeant, how good of you to come," Aunt Rachel rose and curtsied. "Please do come in and sit down. And you've brought flowers, how kind."

"For you, Miss Morton," Henry extended the bouquet to Poppy, who blushed.

"Thank you, Sergeant." She took the flowers and smelled their scent. "They smell wonderful."

"I thought you might like these as a change from the hothouse florals I sent earlier. What do you think? Do you prefer these?"

She gave him a confused look. "What do you mean?"

"The other bouquet of flowers I sent you a few days ago. Did you not like them?" he asked.

Poppy said quietly, "This is the first bouquet of flowers I have received from you, Sergeant."

"Yes, Mr. Terrell gave her a delightful bouquet as well. It looked very expensive," Aunt Rachel said.

Heads looked at Mr. Terrell, who sat there quiet as a toad.

Henry said, "How odd, for I ordered a bouquet of hothouse flowers to be delivered here. Did they not arrive?" He looked at Mr. Terrell. "Where did you purchase yours, sir?"

"Me? I can't remember."

"From a hothouse?"

"To be sure. Only the best for Miss Morton. I wouldn't dream of giving her mere wildflowers," Mr. Terrell said, looking at the simple bouquet in Poppy's hands.

"Indeed. Was it White's Hothouse, on Bury Lane?"

"Yes, I think it was."

Mr. Greene cleared his throat. "You forget, Mr. Terrell, we were there just the other day. There is nothing on Bury Lane but those unfortunate women selling themselves, and the taverns. There are no hothouses there." He frowned at Henry. "Are you trying to confuse my student?"

"Not at all, Mr. Greene, I am merely trying to ascertain where he purchased the flowers from. I wonder how my order was never delivered, yet his was, especially if we both bought bouquets from a hothouse in London."

Mr. Terrell turned red. "I may have mistaken the delivered bouquet for the one I ordered. I'm not saying it is true, but it is possible."

"Pray, what did your bouquet contain?"

"Roses of course. And lilies."

"I see. Mine was very different."

"Oh?"

"Yes, I'm sorry you haven't had a chance to see it, Miss Morton. I ordered you a spray of hollyhocks, honeysuckle, and hydrangeas. The color of their petals change based on the type of soil they are grown in." He sighed. "What I shame you never received them. I shall have to complain to the florist immediately."

Aunt Rachel rose and hurried out the door. In a moment she returned, holding the spray of what most definitely was not roses. "Is this what you ordered, Sergeant?"

"By Jove, it is. You did receive them," he said.

Heads turned to Mr. Terrell.

"You told me these were a gift from you, Mr. Terrell," Poppy said.

"I was mistaken. I was so distracted by your beauty, it's easy to forget things like flower arrangements," he told her, his knee touching hers.

Henry's hand curled into a fist.

Poppy gently moved her knee away.

"I see there has been a misunderstanding." Mr. Greene rose. "Well, I am glad your bouquet arrived, Sergeant. Although to avoid confusion, perhaps you might deliver them in person next time, so as not to get muddled with Mr. Terrell's many gifts." He turned. "Come, Mr. Terrell, we have a sermon to prepare."

The men left, Mr. Terrell not saying a word, but shooting Poppy a backwards glance.

Once the men were gone, Aunt Rachel said, "Well, I never. Imagine that. Your own order being mixed up with his." She took the bouquet from Poppy and said, "I'll just put these in some water. Won't be a minute. Do sit down, Sergeant."

Henry sat. Once Aunt Rachel left them alone, Poppy said, "You knew, didn't you? That he'd taken credit for your bouquet."

"I had an inkling, but didn't know for sure until you confirmed it." He sniffed.

"You didn't have to embarrass him like that."

"He shouldn't have tried to take credit for my flowers."

"My flowers, you mean," she said.

"Yes." He looked at her. "You're annoyed."

"A little," she admitted. "It was wrong of him to do that, but you didn't have to make him a fool in front of my aunt and uncle. A word in his ear might have had the same result."

"And do you think he would have owned up to it? His mistake? Or would he have let you all go on thinking he'd purchased those for you?"

"What does it matter? It's just a bunch of flowers."

"It matters, Miss Morton. It matters to me. I care that another suitor has claimed credit for what I tried to give you. I worry that you'll think I care nothing for you at all, when that's far from the truth."

The look in her eyes suggested her heart had skipped a beat. "You care that much, over a bouquet of flowers?"

"It's more than just a bouquet, Miss Morton. I don't want you to forget about me, even if I can't be by your side."

She looked at him. "Fine words, Sergeant. But I do often see you walking and dancing with other women. Miss Simpkins and Miss Parkinson, for example."

"I have no idea who the first girl is, and as for the second, Miss Parkinson is a guest in my home. It is only politeness and a sense of duty that bids me escort her around. Her father asked me to have a care for her safety, as he cannot be here to look out for her."

"I see." Poppy looked at her knees. "I did hear a rumor that you were courting."

"Miss Morton," Henry started. "I came here to see you. How have you been?"

Poppy told him about finding their names in Harris's List, and about Sarah mentioning she would be investigating with Henry.

Henry started. "Her investigate with me? She's joking. I specifically told her not to get involved."

"That seemed to encourage her, rather than achieve the opposite effect."

"Damn it. I'll have to speak with her again, or her father and put a stop to it. You know as well as I do that for a girl to run around asking questions and sticking her nose where it doesn't belong, she's liable to get hurt."

"What is that supposed to mean?" Poppy asked. "Are you comparing my behavior with hers?"

"No. I'm saying you understand the risks involved in an investigation."

"There was one other thing," Poppy started. "The girls think, although I cannot believe this to be true, that it must be Mr. Grant behind this. Putting our names in the list."

"Mr. Grant? The medical student? Why him?"

"I think you know the history of his connection with the girls, but if not, the girls were all present at the accidental death of his friend, Mr. Horley, but remain close-mouthed about it and refuse to talk. They think he is having his revenge on them by making them the objects of derision."

Henry frowned. "That is a serious accusation. Have they any proof?"

"None. They are just guessing. But they cannot think of anyone else who bears such a grudge."

"I dislike this, Miss Morton, and you in the middle of it. I know better than to ask you to remove yourself from the situation, so I will ask this, promise me you will be careful?" he asked.

She smiled at him. "I will."

"And come to me if you come across any leads. I don't want you going off alone to investigate without me."

"All right."

They smiled at each other, just as Mrs. Greene returned to the room. "There we are." She set the bouquet of wildflowers in the center of the small table between them and sat down beside Poppy. "How goes your investigation, Sergeant?"

"Well enough, Mrs. Greene. But I would rather we speak on pleasanter subjects. Miss Morton, will you be attending a concert at the Fashionable Institution soon? I believe they are holding a concert with a famed soprano there tomorrow."

"You can be sure Poppy will attend," Mrs. Greene said.

"That is excellent news. Then I hope I shall see you there, tomorrow," he said and rose. "I should not keep you any longer. Good day, ladies. Until tomorrow, Miss Morton." He bowed and quit the room.

As he left the parlor, he overheard Mrs. Greene sigh and say, "Oh, you are lucky, Poppy. He's just what a young man ought to be. And those flowers, so charming. They won't make me sneeze at all, I'm sure."

CHAPTER TWENTY-EIGHT

POPPY WAS PLEASED. Henry had paid her a visit, she had received flowers and an assurance of his care and affection, and her aunt was in good spirits too, although that might have been due to the fact that Dyngley's visit had interrupted Mr. Terrell reading to them from his latest sermon.

Poppy sat admiring the wildflowers Henry had brought her when a footman brought a letter forward on a tray. "For you, Miss."

"Thank you, Turner," Poppy said. Despite having a small staff, she was secretly delighted she knew his name. She opened the letter, recognizing the thick wax seal that bore the ornate letter B.

My dear girl,

I hope this letter finds you well. I returned home to discover that the story of my wife's illness has been much exaggerated, and she is the epitome of health. Between Ann's surprise at my returning home out of concern for her health, and Susan's smiles, I am at a loss for what to say. Susan has played a trick on us both, fabricating a story about my wife being practically on her deathbed, in order to bring me away from London, and from you. That was her main desire. Susan and I have quarreled, and I thought the matter was over and done with.

But this morning she has disappeared, and I know not

where. Her brother, James, has no idea, but has agreed to keep this quiet so as not to alarm their mother. We suppose she has gone to London, so I hope this letter reaches you in time. Please do take care of yourself, and be on your guard. For if there was ever a troublemaker with good intentions, it is my daughter, your half-sister, Susan.

Your loving father,
HB

"What is it, Poppy?" her aunt asked.

"It's from my father." She passed the letter to her aunt.

"Who is this Susan? You have a sister?"

"A half-sister. We met briefly a few days ago, but she did not take it well, the fact that we are related." She gave a little sigh.

"I see. This letter makes it sound like she's out to cause trouble."

"I wouldn't put it past her. I did wonder if she had put that addition to the printers about Harris's List, but we had just met, and she didn't know any of us girls."

"Could she not have asked around?"

"I imagine she would have just put my name in. But it makes no difference, for I have heard it was a man who gave the list to the printer, not a woman."

"Could he not have been sent by a woman?" her aunt asked.

"It's possible." Poppy hadn't considered that.

"Well, there's one good thing from all this," her aunt said.

"What's that?"

"I read the retraction in the paper about that list. Now that you girls are acquitted, so to speak, you're all sure to have suitors coming by again. Although I do think Sergeant Dyngley could have come by earlier, to reassure you. But those flowers are very nice," Aunt Rachel sniffed. "Such a shame of Mr. Terrell to get confused about the bouquet of flowers he'd ordered. He'll have to look into that and see what happened with his bouquet."

Poppy agreed, although she seriously doubted Mr. Terrell

had placed such an order at all.

THE FOLLOWING EVENING Poppy dressed for the concert at the Fashionable Institution, thanks to the help of Miss Cooke, who picked out a pretty blue dress of a shimmering satin material, which was shot with glossy white darts of silk. Her high waist was tied with a white ribbon, and with a pearl necklace of her mother's and a pearl comb in her hair, Poppy felt very grand indeed. She wore a pair of elbow length, off-white gloves, and a set of light blue shoes that were so delicate they were clearly meant for nothing else but gracing the rooms of an assembly or concert hall.

Poppy was joined by her aunt, uncle, and Mr. Terrell, and armed with their tickets, they took Poppy's closed carriage to the Fashionable Institution. There were far fewer people than there had been for the masked ball, but Poppy didn't mind. Perhaps a musical concert was not to everyone's taste.

As they climbed from the carriage and Mr. Terrell helped her down, Poppy regarded him thoughtfully. Maybe she had thought about him all wrong. He wasn't such a bad person. And there must be something to him, or else he would not have sought a profession in the clergy.

He offered her his arm and she took it, earning a warm smile from him, that showed too many yellowed teeth. Poppy winced and kept her own mouth closed in a tight smile, and allowed him to escort her inside, after her aunt and uncle.

They stood by in the foyer as other guests began to arrive. Poppy spotted and nodded hello to Sarah, Emily, Lucretia, and Mary.

Emily, looking very pretty in a light green dress, came up to Poppy and said, "Excuse me, Mr. Terrell, but I need to borrow Miss Morton for a moment."

He looked unhappy about this, but could do nothing as Poppy let go of his arm and she followed Emily away to speak by a podium. Other guests filed past as Emily said, "Have you learned anything?"

"No. But I cannot think Mr. Grant was behind this. He doesn't seem like the sort of person to do that kind of vengeful act," Poppy said.

"Then who would?"

"I don't know. Who knows all of us?"

"Well there's him, Mr. Fletcher of course, or..." Emily paused. "It could be one of us."

"Miss Dobbins already accused Miss Haskett, and she's the only one who could have the connections to do that. I'm sure she's innocent. She wouldn't have wanted to expose her background to the group either. It would be too much of a risk."

"I agree, but...There's something strange going on."

Poppy stiffened. In walked Sergeant Dyngley, and on his arm, Miss Parkinson, followed by an older woman of close resemblance, as well as Petunia Dyngley and her husband, John. Petunia looked very large, and not quite fit to be going out, but from what Poppy knew of Petunia's character and force of will, she wouldn't let that stop her.

Miss Parkinson looked very pleased with herself to be on Henry's arm, and she wore a light lavender dress that fitted her figure very well. Her hair was curled and arranged prettily, with some locks hanging loose, and she looked a veritable picture of demure propriety as she led the way past other guests.

"I heard they were courting," Emily said.

"Maybe," Poppy said, watching.

"Does it bother you?"

"A little. But what can I do? He'll court who he wants." But she frowned as she spoke, for she felt she should not be so open and honest with her feelings, despite it being Emily she talked to. It hurt her enormously that Henry was escorting someone else.

But as the gong rang, Poppy and Emily parted ways and hurried to find their own parties. By the time Poppy found her family and were able to find seats, there remained only a handful of open seats in the very back row of the hall. Poppy didn't mind overly, but did rather wish she'd have been able to sit closer, to hear the music and see the performers better. She sat beside Mr. Terrell to her right, and to her left, facing the aisle, Sarah took the last seat next to her. "I hope you don't mind if I join you," she said.

"Not at all, you are very welcome." Poppy said.

Sarah smiled at her and the music began.

MR. TERRELL CHATTED during some of the concert, but Poppy lost herself in the music and enjoyed it, despite his chatter. The interval came too soon and Poppy rose with the other guests, in search of refreshment. With Mr. Terrell at her elbow, Poppy made a circuit, and enjoyed a pleasant conversation with Mary and Lucretia.

They were soon joined by Emily and Sarah, who said, "I've been talking with Mr. Grant. He's very nice and knowledgeable, but he said he's never gone anywhere near Fleet Street, and was quite shocked when I suggested that he might have put our names in the List. He said that if he'd wanted to have revenge on someone, he'd tell them to their face." Sarah shrugged.

"A likely story. That's just what a villain would say," Lucretia said.

"You read too many novels," Mary said. "I don't like this. Someone has been trying to ruin us, and it's been a miserable time."

"What, has the list frightened away some of your suitors?" Lucretia asked.

"Maybe," Mary said.

"Who?"

"None of your concern."

"You shouldn't keep secrets from your friends," Lucretia said.

Mary stuck her tongue out at her. "If I had better friends, maybe I wouldn't."

"I didn't know you had a suitor," Emily said.

Mary shrugged.

"Who cares about suitors? I know who did it," Sarah said proudly.

"You do? Who?"

"I know who killed Miss Grace, and why. And it concerns all of you."

"Tell us. Is someone after me?" Lucretia said.

"I'll tell you after the concert." Sarah tapped her nose and left.

"Do you really think she knows something?" Emily asked.

"I doubt it. Whether she does or not, she's loving being the center of attention, don't you agree?" Lucretia said. "Come, I need a drink."

Poppy looked around. Henry was nearby, talking with his brother and Petunia. Miss Parkinson wasn't far away, but as Poppy watched, she bumped into another woman and apologized, her hands moving swiftly.

Poppy watched with interest for it appeared as though something was amiss. The well-dressed woman nodded and turned away, but a moment later Miss Parkinson joined her party, and on her wrist was a gold bracelet Poppy had not noticed before. Had she stolen it?

Poppy walked over, just as Miss Parkinson was about to rejoin the others. "Excuse me, Miss Parkinson." she took a shaky breath. What did she say?

"Yes? Oh, it's Miss Morton, isn't it?"

"Yes. Um, what a nice bracelet." Poppy looked at her wrist.

Miss Parkinson held it up. "This? My Papa gave it to me as a present before we left for the Season. Isn't it nice?"

"I think it bears a rather close resemblance to the one the lady had over there." Poppy motioned with her head. "The lady you just bumped into."

Miss Parkinson cocked her head. "And just what are you saying, Miss Morton?"

"I saw you. You took that woman's bracelet."

"Did I? I don't know what you thought you saw, but I assure you, I have owned this bracelet for weeks now."

"You're lying."

"What's going on here?" Henry joined them. "Miss Morton, it's good to see you."

"Henry, Miss Morton here is accusing me of stealing." Miss Parkinson pouted.

"What?"

Poppy blushed. "I saw her bump into another woman and...that bracelet she's wearing. I'm fairly certain she took it."

"Yes, I did. From my jewelry box this evening, before I left." Miss Parkinson snapped. "Really, Miss Morton. I knew you disliked me as a bit of competition, but I never thought you'd go so far as to accuse me of a crime." She shook her head at Poppy.

"Miss Morton, is this true?" Henry asked.

"I saw her bump into that woman and then right after, she had that bracelet on her arm."

"Which woman did you see?"

Poppy turned. Now that people were milling about, she couldn't see the woman any longer. "I can't see her..."

"There, see, Henry? She wants your attention so badly that she's accusing everyone of a crime. Just earlier I heard that her little group of friends thought Mr. Grant had put their names in that men's periodical." Miss Parkinson snickered. "As if none of you earned that reputation yourselves."

Poppy stared at her. "Take that back."

"No. I don't know what sort of company you keep, but I have no doubt that if you're the sort of girl who goes around accusing people of theft, you'd better have some proof. And since you don't, I can only assume you're an attention-seeking busybody."

Poppy stared. Her fists curled and she desperately wanted to do something, but did not know what. She had not been raised to think violence was the right way to resolve disputes, but instead calm and measured discourse, as mediated by an adult. Except that now they were adults and she had no one to stand by her, least of all Henry Dyngley.

"Come, Henry. Let's leave her to her family. Maybe they can

talk sense into her." Miss Parkinson turned her back on Poppy and waited. "Well? Are you coming?"

Henry looked at Poppy, who said, "I'm not lying, Sergeant. I saw her do it."

"Unless you can find the woman, or she raises a complaint, I can't do anything," he said.

Her face was hot with embarrassment.

He opened his mouth to speak when they were interrupted.

"Ah, there you are, I've been looking for you. Not causing any trouble, are we?" Mr. Terrell joked. He looked from Dyngley to Poppy and said, "The gong just rang. We should return to our seats, Miss Morton."

Poppy shared a glance with Dyngley but felt powerless. At the same moment, he turned away, just as Mr. Terrell took her arm and steered her from him, back toward the seats, just behind Emily, Lucretia, and Miss Gibbs.

Poppy was just about to sit down when something splashed onto her face and side. "What?"

She turned. There stood Susan, with an empty wine glass in hand, grinning from ear to ear. "Dear me. How clumsy I am. I seem to have spilled my drink."

"You did that on purpose," Poppy snapped, stock still. She stood rigid with anger.

"Oh no, that is unfortunate. That was very clumsy of you, miss," Mr. Terrell said. "Your dress is quite ruined, Miss Morton."

"I know." She met Susan's gaze. She didn't know what to say. She wanted to punch the girl in the face, or pull her hair out, or scream. But she had been too well bred to do any of those things, and didn't know what to do. She couldn't even defend herself.

"Oh my goodness," Aunt Rachel and her uncle came up to her. "Whatever happened?"

"This girl has spilt her wine on me," Poppy said.

"What an unfortunate occurrence. It is rather all over you." Aunt Rachel said. "I suppose we shall have to go home. And I did so want to see the rest of the concert."

Poppy stood, seething. She could see Miss Parkinson laugh out loud at the sight of her, and her face grew red. Could the evening get any worse?

Susan said, "I'm dreadfully sorry. So dashed clumsy of me." The words were right, but her tone was syrupy sweet, and so off-color that her tone made Aunt Rachel look up.

Her eyes narrowed and she said, "What is your name, girl?"

"Susan Blackwood. My father is Sir Hugh Blackwood, of Somerset."

"What a shame that he did not raise his children to be more careful with their drinks," Aunt Rachel said. "If I had a child like that, I would teach her to be more considerate of others, and to have a more civil tongue."

Susan smiled sweetly, causally dropped her glass to the floor, sending shards flying, and walked away.

Poppy stepped toward her.

"Poppy, no." Her aunt said, holding her arm. "Young ladies do not resort to violence."

Susan turned back around, a smirk on her face. "Too bad, Miss Morton. I did rather think it suits you. But then I suppose you'd be used to drunken looks from your mama."

Aunt Rachel went up to the girl, pulled her hair and slapped her across the face with a loud smack. Susan screeched.

"You may have had the misfortune to spill your drink, but no one insults my niece or my sister. Get out, and pray to God he may have mercy on you." Aunt Rachel gave the girl a swift shove, and Susan stumbled back, crying and screeching curses. She fell into the arms of a young, smartly dressed man, who took her firmly by the arm and led her away. He looked hard at Aunt Rachel and Poppy, and left.

Poppy let out a little sigh and brushed away the single tear that fell down her cheek. The entire room was silent. Everyone was staring at them.

"Miss Haskett?"

Poppy looked. Sarah fell out of her chair, covered in wine.

"Oh, the girl's fainted. Some of the wine must've splashed on her." Aunt Rachel said.

Now dripping wet, Poppy glanced at Sarah, as did Mr. Terrell, Emily, Mary, and one to two others in the vicinity.

"Step back, step back. Make way." Peregrine's voice cut through.

Poppy stepped away and let him attend to her. Emily held Sarah in her arms. "Miss Morton, I think she's hurt."

He and Emily laid Sarah to the floor. He touched her cheeks. "Miss Haskett? Miss? Miss Haskett?"

He touched a fingertip to her wrist, and then two fingers to beneath her chin, against her neck. Her eyes were closed and her face was pale. As he turned her over, a dark stain was spreading across her front, blood pooling down from her neck.

"This girl is dead," Peregrine said, "She's been stabbed."

Chapter Twenty-Nine

THE CONCERT ENDED abruptly. Men shouted, women fainted, people left in a hurry. Someone called the watch, and the magistrate. Poppy stood by as the men of the watch covered Sarah's body with a sheet, and carried her out. Soon the only people who were left present were Poppy and her family, as well as Henry, Peregrine, Emily, Lucretia, and Mary, besides the concert performers and the organizers.

Magistrate Tomlinson and his men questioned everyone, but no one seemed to have any answers. No one knew how Miss Haskett had been killed.

"You mean to tell me that a girl was killed right in front of you all and no one saw it? How did that even happen?" the magistrate asked.

"There was an accident. We were all distracted by it," Emily said.

"What accident? Oh." His gaze landed on Poppy. "You're covered in blood."

"It's wine. A girl spilled her drink on me," Poppy told him.

"That's unlucky."

"Yes," Poppy said.

"Dyngley, take me home. Let's leave this in the hands of the authorities," Miss Parkinson said.

Henry looked ready to protest, but Miss Parkinson put a hand on his arm and said in a breathy voice, "Please, Henry. I feel ill."

Dyngley said, "Very well." He told the magistrate, "I'm staying in town on Park Street if you need me."

Once the Dyngley party had left, an older woman came up to the group.

"Excuse me," she said to the magistrate.

"Now if only we had a murder weapon," he said, stroking his beard.

"It's there on the floor, sir," one of the constables said. "Look. There's a piece of glass shard there, covered with blood."

"Where?" the magistrate asked.

"There." The man picked it up. "See?"

"Excuse me," the older woman said.

"Ugh, that's disgusting. Could it have been an accident? There's wine on the floor. Could the girl have slipped and fallen?" the magistrate asked.

"It's possible, but unlikely," Peregrine said.

"And just who are you?"

"Peregrine Grant. I'm a student at the medical college at St Bartholomew's Hospital."

"Uh huh. Lucky to have a doctor here, eh? Coincidence?"

"Um, doctors like music too, sir," Peregrine said.

"So they do, son, so they do. But I'll be watching you." The magistrate crossed his arms.

"Excuse me," the older woman raised her voice.

"What?" the magistrate turned around. "What is it?"

"I wish to report a crime."

"We know, a girl died here."

"No, a different crime. My bracelet has been stolen," the woman said.

"Your what?"

"My bracelet. It's gold and has engraved letters LM on its band. They're my initials, you see, Lillibet Montrose," the woman said, "I wore it tonight and now it's missing."

"Mrs. Montrose?" the magistrate said.

"Yes."

"Go talk with one of my constables. They'll help you." The

man turned his back on her.

Poppy heard Peregrine say, "The wounds on her body are consistent with a stabbing. It looks to me like someone took a piece of glass and cut her throat, or she did it herself."

"Would the girl have done that?" the magistrate asked.

"No. Suicide attempts are often a cry for help, but I've never seen something like this. I think the girl was killed."

Poppy asked, "When the girl dropped her wine glass, I saw shards of glass fly out when it hit the floor. Could one of the shards have flown and cut Sarah?"

Peregrine thought on this. "You mean a random accident? It's possible, but I doubt it." He asked, "When you first noticed her, where was she?"

"In her chair, sitting."

"Which way was she facing?" he asked.

"A little to the side, I think. Why?"

"It doesn't make sense," Peregrine said. "When I examined her, I saw the cut is to the center of her throat, and down. But if a glass shard had gone flying, it would have struck her on the left side of her neck, or on her face, or hair. The cut is in the wrong place for it to have been an accident."

"Then it's murder," the magistrate said grimly.

THE MAGISTRATE AND his men took the names and addresses of everyone present, but with nothing left but a body, blood, wine, and glass on the floor, there seemed to be little more to accomplish. The organizers were told and servants were brought in to clean. Everyone was told to go home, and an arrest would be made soon. Mr. Terrell escorted Poppy, her aunt, and Mr. Greene back to the townhouse.

In the carriage ride back, Poppy said, "Thank you, Aunt. For defending me."

"It was nothing that girl didn't deserve. The cheek of her. And you in your beautiful dress. It's ruined."

Mr. Terrell was sour-faced. "Who was that girl?"

Before anyone could speak, Poppy said, "My half-sister."

There was silence.

"You attract a lot of unwanted attention, Miss Morton," he said.

Poppy shrugged. Her dress was ruined and had begun to smell. The scent of wine and blood assailed her nostrils and all she wanted to do was strip it off and get clean. She gave her aunt a smile. "It was something to see, wasn't it?"

"That girl should learn she cannot bully others. Having a good name and a pretty face will only get her so far. With an attitude like that, she'll have no lack of critics."

"Is that all you can think about?" Mr. Terrell asked, looking at the two of them. "About a girl spilling wine on your pretty dress? A girl died, ladies. You must think less of your material possessions and more about others. Where is your Christian charity?"

Mr. Greene cleared his throat. "Mr. Terrell, we have all had an eventful evening. I think the ladies are in shock."

Poppy frowned at her uncle. She did not need him to explain her actions. She was not in shock.

"When I think of my future wife, she will have no use for such material things, and will instead be attuned to my wants and needs, and that of our church," Mr. Terrell said.

Poppy couldn't help it; she rolled her eyes. Her aunt snickered, but wisely held her tongue.

Upon arriving at the townhouse, Poppy ordered the servants to prepare her a bath, despite the late hour, and in the safety of her bedroom, stripped off the beautiful dress, stays, and chemise, all of which were stained. She handed them into the careful arms of Miss Cooke, who stood with her back to the door and listened as Poppy sat in the bathtub, scrubbed herself with sweet-smelling soap, and relayed her account of the evening's events. Poppy was sad about Sarah's death, but was too tired and exhausted to think much, and fell asleep, finally clean, dreaming of her sister's sneering face and bloody glass shards that aimed for her throat.

THE NEXT MORNING over breakfast, Poppy munched on a slice of toast and jam, and thought as Mr. Terrell and her uncle debated their latest sermon, and her aunt drank tea.

There was much to think on. Sarah had been killed right next to her, and no one noticed it, least of all herself. She had been too shocked and embarrassed by Susan's wretched display. But why had Sarah died at all? It was definitely murder, not an accident, but had the killer planned it? Were they working with her sister to take advantage of a distraction?

No, Poppy couldn't believe that. But why did Sarah have to die? Poppy frowned over her toast and drank some hot tea, feeling the warmth in her bones. Sarah had learned all she could about the printing of Harris's List, and whilst she did love a bit of gossip, was that any reason to for to be killed? Unless she'd stumbled across something else in her inquiries, some vital piece of information that a person would do anything to keep secret. Like the private relationship of Miss Gibbs and Mr. Fletcher, or who was really behind the death of Mr. Stuart Horley. Maybe it wasn't an accident at all.

THAT DAY POPPY paid a call on Lucretia, who was morose. She sat on a plump sofa eating candied sweets. Her red hair was arranged prettily, but her skin was pale, her eyes dark with worry. "Miss Morton, hello."

"What's wrong, Miss Dobbins? Are you thinking about Miss Haskett?"

"No. I mean, I should be, I suppose, but no. I was thinking of the great injustice that has befallen me."

"What do you mean?" Poppy asked.

"After the addition of Harris's List was printed, I wrote to Mr. Fletcher, telling him it was all false. He returned all my letters and notes, even the lock of hair I bestowed upon him, and said that he could not in good conscience court a girl of dubious reputation." She slumped against the sofa cushions. "I didn't want to tell Sarah, of course. I have some delicacy. She had enough problems."

"Miss Haskett?"

"Yes, didn't you know? She threw herself at Mr. Grant and got rejected. In a bookshop, of all places. Can you imagine? With some crotchety old bookseller looking on? Ugh, it gives me chills just thinking about it."

"When was this?"

"The day before yesterday. She may have seemed all keen on your sergeant, Miss Morton, but she's got a roving eye." Lucretia pouted. "I'm not giving up. Mr. Fletcher and I are perfect for each other, he just needs to see that. But I haven't heard from him since then. By the way, have you heard from Miss Gibbs at all? I haven't seen or talked to her since last night."

"No, I haven't."

"I'll pay her a call. But it's the strangest thing. Every morning we would normally take a tour of the parks together. When I went to meet her, she never showed up. You don't think something has happened to her, do you?" Lucretia asked.

"I don't know."

Lucretia gave Poppy Miss Gibbs's address and Poppy left. But when she called at the respectable townhouse, she was to find it in an uproar. She was admitted and shown in to see Mrs. Gibbs, Mary's mother, a thin, narrow-faced woman of middle age who with her pointed chin and black hair, was no doubt be the spitting image of Mary in a few decades. The woman was tearful and invited Poppy to sit down in a small but comfortable sitting room. She twisted some of the cloth of her dress in her hands and forgot to offer Poppy tea. "I'm so sorry my daughter isn't here to receive you. She's normally so chatty and loves seeing her friends. Are you a new friend of hers?"

"Yes," Poppy said and introduced herself. "We socialized with the same set of girls this Season. We went to many of the same parties together."

"Oh, how nice." Mrs. Gibbs sniffed and dabbed a handkerchief to her eyes. "I'm afraid I don't know what has happened to her. It's the strangest thing. Last night she came home from the concert with some wild tale about a girl dying, and then this morning she never came down to breakfast. When her maid went up to check on her, she was gone."

"I'm so sorry."

"No, I am. I should have kept a closer eye on her. You don't know where she might have gone, do you? I mean, she might have gone to see those friends of hers."

"Miss Dobbins did say she went to their usual meet-up spot but she wasn't there."

"That's not right. She always went on her morning walk with Miss Dobbins. A creature of habit, my girl." Mrs. Gibbs's face fell and she bit her lip. "So orderly. Even her bedroom, she always kept it clean. Never any need for the servants to touch it, really."

"Mrs. Gibbs, did your daughter have any beaus?"

Mrs. Gibbs blinked.

"Any gentleman suitors she was seeing, or any followers?"

The lady frowned. "No. No one. We had rather hoped that she might find someone this Season, but ever since that accident involving that young man, I don't think any other gentleman has been interested."

"What accident?"

"Did you not hear of it? It happened a few months ago."

"Do you mean the death of Mr. Stuart Horley?"

"Yes, that's it. Dreadful shame, that. A young man in the prime of his life, falling from a balcony when he had too much to drink." She shook her head.

"I wonder, Mrs. Gibbs, would you mind if I had a look in your daughter's room?"

"Whatever for?"

"There might be some notes or a clue lying around that might reveal where she has gone."

"What are you, a girl of the watch?"

"No, but I am observant. Would you mind?"

Mrs. Gibbs looked at her. "Normally, I would say no. This is highly irregular. But in this case...all right. Come with me." She rose and led Poppy upstairs and then to an immediate left, where they stood outside a bedroom. "I'll leave you to it. Do let me know if you find anything. I don't know where she could have gone, and if something's happened to her, I don't know what I'll do." She sniffed and walked away.

Poppy entered the room. It was a typical girl's room, in that it bore a vanity table with a large mirror, a simple single bed with many pillows, and a comfortable-looking duvet. The wardrobe held many dresses, but the state of the room was a bit haphazard. Clothes were strewn across the floor and the doors of the wardrobe were wide open. Shoes lay on their side and as Poppy approached the vanity table, she could see a jewelry box that had been raided. But something stuck out of it. She looked inside the wooden box and could see an inner compartment that could be removed. She took it out and saw a series of letters, folded up tight. *Ah-ha,* she thought. She unfolded the letters and opened up the first one.

I saw you two last night beneath the shrubbery. Pay me £20 or I'll tell everyone. – SH

Poppy gasped. Blackmail. The second note read:

My favorite little naughty girl. What would your mother say if she knew you were giving away your virtue? Pay me £20 or I'll tell her and your father.

And another: *Do you not believe me? Pay me £20 or I'll tell everyone about you two. Good luck finding a husband when the world finds out you've been giving it away.*

Poppy breathed in. Mr. Stuart Horley was not such a nice person after all. Alongside the notes was a little list, where Mary had lined the paper and written a table of the date, and amounts paid. She'd been paying Mr. Horley for weeks. "Oh, Miss Gibbs," she said.

She folded the notes and hesitated. Should she take them with her or not? Perhaps just for safekeeping. She pocketed the lot.

Chapter Thirty

Poppy sent out a note to Tom, who invited her to meet him for a stroll of St James's Park that afternoon.

When they met, his face fell. "Miss Morton? What's wrong?"

Poppy told him about the missing Miss Gibbs. "I spoke with her mother. She's normally a very tidy and clean person, but her room was in disarray and her clothes were strewn about it in a mess. I wonder if…"

"She's run away?"

"Exactly. Have you heard anything?" Poppy asked.

"No. But it's odd you mention it, for no one has seen Mr. Fletcher either for a few days now. You don't think they…"

Poppy bit her lip. "Could they have run away together?"

"I'll find out. I'll make some inquiries. I'll write to you at home."

They parted ways.

Poppy was about to leave the park when she spotted Lucretia and Emily and walked over to them. Lucretia was saying, "I can hardly believe it, but it must be true if it's in the paper."

"Hello," Poppy said in greeting.

Lucretia's mouth dropped open, and she stuck her nose in the air. "I cannot believe you would show yourself in public."

"What?"

"What?" Lucretia mimicked. "You're completely shameless.

It's worse than coming from trade, it's… just wrong. You deceived us. You deceived all of us. You deceived me."

"What are you talking about?" Poppy asked.

"You haven't seen. Miss Dobbins, she doesn't know." Emily's face was a picture of worry. She took Poppy by the hand and led her a little way away. "Is it true?"

"What?"

"That you're the daughter of… a mistress?"

Poppy stared at her. "Where did you hear that?"

"I read it. Everyone has. It was in the paper." Emily looked at Poppy. "I'm not surprised you hid it, but you had to know it was going to come out at some point. News like this always does."

Poppy went home, pulling her bonnet tightly over her head to shield her face. Inside, the house was in an uproar.

Her uncle stood by the foyer, his face red. "I knew this would happen. Pack your bags, Poppy, we're leaving."

"What?"

"We are returning to Hertford."

"Now?"

"This very instant. I stood by and let you play your game, to give you a chance at finding a good husband, but this…" He shook a newspaper at her. "This has done it. How did the editor find out? Did you tell them?"

"What?" she took the paper from him and started reading.

A scandalous debutante this season

The editor of this paper has been made aware of an alarming piece of information regarding the birth and background of one of this Season's debutantes. As some may know, Miss Poppy Morton, the new arrival from Hertfordshire, who has graced many of our humble assemblies at the Fashionable Institution this season, is none other than the daughter of The Grace, Celeste Grey, a woman of private means, and her lover, the owner of Blackwood Manor in Somerset. It is understood by this editor that their relationship, which has lasted happily these past 20 years until her untimely death last year, resulted in Miss Morton's birth. No doubt the girl was advised to keep the humble nature of her origin a secret, but this editor wishes to know, would any suitor wish to take on a girl of such dubious origin, or would he hope to connect himself with a man whose extramarital affairs became the source of news and entertaining reading for the local population?

Poppy lowered the newspaper. "So that's it, then."

"That's it? Yes, that's it. You're done. Your Season is over. Pack your things, Poppy. We leave immediately," her uncle said.

"No. I need to think."

"What is there to think about? You're ruined. Your Season is over. No one will want you now. You're the daughter of a whore and everyone knows it."

"Is that how you see me, Uncle?"

"I see your situation as an unfortunate mistake," he said grimly. "And one I should have rectified from the start. We should never have come here."

Tears came to her eyes and she went to her room and shut the door. She looked for the letter from her father. Even just to read his handwriting would make her feel better. But oddly enough, she couldn't find it. She must have misplaced it somewhere.

Poppy went to the parlor to sit by her aunt, who took her hand and squeezed. They ordered tea but were too ill-composed to drink it. And then the notes arrived.

Poppy received a short, precise one from Mrs. Devenshaw, saying that unfortunately, due to recent events, she and her family were no longer welcome at the Fashionable Institution.

Another came from Lucretia, who wrote to say that she was embarrassed for her, and could not consider herself friends with a girl who kept her birth and extremely undesirable origin a secret, so as to willingly connect herself to her betters. Poppy tossed this one to the floor.

Her uncle came in, "I've told the servants we are closing up the house."

"What?" Poppy said.

"Reginald, please. There's no rush," Aunt Rachel said.

"There is every need. You have no idea how this news affects the rest of us."

Poppy looked up. "Uncle?"

"I know you may feel embarrassed now, but it is not just your name that is blackened by this news, Poppy. All of us under this roof are brought down with you."

Poppy felt as if she'd been punched in the gut.

"I will forever be known as the man who raised a whore's child, and allowed her to carry on in her mother's footsteps. Or worse, put her up for a London Season. This will be the gossip from here to Hertfordshire, you had better believe it."

"Uncle…" Poppy started.

"I will call for the carriage. I've told your Miss Cooke you no longer need her services, and to take herself off once she's done packing your bag."

"Uncle," Poppy said, rising to her feet.

"Once you both are packed, we are leaving. I don't feel I need to stress how important it is that you do not speak of this to anyone. Mr. Terrell, of course, has already been made aware of the precarious situation you have placed us in."

"*Uncle,*" Poppy snapped. "Enough."

Her uncle stopped, an enquiring look on his facc.

"This has been one of the more horrid days of my life," she said.

"As well I can imagine. I—"

"That is in part due to your behavior."

He stopped as if struck.

"Do you think I like being reminded of my mother's profession? Or to hear her name, mine, and my father's dragged through the mud? To hear your complaints again and again of being connected to her, and me?"

"Poppy, I have said and done as any parent would have

done—" he started.

"No." She held up a finger. "For weeks now, you have humored me with a London Season. I appreciate that. But as you can see, that is now at an end. I will accept that failure as my own. However," she added, seeing his resolute face, "I will not accept you ordering the servants around, or making decisions regarding my household in my name, without consulting me."

Aunt Rachel's eyes widened.

"You seem to forget that this house, the furnishings, the bed you have slept on, and the food you have eaten have all come from my mother's annuity for me, from the mistress you so claim to despise."

Her uncle began to turn pink.

"This is my household. The servants employed here are not yours to order around, or to relieve from their services. If I decide that needs to be done, that duty will fall to me, and to me alone."

"You are nothing but a child with a pocketbook. You have no concept of money. Without me to guide you, they would cheat you out of your house and home," Uncle Reginald said.

"My father has already introduced me to my solicitor, who is guiding me in my finances. If I run into trouble, I will go to him for advice," Poppy said.

Aunt Rachel snorted. Uncle Reginald turned very red. "You are a child."

"I am twenty. I may be young and naive in the ways of the world, but this is my household, and I am not leaving."

He breathed in through his nose and out again, noisily. "Do you realize that you are blacklisted now, from all good society? No hostess will let you darken her door, no host will accept you. You cannot attend concerts, or assemblies. No one will invite you. Your friends have forsaken you. What other recourse is there but to go home?"

"This *is* my home," Poppy said.

"This is an empty house your mother left you. If she'd had any sense, she would have returned it to your father, where it belongs."

"Reginald…" Aunt Rachel started.

"Uncle, you may leave as soon as you wish. I am staying," Poppy said.

"Why? There is nothing for you here."

"A fellow debutante has gone missing. One of the girls has suffered accidents and another two have died. I want to resolve this."

"Hah, I should have known. No doubt you're wanting to impress that constable fellow by throwing yourself into other people's private affairs and calling it investigations. Why you bother, I don't know. But who am I to tell you what to do? You've made it perfectly clear I have no place in your life. Fine, Poppy, I will go. God help you." He turned and made for the door, coming face to face with—

"Sergeant Dyngley," Poppy said.

"Oof, what are you doing here?" Uncle Reginald asked, backing up.

"Forgive me for intruding, but I wondered if I might have a private word with Miss Morton. Alone."

"Of course, Constable, or Sergeant. Whatever your title is. She could use a voice of sense right about now," Uncle Reginald snapped and left.

Aunt Rachel rose and said, "I'll be right outside if you need me, Poppy."

Poppy let out a shaky breath, and bid Sergeant Dyngley sit. He sat and said, "You can have no doubts as to why I have come."

"I can only assume you have read the newspaper today," Poppy said.

"Yes. The news there is… It gave rise to an unfortunate discussion amongst my family, the result of which I am honor-bound to obey."

"And what is that?"

"I must stop seeing you," he said.

CHAPTER THIRTY-ONE

HENRY HATED SEEING her face at that moment. It felt as if he'd taken a knife and gored himself on its point. From his simple words, her face fell and with it, his hopes and dreams.

"What?" Poppy asked.

"I'm sorry I...Sorry doesn't even begin to say how I sorry I am. I came here wanting to comfort you, but...With every step, I realized, to continue our relationship as it stands would be to court further scandal. It would be a lie."

"A lie?" she repeated.

"Only one of us would be happy. I have a reputation to uphold. Do you think I can happily go around Town with a woman whose unfortunate circumstances have been made public?" He spoke quietly, and it hurt more than if he'd yelled at her.

"That is not my fault. I don't know who told the paper."

"It doesn't matter who did it. The fact is that everyone knows you are the illegitimate child of a mistress and her lover." His tone was cold.

"I didn't think you cared about that."

"If it was just us, I wouldn't. I don't. But my family does care, and we have the Dyngley name to uphold. Petunia almost had a fit when she read the paper."

"So you're leaving me because your family does not approve? I cannot help the circumstances of my birth," Poppy said.

"No, and it is unfair to hold that against you. But I never said life was fair." He paused. "I will be honest. For a long time I have needed to look after my family, and being a county constable doesn't pay well."

"You're a sergeant."

"That pays little more, and it's not enough to support me, my family, and a wife. My family depends on my income to survive."

"But your father…Your brother…" Poppy started.

Henry shook his head. "My father is getting on in years and has looked after the estate as best he can, but there are few tenants left. My brother has debts and needs to look after Petunia. She's due any day now. My brother is a gentleman, he cannot work, and my father would have apoplexy if he did. It just isn't done." He paused. "We thought Petunia's dowry would help, and it did, a little. But the estate needs more. The tenants need help, the manor house needs refurbishment, and the servants need paying. We have all the little problems that come with owning a house, but tenfold. We look after not just each other, but the families who live on our lands. In short, I need an heiress, Poppy."

She let out a breath and sat down.

He said, "I care for you, very much. But when I take a wife, I need the income her dowry will bring to my family's estate." He looked at her face, so forlorn. "Forgive me for speaking so plainly about money, I know it is not done. But I felt I needed to explain myself."

"And what about Miss Parkinson?" she asked.

"What about her?"

"She is a thief."

"What gossip are you listening to? She has stolen nothing I am aware of," he said.

"After you left, the lady whose bracelet she'd taken reported it missing."

"A coincidence. These things happen."

"Why are you so determined to ignore her guilt?" She rose.

"Why do you refuse to believe in her innocence?" he came over, 'til they stood a foot apart. As he met her steadfast gaze, he wanted to take her in his arms. But he didn't dare.

"I believe what I saw, that she stole from that older woman," Poppy said, "If you don't believe me, fine. But check the bracelet itself. The woman said her initials were engraved on it, 'LM' for Lillibet Montrose."

Henry removed his hat and ran a hand through his hair, raking the dark locks. "If that is what it will take to convince you of Miss Parkinson's innocence, then very well. But I don't like you at this moment, Poppy. Jealousy doesn't become you."

"Hah. As if I could be jealous of the woman who steals and seeks to put her hands all over you at every opportunity," she snapped.

He glared at her as she frowned back at him. They were at an impasse, and he knew it. "Very well. I will take up no more of your time. Farewell, Poppy."

"That's Miss Morton, sir. Only my close friends and family may call me by my Christian name."

That stung. He stepped back, bowed stiffly, and left without a word.

HE STORMED OUT of Poppy's townhouse, raging with every step. He didn't care who got in his way, his ground-eating pace took him back to the steps of the Dyngley townhouse in no time at all. He was not fit for company, and yet as soon as he walked into the house, he heard the women's voices calling for him.

He said, "I'll just be a minute," and practically flew upstairs. He flung his bedroom door open and threw himself into the old wooden, rickety chair before his desk. Its aged legs snapped beneath the force of him and he crashed to the floor. He cursed.

"Sir, are you all right?" His manservant, Geoffrey, appeared in the doorway.

"I'm fine," Henry growled, picking himself up from the floor.

Geoffrey said, "I'll just dispose of this." he came forward.

"Leave it. I don't mind it right now," Henry said.

Geoffrey stopped. He glanced at Henry and said, "I wonder, sir, if you'd taken your cufflinks away? I can't seem to find them."

Henry looked up. "What do you mean? They should be here." He dusted himself off and looked over to his box of cufflinks that sat on his desk. He flipped it open but strangely enough, a pair was missing. He glanced at the pair on his shirt cuffs, but these were not the missing ones. "Where are the gold ones with the Dyngley crest?"

"I'm afraid I do not know, sir," Geoffrey said.

"Find them."

"Yes, sir."

"They're dear to me."

"Right away, sir." Geoffrey bowed. "Begging your pardon, sir, but Mrs. Dyngley did say a locket of hers had gone missing. Perhaps you've seen it around the house?"

"I have not."

Geoffrey left the room.

Henry felt a nagging suspicion at the back of his mind but he ignored it. Poppy was being jealous, that was all. There was no proof that Miss Parkinson was a thief.

He walked down the corridor, over to the guest rooms where Miss Parkinson was staying. He paused outside her door, then opened it and walked in. The room looked tidy, but with his heart beating in his throat, he saw one of her travel bags open. He bent down and began rummaging through, stopping when he heard a clink.

He carefully moved some layers of clothing aside, and found a small velvet reticule. He dumped the contents of it into his hand. Out fell coins, paper money, rings, a lady's hair comb, a locket, some cufflinks, and a gold bracelet. He blinked and turned the bracelet over in the light. It was engraved. He looked at the cufflinks, peering down at them. But he could not deny recognizing the ornate crest of the Dyngley name on them, or mistake the initials on the golden bracelet for anything other than "LM."

"My god, you're a thief."

With trembling hands, he took his cufflinks back, pocketed the gold bracelet and returned her reticule to its rightful place. He shut the bag and left the room, walking down the stairs.

"Henry, come into the parlor. Where have you been?" Petunia called.

Henry entered the parlor, where Petunia sat holding a plate of biscuits over her protruding stomach. "Hello Petunia."

"What have you been doing? You look a bit...weathered."

She was never one to mince words, Petunia.

"I have just broken it off with Miss Morton."

"Her? Good God. Thank goodness for that. If I'd known you were seeing her I would have put a stop to that right away. She's wholly unsuitable. What would Miss Parkinson say?" She touched a hand to her abdomen and winced.

"I neither know nor care. Miss Parkinson is a thief."

"What? Don't be callous, Henry, it's rude. She is a guest. She may have pinched a biscuit or two, but there's no need for name-calling."

"I mean it." He dropped her locket onto the sofa cushion beside her.

She set down the biscuit plate. "My locket. Where on earth did you find it?"

"In Miss Parkinson's reticule."

"What was it doing there?"

Henry gave her a look. Was she really so clueless as to mistake the obvious? "I can only assume she took it."

"Well, that's very odd. She probably wanted to get it polished and return it to me as a gift. Sweet girl."

"Mrs. Dyngley, I am a sergeant of the law. I cannot continue to court Miss Parkinson."

Petunia coughed, spitting out biscuit crumbs everywhere. "But what about your engagement?"

"What?"

"You and Miss Parkinson. You both are engaged, are you not?

She has gone this very afternoon to order her wedding clothes." She stood up and froze.

"We are not engaged, madam."

"Oh." Petunia put a hand on her abdomen. "Oh my. Henry..."

"What is it?"

"Call the doctor."

"Why? I need to call the watch and take her away."

"No, call the doctor."

"What for?"

"I need a doctor now, Henry. The baby is coming."

He gaped at her.

Chapter Thirty-Two

Poppy found herself sitting on the floor of her mother's sitting room. The plush carpet dug into her hands and the light fabric of her dress. She stood, just as her aunt came back in. "Poppy, are you all right?"

Poppy gave her aunt a watery smile.

"I heard everything. To think, I had such hopes for Sergeant Dyngley. Well, never mind him. You'll do better than that, I just know it." She wrapped Poppy in a warm hug, holding her close.

Poppy felt like a twig that had been snapped. Within a single day, her reputation had been besmirched with the truth, she had lost her friends, possibly her servants and household, and the only man she'd ever loved. What more could the day bring?

Poppy went downstairs to the servants' hall. She found the staff drinking tea in the kitchen. They stood up as she entered, and she said, "I'm sorry to have disturbed you." She cleared her throat. "I believe my uncle has said that my family will be leaving shortly and that your services are no longer required."

From the housekeeper, Mrs. Pratt, to the dour faces of the scullery girl and pot boy, it was clear they expected her to reiterate her uncle's commands. She said, "My uncle was mistaken."

She heard an intake of breath.

"I have no intention of leaving. And I hope you will all stay in my employ. We have all enjoyed our stay here very much. The rooms are exceedingly comfortable and the food delicious." She looked around the room. "Thank you."

She turned and left, taking a few loud steps out of the servants' hall and up the back stairs. As soon as she heard the first sounds of tea cups, chairs being moved, and low chatter, she exhaled and fled to her room. Once the door closed behind her, she leaned against the door, her body trembling. The first tears started to fall, and she locked the door, putting a chair beneath the handle.

She crossed the room, went to her writing desk, and looked for her father's letters. She looked and opened drawers, and moved aside invitations and newspapers but there was nothing. They were missing. Tears rolled down her cheeks as she stood there forlornly, looking at her writing table. Not even her father's letters could console her.

She fell on her bed and cried into her pillow. Henry, gone. Henry, abandoning her in pursuit of an heiress. Henry, with Miss Parkinson on his arm, all smiles. It made her sick to her stomach.

She fell asleep. When she woke, it was nighttime, and Miss Cooke was quietly rapping on her door. "Miss Morton? Miss Morton, are you in there?"

Poppy rose, removed the chair, and unlocked the door. "Yes, Miss Cooke, I'm here."

"Oh thank goodness. I thought you might've done yourself a harm. Are you all right, Miss?"

"I'm fine, thank you." She stood back to let her maid enter.

Miss Cooke came in with a candle. "Lord, it's dark in here." She came in and began lighting candles around the room 'til it was warm with light.

"Come to dinner."

"I'm not hungry." Poppy turned her back and sat on her bed.

"Why? Because your uncle tried to dismiss us all, or because the newspaper said you're the daughter of a whore?"

Poppy's head snapped back around. "How dare you? She was

your mistress."

"I call it like I sees it. But it makes no difference to me what she did for a living. Missus Grey was a good and proper woman, and your father loved her. Make no mistake about that." Miss Cooke motioned for Poppy to stand, and she helped her into a dress for the evening.

Poppy stood stiffly as Miss Cooke helped her. "Did you like my mother?"

"She treated us kindly. I liked your mum well enough. No airs about her, unlike some ladies I've worked for before. Now let's fix your hair, straighten your shoulders, and join them downstairs. They'll all be thinking about you."

Poppy stared into the looking glass. "I wonder what my mother would do at a time like this."

"Missus Grey? That's easy. A few years ago, some ladies found out about her and made life difficult. They spread rumors about her and for a while, she was the victim of some nasty gossip."

"What did she do?"

"Privately, she had her cry. But only once. Then she planned how to get revenge. She couldn't, of course, not really. But she made life difficult right back, until they stopped and left her alone. Missus Grey never did hide from her problems. She faced them directly. You should too."

Poppy looked back from Miss Cooke's honest face to herself in the reflection of the looking glass. She had her mother's long swanlike neck, her high cheekbones, a wide forehead, and a pert nose. Thin lips and fair skin, and her soft brown hair was pulled back and expertly arranged to be up and out of her face, yet hung down in pretty ringlets over her shoulder. And just like that, Poppy decided what she would do.

Her uncle tapped on her bedroom door, and she looked at him, standing there. "Come in."

Her uncle entered and shut the door behind him, as Miss Cooke left them. "I came to talk to you about your situation here."

Poppy gripped the hard wooden back of her chair. "Uncle, are you ashamed of me?"

"Why would I be ashamed? What have you done?"

"Nothing. I just mean, are you embarrassed by me? To have me as your niece, because of what my mother was? Is that why you didn't want me to go to London?"

"No. I was most afraid she'd want you to take after her when you were together, but there is no danger of that now. Her influence over you is gone, and I am glad to see her gone."

She must have looked hurt. He said, "I mean that she lived a life of luxury and idleness and I do not want you to follow in her footsteps. But I have never been ashamed to have you as my niece. I might not have approved of your mother or her wicked ways, but that does not reflect on you. Only your words and actions show the world what you are." He adjusted the horn-rimmed spectacles on his nose. "I am proud of you, and the young woman you have become. I only wish that you would settle down and become a clergyman's wife. You already know all it entails."

Inwardly Poppy couldn't think of anything duller. She had no desire to spend her days visiting the poor and sick and being a sounding board for a county rector, only to sit in the pew like a good little church mouse as he droned on about propriety and goodwill toward others. She wasn't feeling very good natured toward anyone at that moment.

Her uncle continued, "You have a smart head on your shoulders. That is why I know you will make the right decision in your choice of a husband, whomever he may be. You know who I would choose for you."

Dinner was a quiet affair, with little sound but the clinking of spoons and cutlery as the small party ate and drank. Uncle Reginald hardly spoke to Poppy. But the servants were pleased, and so provided a rich consommé, hot chicken with crispy seasoned skin, boiled herb potatoes, and a full-bodied red wine.

The cook even made a blackberry trifle for dessert.

Poppy heard little of the conversation, and instead thought hard about what she would do. She might feel humiliated by the newspapers, but that didn't mean she had to act like it. She was not a leper out of some medieval tale. She was Poppy Morton, and by god, she'd let the world know it.

She looked up at her family and Mr. Terrell. "I have decided to stay here in London for a time. I hope you all will too."

Her uncle grunted, her aunt coughed, and Mr. Terrell looked delighted. "I normally would not involve myself in your family affairs," he began. "But I feel as though we are family already, and cannot but think that while I disapprove of your disobedience toward your uncle, once you finish your business here in Town, you might reconsider your uncle's suggestion to move back to Hertfordshire."

Poppy glanced at him. From what she had seen, he had done little else but involve himself in her family's affairs.

Aunt Rachel coughed delicately and said, "That is very kind of you to say, Mr. Terrell, to think of us all as family. I am sure Poppy will make the right decision." Her aunt added, "for her."

As the family finished dinner, Poppy sat at the table still, nursing her glass of wine. Her uncle had taken himself off the moment the meal had finished, muttering about a sermon to write. Mr. Terrell followed, shooting a look at Poppy.

She sat, facing her aunt when her uncle and Mr. Terrell came back into the room. "Poppy, Mr. Terrell has something he wishes to say to you. Alone."

Poppy looked up. "What? All right." Whatever it was, she didn't care. She didn't feel up to a fight.

Her aunt started, and rose, squeezing her shoulder as she left.

The door to the parlor closed behind them, sealing Mr. Terrell and Poppy in the room alone. He stepped forward. "Have you given any thought to my offer, Miss Morton?"

"What offer is that?"

"My offer of marriage," he said.

She stared at him. "I beg your pardon?"

"A short time ago I offered to look after you and take care of you. As my future wife. I think you've had enough time to come to a decision."

"I..."

"No doubt you are overcome. I understand this is common amongst young ladies. If you wish to faint, do not worry, I will catch you."

"I am not feeling faint, Mr. Terrell."

"Then what is your answer?" he asked.

She looked at him. He wasn't a bad fellow, just a bit annoying and presumptuous at times. Arrogant, even. He had made no attempt to look well, and his hair bore traces of white dander from his scalp. His brown clothes looked worn and needed mending, his skin looked sallow and pale, and his dark hair was limp. He needed a bath. Could she love such a man?

"I promise you, once we are wed, you will have no need to remain in Town, and with the money from the sale of this townhouse, we will be able to live comfortably. We could even add a new room to the parsonage," he said.

"I beg your pardon?"

"The parsonage in Hertford. There is no living available just yet, but in a few years, once your uncle passes on and the living goes to me..."

Her eyes widened.

"...I promise to look after you and your aunt, and we will all live together in the parsonage. It will be a comfort to yourself and your aunt not to move somewhere else. If you like, you may keep Miss Cooke as your maid. Is she like her namesake, can she cook?"

"I hardly know."

"Well, we'll have to find that out. And no need to worry, once we are engaged, I see no reason for you to keep looking into these little disturbances and accidents of your friends. It is high time, and your uncle agrees with me, that you take on more ladylike pursuits. You can sew, and I have shirts that need mending. Not to mention socks. You can do that, I suppose?"

How very romantic, Poppy thought. No exclamations of how he was in love with her or how overcome he was by her beauty or charms. Not a word of how he wanted to spend every waking moment by her side. No. Instead, he wanted her to darn his socks. As if that was a fulfilling pursuit for her days.

The damned cheek of the man.

"Sir," she began, "I am very conscious of the honor you do me."

"Very good. That is a very good answer."

"But I regret I am unable to accept you," she said.

He stared at her. "What?"

"I'm sorry. I do not think we are suited, and I do not love you."

"I don't love you either. What does that have to do with anything?" he asked and scratched his head.

She let out a breath. She'd made the right decision. "Love normally plays into whether two people marry, I've heard."

"It's that constable, isn't it? You like him," Mr. Terrell accused.

"I do like him."

"And where is he now? Gone. I was listening to your conversation and I heard it all. He abandoned you as soon as your unfortunate birth made the newspaper."

"My unfortunate birth," she repeated.

"Yes. Thanks to the paper, no one will want you now, least of all him. I hope you realize that I am doing you a favor by even asking for your hand, but here I am. I will have you. I will look after you, Poppy. Me and no one else."

Seeing her face, he added, "Once we are married, there will be no mention from me of your unfortunate birth, or the circumstances in which you find yourself. No, once we are engaged, we will return to Hertford as your uncle said, and we will marry, quietly. Your uncle and I will share the living and you will take on your new role as my wife, to look after the parishioners and tend to them. And me."

Her mouth hung open a little.

"It is a good life, Poppy. Many girls would love to be in your shoes right now."

"Sir, I cannot accept you."

"Poppy, why not?"

She stood from her seat, the chair falling back. "How could I accept the man who talks about me and 'my unfortunate birth', or who would rather see me darn his socks? Or who points out that he is doing me a favor by asking for my hand? As if I should be grateful or indebted to you? No, sir, we are most definitely not suited. We do not love each other and I think that, more than anything, is reason enough for us not to marry. Do excuse me." She started to sweep past him and turned. "And for god's sake, stop calling me by my Christian name. We are acquaintances, nothing more. Good evening, Mr. Terrell."

"Miss Morton, stop." His voice was sharp.

She looked at him.

"You forget that you are in a precarious position. The entire world now knows of your unfortunate birth, and the inappropriate circumstances of your mother and father. You seem unable to understand how low you have fallen in the eyes of society."

"And this is how you wish to convince me to marry you?"

He turned pink. "You may never receive another offer. Take it while you still can."

"I think I can do better without." She turned when he gripped her arm. "Let go of me."

"Not until you come to your senses. You will marry me, Poppy."

She slapped him upside the head, and boxed his ear.

He fell like a bag of potatoes, and held a hand to his ear. "You hurt me," he whined.

She looked down at him, her body trembling. "Don't you ever lay a hand on me again. Get out."

She walked out to find her aunt and uncle listening by the door. They had witnessed or overheard her entire humiliating experience. She said, "Do not ask me to reconsider. I am staying and I do not care if I end up an old maid. I will not marry anyone so insulting as him."

She went to bed, locking the door behind her and as per her daily practice now, lodging a stiff and sturdy chair beneath the handle.

THE NEXT MORNING Poppy couldn't bear to see her family over breakfast, much less Mr. Terrell, and asked for a tray to be brought up to her. Miss Cooke brought it up, along with a note from Mr. Grant, asking her to meet him at McNally's bookshop. She dressed quickly and quietly slipped out the backdoor of the house. Keeping her bonnet pulled low over her face, she made the quick walk to the bookshop, the bell on the door signaling her arrival.

She nodded hello to Mr. McNally, who bid her good morning, and she began to wander around the stacks of books. She heard a whispered, "Miss Morton."

There not far away stood Mr. Grant, behind a wall of books. He bowed and said hello.

"Hello, Mr. Grant."

"Hello. I wasn't sure you'd be moving around in society."

She nodded. "I needed to get out of the house. Your timing was perfect."

"I'm glad. I wanted to tell you the news. Miss Haskett is alive."

"What?" She stared.

"I wanted to tell you in person. She is staying at her family's shop in Town. Would you like to visit her?"

"Yes."

They went together to see Sarah. Her parents were understandably concerned but happy to see a friend, and at the introduction of Mr. Grant, they let her into the back of their shop, where Sarah lay resting in bed. She lay covered in blankets up to her neck, which was wrapped in bandages. Poppy quietly approached Sarah's bed and said, "Miss Haskett?"

Sarah's eyelids fluttered and then opened. She smiled weakly and waved a few fingers at Poppy.

"How are you feeling?" Poppy asked.

"She's been through a lot. I've told her not to speak," Peregrine said.

Sarah smiled at her and winced.

"Do you know who did this to you?"

Sarah nodded.

"They were all there. It could have been anyone," Peregrine said.

"This was no accident. That evening, Sarah told us girls she knew who was behind it all," Poppy said. "Excuse me just a moment." She went downstairs to the shop and borrowed one of the books, a printed copy of a book that was dirty and unsuitable to sell. She put it in Sarah's hands. "Point to the letters and tell me who did this to you."

"I say, that's smart," Peregrine said.

Sarah pointed at the first letter and began spelling out a name.

THAT AFTERNOON, POPPY sent out invitations. She wrote to the magistrate, Henry Dyngley, as well as Peregrine, Tom, Lucretia, and Emily. She also invited her aunt, uncle, and even Mr. Terrell, who was still present in the house, to join them all.

At the appointed time and when people began to arrive, her uncle, aunt, and Mr. Terrell joined her in the parlor.

"What is this, Poppy?" Uncle Reginald asked. "Why have you invited all these people here? This is no time to celebrate."

Poppy said, "Just wait, Uncle. I'll explain once everyone is here."

They did not need to wait long. Even Lucretia arrived, although she looked around her disdainfully and spoke to no one.

Poppy said, "A series of events have affected all of us girls. I called you all here because I know who was behind it. But first, let me relay the events in order."

"Oh lord, we're going to need refreshments for this. Miss Cooke, please bring in tea," Aunt Rachel said.

Once everyone had tea and biscuits and was sitting comfortably, Poppy began. "A few months ago, there was a dance, where Mr. Stuart Horley, a good friend to Mr. Grant and Mr. Fletcher, sadly perished. It was known that he'd had an unfortunate fall from a balcony that evening, whilst in the company of a few debutantes and that he had been drunk when he fell."

"You're not telling us anything we don't already know," the magistrate said.

"The debutantes present were Miss Dobbins, Miss Gibbs, and Miss Munden."

Faces turned to look at the two girls. Lucretia turned pink. "I didn't come here to be accused. I'm innocent."

"We all are," Emily said. "I don't like that you're bringing this up, Miss Morton. What's done is done. The man is dead."

Poppy said, "What is less known is the fact that Mr. Horley was a blackguard."

Peregrine protested, "That's my friend you're slandering."

"You'd better have some proof, Miss," the magistrate said.

"I do. For weeks, Mr. Grant has been asking questions, trying to figure out why none of the girls who were present at Mr. Horley's death would say anything. It might be thought that witnessing a man's death would be too distressing for three young women. But I have lately learned that each of these women had a reason for wanting Mr. Horley dead."

"Miss Morton, what are you saying?" Emily asked.

"You told me yourself that you and Mr. Horley were courting. If that were true, then why would he not tell anyone? Why would he keep it a secret? You come from a respectable family, so why would he not make it public?"

"I don't know," Emily said.

"Is it possible he was ashamed of you? Your family is wealthy and titled, but they didn't start out that way. You told me with pride how your family owns an apothecary's shop in London, and how your father is a proud member of the Royal Society of Apothecaries."

"So what if he is? I am not ashamed," Emily said.

"No, but Mr. Horley may have been. You are young, pretty, and have money. Why would he not tell anyone he was courting you? It doesn't make sense."

"Then Miss Dobbins," Poppy began, "ever since we met, you have been singularly loyal to Mr. Fletcher, even when he has come under suspicion of being party to a crime. Why is that?"

"We are courting. Simple as that." Lucretia said.

"Then why is it I have never seen you together? It appears as though all the romantic overtures are on your side, not his."

"So what? Courting is a complicated matter. I wouldn't expect you to understand," Lucretia scoffed.

"I think that on the day of the dance, Mr. Fletcher caught Mr. Horley trying to seduce you. Mr. Grant himself told me they had had a fight, but Mr. Fletcher said it was a private matter concerning a lady. I think the lady was you."

"No," Lucretia said.

"I think they fought, and since he rescued you, you have sought his affection ever since."

"It's not like that," Lucretia said. "He loves me."

"Then where is he now?"

"I don't know. But he didn't do it! He didn't kill Mr. Horley." She growled, "Even if he did deserve it."

"What happened next was a series of unfortunate accidents. Miss Dobbins was pushed down a flight of stairs. She almost drank poison that led to the death of Miss Grace. And on top of that, all of our names were given as a special addition to be printed with Harris's List."

Grim faces were all around the room.

"Why are you bringing this back up, Poppy?" Uncle Reginald asked.

"Because all of us girls were trying to think of who could have done it. Who knew all of us, disliked us so much they wanted to ruin our reputations in print? Who wanted to bring us down so low no one would have us?"

"Do you know?" Peregrine asked.

"I do," Poppy said. "As you all know, I was recently the subject of a newspaper article, one which you may think besmirched my character. But the fact is, it is true. I am the illegitimate daughter of Lord Blackwood and his mistress, Celeste Morton."

A gasp or two, but mostly silence, answered her. Lucretia's eyes grew wide and she bit into a biscuit.

"No one knew this fact but a select few. I wondered if it was perhaps my half-sister, out to cause trouble. But she knew that to do so would risk damaging her own reputation and causing harm to her family, so I knew she wouldn't do it, no matter how much she disliked me. I wondered perhaps if one of the girls I socialized with had found out. But then I also realized that if they had known, very few of them would have remained friends with me. For as unlikeable, perhaps, as a family that comes from a trade background is, coming from an illicit union and having a mother as a mistress is worse. None of the girls I called friends knew my secret. And as anyone knows, the way to keep a secret is to not tell anyone. So who knew?"

The magistrate and Henry gazed around the room.

"I can tell you. My immediate family, the servants who had been with my mother for a long time, and one other person. And as this person has consistently told me, no one would want me now," Poppy said.

"Who?" Emily asked.

Poppy looked around the room. "The person who gave all our names to the printer, and who told the newspaper about my birth, is none other than Mr. Terrence Terrell."

Chapter Thirty-Three

Mr. Terrell shot up out of his seat. "Me? Why on earth would you think I had anything to do with that?"

"Because, Mr. Terrell, you are the only other person who knew. You are the one who disliked my having other suitors from the beginning of our acquaintance back in Hertford. Even when my father paid a visit, you asked my uncle if he was a new suitor of mine, and I learned from Miss Cooke that my uncle told you the whole of our relationship. It could not have been anyone but you."

He glared at her. "Your imagination knows no bounds. Rest assured, once we are married, I will put a stop to that kind of willful behavior."

"We are not going to marry."

"What makes you think it was this man, Miss Morton?" the magistrate asked.

"He is the only one who knew all of our names, and who knew of my background. Outside of my immediate family and Sergeant Dyngley, no one else did."

"When your men apprehended the printer, Magistrate Tomlinson, you recall that the man who gave the addition and the old list to the printer was described as a young man dressed in brown," Henry said.

Everyone looked at Mr. Terrell, who stood in head-to-toe

brown clothing. "What? Wearing brown is not a crime."

"Not at all. But most men wear different articles of clothing, in varying shades and patterns."

"I cannot help being poor."

"The newspaper would've wanted a source, though. They wouldn't just accept anyone's word as gospel," Magistrate Tomlinson said.

"Just yesterday, I noticed that all the letters from my father had gone missing. All of them. I suspect that Mr. Terrell stole them and used them as evidence for the newspaper, to prove my relationship with Lord Blackwood."

"You haven't a shred of proof," Mr. Terrell said.

"Miss Cooke," Poppy said.

"Yes, Miss?" Miss Cooke walked inside the room.

"Go into Mr. Terrell's room. I believe he has some letters of mine. If you can't find them, do come back."

"This is unpardonable!" Mr. Terrell said, stamping his feet. "You have no right to go into my room. Rummaging amongst a man's things is beneath you, Poppy."

"And yet that did not stop you from entering my room the first night we arrived in London, or from going through my personal effects from time to time. How often did I find a note of poetry on my pillow, a sign that you had entered my room? And please, sir, call me Miss Morton. Thanks to you, I have had to lock my bedroom door and put a chair under the handle every night, just to be able to sleep in peace."

"What?" Uncle Reginald asked.

"It's true, Uncle. I know this man is your student, but–"

"This has gone on far enough. First, you disobey me and refuse Mr. Terrell's generous offer of marriage, but now you accuse him of a crime? And suggest he has harassed you? How low can you fall, Poppy?" His face grew dark.

"Yes, exactly what I said. The world deserves to know." Mr. Terrell rubbed his hands together.

Miss Cooke re-entered the parlor. "I found the letters, Miss.

Right where you said they'd be. He didn't do a good job of hiding them at all," Miss Cooke said, holding up the letters.

Mr. Terrell turned pink.

"Well, Mr. Terrell? Will you tell us why my private letters were in your room?"

He glared at her, then, and looked rather like a thin brown toad. "I was checking the correspondence, to make sure that man didn't try anything inappropriate with you. He had already led your mother into sin, what's to say he wouldn't try to sell you off to one of his friends? Yes, I did look through your letters, but it was with the best intentions."

"There, you see? Mr. Terrell has been nothing but honorable and good since he arrived," Uncle Reginald said.

Aunt Rachel barked a laugh. "Oh, Reginald, you are fooling yourself if you believe that. The first night the man wandered into her room. Poppy was scared out of her wits and has been sleeping with a poker beside her bed every night, afraid he might try and attack her."

"Mr. Terrell attack Poppy? Whatever for?"

The women all exchanged glances. "To compromise her person, sir, in order to force her into marrying him," Miss Cooke said, glaring at Mr. Terrell. "He wants the living in Hertford once you pass on. The letters in his room are just extra proof he's guilty of wrongdoing."

Mr. Terrell looked at them all, and crossed his arms and sulked. "All right, have it your way. Yes, I did it. Yes, I wrote to the paper and gave the printer that list."

"You snotty little rat!" Lucretia lunged at him, toppling him to the ground. She kicked and clawed at Mr. Terrell, shrieking, "Do you know what damage you have done? You've ruined all of our reputations, you twit! None of us will find good husbands, all thanks to your lies, you selfish, obnoxious…"

"All right, all right. That's enough." Magistrate Tomlinson picked up Lucretia and sat her back down on the sofa. She snarled at Mr. Terrell and rearranged her dress. "I'm going to sue you,

you vermin. You will be hearing from my father's solicitor."

"And mine," Emily said.

"Mr. Terrell?" Uncle Reginald asked. "Is this true? Did you really do these things?"

Terrence looked at Uncle Reginald and said, "You don't understand. She's a good girl, but she's no better than me. She's the daughter of a whore, for Christ's sake. Why on earth should she be dallying with suitors far above her station, when we both know she should be with me?"

Uncle Reginald's mouth dropped open.

"You knowingly did this to my niece? You befouled her reputation. Just so you might win her hand?"

"I knew you would understand. You're always telling me what a good, obedient girl Poppy is. She just needed to be brought down a peg or two and reminded of her place in the world."

"My God. You really are a blackguard. How despicable," Aunt Rachel said.

"And to think, the man I have welcomed into my home for so many weeks, is none other than a miserable sod. Get out of here," Uncle Reginald said.

"What? Sir, you can't mean that," Terrence said.

"I do. Leave here at once."

"But I have nowhere to go. I have no money. Besides, what choice did I have? You know as well as I do that she's got no right to go around dancing with lords and gentlemen like she's one of them. She's as common as dirt. Lower than, if you ask me."

"Poppy, you were right to refuse this man. Magistrate, I want you to arrest this man. Take him away."

Magistrate Tomlinson had a wide smile on his face. "With pleasure, sir. You can share a cell with your old friend, the printer. He'd love to see you again, eh?" Together with a few men of the watch, Mr. Terrell was removed, still protesting his innocence.

After the ruckus ended, the magistrate had returned, and the group was back and sitting comfortably, Lucretia asked, "But I don't understand. We know he was the one who gave our names to the printer and who told about you to the paper, but who killed Miss Grace? Who has been after me this whole time? And who killed Miss Haskett?"

"I think the answer to that lies with Miss Gibbs, whom Mr. Horley was blackmailing," Poppy said.

"What?" the magistrate, Peregrine, and Lucretia said.

Poppy said, "I went over to see Miss Gibbs, the night after the concert. She has disappeared and her mother was worried sick about her. This morning I received a note from my friend Mr. Markham, who found her."

"So Miss Gibbs did it," Lucretia said.

"No, she didn't. She ran away."

"What? Is she all right?"

"Yes. She is fine. She will be in Scotland for a few days."

"Scotland? Whatever for?"

"Miss Gibbs has eloped," Poppy said quietly. "When she returns, you may call her Mrs. Fletcher."

Lucretia's mouth dropped open. "Mrs. Fletcher? You mean..."

"Miss Haskett told us a rumor a few weeks ago that we barely believed to be true," Emily said. "That Miss Gibbs was secretly engaged to Mr. Fletcher, and had been for some time. They were just waiting for the right moment, I suppose."

"No. You're wrong. You're lying." Lucretia's voice grew shrill.

"She isn't. I was there when Sarah told it. And she's not the only one who knew. Mr. Horley saw them at some point, and started blackmailing Miss Gibbs for money, or else he would tell her family and ruin all chances of her marrying Mr. Fletcher."

"How could this be true?" Lucretia asked.

"I found the letters from Mr. Horley, blackmailing her," Poppy said.

"So she did it. She must have done it."

Emily shot Lucretia a dirty look.

"I think you all did it," Poppy said. "You all killed Mr. Horley."

The girls looked at her in dismay.

"Tell me if I'm wrong. I think that during the dance that night, Mr. Horley had too much to drink. He was paying Lucretia unwanted attention, and he didn't stop. Out on the balcony, Emily found them."

Lucretia turned pale.

"He'd already been blackmailing Miss Gibbs. She had reason enough to want him dead. But you, Miss Dobbins, I think he wanted to seduce and wasn't willing to take no for an answer. Out on the balcony, with him drunk, it was just the three of you. No one would ever know if he'd actually just slipped and fell, or if he'd been pushed."

"Stop it," Lucretia said. "Stop this at once."

"I think all three of you know what happened. One of them caught you in a compromising position and to protect you, did away with the drunken Mr. Horley. And to protect each other, you agreed not to say a word to anyone, and to say he'd had an unfortunate accident."

"No," Lucretia muttered. "You're wrong."

"Am I? Because one of the people who was there that night thinks that you're going to give them up at any moment. That's why they've been watching you at parties, pushing you down stairs, even giving you drinks that have been drugged. You're right in that you were the intended victim. But the night of the concert, they panicked."

"What do you mean?" Lucretia asked.

"That night, Miss Haskett told the group of us that she figured out who was behind it all. She was going to reveal the answer later. The killer couldn't take the chance that Miss Haskett was right."

"Who?" Magistrate Tomlinson asked, "Oh, you mean the dead girl. Miss Haskett."

"Yes. That night, the killer used the opportunity of me being embarrassed before the entire assembly to pick up a piece of glass and stab Miss Haskett in the neck. The girl fainted and everyone thought she was dead. But she didn't die."

Lucretia and Emily stared at her.

"Today Mr. Grant and I visited her. She is badly injured and cannot talk, but she pointed out the name of the person who tried to kill her. The same person who tried to stop Lucretia from talking." She looked at the killer. "Miss Emily Munden."

Emily laughed at her.

"Miss Munden, I'm not joking."

"Oh, but you are. I cannot believe you would accuse me of this. We are friends, Miss Morton."

"You... I knew it was you." Lucretia said, edging away from her on the sofa. "I didn't do it. You told me everything would be fine if we didn't say anything."

"Oh please, you fretted everyone would know it was you who let Mr. Horley put his hand down your dress." Emily turned to Poppy. "There, are you happy? Lucretia did it. I was going to break it off with Mr. Horley anyway when I'd found them kissing. There was no need for him to fight over her, but at that point, I didn't care."

Poppy looked at her friend. "But you did. Otherwise, why would you have tried to kill Lucretia at the dance with the poisoned drink, or push her down the stairs?"

"That was Miss Gibbs. So clumsy."

"But the drink was poisoned with strychnine. Only someone who knew their way around drugs and poisons would be able to access that, and know how to administer it," Henry said.

"Someone perhaps, whose family was in the apothecary business?" Poppy asked.

"I'm going to pretend you didn't just say that," Emily said. "Shame on you, Miss Morton. I am the one friend who sticks by you and what do you do? Accuse me of murder. This is beyond the pale. For days the girls said nasty things behind your back. They even wondered if you had put your name in the paper for the notoriety."

"What? Why would I sabotage my own reputation?" Poppy asked.

"Everyone likes a rebellious sort of girl. You pretend to be all quiet and meek, but we all know you've got the mind of a criminal."

Poppy ignored her. "Magistrate, Miss Munden is the girl you want. She did it. She attempted to kill Miss Haskett, and has tried to hurt Miss Dobbins, repeatedly."

Emily snorted at that.

"Uh, right. Miss Munden, was it? Could you just come along with me? We'll just have a little chat," Magistrate Tomlinson said.

Emily looked up at the man and said, "I'll go. But you will all be hearing from my father. He will sort this out." She spared a dirty look for Poppy and calmly allowed the magistrate to take her away.

ONCE THEY WERE gone, Aunt Rachel let out a noisy breath. "Good lord. What an afternoon. I swear, this is better than the stage. Who's for more tea and biscuits?"

Lucretia said, "I think I need to lie down after that." She left, along with Mr. Grant.

Uncle Reginald glanced at Poppy and his wife. "Well, Poppy, you've done it again. I distrusted your character and good judgment, and you've not only proved me wrong, but also caught a killer." He ran a hand through his thinning hair. "I need a drink."

"Make that two," Aunt Rachel said, following him out of the room. Miss Cooke glanced at Poppy and Dyngley and said, "Do you want me to stay, Miss?"

"No, I'll be all right. Thank you," Poppy said.

Once they were alone, Poppy looked at him. He sat there, looking at the floor. He said, "Mrs. Dyngley has had a child. A little boy. His name is Arthur."

"Congratulations. She must be thrilled."

"She is. But very tired, too." He looked at her and said, "I'd told you not to get involved in this investigation, and instead you uncover a killer and get rid of that odious Mr. Terrell."

She opened her mouth to apologize, when he said, "Well done, Miss Morton."

"Thank you."

Henry looked down at his hands. "I've been meaning to–"

Miss Cooke entered the room. "Excuse me, Miss Morton, but there's a visitor here for you. A Mr. James Blackwood, of Somerset?"

Poppy stopped. "I…"

Miss Cooke let in a young man into the parlor, in his early twenties, with dusky blond hair, long legs, and a good-natured smile. He had fair skin, tanned by the sun, and wore a smart day suit of green and brown. He said, "Forgive me for intruding."

"I'll see myself out," Henry said.

"All right."

Henry left, and Poppy bid Mr. Blackwood to sit down. He said, "I wasn't sure whether to come in or not. I saw a lot of people leave, including a man of the watch. Was there a crime or something?"

"Something like that," Poppy said. "Biscuit?" She offered him a plate, and he took one.

"This isn't easy for me to say but…I think I'm your brother."

POPPY LOOKED AT him. In his face, she recognized the same eyes as her father, the same tilt of his face and cleft of his chin, and when he walked in, the same stance as her father often took. "I think you are."

"Forgive me for intruding upon you. I just…wanted to meet you."

"You saw the paper, I assume," she said.

"Yes. I wanted to come and apologize. My sister…"

"Your sister did it?" Poppy froze. Had she accused the wrong person?

"Susan? No. God, no. I talked her out of that, you can be sure. No. I explained to her that if she breathed a word about you to anyone, she would hurt our Mama irrevocably, and she would damage her reputation, mine, and that of the entire family. She's come to her senses."

"Thank goodness. I thought I had figured out who did write to the paper about it, but you've shaken me for a moment." She gave a little sigh of relief.

"Really? Who was it?"

"A man who was up to no good. He's on his way to jail now."

"Jolly good." James bit into a biscuit and said, "That is good news. But I also wanted to apologize for the trouble my sister has caused. When she told me about you…" He ran a hand through his hair. "The fact is, I've known about you for months. Since father came back this autumn. He took me aside and told me, and said that if anything ever happened to him, I was to look after you."

Poppy's eyes widened.

"It was a shock. I was angry at him for quite a while. I wanted to tell Susan, but he forbade me from doing so. And seeing her reaction since learning the news of our half-sister, I think he was right." He swallowed. "When she came home and told me, I admitted that I'd known. She was furious, with me and with Papa, and fled back to London. None of us dared tell Mama, she just thought we were squabbling. She was especially surprised to find our father worried about her health. He thought she was on her deathbed. So whilst of course, we are all pleased that Mama is healthy…" He shrugged.

"I'm glad your mother is in good health," Poppy said.

"Thank you. Anyway, I followed her back to London and found her at the concert, causing a scene."

"You were the one, that night of the concert. You dragged her away," Poppy said.

"Yes. I'm sorry about her behavior toward you. She is angry at everyone, but mostly my Papa, and she's looking for someone to blame. She's chosen you as her target, and it's not fair, since you've done nothing wrong. You seem quite nice, in fact."

Poppy smiled at him. "Thank you."

"Did you know about our… relationship?" James asked.

"Not until a few months ago. But I'm glad to have met your father. And you."

"Don't worry about Susan, she'll come around." He blushed. "In the meantime, if you'll give me your stained dress, I'll have it cleaned and mended."

Poppy shook her head. "It's already been taken care of. But thank you."

"Um, now that the news of our familial relationship is common knowledge, perhaps we might see each other again sometime?"

"I'd like that," Poppy said.

CHAPTER THIRTY-FOUR

HENRY WALKED HOME. What an afternoon. He felt like so much time had passed, and yet hardly an hour or so had gone. It seemed as if he had walked through a whirlwind of emotion. Miss Dobbins, being seduced by a layabout and then rescued by her friends, but with disastrous ends, that miscreant Mr. Terrell being behind Poppy's fall from grace and ruining her good name, just to suit his own ends, and even a girl having eloped. He shook his head and walked up the steps to the Dyngley townhouse. How different life would be without Poppy around.

He paused on the top step, his gloved hand poised above the door handle. He had broken Poppy's heart, he was sure of it. And his own in the process. What good could come of a union between them? They shared similar minds and tastes, but he needed money, and she brought nothing to the relationship, not even a good name. Not anymore.

He hadn't cared about her background, but his family surely had. And yet, he had come immediately when she sent for him. He hadn't a spare thought but to see what she wanted. And once a murderer had been caught, what had he done? Sat in her parlor and ate biscuits, whilst her brother came to see her for the first time. He let out a small sigh. He felt like a poor excuse for a gentleman.

He walked inside, to hear Petunia call, "Henry, is that you? Come inside and see."

He dutifully walked into the parlor. There sat Petunia, holding little Arthur in swaddling clothes, as Miss Parkinson stood, holding up layers of white lacy fabric. "Oh, you're not supposed to see it before the wedding," she chided, holding the material behind her back.

"What wedding might that be?" he asked.

"Why ours, silly," Miss Parkinson said.

He looked at her. "How strange. I don't recall a proposal."

She paled. Petunia and Mrs. Parkinson exchanged a look.

"Henry, don't be coarse. The games these young men play today, honestly..." She rocked little Arthur in her arms and smiled at Mrs. Parkinson.

"Shall we talk for a moment?" he asked.

"Of course." Miss Parkinson set the gauzy material aside and followed him out of the parlor. He started walking and realized he didn't know where to go. In the parlor was where Mrs. Parkinson and Petunia were, and it felt like if he were to go anywhere else and close the door, that would be putting her reputation as a young woman into question. Instead, he went into the dining room, where his brother, John, sat asleep in a chair, a newspaper on his lap.

"Your brother will hear us," she said.

"My brother is dead to the world. He wouldn't wake up if you danced a jig next to him."

"Fine. What is it you want to say? You embarrassed me in there," she said.

"That's a funny thing, coming from you. How did my family come under the impression that we are engaged?"

"Why, you promised me yourself. When we agreed to court."

"Ah, yes. We agreed to court for pretend, to get your mother's nagging off your back, and to prevent me from having to go on more romantic meetings with women. We never agreed to become engaged," he said.

"But I thought…" she started. "It's no matter. I've not found anyone suitable, and neither have you."

"Haven't I?"

"Don't tell me Miss Simkins caught your eye at the dance before."

He gave her an even look.

"You're not possibly thinking of that girl, Miss Morton."

He cocked his head.

She laughed. "Are you really? What a joke. She's as tall as a beanpole and accused me of being a thief."

"You are a thief."

She stared at him. "That is not funny."

"I'm not joking. I certainly didn't think it funny when Mrs. Dyngley's locket went missing. Or my cufflinks, or the gold bracelet that went missing at the concert the other night."

"Do you really believe what that beanpole told you? It was a gift."

"With the letters engraved 'LM' on it? Pray tell, Miss Parkinson, what do they stand for?" He looked down at her.

"Loving Memory. It was in memoriam of my grandmother."

He remained unconvinced. "You are lying to my face. I went in your room and found Mrs. Dyngley's locket and my cufflinks. You are a thief and a liar, and I have no wish to know you."

"But what about our engagement?" she asked.

"We have no engagement. Our courtship is at an end. Pack your things, and only your things, Miss Parkinson. You and your mother are returning to Hertfordshire, tonight."

"Please, Mr. Dyngley. Please reconsider." Mrs. Parkinson stepped into the room.

Henry glanced at the older woman. "I'm sorry you had to witness this, Mrs. Parkinson, but…"

"It's my fault. I should have been honest with you from the beginning."

"What do you mean?" he asked.

"For years now, my daughter's condition is of such a nature that I…"

"Condition? You mean you knew about this?" he said.

The woman stiffened. "Yes."

"I want you, Henry." Miss Parkinson came close and took his hand, pressing it to her chest. "I love you. I've wanted you since I saw you a year ago."

"What?" He removed his hand and stepped back.

"Last year, when your investigation made the paper. My father invited you to our home to congratulate you and you came to dinner. Did you never wonder how you were made sergeant?"

He stared at her.

She snorted. "And with an improved income?"

Henry's mouth dropped open. "What are you saying?"

"It was all my Papa's doing. I told him I wanted you as a husband. He said you were a poor county constable. I told him to raise you up. You come from a titled family, after all, you just needed a bit of help. And money."

Henry swallowed. "My thanks to your father. He must allow me to repay him."

"Oh, he doesn't want your thanks. You can thank him in other ways," Miss Parkinson said. "By marrying me."

"Our courting was a fiction, nothing more. You overstep yourself, madam," Henry said.

"On the contrary. That was my sole purpose in coming here. Mama and I came with no other intention than to secure my hand in marriage to you."

Henry stared. "You have played me for a fool. And you have abused my family's hospitality."

She shrugged. "How else was I to get close to you? You had all those other women sniffing around you. Besides, you're all I've wanted. Please, Henry, marry me." She paused. "I realize that in proposing to you, I am acting more forward and in an unladylike manner. But I cannot help myself. From the moment I laid eyes on you, Henry, I wanted you. That hasn't changed."

"Neither has your stealing."

"Then help her," her mother said. "Help my daughter. We thought that with you looking after her, she might stop stealing and become a better person–"

"People who steal won't be helped by marrying a member of the constabulary. It's a condition that she must work through herself," he said.

Mrs. Parkinson's face was a study of disappointment.

"I am sorry to disappoint you, but I came here to tell you that we are not suited. I love someone else," he said.

Mrs. Parkinson's shoulders fell. Miss Parkinson laughed. "Not that beanpole of a girl?"

"It is no concern of yours. Please, save me the trouble and see yourselves out. I am sure Miss Parkinson has taken enough for you to be able to afford the journey."

"That's it? You'll leave us, in the middle of the Season? How is my daughter to find a good husband now?" Mrs. Parkinson asked, her hands on her hips.

"I rather think she should find a good doctor instead." Seeing the older woman's mutinous face, he felt sympathy for their plight, and said, "You can say we simply were not suited, and that your family did not approve of the match. I am, after all, a mere poor county sergeant."

"Henry, won't you reconsider? We could be a good match. And with my father behind you, you could be a magistrate or judge soon enough."

Henry shook his head. "I would rather get advancement through my own merit."

Mrs. Parkinson gave him a pitying look. "Come, Julia. We're leaving." The ladies walked out, whispering, and shooting him little glances.

Henry stood by to watch them go. Only when they exited the room did he let out a breath.

"Well done, Henry," his brother said behind him.

"John? You were listening?" Henry turned.

"Heard the whole thing, little brother. I was awake the whole time. I never did trust that Miss Parkinson. Always seemed a bit funny, if you take my meaning."

Henry smiled, then his face fell. "John, I've got to go."

"Now? Henry, it'll be time for dinner soon. Where do you have to go?"

Seeing his face, John said, "It's that Poppy girl, isn't it? Poppy Morton. You like her."

Henry's face lit up in a smile. John smiled back. "How will you—never mind. Go on, I'll tell the cook to keep you something warm for dinner. Have you met little Arthur yet?"

"I have."

They could hear the baby scream from across the hall.

"Well, I'll just be going," Henry said.

"Are you sure you wouldn't want company? I can give you morale," John said.

"No. I wouldn't dream of keeping you from your wife and child." Henry grinned.

John muttered a curse as Henry laughed and got his hat.

HENRY RETURNED TO the Morton household, flowers in hand. It was a small bouquet, nothing so fine as he'd find in a hothouse, but he couldn't wait another moment. He had to tell her.

Once shown into the parlor, he met Poppy's aunt, who sat nibbling a biscuit. "Sergeant? What are you doing here at so late an hour? It's after five o'clock."

"I need to speak with Miss Morton. Where is she?"

Seeing the flowers in his hands, Aunt Rachel gave a little smile and said, "I couldn't tell you." Then she called, "Miss Cooke."

Poppy's lady's maid entered the room. "Yes ma'am."

"Fetch Poppy for us please, the sergeant wishes to speak to her."

Moments later, Miss Cooke reported Poppy was gone.

"Gone? Where is she?" Henry asked.

"She's not in her room, sir. I found this on her writing desk." Miss Cooke held out a small note. Henry read:

Come to where we first met. I have the answer to both our problems.

-Emily

Henry set down the flowers on the small table in the parlor. "Where did they meet?"

"I don't know. I wasn't with her," Miss Cooke said.

"What's happened? Sergeant, why are you still here? I thought you'd left." Uncle Reginald entered the parlor.

"Poppy's gone, Reginald," Aunt Rachel said.

"What? Did she run away?"

"No." Henry handed him the note.

"Good Lord. Where could she be? Where is this Emily person? She was the one the magistrate apprehended, wasn't she?"

"Apparently she's no longer in their custody," Henry said grimly. "I must find her."

"I'm coming too," Uncle Reginald said.

"Sir, you should stay here, in case she comes back," Henry said.

"Nonsense. I'm not going to sit here and twiddle my thumbs whilst Poppy's in danger."

Henry shot Mrs. Greene a look.

She said, "Reginald, please. You need to go for the magistrate. That girl could be anywhere and she's with Poppy."

Reginald left to get his coat and hat. Dyngley said, "Where is she? Where could she be?"

"I know. We met those girls at the Royal Academy. Go there and you'll find her."

"But Mrs. Greene, it'll be locked for sure. It's after hours."

"If that girl found a way in, Sergeant Dyngley will too. Go," Aunt Rachel said. "Bring her back, Sergeant."

He bowed and turned to leave. Just outside the parlor, he overheard Aunt Rachel say, "I'll just put these in some water. So nice of him to bring flowers."

CHAPTER THIRTY-FIVE

POPPY BARELY HAD time to pull on a hooded cloak before she stepped outside the townhouse and skipped down the front steps. Being late June, the sun was low to set in the sky, despite the advanced hour. Poppy walked, and holding her hand up against the sun's golden rays, hailed a hackney cab.

Within a short while, it dropped her outside of the Royal Academy. Poppy stood there off to the side, looking at the building, now closed. She walked up to the entrance, but as she thought, the doors were locked. She walked along the inside of the main courtyard, trying each and every door. Then farther down a walkway, she saw a flicker of light.

She followed it and walked through an open door into a main gallery room. The room itself was eerie, with just silent statues and pictures hanging on the walls for company. There on the floor sat Susan, tied up, her mouth stuffed with a gag, whilst Emily sat next to her with a bottle of wine and two glasses.

"Ah, you finally decided to show up. I was beginning to think you wouldn't make it."

"I'm here."

"Good. Now we can begin." Emily patted the seat near her and said, "Sit."

Poppy sat. "What are you doing?"

"Solving our little problem. You see, I was being escorted

away by the magistrate, when I thought, this isn't right. I shouldn't be carted off to jail. He had no evidence to hold me, and had to let me go. Someone else should pay. And I knew who. She wasn't hard to find, your sister I mean. I spotted your brother leaving your townhouse–"

"You were watching me?" Poppy asked.

"Of course. And when I followed him, he led me right to her." Her smile toward Susan was nasty. "When I told her I had a plan to hurt you, she came willingly. Once she'd had a few drinks, she didn't know what I was doing until it was too late."

Susan glared at Emily and Poppy through her gag.

"This is your way of punishing me?" Poppy asked.

"Not you. Her," Emily said.

Susan made a muffled voice of protest.

Emily tugged down the girl's gag.

Susan began snarling, "Half-sister, you idiot. When I get out of here I'm going to slap you so hard—"

Emily calmly backhanded her across the face, sending Susan tumbling over.

"Miss Munden!" Poppy said.

"Stop right there." Emily pointed a small pistol at Poppy. "Don't move." She leaned over and tugged the gag back over Susan's mouth.

"Why are you doing this?" Poppy asked.

"Because I'm not going to prison, and you've had enough shit thrown your way for a year. I'm not going to let this little snot-nosed hussy get the better of either of us, so we're going to deal with this, here and now."

"What do you mean? Let her go."

"In due time. Drink?" Emily offered Poppy a glass.

Poppy stared at it. "I don't think so."

"Suit yourself." Emily poured herself a glass and drank. "Miss Blackwood here can help us both out. Can't you, dear?"

"What do you mean?"

"She's had it in for you since she arrived. I saw her throw dirt at you in the park, and I was there when she threw her wine at you in front of everyone."

"Right when you attempted to kill Miss Haskett."

"Miss Blackwood has been nothing but trouble since she got here. I thought I'd do you a favor."

Poppy balked. "Are you joking?"

"No. This is all for you. Why do you think I killed Miss Grace?"

"But that was to harm Lucretia."

"No dear, that was me. Who do you think doctored Lucretia's drink, and told Miss Grace she seemed awfully thirsty?" Emily tapped her chest. "Me."

"Why? What did Miss Grace ever do to you?"

"Nothing. But she stood in your way for you to be with your handsome sergeant, and I wasn't going to let her ruin your relationship. Besides the things she said about him were horrible and I couldn't stand her. She had to go."

Poppy stiffened. "I can't believe this."

"Oh yes. That's why I thought, ah-ha, Miss Blackwood will solve all our problems. We can say that when she threw her wine on you, the glass flew into Miss Haskett's neck, cutting her."

Susan gave a muffled shout in her gag.

"Hush, you." Emily said, leaning forward. "Don't you see, Miss Morton? This was for you. I always look out for my friends."

Poppy said, "Miss Haskett is alive and well. She's recovering. And she knows it was you who tried to kill her. We all know."

Emily's mouth pursed into a frown.

"You won't get away with this, you know. My family will notice I'm gone. They'll send someone after me."

"I doubt that. Your family seems nice and all, but it can be hours, sometimes days, before they notice a young woman is missing. We're always left alone to spend our attention on quiet, womanly pursuits." Emily looked at her with a growing smile. "No, I don't think anyone is coming." She poured the second glass of wine.

"I told you I didn't want any."

"This isn't for you, silly." Emily fetched a small white bottle from her pocket.

"What's that?"

"What do you think? Strychnine, of course." She aimed the gun at Poppy and said, "Don't even think about doing anything stupid. I wouldn't want to shoot you."

Poppy froze as Emily unstoppered the bottle with her thumb and daintily poured a white powder into the glass. She gave it a swirl. "Now, the way I see it, this can solve both our problems."

Poppy stared at her.

"I'll undo this gag, and you can help our friend have a little drink. Once she does, I'll untie her and we can go our merry ways. I even have a note."

"In your handwriting?" Poppy snorted.

Emily frowned at her. "As I was saying, she'll drink, we'll leave the note and anyone who finds her will think she killed herself. See? Problem solved."

"Except that it's wrong. And murder."

"What does that matter? By the time anyone figures it out we'll both be long gone. No one will suspect you."

Poppy looked at her. "Why?"

"Because you're my friend. And I don't let anyone hurt my friends."

"It's why you hushed up Mr. Horley's death, isn't it?"

"That, and I didn't want to go to jail. What do you say, Miss Morton? Is our friend feeling thirsty?"

Poppy stared. This girl, whom she thought was a friend, had presented Susan in a nice little parcel.

"Think about it, Miss Morton, with one drink, your problems would be over. No one would harass you any more about your birth, your mother, or your father. No one would dare."

Poppy charged Miss Munden, who toppled over. The gun went off, a clear shot ringing around the gallery.

"Oof! You bitch!" Miss Munden grappled with Poppy.

Poppy pinned her down and grabbed the gun, tossing it away. It went skittering across the floor. Poppy elbowed her, but Emily headbutted Poppy in the face and she reeled back, seeing stars.

"You stupid bitch. What do you think you're doing?"

They could hear the sound of breaking glass. Men's voices called out, and Poppy cried, "Here!"

"Shut your mouth, bitch, no one can hear you."

"We're in here!" Poppy called.

But the voices died away. The sounds of men and footsteps disappeared.

"Ha. Where are your rescuers now, eh?"

Poppy backed up. "It's over, Miss Munden. You're done."

"Not at all. I came prepared. If you're too cowardly to take care of this, I'll do it myself." Emily unearthed a small dagger from her sleeve and got to her feet.

Susan mouthed a shriek through her gag and tried to right herself.

"Stop!" Poppy cried. "I'll do it. I'll drink the wine."

"You? Why would you do it? This whole plan has been to support you."

"Don't kill her. I'll drink it. You can go and say I did it all. Blame it on me," Poppy said.

"What about her?"

"She won't say a word. She's too scared. And besides, as you said, she wouldn't care if I was dead anyway. She'd probably thank you for doing her a favor," Poppy said. "With me out of the way, she won't need to worry about me causing any trouble to her family."

Emily stared at her. She approached Susan and pulled her up by her hair, earning a muffled squeal.

"Stop!" Poppy shouted.

The sound of men's voices grew nearer.

The lantern's shadows lit up Miss Munden's face like a horrific creature of nightmares, made wickeder by her smile.

"You can say you found me here, and I'd tied her up. You

caught me planning to kill her and tried to stop me." Poppy took one of the wine glasses. "A toast? To your success? You've won, Miss Munden."

Emily dropped Susan and flashed Poppy a triumphant smile. "Why not? I'm glad you're finally seeing sense. I'm sorry to lose you, but I can't go to jail."

The girls clinked glasses and drank, every single drop, just as the men burst into the room.

"Poppy!" Henry cried, coming for her.

"She did it. It was her all along...." Emily said, then choked. The dagger fell from her hands. Her limbs stiffened and her eyes widened. "You... drank the wrong glass."

Poppy said, "What? But I?" she looked down at her hands. The glass she held was free and devoid of all white sandy crystals. She looked up at Emily. "You drank the strychnine."

"I thought we were friends. You bit—" Emily began convulsing.

"Oh, my god. Emily," Poppy said, as Henry pulled her away.

"No, we have to help her," Poppy said, reaching for her.

"There's nothing you can do. Not if she's drunk strychnine. Look at her," Henry said.

Emily convulsed, gagged, her arms and limbs stiffened and locked, and stilled.

Tom pulled the gag from Susan's mouth as she screamed.

Poppy sat in Henry's arms and looked at the body of her dead friend. Her only friend, gone. A tear rolled down her cheek. "It should've been me," she said. "I drank the wrong glass."

HER HALF-BROTHER, JAMES, Tom, her uncle, and the men of the watch, with the magistrate, all converged on the room. One of them found the gun, which had shot a small hole into the wall. The other men surrounded them. As one surveyed Miss Munden's body, the magistrate demanded answers. "What happened here?"

Poppy was helped to her feet by Henry and told them everything, as Tom took the dagger and began slicing through the rope around Susan. He helped her to her feet and she held onto him for balance. "Steady there," he said.

"Thank you," she told him, looking into his eyes.

His mouth crinkled into a goofy smile, and in that moment, Poppy knew he was a man gone, even if he didn't know it himself.

"How did you know we were in trouble?" Poppy asked.

"Something didn't sit right with me and I went to the magistrate to talk to him. When he said he'd had to release Miss Munden, I knew she'd try to come after you. I was there when your uncle came and said there was trouble at the academy, and I hitched a ride with the watchmen. So here I am. And glad I am too," he said, looking at Susan, who blushed.

Poppy stood by her as the men were all talking.

"Who is that man?" Susan asked her, as Tom walked away.

"A rake."

"Yes, please."

James gave Poppy a nod and smile before taking Susan away.

Poppy's uncle came up to her and said, "We were worried sick, child. Your aunt and I were terrified something had happened to you."

Poppy looked at him. For all his fault, he was still the main father figure in her life. Even though they had their disagreements, she still loved him, as the doting uncle she had always known, and knew she would love him still. "I'm all right."

"Well that's fine. Come away and let's go back to your townhouse. Rachel will be in fits until you're back."

"I'm surprised to hear you call it my townhouse. I'd have thought you'd want to go to Hertford."

"I do, but I know it's your home too. Your London home. I'll not stand in your way," he said quietly. "Come, Poppy, let's go."

"Mr. Greene, if you wouldn't mind, I would like a word with your niece. Please," Henry said.

Uncle Reginald turned. "Oh. All right. But make it quick. I

don't want to stay in this place a moment longer than necessary. It gives me chills."

Poppy walked to Henry, her arms hugging herself. "What did you want to speak to me about, Sergeant?"

He said, "I... You have been through an ordeal. And I am a fool. I've been a fool this entire time. May I call on you tomorrow?"

Poppy looked at him and stifled a yawn. "Yes, if it pleases you. Good night."

"Good night, Miss Morton." He bowed.

Chapter Thirty-Six

The next morning, Poppy, her aunt, and uncle were just finishing a late breakfast when a footman announced that Miss Morton had a caller in the parlor.

Poppy wiped her mouth free of marmalade and hurried to the parlor, where she said, "Good morning, Mr. Blackwood."

Her half-brother bowed. "Hello Poppy. I can call you that, can't I?"

Poppy nodded. "Only if I can call you James."

His smile was warm. "Absolutely."

"Please, sit." She gestured to the sofa, and he sat across from her.

He ran a hand through his blond hair and said, "I don't know quite the ordeal you've had, but I gather from Susan it was very bad. I wanted to thank you."

"It was—"

He held up a hand. "It was no small thing. Susan said you saved her life. I gather that other girl was about to kill her when you stopped her. Whatever possessed you to drink the wine? It was poisoned, wasn't it?"

"It was. I thought I could stall and give Susan enough time for the men to arrive, so she would be all right and be rescued."

"Susan's never liked you. What if she had decided to say it was all your fault?"

Poppy shrugged. "It was a risk I was willing to take. I just wanted to give her more time."

"It was smart of you to trick her."

"I didn't. I never thought that I'd take the wrong glass, or that Emily would drink the poisoned wine."

"So it was an accident, then." He looked haunted. "You meant to drink the poison. You would have died for Susan. For another few minutes."

"Yes," Poppy nodded.

It should have been me, she thought. *It should've been me.*

A shudder ran through James. "You don't even know her. And after all that she's done to you..."

"She's the closest thing I have to a sister. Wouldn't you? If it meant she might have a few more minutes to live?" Poppy asked.

He blinked hard. In seconds, his eyes turned glassy with unshed tears.

He coughed and said, "I wanted to tell you that Susan expresses her thanks. She wanted to come here but—no. I won't lie to you. She's too embarrassed to come to tell you in person, and she's still trying to reconcile the image of you as your mother's daughter, whilst also being the woman who saved her life. It's a lot to take in at age eighteen, I suppose."

"That's all right. I understand."

"She won't make your life difficult anymore. She's promised me that. She's asked that you keep a distance from our family, and she will not trouble you," James said.

"I would, happily, but... what about you? What about my father?"

"We'll figure something out. I know he wouldn't want to lose you, and now that I've gained another sister, I don't want to lose you either. I don't know what the future holds, but..." He took her hand. "You don't have to be alone, Poppy. You've got family now."

Poppy felt tears come to her eyes, and she gave her brother a watery smile. "That means a lot."

They were interrupted by Sergeant Dyngley, who came walking in and stopped at the sight of them holding hands. "Oh. Pardon me. I thought Miss Morton was alone."

"No, I should be going. Talk soon, Poppy." James rose.

"Yes. Good bye, James."

He bowed, she nodded, and he left.

Henry stood there awkwardly.

"Please, sit down, Sergeant," she said.

"Is that another one of your suitors?" he asked.

"Hmmm?"

"You were holding hands. He called you by your Christian name." Henry said accusingly.

"I…Yes, he did."

"So? Are you courting?"

Poppy laughed. "I am many things but I won't go so far as to court my own family members, Sergeant. That man you saw is my half-brother, James, the son of Lord Blackwood."

Henry let out a breath of relief. "Thank goodness for that. I thought… I don't know what I thought."

"Why are you here, Sergeant? Did you come to discuss the investigation?"

"No."

"Then what is it—"

"I love you," he said.

Poppy froze.

"I have tried not to care, as you had other suitors. Even that miscreant Mr. Terrell, whom I knew was no good from the start. I knew he was bad for you." He looked at her.

"You came here to tell me Mr. Terrell was a bad person?"

"No, I, dash it, Poppy." Henry removed his hat and raked his fingers through his dark hair. He crossed the room and stood before her. "I don't want to be parted from you, ever."

He came face to face with her. "I don't care what other people say or think. I don't care if you're an heiress, a companion, or a clergyman's niece without a penny. I don't want anyone else. I don't want anyone but you." He breathed, his voice low. His eyes were red, as if he had spent hours agonizing over this.

She didn't know what to think. She was speechless. "I..."

"Marry me," he said.

"But what about your family?"

"They will have to deal with it. John already likes you, and Petunia will come around. And my father... They were prepared to take a thief into the family, so you'll be a welcome addition after that almost disaster."

She raised an eyebrow at him.

"Sorry, I mean to say..." He took her hands in his. "I love you. I don't care what anyone says, and if anyone raises so much as a finger against you, I'll knock them flat on their face. Or skewer them with my best insult." He smiled. "I am a poor sergeant, likely to be demoted to a poorer county constable. I have no prospects, little family, and I... don't want to be with anyone else. I don't want to solve crimes with anyone else. Just you."

Her heart lifted.

"Will you?"

She looked at him. His brown eyes looked so vulnerable. He was going against his family, society, everyone and everything against the match, in order to be with her.

"Marry you?" she repeated.

He nodded.

"Yes," she whispered, "I will."

WHEN HER AUNT and uncle walked into the parlor a few minutes later, they interrupted Poppy and Henry kissing. But despite Uncle Reginald's protests, Aunt Rachel firmly closed the door and stood with her back to it, crossing her arms over her chest. "She'll come out in good time. You need to tell the servants to break out the good wine, and order a haunch of pork. We'll need all our strength, Reginald. We have a wedding to plan."

The End

Historical Note

I appreciate that the word "debutante" as I've used it for this book's title and its contents isn't entirely historically accurate. Whilst the term "debutante" originates from 1801, it refers to an actress's debut performance on stage. The meaning of the term I'm using didn't come into the regular vernacular until 1817. On the plus side, the words "snack" and "chatty" originate from the 1700s, so those are accurate.

With Poppy's character in this story, I particularly wanted to show the imbalances and subtle pressures her relationship with her father as her patron puts on her socially. Other girls of good fortune and breeding would have been presented to the Queen, but as the illegitimate child and formally unrecognized by her father, Poppy would not have been allowed that opportunity as a girl in the London Season. That being said, this book does have its Cinderella moments, which I love. I hope you enjoyed it.

Historical Sources

Online etymology dictionary: www.etymonline.com

On masquerade balls in regency London:
www.regencyhistory.net/2018/11/masquerade-balls-in-regency-london.html

I also read historic newspapers for more accurate details of the Fashionable Institution and the sort of parties they hosted during the time this book is set.

Acknowledgments

The team at Dragonblade is wonderful. I'm very grateful to Kathryn, Shawn, Evelyn, Elizabeth, and my incredible editor Amelia. I'm also grateful to the wonderful authors I've met along the way. Thank you to my family for their ongoing support, and my husband for pointing out plot holes, despite my grumpiness in response. And thank you to my readers, for reading this far. I hope you've enjoyed this series.

About the Author

E. L. Johnson writes historical mysteries. A Boston native, she gave up clam chowder and lobster rolls for tea and scones when she moved across the pond to London, where she studied medieval magic at UCL and medieval remedies at Birkbeck College. Now based in Hertfordshire, she is a member of the Hertford Writers' Circle and the founder of the London Seasonal Book Club.

When not writing, Erin spends her days working as a press officer for a royal charity and her evenings as the lead singer of the gothic progressive metal band, Orpheum. She is also an avid Jane Austen fan and has a growing collection of period drama films.

Connect with her on Twitter at twitter.com/ELJohnson888 or on Instagram at instagram.com/ejgoth.

www.ingramcontent.com/pod-product-compliance
Lightning Source LLC
Chambersburg PA
CBHW071414200726
48294CB00002B/390

* 9 7 8 1 9 6 1 2 7 5 2 5 6 *